Return to TOBACCO ROAD

a novel

CHARLIE FIVEASH

2013

This Book is dedicated to John W. Liles, the Squire of Tobacco Road and the best uncle a boy could ever hope to have. And to Virginia L. Liles, an aunt who always put family first and has continued to promote our family's heritage, which will bind us together for generations.

The Road

Prologue

Roads lead us to where we're going in life. Roads are everywhere: high roads, back roads, cross-roads, road-trips, roads to success, roads of destruction, and roads that lead to nowhere. Then there are twisted roads, roads less traveled, country roads, long roads, bumps in the road, back roads, and roads to recovery.

Some roads lead to nowhere, but all roads lead somewhere. Most follow the road that others have paved. Some get off the road — to rest, reflect, or pave a different path. Just because one leaves the road doesn't mean he is lost. The Bible speaks often of roads. Saul, the antagonist toward the teachings of Christ, found God on the Road to Damascus, and the disciples encountered Jesus on the Road to Emmaus after the resurrection.

People travel on highways and live on streets, but it's the roads that take us home. At times, we get off the road, only to get back on. Some never return, while others never leave the road. Some never even cross the center line.

It's been said that life is a highway, but it's really more like a road, with many turns and twists and obstacles. Then there are decisions about what road to take – decisions that impact our lives. Some roads are named for people, for places, or for landmarks. Other roads describe a region, an era, even history, while other roads are not even roads at all.

Tobacco Road is one of those roads. Tobacco Road is more than a road, but a place that defines a region. Still, Tobacco Road is more than a region or a place. It's an iconic name that carries with it a mystique that lives in the hearts of those that have walked along that Road. One can walk it, but a walk along Tobacco Road really has to be lived and experienced. Tobacco Road is more than a historical sign placard posted on the side of the road; it is a way of life, a pride of ownership that belongs to those who have walked the road. Tobacco Road is a legend that will stand the test of time for generations to come. When it comes to roads, it's been said:

If you don't know where you are going, any road will get you there.

When you come to the fork in the road, take it.

Don't follow where the road may lead; go instead and pave your own path.

There are no shortcuts to any place worth going.

The distance a person goes down the road is not as important as the direction.

No matter how far you have gone down a wrong road, turn back.

Roads, like decisions in life, lead us to where we're going or where we think we should go. Good decisions, bad decisions, even indecision can lead to a road of success or a road to destruction. Choose the road you will travel.

The Tournament

Chapter 1

The afternoon's summer heat scorched the infield of the baseball diamond, the green grass in the outfield reflecting the sun's bright rays into the eyes of the young players. The spectators fanned themselves from the 95-degree heat with paper fans provided by the tournament sponsor. With a catchy play on words, the air circulators waved in systematic fashion in the wooden bleachers, each printed with the phrase, *"I'm a fan of White Lake baseball!"*

With little or no tree cover surrounding the fields, a coveted summer breeze was just an illusion in the flatlands of eastern North Carolina this Saturday afternoon. Like barbeque spare ribs on a hot grill, the July heat burned the hardpan red clay surface of the infield at the Bladen County Recreation Park.

The afternoon's match-up paired two All-Star teams of eight-year-olds from the surrounding region, in hopes of advancing to the championship game the following afternoon. With the score tied at eleven, a solid grounder propelled the baseball toward the shortstop. Glove down, a quick release, and an accurate throw toward first base secured out the third out. A tie game in the bottom of the last inning meant that the Wilmington Bulls needed only a single run to end the game and return on Sunday afternoon for the championship game.

"Good throw, Will," called a voice from the stands.

"Great job, guys! Way to hold 'em," said another.

"All right, let's get that run, boys," came encouragement from one of the moms in the bleachers.

Ten faded blue jerseys trotted off the field towards the dugout, baseball gloves tucked under their arms, fatigued by the blazing sun but ready for battle in the bottom of the final inning of play that afternoon. It had been a long day for the weary players. Up before 7:00, in uniform with gear packed by 7:30, the team traveled inland fifty-four miles to Bladen County, North Carolina, followed by play in three baseball games in the summer heat.

With the rising sun at their backs, the convoy of station wagons, loaded with baseball equipment, players, and fans, left the Wilmington Recreation Center at 8:00, resembling a regiment of army tanks rolling to an early morning attack. The excitement of a playing three baseball games in one day and spending the night together as a team trumped any complaints about an early departure that morning.

The year was 1974, and this was summer baseball in the South. This select group of eight year-olds was All-Stars, the best of the best in their age group, chosen by their coaches to represent the Wilmington, North Carolina Recreation Center in four organized Little League tournaments during June and July. Between the practices and tournaments, baseball had consumed most of the summer for the boys - and their families. By the second week in July, the players had practiced four days a week and played in three All-Star tournaments since school ended in June, including one competition last week over the Fourth of July weekend.

Charlie Fiveash

The White Lake All-Star tournament was a smaller event, with fewer teams and less competition than the Bulls were accustomed to facing in summer league play in the southeast region of North Carolina. While most tournaments started on Thursday night and ended with a championship game on Sunday evening, the White Lake competition was confined to just weekend play, starting on Saturday morning and ending with the final two games on Sunday afternoon.

The Wilmington Bulls had yet to win a tournament this summer, but the fledgling team had made it to the semi-finals in two previous tournaments. The team had high hopes for a strong finish to the season in the White Lake Invitational. More important than the win-loss record was the fact that the boys were learning more about baseball and honing their skills in June and July during the abbreviated summer Little League season.

Although only eight years old, the All-Stars were taught that baseball was about execution, repetition, and situational decisions in the field. The coaches instructed each player with tips on batting and on the art of fielding. These instructions were etched in the minds of the Wilmington Bulls at a young age. T-ball was last year's sport, now a distant memory for the boys. This was real baseball, like the Durham Bulls and the Atlanta Braves played. These twelve boys were All-Stars, a summer travel team with high hopes to win its last tournament of the season in the farmland of eastern North Carolina at the White Lake All-Star Invitational.

The tournament was hardly an invitational. In fact, the organizers at the Bladen County Recreation Department in nearby Elizabethtown usually had to solicit help from the rec directors in nearby counties to ensure the annual tournament had enough teams to fill sixteen slots in the brackets. To perpetuate interest, the tournament was moved from the rec fields in downtown Elizabethtown six years ago to the shores of scenic White Lake in 1968 to give the tournament an added draw to All-Star teams from out of town.

Located just four miles east of Elizabethtown, the county seat, White Lake was the recreational epicenter of Bladen County. The lake was renowned in the region for its clear, spring-fed water and beach-like shores. Even at its deepest point, one could see the white sand at the lake's bottom, hence came the name White Lake.

Located about sixty miles inland from the North Carolina Outer Banks, White Lake was surrounded by farmland, a picturesque snapshot of the rural south. Amidst its sandy soils, the flatlands of southeast North Carolina were known for several row crops, including blueberries, soybeans, and corn, but one crop stood out above all the others - tobacco. Tobacco farming had been a way of life for generations in the southern Atlantic region, dating back to the late seventeenth century. The green leafy plant was grown in several states in the South including Georgia, South Carolina, and Virginia, but nowhere was it more prolific than in eastern North Carolina. Known at the time as the Tobacco Belt, certain counties in the eastern part of the Tar Heel state produced more tobacco in the 1940s than all other states combined.

Georgia had its peanuts, South Carolina its peaches, Florida had oranges, but tobacco was king in North Carolina. Even when cotton was the primary crop in the south in the 1800s, tobacco still ruled as the dominant crop in North Carolina. Farmers and citizens alike in the tobacco region took pride in the short and full leafy crop that covered the flat fields of Carolina from Greensboro to Wilmington. Located in the heart of the tobacco region, Bladen County was the axis of tobacco farming in the Tar Heel state, at least according to the locals.

Consequently, smoking cigarettes and chewing tobacco were not frowned upon in eastern parts of North Carolina for several reasons. First, tobacco was the lifeline of the community and second, prior to the 1970s, the adverse effects of smoking and chewing tobacco products had not surfaced.

What generated such community pride in tobacco farming was the fact that so many, from young to old, were a part of the tobacco farming culture and process. Unlike other major commercial farming operations, tobacco production was a hands-on endeavor, requiring various forms of hard labor. At the hottest point in the summer months, tobacco leaves reached their optimal harvest time, and the work began.

As the school year ended, the tobacco harvest represented a rite of passage in eastern North Carolina. Teenagers, teachers, mothers, daughters, migrant workers, and families all converged on the tobacco fields in June, signifying that summer had arrived. Tobacco was the most labor-intensive of all harvests. Like picking cotton, working tobacco required a strong back and a high tolerance for enduring the sun's brutal summer heat. Harvesting tobacco required wearing, long pants, gloves and a long-sleeve shirt because the full-grown tobacco leaf's nicotine content was known to cause sickness among the handlers. Overexposure of the skin to the green and yellow leaf was known to cause "tobacco flu," which could result in headaches, vomiting, and difficulty in breathing.

Before the 1960s, the only way to harvest tobacco was to bend over the eighteen to twenty-four-inch plants and remove the large leaves off the stem. Hours spent bent over in the heat was not suited for those who shied away from laborious work conditions. Soon after the advent of the farm tractor, a tobacco harvesting implement was devised that sat low to the ground, enabling the harvesters to sit at eye-level to the leaves without the arduous task of bending over in the fields all day.

Because it was such a labor-intensive crop, tobacco harvesting meant that every family member on the farm was required to work in the fields and barns once he or she turned thirteen years of age, and women and young girls were known to be some of the best workers in the tobacco fields.

Due to the many hands required to harvest tobacco, migrant workers would come from as far as Florida and Texas to harvest tobacco in North Carolina. The locals flocked to the fields at harvest time to help the tobacco farmers and generate extra money in the summers. Many college and high school students never even applied for a different job in summer. Jobs in tobacco were plentiful for those willing to work – and work hard. Tobacco was more than a crop, but a way of life in eastern North Carolina for centuries. The tobacco harvest kept the community working together each summer.

Tobacco farmers raised their children to be tobacco farmers, like their fathers before them. Most tobacco farms in eastern North Carolina were generational farms, spanning three generations with over a century of history. Winfield Farm in Bladen County was one of those quintessential generational farms that thrived during the proliferation of the tobacco industry. Large families were almost a mandate to run a tobacco farming operation, and the Winfield family met that requirement for generations.

The family farm was purchased by Malcolm Winfield as an existing tobacco farm in 1893. While the land had been in tobacco production for several centuries, the Winfield family had owned and operated the farm for eight decades by the time the Wilmington Bulls came to Bladen County for the White Lake Invitational Little League Baseball Tournament in the summer of 1974. The eleven hundred acre Winfield farm was in its third generation of owner-ship when John Winfield, the oldest son of Julian Winfield, took the reins of the farm after his father died in 1968. John's grandfather, Malcolm Winfield, initially purchased just over four hundred acres along the South River to farm tobacco in the 1890s.

Located just eleven miles north of White Lake, an overnight visit to Winfield Farm was a major factor in the Bull's decision to participate in the White Lake baseball tournament this summer, and the perfect way to end the summer all-star season. The team's shortstop, Will Jordan, was John Winfield's nephew. Will's mom, Rachael Winfield Jordan, was born and raised on Winfield Farm, along with her six brothers and sisters. All seven siblings had worked in tobacco on Winfield Farm since Will's grandfather determined they were old enough to work.

The tobacco harvests used the phrase that laborers "worked in" tobacco, rather than "working on" or "working at" a vegetable farm. Due to the lack of automation, working in tobacco meant that a laborer literally "worked in" tobacco, meaning you either harvested the leaves in the fields or worked in the tobacco barns where the leaves were stored to cure. "There's nothing harder than working in tobacco in the summers," Rachael Jordan told her boys when they complained about work of any type around the house in Wilmington. "I'm going to send you boys to the farm with your uncle for the summer to learn what hard work is all about."

After meeting at the University of North Carolina, Rachael Winfield married William Jordan, an insurance agent from Wilmington, eleven years ago. The wedding ceremony was held in downtown Elizabethtown at the historic Trinity Methodist Church, about fifteen miles south of Winfield Farm. All the Winfield girls were married in Elizabethtown and celebrated their nuptials with a reception at the farm after the ceremony.

By the 1970s, tobacco production in the United States was at full throttle. John Winfield, a third-generation tobacco farmer, made the decision to add more tobacco acreage in the crop rotation during the fifties, and as a result, Winfield Farm evolved as one of the largest tobacco farms in Bladen County.

Now in his early forties, John was the only one of the seven siblings that stayed on the farm. He left for a few years to serve his country as an Army infantryman in World War Two, attended college on the GI bill, and worked as an accountant in nearby Elizabethtown for three years. Still, John's true calling was farming. Never married, John Winfield dedicated his life to carrying on the legacy of the family farm.

Living on the coast of North Carolina, most of the young Wilmington Bulls had never experienced life on an operating tobacco farm. The weekend trip to the White Lake baseball tournament served two functions: a visit to Will's family farm and the chance to play in another Little League baseball tournament this summer. The occasion for an eight-year-old to run around in wide-open fields at a real farm with eleven of your best friends was more fun than spending the day at an amusement park. Playing in the tournament at White Lake was a thrill, but secondary to spending the night at Winfield Farm.

After a walk-off single by second baseman Ronnie Downey on Saturday afternoon, the Bulls advanced to the tournament semifinals with a 12 to 11 win. Tournament play would resume on Sunday afternoon with two semi-final games and the championship at 4:00 pm. For now, it was off to Will's family farm to celebrate. Will's uncle and grandmother would be at the farm to welcome the victors and their families for a cookout.

The convoy of station wagons pulled out of the White Lake Rec Center in a line that resembled a funeral procession on a country road. Twenty minutes later, the station wagon brigade, loaded with players, siblings, overnight bags, and baseball equipment, turned left off Highway 210 on to the long dirt driveway that led the team and their families to Winfield Farm. The wagons parked in the grass to the right of the house near Will's grandmother's garden. On cue, car doors opened and mayhem ensued as twelve boys in full uniform hit the ground like soldiers dropped in a Viet Cong rice field, ready for action. The players scrambled like ants on a picnic table until Will commandeered the troops toward the front porch of the house.

Will hugged his grandmother, standing on the front porch, prepared to greet the convoy. A few of the Bulls said a quick hello to Grandma Winfield, while others ran across the porch to claim one of the four wooden rocking chairs spaced evenly between the two front doors of the farmhouse.

"Did your team win?" Nanny asked Will, smothering him in an embrace.

The distinct fragrance of his grandmother's hand lotion always brought back memories of Will's visits to the farm. Now in her mid-seventies, she was still the gracious host, the master cook, a grandmother to eight, and patient in all her ways. The sound of Nanny's voice and rural Eastern Carolina dialect invoked a soothing effect on Will. The familiar activity of children playing at the farm still inspired her, even at her age. "Where's Uncle John?" Will asked, in anticipation of seeing his favorite uncle.

"He's in the fields, but he should be here soon. He probably didn't expect you quite this early," Nanny explained.

"Aaaw," Will said, disappointed that his uncle was not there to greet the team.

"Go inside and get your things put away," Nanny said gently. "Uncle John will be along shortly, dear."

The six-bedroom farmhouse was just scalable enough to accommodate the twelve-man Bulls roster and Will's parents, the designated chaperones for the night. Parents and siblings would be housed near the tournament site at the White Lake Motel, secondary accommodations to the privilege of staying at Winfield Farm and reserved exclusively for the team and the Winfield family.

After Will's dad gave the team the house rules, the boys stormed upstairs to the bedrooms. Mr. Jordan ended with, "No jumping on the beds! This old house might not be able to stand the weight and you and the beds could come crashing down to the first floor."

The reverberation of twelve eight year-olds running up the wooden stairwell in baseball cleats sounded like a herd of buffalo stampeding through Wyoming. Once to the top of the stairs, one by one, the boys realized they had three bedrooms to choose from on the second level. First baseman, Mason "Bud" Miller, made the first proclamation.

"I'm in Will's room!"

Several other players chimed in.

"Me too!"

"No, I called it first!"

The competition commenced as the boys created mayhem by diving on the two double beds in the middle bedroom to secure a position in Will's room. The battle for who slept in which room ensued for several minutes, until Will's dad intervened and assigned the boys to beds and cots set up to accommodate the team.

"Let's go outside," Will announced. "Y'all need to see the tobacco barns. It smells like nothing you've ever smelled before in your whole life."

Still in uniform, the Bulls charged down the stairs and out the side door of the farmhouse in single file. Once outside, the pack of boys broke into a full sprint, with Will leading the way, down the dirt road behind the house through the tobacco fields. The tobacco barns could be seen beyond the first field behind the house, a good three hundred yards down the dirt road, a lengthy distance for twelve Little League players who had already played three baseball games in the July heat.

Will led the Bulls down the sandy road, but stopped dead in his tracks when he saw the red and gray Ford tractor moving slowly toward the speeding baseball team. Will turned around and waited as all eleven of his teammates joined him in a covey, just short of their destination. "There he is!" he announced, out of breath. "It's Uncle John, coming this way on the tractor. Let's go stop him!"

Flailing his arms in the air in an attempt to garner John's attention, Will yelled. "Uncle John, Uncle John! We're here!"

As twelve blue jerseys ran toward John's tractor, he needed no help from Will to indicate that the pack of Bulls had arrived. Will led the team toward the oncoming tractor and stopped as they approached the hum of the diesel engine. Carefully, John put the tractor in neutral and stepped down to greet young Will and his teammate, opening his arms as Will ran full speed toward him. Will plowed headfirst into his uncle's stomach, and the two hugged.

"Where are you boys headed?" Uncle John asked, surveying the dirty dozen players.

"We're going to the tobacco barns," Will answered, still out of breath from the run from the house.

"Let's see the barns tomorrow morning," John suggested. "I have another idea, but first, introduce me to your teammates, Will."

"Yes, sir," Will responded in military-like fashion, and then named each player and their respective positions. After the introductions, Will turned back to his uncle. "Uncle John, can we go on a tractor ride?"

"Sure, let's go back to the barn and get the trailer. I'll hook up the trailer while you guys get your swim suits on, and we'll head down to the river and let you guys cool off. We'll take a couple of fishing poles and see if we can catch us some fish for supper." He turned to the group of boys clustered around Will. "You guys hungry? We don't have anything here to eat, so I hope you boys know how to fish," he quipped, looking for a reaction to his comments.

"I thought you said we were having hamburgers, Will," outfielder Robinson Adams frowned, seemingly disappointed with the idea of fish for dinner.

Will looked at his uncle, knowing well his sense of humor, especially when in the midst of a crowd. "He's kidding guys, but there are some big fish in the river. We caught some last summer," Will exclaimed in an effort to solicit support for the fishing expedition.

"You guys run back to the house and get changed, and I'll get the fishing poles and hook up the trailer," John said with a clap of his hands.

"Can I ride back with you?" Will asked his uncle, eyeing the tractor. Ever since Will was a toddler, John had granted his nephews and nieces rides on the tractor, straddled tightly between his legs, holding firm to the steering wheel.

"Okay, but you should ride on the trailer with your team when we go to the river," John suggested. He turned to the others. "All right boys, first one to the house gets to eat the first fish for supper," John announced. "Will's riding with me, but I think you guys can outrun this slow tractor. On your mark, get ready, set ... go!" The boys took off in a full sprint down the dirt road back to the house.

Will mounted the tractor with some help from his uncle.

"Let's go, Uncle John! You gave them too much of a head start. We gotta' catch 'em."

"We'll get 'em, you watch," John proclaimed as he put the vintage Ford 8N in first gear. "Hang on, let's go get those rascals."

"Can I drive?" Will asked, looking up at his uncle.

"Sure," John smiled down at him, shifting into third gear as the tractor puttered toward the barn. "But you gotta' keep the wheels on the road so we can catch those boys,"

While John controlled the speed, Will kept both hands on the bottom of the tractor's steering wheel, independent of his uncle's assistance. Eyes straight ahead, Will saw the numbers of each player on the back of their jerseys as the tractor followed at a safe distance. Will predicted who would get to the house first and most likely which player would be last. As one of the faster players on the team, Will would've liked to be in this footrace, but he much preferred his place seated high on the seat of the tractor, bouncing along the dirt road with his uncle's foot on the throttle.

Will smiled as the tractor chugged its way down the dirt road in an effort to catch the boys. Though the tractor never quite caught up with the runners, Will's teammates envied him driving the tractor, while they had to run back to the barn. Winded by the race, the boys stood on the dirt driveway between the white frame house and the tractor barn as the tractor approached the pack of boys, now doubled over in exhaustion from the sprint to the barn. Will stood between the clutch and his uncle's legs and snapped out a quick salute in the team's direction as the tractor passed the host of blue jerseys. The players cheered in exhilaration as the tractor came to a stop in front of the maroon-stained barn.

What a great day, Will thought as he jumped off the tractor to join his teammates.

The Win

Chapter 2

Will and his teammates were up early Sunday morning, awakened by the excitement of exploring more of Winfield Farm and the anticipation of playing in the championship game of the White Lake Invitational that afternoon. The third baseman, Nick Jacoby, was the first of the players out of bed this morning, inspired by his civic duty to rouse the rest of the team to start the day's activities as early as possible.

One by one, Nick roused the boys out of the sheets and onto the hardwood floors for an early morning raid on the tobacco barns. Tired from a late night of antics and horseplay, the team members gradually rose one by one to meet the day's call of duty. Thompson Wellesley, the Bulls catcher, was the only teammate who preferred the lure of additional sleep over a morning mission trip to the barn. However, the rambunctious morning rabble-rousers would not allow Thompson the additional rest he craved.

"Get up, you slug," outfielder Michael McLean yelled.

His voice was loud enough to wake the roosters on the adjacent farm. Without prompting, three of the boys climbed on the double bed and started a slow jump on the mattress surrounding their catcher. Covered by bed-sheets, a faint cow-like moan was the only response the boys could garner from under the pillow that covered Thompson's head.

"Come on, Sluggo, it's time to go see the tobacco barns," Ross Sanders pleaded. He sprang higher and higher, landing closer and closer to the catcher's head with each jump.

Finally, the sleeping giant emerged. First, the blonde bristles of Thompson's summer crew cut appeared from under the pillow, the tips of his hair resembling the end of a broom. Swinging arms followed, in hopes of striking one of his aggressors charged with waking the lone sleeper. Seeing themselves in immediate danger, the three pajama-clad 'attackers' parachuted from the mattress, landing with a thud one by one on the heart pine floors.

"Mr. Jordan said no jumping on the bed, you morons," Thompson announced. "Don't you idiots remember the rules? Now get outta here!"

The battle began as Thompson emerged from the sheets inch by inch, his Red Sox pajamas clinging tightly to his hefty torso. Clearly not the fleetest of players on the team, the catcher rolled off the bed and stormed out of the bedroom in search of his teammates. The aggressors and other awak-ened players had already scattered in fear to safer quarters downstairs in an effort to avoid the wrath of the awakened mammoth.

Most of the team found a safe haven under the roomy dining room table on the main level, but after a short search mission on the second floor, Thompson made his way down the stairs and followed the whispers into the dining room.

"Ha, found you guys!" Thompson proclaimed sarcas-tically. "You call that a hiding place?" he asked, and kicked one of his feet under the spacious table in hopes of striking a random player.

Uncle John appeared at the entrance to the dining room fully clothed, though still barefoot. A pair of socks and shoes dangled from the fingers of his hand. "You boys are up early," he commented, eyeing the boys clustered together under the table. "Who are we hiding from?"

"They're hiding from me," Thompson responded. "Because they know I'll hurt every one of them. Look at them, trying to hide. See? They're all afraid of me."

"What did you guys do to make him so mad?" John asked, stooping down to peer under the table.

Will shrugged his shoulders and spoke for the group. "All we did was wake him up."

"Well, I'm with you then, Thompson," John said, looking at the catcher, a grin turning up the corners of his mouth. "They woke me up too. Let's get these guys!"

Socks and shoes discarded, and now down on his knees, Uncle John waved Thompson to join him under the massive mahogany table. "Attack!" John yelled just before he tickled the first Bull he could reach.

Half of the team escaped the makeshift hiding place and ran for higher ground, while the rest endured their punishment with tickles from Will's uncle and softened punches from Thompson.

Once the battle subsided, Uncle John called for the troops to reassemble in the dining room. "Let's go get dressed, and I'll take you guys on a tractor ride to see the rest of the farm. By the time we get back, I bet we'll have a big breakfast waiting for us."

"We want to see the tobacco barns," one of the players suggested.

"Yeah!" was the consensus among the team, as the players scrambled upstairs.

"Let's eat first," Thompson suggested, his face breaking into a sly smile.

"I'm hungry myself," Uncle John agreed. "But first, we need Will's grandmother to cook us some of her good bacon and eggs. I promise it'll be ready when we get back. So, let's go get ready. The tractor leaves in five minutes." The boys stared at him as he retrieved his shoes and socks. "Move it!" John barked like a drill sergeant.

The sound of twenty-four bare feet running up the wooden stairwell insured that no one intended to get left behind, including Thompson.

"Mama, we're off to the tobacco fields," John called to his mother, already in the kitchen and preparing the fixings for breakfast. "We'll be back in an hour. I'll help you feed this group when we get back. They'll need a good breakfast before they head to the ball field."

Nanny smiled. "That's fine, I'm used to feeding big groups. I'll get breakfast started. You just keep them entertained and out of the kitchen."

"Yes ma'am," John said to his mother. "I'm going outside to crank the tractor. We'll be out of here in a matter of minutes."

For the last four years since Pop-Pop Winfield died, just John and Nanny had lived in the roomy farmhouse. In addition to running the farm, John was also his mother's caretaker. Though seventy-six years old, Nanny was still in good health and could take care of herself, but having John in the house was helpful when it came to chores, maintenance, and driving her to town to shop or see the doctor.

Outside, the sun sparkled over the open acreage of Winfield Farm, signaling a new day. It rose to its full majesty, absorbing the morning dew from the bright green and yellow tobacco leaves. It was just after eight o'clock, so the sun's July heat had yet to fully manifest itself. The summer tobacco harvest was nearing its end, as the leafy green plants transitioned into a spotty yellow.

John had hooked up the trailer to the tractor in no time, and by the time the gaggle of boys emerged from the house, he sat in the tractor seat, ready to provide the full tour of the farm.

The oversized tires of the Ford tractor trudged along the familiar path down the dirt road pulling and bouncing the trailer-load of boys past the tobacco fields toward the curing barn. John looked over his shoulder to make sure the kids were seated safely on the bed of the trailer, and then smiled as he steered the tractor just off the dirt road, knowing the boys anticipated their visit to the tobacco barn. The diesel engine soon sputtered to a stop, and the boys rapidly deployed from the trailer and raced toward the closed barn doors.

John shook his head in amusement and then climbed down from the tractor. He strolled toward the doors, fighting back a laugh as the boys shifted from one foot to the other in growing impatience and anticipation. He reached for and swung open the wide barn door. Immediately, the distinct smell of curing tobacco overwhelmed the boys as they curiously peeked inside. Uncertain of what they would find inside the cool darkness of the barn, each player tentatively stepped through the barn door, observing the golden tobacco leaves hanging from every corner of the barn's rafters.

Once all twelve were inside the barn, the look on the players' faces revealed the unique stench of the tobacco curing process.

"I told you it stunk in here," Will whispered to the players that stood closest to him.

Despite the odor, and their wrinkled noses, the boys displayed a sense of homage as they stood quietly on dirt floor in the center of the barn. The team stood in reverence, circled around Uncle John. Finally, Harper Stephens, the Bulls right fielder, broke the silence.

"Why does it stink so bad in here, Mr. Winfield?"

After a few murmurs of agreement from the boys, John spoke up. "That's the smell of money. I love this smell. I've been smelling tobacco cure in this barn since I was half your age. It brings back good memories for me. I used to think this barn stunk too, but now I love the smell of it." He took a big breath, inhaling the fragrance of the dark brown tobacco leaves hanging from the barn roof like moss off an old oak tree, and smiled. The boys watched him as he took another deep breath, his head tilted back as he inhaled the fumes through his nostrils. The smell was like sweet nectar to him. Finally, he lifted his head and adjusted his thick black frame glasses like a professor, prepared to instruct the boys in the tobacco curing process. Suddenly, he felt like one of the boys' coaches, addressing the team before a game.

"This is where we hang the tobacco to let it dry out. The heat in the barn turns the leaves from the green and yellow color you see on the plants outside to this brown tint once it begins a process called curing."

"Do you eat it?" one of the boys asked.

John chuckled. "No, we use tobacco for a number of things. Some people chew it, but you don't swallow it. Some smoke it. It's also good to rub on bee stings."

"My dad smokes," one of the players piped in.

"So does mine," Wilson Davis commented. "*And* my mom."

"I smoke too, but it's not a habit I'm proud of," John shared. "Smoking is not something you should start. It's bad for you, especially for you athletes."

"Why do you do it then?" one of the players asked.

"I've been smoking and chewing tobacco since I was four-teen. When you grow up around tobacco like I did, it's what most folks around here do. I should'a quit a long time ago,"

John sighed. He watched as two of the curious players broke off from the group and wandered behind the low-hanging bundles of leaves. "Don't go back there, boys," John warned them. "There are snakes that live in the back of the barn. Sometime you can see 'em hanging from the rafters."

The two players quickly scurried back to join the rest of their teammates standing in the center of the barn.

"I've seen the snakes myself," Will said with his blue eyes wide. Black snakes. Big ones. My grandma killed one in her garden last summer. It was as long as the hoe she killed it with." Will stretched his arms from his sides as wide as possible, attempting to reveal the full length of the snake.

The boys inched closer together in the center of the barn toward Uncle John, intrepid at the news that large snakes might be looming in their midst.

"Those snakes keep the rats out of the barn," John explained, noting the fear that swept through the circle of eight year olds. "Just stay close to me. You'll be fine."

The boys inspected the rafters above them, in search of the phantom slithering creatures that ruled the tobacco barn. Instead, they found bundles of golden brown tobacco leaves hanging well above their reach.

"See, it doesn't smell so bad in here any longer, right?" John asked. "It's not a bad smell once you get used to it." He watched them turn in slow circles, studying every inch of the barn. "Let's get back in the trailer and go see some other parts of the farm before you guys have to suit up and get out to the ballpark," John suggested.

With all twelve boys seated safely in the open trailer once again, John drove slowly down the dirt road past seemingly endless rows of tobacco plants. Most of the acreage had already been harvested, leaving the stalks barren until planting season next spring. From the open fields, the tractor pulled the team over the sandy white road into another large field where waist-high tree saplings grew in perfect rows that seemed to stretch to the end of the earth's surface. John stopped the tractor, shifted the gear into neutral, and left the engine idling. As he dismounted the tractor, his boots hit the dirt road like an astronaut landing on the moon. He walked back to the flatbed trailer, typically used for hauling bales of hay. "You boys okay back here?" John asked, surveying the team, seated Indian-style on the trailer's wooden surface. They nodded. "We grow mostly tobacco on our farm, but we also plant corn and soybeans." After explaining what a soybean was used for, John pointed over his shoulder in the direction of the field behind him. "Who knows what crop this is behind me?" John asked the boys, staring into the field of scrawny tree saplings.

"They look like little Christmas trees," Lawson Nixon, the team's center fielder, responded in hopes of being the first to answer.

"Good guess. These are actually pine trees. They look like little Christmas trees when they're first planted. See that forest of big trees beyond the little trees?" John pointed to the wooded forest of loblolly pines standing majestically in the path of the morning sun. "By the time you guys are out of college, these little trees will be almost as big as the trees over there." Pine trees are different from tobacco and other crops. These trees take fifteen years or more to grow to full height, but tobacco and corn grow in one season. We harvest tobacco in the summer when it's hot, and corn and soybeans are harvested in the fall. Some of these pine trees will grow as long as twenty to twenty-five years before we cut 'em," John explained.

The boys made appropriate sounds of awe. John grinned and swung his arm toward the bigger trees. "Let's ride up a little closer to the big pines. I want to show you guys something interesting," John said as he headed back to the idling tractor. He pulled the trailer down the road about a quarter of a mile past the planted saplings, lining both sides of the road. The dirt road became slightly opaque and dim as the tractor entered the imposing tree-lined forest, which partially blocked the morning sunlight.

The diesel tractor slowed to a stop, the sun making more of an effort to sheen its way through the endless rows of regal pines. The rays of light resembled the beam of a laser, forcing its way to the pine straw beds that covered the forest floor. "You guys can get out here," John instructed, opening the gate at the rear of the trailer. The boys rapidly exited the trailer like twelve English pointers tracking quail on a morning hunt.

Once assembled on the ground, the boys listened as John began his next tutorial. "You guys see how these trees grow in a straight line for as far as you can see?" John said, pointing down the rows. The boys nodded. "My dad and I planted these trees when I was just out of the Army. We cut some of the trees four years ago. That's called thinning. These trees could grow for a long time, but we cut them down when they grow to a certain size. Who knows what we make from trees?"

"Houses," Billy Harvey, one of the outfielders, answered quickly.

"That's right. We make lumber for construction, but a lot of people don't know that trees are also used for a number of things, like paper. All kinds of paper - newspaper, paper you write on at school, even toilet paper. It's hard to believe that a big 'ole tree like this can produce something as thin as toilet paper," John shared, lifting his eyebrows. Again, the boys expressed their awe.

"Now, follow me." The entourage walked single file like soldiers between two rows of the massive planted pines until John stopped and motioned for the boys to circle around a single pine tree. "You see this metal box jammed into this tree?" John asked, placing his hand on what looked like a metal birdhouse penetrating the bark of the tree. "This box is there to collect the gooey sap that comes out of the pine tree. Have you ever picked up a pine log and got that sticky glue stuff on your hands or your clothes? Well, that sap is collected in these small boxes on the pine trees and put in big metal drums and hauled into Elizabethtown near where you guys are playing baseball today."

John saw that a few of the boys were growing restless at the length of his story, so he decided to shorten the narration. "The glue is processed into turpentine or tar. The tar is black, and that's why your parents may describe something really dark as 'black as tar.' A long time ago, even before I was born, the drums were shipped down the Cape Fear River to your hometown of Wilmington, where the drums were sent all over the world from the port. Now listen to the rest of the story," he urged. "This is where it gets good. That sap out of the trees is distilled or cooked to create the tar. When the tar was made at the factories, it would ooze out on the floor and the workers would step in the tar. The workers got the black tar on their boots. That's where the name Tar Heel came from," John explained, finishing with a smile as he looked each player.

"Like the North Carolina Tar Heels?" one of the players asked.

"Yep, that's where the name comes from," John confirmed.

"Wow!"

"Cool!"

"That's neat."

John figured the boys had been given enough instruction for the day, though the Tar Heel story had intrigued them and kept their attention. "All right, let's get outta here and go back to the house for breakfast," John announced.

A race ensued as the boys bolted through the pine forest in the direction of the tractor. By the time the farm tour ended, the station wagon entourage had resurged on Winfield Farm. After a hardy breakfast, it was time to suit up in the Bulls' attire and get some batting practice in over at the fields before the first semi-final game started at one o'clock. The boys thanked Uncle John and Nanny for their hospitality as they left the house.

"I'll be there this afternoon to watch you guys win this tournament," John announced. "I want to see you guys win both games today."

"Yes sir!" the players responded in unison before they loaded up in the station wagon brigade.

The mid-day heat pushed the temperatures into the mid-nineties again today by the first pitch at one o'clock. Uncle John found a seat next to his sister, Rachael, and husband Bill in the bleachers among the Wilmington fans. "This is why the professionals play most of their games at night," John commented to Rachael and the other Bulls' parents seated close by, referring to the blazing summer heat.

John had never seen his nephew play baseball, but he knew from his sister that Will had a special talent for the game. John's expectations of his nephew's baseball skills were not disappointed. Will played a spectacular game with two hits and an impressive double play at shortstop. His bat, glove, and throwing arm proved to his uncle that Will was indeed an All-Star. "I think I see now why they call him the Human Vacuum Cleaner," John laughed to his brother-in-law after the double play.

"He didn't get it from me," Bill commented. "It must come from the Winfield side."

"He may be playing in Durham for the real Bulls before it's all over," John commented on Will's talent for the game.

"For now, we'd just like to get to the finals of today's tournament," Will's father responded with a laugh. "We'll work on getting him in the major leagues next spring."

The Wilmington Bulls took care of the Clinton Reds by a score of eleven runs to five, propelling the Bulls to the championship game at five o'clock. The Bulls were scheduled to play the winner of the following game, matching the Lumberton Indians and the local favorite, the Elizabethtown Astros.

After the game, John made his way to the winning dug-out and congratulated the team, shaking each player's hand. "Great game, guys! That's good baseball. Good job! Now, let's go cool off in the lake before your next game," John offered as they gathered the equipment from the winning dugout.

The brigade of station wagons made the short drive to Goldston's Marina for a quick change into swimsuits for some time at the lake before the championship game.

"Hopefully this down-time before the finals will give us an edge over the winner of the next game," Will's father commented to one of the coaches.

While the Wilmington Bulls enjoyed a cool dip in White Lake, the Lumberton Indians pounded the local Elizabethtown team in a one-sided contest seventeen to four in the three o'clock game. Hoping the afternoon sun had taken its toll on the Lumberton All-Stars while the Bulls enjoyed a two-hour respite at the lake, the Bulls sought any advantage to prepare themselves for the finale against the power-hitting Indians.

"Based on the amount of sleep the boys got last night, I hope they don't run out of steam," John commented to Will's dad.

"We've won most of our games this post-season, but we've yet to win a tournament. I hope these guys don't let their nerves get the best of them," Mr. Jordan responded.

The contest between the finalists was one for the record books. The Bulls brought their best game, but it was not enough to take down the mighty Indians from nearby Lumberton. The Indians' bats were too much for the Bulls, and the Lumberton All-Stars took the championship trophy back to Robeson County with a final score of nine to four.

The White Lake tournament proved to be best weekend competition of the summer season, with a second place finish, an overnight stay at Winfield Farm, and an *esprit de corps* among the players and families that made for the perfect ending to a series of summer tournaments for the Wilmington Bulls.

The Farm

Chapter 3

The summer tradition of playing in the White Lake Invitational All-Star Little League Tournament continued for the Wilmington Bulls in a three-year succession until Will and his teammates aged out of Little League. By age twelve, Will had advanced to middle school baseball and was no longer eligible for recreation league play.

However, Will's baseball skills as an infielder and a line-drive hitter, coupled with his love for the game, insured a place for Will on his school teams. Baseball had become his passion, and when not playing himself, Will enjoyed watching his younger brother play. Will's brother, Clay, played summer All-Star baseball, so the White Lake and Winfield Farm tradition continued for another three years after Will's era of summer baseball ended.

As the boys' baseball schedules ended in July and freed up family time, the Jordan family was able to spend more time at Winfield Farm and White Lake. While many boys in Wilmington traveled to summer camps in western North Carolina, Will and Clay rarely attended the overnight camps with their friends. The Jordan's home away from home in the summers was Winfield Farm and White Lake.

The Jordan family typically rented a cabin on the shores of White Lake for a week in late August, and then left Will and Clay with Uncle John and Nanny at the farm for the following week. August was the ideal time to visit Winfield Farm, when the tobacco harvest was complete and Uncle John's workload at the farm eased.

During the Jordan's extended stay at the farm, six other Winfield cousins converged on Winfield Farm at various times every summer. Three of the eight cousins lived only a twenty-minute drive across the South River in Sampson County, Bladen's neighboring county to the north. The other three cousins lived in Asheville, three hundred miles west of the farm, but the western Carolina cousins always planned a trip to Winfield Farm when they knew the other cousins were visiting. The eight cousins looked forward to summers at Camp Winfield Farm, but most of all, they enjoyed spending time with each other. Days at the farm involved no structure, no planned activities - just old-fashioned fun. With eleven hundred acres as their playground, the cousins always found fun activities to fill their days.

Without children of his own, John treated the Winfield cousins like the children he never had. Of the seven children in John's generation, only three siblings had children. One brother had died of pneumonia at the age of eleven, a sister could not bear children, and two, including John, never married.

When the cousins were at the farm, Uncle John typically worked mornings and spent time with the cousins in the afternoons and evenings. John relished the time with his niece and seven nephews, especially when all eight were around the farm. As the unofficial 'camp counselor', John instructed the cousins in outdoor activities like fishing, hunting, target shooting, firearm safety, and driving the tractor or the pick-up.

John was all about having fun, but he also emphasized safety, especially around firearms and farm equipment. Always the teacher, John also taught the cousins about farming and taking care of the land. Based on his love for farming, John instructed the cousins on crop rotation, when to plant and harvest various crops, and how to approach timber management. When it came to tobacco, John spent time explaining the process of planting, cultivating, harvesting, and curing, and why tobacco grew so well in the soils of Bladen County and eastern North Carolina.

When not farming or teaching the cousins about farming, Uncle John fished. He kept a 14-foot jon-boat on the property that he used to fish in the various lakes around the farm. Known as the Land of a Thousand Lakes, Bladen County's landscape was dotted with fresh-water lakes of assorted sizes, and John had fished many of the lakes in the county. When the fish were not biting in the South River, along the northern border of the farm, John hooked the jon-boat to his truck and found a lake in Bladen County where the fish were feeding. Whether fishing on the farm or in the area lakes, the Winfield cousins had fond memories of long afternoons fishing with their uncle.

Though not known as a fishing lake, White Lake was a spot where the cousins spent most of their time in the summers when not at the farm. On the eastern shores of White Lake were Goldston's Pier and Crystal Beach, two commercial amusement centers that shared a fifty-foot common dock. Restaurants, arcades, skeet-ball, Putt-Putt, shops, bingo, a mini-beach area, and a midway with roller-coasters, bumper-cars, and other fun made up the landscape of Goldston's and Crystal Beach. Two glass-bottom tour boats, the *Lily* and the *Crystal Queen,* left on the hour from Goldston's Pier for summer cruises around the clear waters of the 1,100-acre lake. On most summer nights when the cousins visited, Nanny prepared a big supper. Afterwards, Uncle John loaded his truck with the Winfield cousins and made the eleven-mile pilgrimage south to White Lake.

Cousin Virginia usually rode in the cab with Uncle John, while the boys gladly sat in the bed of the pick-up and let the speed of the truck on Highway 701 cut through the summer's evening heat. Before the cousins were old enough to drive themselves, John enjoyed the trek to White Lake with the cousins, leaving the adults at home to drink wine and keep Nanny company.

The amusement parks at Goldston's and Crystal Lake provided a nighttime worth of entertainment and a lifetime of memories for the Winfield Cousins. White Lake's amusements were inferior when compared to Six Flags or Disney World, but the lake had its share of family activities that broke the monotony of staying at the farm, and the nightly trips to White Lake in the summers never got old, especially if the cousins were together.

The cousins' favorite story from their childhood took place on one balmy summer night at White Lake when Will was twelve. Old enough to hang together at the pavilion without parental supervision, five of the eight cousins stood in a long line waiting to ride the roller coaster, when a catastrophe of minor proportions transpired at the midway. As the story is told, the roller coaster's speed and gyrations were apparently too much for one young rider. Add to the fact that she had most likely been over-served with too many treats from the pavilion that night. Just as the roller coaster jeered around one of the steep turns in the track, the young girl leaned over the side of the open car and projectile-vomited the sweets from her stomach.

The projection sailed through the air and showered several of those below, patiently waiting their turn in the roller coaster line. Like acid rain, the emission dropped down twenty feet and struck at least four of the Winfield cousins standing in line. Most impacted by the air attack was Cousin Virginia Winfield, known to have a weak stomach herself. Almost on cue, after realizing what had just transpired, Virginia hurled the remnants of Nanny's pork-chops and fried okra on the pavement at her feet. The Winfield boys in the path of the "puklear attack" retreated in an immediate sprint to the nearby lake and jumped in without hesitation – clothes and shoes included. Fifteen year-old Virginia was left alone under the roller coaster to recover from her own sickness and assess the damage to her clothes and hair. In a matter of seconds, the roller coaster ride and the remaining night of fun at the midway were cut short for the cousins.

On the ride back to the farm, Uncle John relegated Virginia to ride in the back of the truck with the four boys, who hovered in one corner of the truck-bed, keeping a comfortable distance from their rancid cousin. Humiliated like a scalded dog, Virginia sat on the elevated wheelbase, unable to look at the sneering boys, while fuming at the misfortune of standing in the target of the vile shower. The boys, still dripping wet from the lake's cleansing baptism, stared at Virginia like she was a leper covered in boils. After a hot shower that night, Virginia was able to itemize all the treats the rider had enjoyed before the incident. "I found chunks of hotdog and bits of a chocolate dip-cone in the shower drain, and my hair is still sticky from what I think was cotton candy!" Virginia shared in the dramatic fashion of an embarrassed teen.

While White Lake was known for its nighttime fun at Goldston's and Crystal Lake, a favorite daytime activity in the summers for the Winfield cousins was water skiing. As the cousins grew older, Uncle John rented a ski boat from Goldston's Marina for a week every summer, and a skilled skier himself in his younger days, John taught all eight cousins how to water ski on White Lake. Each cousin became proficient at water skiing with Uncle John's instruction - and some even learned a few tricks. As the cousins grew older still, John allowed Henry to drive the ski-boat, while John stayed behind on the farm.

In the late seventies, mooning was a popular teenage pastime common throughout the United States. Mooning was particularly easy in the summertime when guys only wore a swimsuit. One summer afternoon, Will and the Winfield cousins devised a prank on White Lake that was sure to entertain the tourists and themselves. Just as the glass-bottom boats cruised to the middle of the clear waters of White Lake, the boys pulled the ski boat to within viewing distance of the passengers and dropped their trunks, hanging a moon off the edge of the boat for the viewing pleasure of the spectators on the *Lily* and *Crystal Queen*.

When not on the farm or at White Lake, the cousins often rode with John into town. Elizabethtown was the county seat of Bladen County, located eighteen miles south of the farm and just seven miles past White Lake. Trips into Elizabethtown typically meant a stop at the grocery, the feed store, and lunch and ice cream at Melvin's, home of the best hamburger in North Carolina, according to Uncle John. The feed store carried items that Will never saw in other stores back in Wilmington. There were all kinds of tools, farm equipment, clothes, hats, work gloves, hay, animal feed, hay, and books on farming. There were even toys for kids, like small cast iron tractors, just like Uncle John had on his farm. Will was fascinated with the feed store and its vast inventory.

Located along the banks of the Cape Fear River, Elizabethtown was rich in North Carolina tradition and history. Still the largest county in North Carolina in land mass, Bladen

County was known as the Mother County of North Carolina, because over fifty counties in eastern North Carolina had been formed over the years from massive Bladen County, which covered most of the eastern portion of the State in the 1800s. Initially founded in 1663, Bladen County had long stood as an agricultural region, even by the early settlers.

The Cape Fear River, which runs directly through downtown Elizabethtown, was a vital conduit of trade for agricultural products shipped to other parts of the eastern seaboard and overseas. Tobacco was grown as early as the seventeenth century in Bladen County, and shipped down the River to Wilmington for export to Europe, as Uncle John had explained to Will and his baseball team.

Elizabethtown, population four thousand at its peak, was the epicenter of Bladen County and the mecca of shopping for the rural farmer and his family. The courthouse stood directly in the center of the town square as the tallest building in the county. Under the shadows of the county courthouse stood the Trinity Methodist Church, built in 1832, and the church home to the Winfield family for three generations.

Since the late 1800s, the Winfield family occupied one or more pews on most Sunday mornings. The church stood as one of the oldest structures in the county, always well maintained, manicured. Not only was it a historic landmark in the county, but a place of worship for many in Bladen County.

Just off the town square, in a small white frame house within walking distance of the church and courthouse square, stood the home of Martha Joiner, a widow and mother of two children. Martha was a native of Bladen County, born in Elizabethtown. She also grew up swimming in White Lake in the summers, and married not one, but two locals. Martha's first husband, the father of her two children, died in his twenties on a hunting trip, leaving behind a four-year-old and a two-year-old. Widowed for two years, Martha then married Mr. Sam Parks, a local banker, in 1961. Married less than two weeks, Parks drove his car off McGirt's Bridge in downtown Elizabethtown and into the Cape Fear River, leaving Miss Martha a widow for the second time in a short two-year span.

Her beauty was timeless, her spirit as sweet as the nectar from a honeysuckle stem, and her demeanor as pleasant and pleasing as a rabbit's coat, despite the adversities that life had dealt her. She was revered by the residents of her hometown, composed in her ways, and spoke with compassion to all she encountered. Tall and thin, she always wore a friendly smile on her face each time Will remembered visiting her. For those reasons, and others, John Winfield called Martha Joiner his girlfriend.

John and the cousins visited Martha when their travels took them from the farm into Elizabethtown. Occasionally, she would join John and the cousins for lunch at Melvin's. Martha would sometimes visit the farm as well when Will and his cousins were in town. For years, the extended Winfield family contemplated whether Martha and John might get married.

"Why aren't they married?" seven-year-old Will once inquired, puzzled as to why John would have a girlfriend and not be married.

"Maybe one day they *will* get married," Will's mom replied as the Jordan family left Winfield Farm after a weekend visit.

"She's nice, for a girl. Uncle John should marry her, if he wants to get married. But I'm never getting married," Will announced.

"Martha was married before she was John's girlfriend," his mother explained.

"She had two husbands that died," his dad interjected. "Uncle John may be afraid to marry her because she already had two husbands that died."

"We don't want John to marry her and die too. That would be bad," Will commented from the back seat of the station wagon, seated next to his five-year-old brother.

"We want Uncle John to live forever," young Clay announced.

"So, if Uncle John doesn't marry, does that mean he won't have kids?" Will asked his parents.

"That's the way it's supposed to work," his dad responded with his quick wit.

"Uncle John would be a wonderful father, but he has both of you boys and all your cousins," his mom explained. "Plus, he's like a father to Miss Martha's children, although they are older than you two."

"I would like to be like Uncle John and have a lot of kids around, but not be married," Will pontificated.

"Sounds like a good arrangement to me," Will's dad interjected, cutting an eye toward his wife, sitting next to him in the passenger seat. She stared back at him without having to say a word.

"Uncle John does have it pretty good," Will reasoned. "He gets to live on the farm all the time, and he doesn't have a wife. He also has Nanny to cook for him." Will nodded as if he'd just made a profound decision. "I think I'd like to be like Uncle John when I grow up," he said, staring out the window of the family station wagon. Imagining what it would be like to live at Winfield Farm when he was older, Will started counting every telephone pole along Highway 210 on the road back to Wilmington.

The Island

Chapter 4

As Will and Clay entered their teenage years, other summertime activities took the place of trips to Winfield Farm. As her health failed, Nanny relied on John as her primary caretaker. To help her brother, Mrs. Jordan often drove from Wilmington to the farm for the day during the week, as Nanny became too frail to take care of herself.

"Don't you boys want to ride to the farm today to see your grandmother? Mrs. Jordan asked.

"Not today, Mom, we want to stay here. It's not as fun at the farm anymore, now that Nanny is sick," came Will's excuse to avoid making the trip - a trip he had always looked forward to in his younger years.

Nanny died at the age of eight-two, when Will was fourteen, leaving Uncle John alone on the farm. Though only an hour's drive from Wilmington, trips to the farm for the Jordan family became less and less frequent after Nanny died. The traditional summer trips to White Lake and the farm nearly faded from memory when Will and Clay entered high school.

Occasionally, John traveled to Wilmington to watch Will and Clay play in a baseball game, and usually came to

visit the Jordan's in Wilmington during the Christmas holidays. Nevertheless, the farm became less of a destination for
the Jordan family, particularly as Will discovered the thrills
of his teenage years, a summer job, and the independence that
came with a driver's license and the keys to the wood-paneled
family station wagon. Hanging out with friends and working
a part-time job took the place of time spent at Winfield Farm
in summers past.

Wilmington, North Carolina, was a teenager's haven
in the early eighties. Will and his high school harem found
plenty of trouble in New Hanover County during this era,
and if high school students with access to a car could not find
trouble, then trouble would find them. Maybe it was something about growing up on the coast, or possibly the laid-back
lifestyle of summers at the beach. Regardless, combined with
an influx of tourists at Wrightsville Beach during the summer,
New Hanover County in the 1980s was the place to be for a
teenager with access to a car.

Beer and alcohol were easy to attain for a sixteen year old
with a fake ID. Some stores in Wilmington sold beer without
even checking for identification. The authorities were lax
when it came to selling alcohol to minors in the late seventies
through the early eighties, so the convenience and package
stores did what was necessary to capture additional revenue —
even if it meant selling beer and liquor to those under the legal
drinking age at the time. Local authorities in New Hanover
County turned their heads to certain stores that were known
to sell alcohol to minors. Therefore, the unwritten rule of the
day became, 'If you were old enough to drive, you were old
enough to buy beer, wine and liquor — as long as you knew
which store to patronize.'

Will and his friends in Wilmington discovered one particular convenience store that became a favorite stop for beer on

the way to Wrightsville Beach. The boys knew the clerks by first name, and cash was all that was required. No matter which demographic category or clique a high school student fell into, finding a party somewhere in New Hanover County on most weekends was easy. No barriers to entry or exclusive "invitation only" parties existed for the teenagers in New Hanover County. The only uninvited guests were parents and police.

Wrightsville Beach, a mere fifteen-mile drive from Will's neighborhood, became a summer playground for Will and his classmates. Included among the popular places to hang out were other nearby islands, as well as the Downtown Wilmington waterfront, but the real action in summer and on the weekends was undeniably Wrightsville Beach. Wrightsville Beach was more than a beach, but a pristine barrier island just across the intercostal waterway from downtown Wilmington, known as a summer destination for North Carolina's upper middle class. A small, narrow island with less than three thousand permanent residents, Wrightsville Beach offered impressive waves for surfers, white sandy beaches, a selection of second homes, and a handful of nice hotels.

Wrightsville Beach represented a paradise for anyone who enjoyed being outdoors. First, water was everywhere, and the beach, surfing, boating, skiing, and fishing were among the many activities that made Wilmington and its barrier islands attractive to the locals as well as summer visitors. As a resort island and destination for tourism in the warmer months, the area provided summer jobs for high school and college students working at the hotels or as a lifeguard at one of the pools or on the beach. Summer tourism was the major economic driver in the New Hanover economy. For Will and his friends, the hotels were magnets for families on summer vacation, and girls from all over the southeast flocked to Wrightsville Beach.

The Blockade Runner, a three-hundred-fifty-room hotel in the center of Wrightsville Beach, served as Ground Zero for Will and his comrades those summers. The largest, oldest, and arguably the nicest hotel on the island, the Blockade Runner offered spectacular views of the beach on one side and the intercostal waterway on the other. The expansive pool area between the beach and hotel could accommodate up to three hundred guests. The grounds at the Blockade Runner were meticulously manicured and maintained for major events throughout the year, but summer was by far the peak season.

Will and his comrades learned early during their high school years that access to the Blockade Runner was mostly unrestricted, open to any and all - and not just to paying customers. The hotel employed no security guards or check-points to enter the hotel or pool area, and no parking fees to enter the resort. Guests were not required to carry access cards or badges, so Will and his companions blended right in with the summer crowds.

As self-appointed local ambassadors, Will and his fellow gatecrashers at the Blockade Runner deemed it their civic duty as residents of New Hanover County to inform the teenage guests of the hotel regarding nighttime activities available on Wrightsville Beach, in an effort to enhance the younger visitors' vacation experience.

In the summers, a typical day for Will included afternoons hanging out at the Blockade Runner after working his morning job at Pine Valley Country Club as a landscaper. When his shift at the Club ended at 12:30, Will's time was open for leisure activities, typically spent at the Blockade Runner. Though sweaty and covered with grass and pine straw, Will often elected to skip his post-work shower, drive straight to the beach and bathe in the salty seas of the Atlantic to maximize his time there. Will and his Resort Crashers

Club were not the only locals that called the Blockade Runner their home away from home. The beachhead in front of the hotel became a destination for the New Hanover High School students to meet. An imaginary line on the beach ran perpendicular to the ocean, separating the locals from the Blockade Runner patrons. The locals brought towels and suntan oil, while the tourists sat in expensive wooden chairs under expansive green umbrellas.

For Will, the Blockade Runner surf represented the best of both worlds. The local New Hanover girls clustered in one section of the beach, and the Blockade guests congregated within contiguous viewing distance, just on the other side of the imaginary line. At times, the two worlds collided. It didn't take long for New Hanover girls to catch on to the fact that the high school boys were not always at the beach to be attentive to their New Hanover classmates. For the boys, the New Hanover girls were a known commodity, while the mystique of the guests at the Blockade Runner represented the unknown.

Sun tanning was the favorite beach time activity for the girls. Sporting scant two-piece bathing attire, the local girls would lie in their beach chairs for hours, lathered in baby oil. Sunscreen in New Hanover County had yet to be discovered. After all, it was the 1980s, and the effects of overexposure to the sun had not yet been fully documented, at least not to the girls of New Hanover High.

For the high school boys, sun tanning was a lower priority. The beach near the Blockade offered too many other activities, with some of the best waves on the eastern seaboard. Surfing was a popular form of recreation, although a game of volleyball or touch football was also commonplace on the sandy beaches in front of the Blockade Runner. On occasion, Will and New Hanover High outfielder Lawson Nelson brought their baseball gloves and practiced catching fly balls along the surf.

The tourists enjoyed finding shark's teeth and sand dollars that had washed ashore along the beach, and while surf fishing was popular on Wrightsville Beach, the locals preferred fishing offshore or in the marsh-laden creeks and rivers between Wilmington and the barrier islands. For all the fishing opportunities in New Hanover County, Will and his friends adopted a different type of fishing: trolling for girls along the beach and poolside around the Blockade Runner. This sport did not require a license, a surfboard, or a glove. It did require some skill, charm, confidence, and humor, however. Trolling did require certain rules of engagement. First, a good fisherman first knows where the fish are located. Between the local girls on the beach and the summer guests at the Blockade Runner, the New Hanover fishermen were able to identify sizable schools of fish.

Second, the fisherman must know his waters. The New Hanover anglers knew every square foot of the Blockade resort, from the beach to the hotel. They also knew most of the summer employees at the Blockade, for many of the summer employees at the resort were friends of the fishing contingency. The Blockade Runner and Wrightsville Beach represented the boys' summer fishing domain. Though their fishing rights were not exclusive, Will and his friends were known as angling experts when it came to waters of Wrightsville Beach.

Third, it was imperative for the fisherman to know the best times to fish. For Will and his comrades, their genre of fishing was best suited to warm afternoons. Schools of fish converged on the Blockade Runner grounds from early June through Labor Day, and sunny afternoons proved to be the best feeding times. As for bait, the boys carried in their tackle-box the gift of hospitality, bulked up biceps, good looks, a bronze suntan, and the confidence to approach a fish swimming alone or in a school. Female fish that swam with parent fish were considered uncatchable. Fish with their siblings were considered a more challenging catch, but tough conditions fueled the fisherman's creativity for ways to chum the waters. A football was often used as effective bait when trolling the waters near the Blockade Runner. A toss to the younger brother was a persuasive method to "lure" the attention of the older sister.

The fishing line represented importance for the angler. The lines that the boys used to attract the fish came straight from their mouths, and the boys learned early that lines were important. Strong lines were key to effective introductions and good first impressions. Sometimes, the use of an irrelevant question was enough to start a dialog with a fish. "Do you know where we could find a payphone?" was a line used by an angler in Will's fishing expedition before the days of cell phones. Asking for directions was also often effective, however, "Which way to the beach?" was considered a question too ludicrous to ask, revealing that the fishing line was ineffective.

The use of unassuming items was also known as effective bait. Davis Butler, one of New Hanover's wide receivers on the football team, found an earring on the Blockade Runner boardwalk one summer and used the unassuming silver piece of jewelry as a fishing lure for an entire summer. Holding the earring in full view of the fish, Davis asked, "Did you drop this earring?" It was a simple question Davis posed to any girl he thought he might like to meet. He used the line daily for most of the summer. There were many nights that particular summer that Will would lie in bed trying to fall asleep, and all he heard was Davis' voice asking, "Did you drop this earring?"

The cheesy pick-up lines used in the bar by the guy wearing gold jewelry and the unbuttoned polyester shirt were extremely ineffective. For example, "Can I buy you a drink?"

was never a line used by a New Hanover fisherman. Using bad lines was like fishing with live shrimp in a fresh water pond. The boys were far more cunning fishermen than to use substandard fishing lines. Although Will was known to fish on occasion by himself, fishing with friends in teams proved to be more effective, especially when encountering schools of fish. Fishing with friends was definitely more fun too.

Will and his fishing buddies had different objectives when fishing. Some kept score and tallied the number of fish caught during a given summer. Others were out to simply enjoy a day of fishing with friends. Will enjoyed the actual "sport" of fishing, while comrade Corey Smith, a more aggressive angler, was more about getting the fish in the boat. Corey was out for one thing, and that one thing was to bed the fish. He found little value in the catch and release program. Once Corey had a fish hooked on the line, he was going to make sure he filleted that fish or had it mounted.

Will had a different perspective. A successful fishing excursion for Will was to approach a group of girls at the Blockade Runner, introduce them to his fellow fishermen, invite them to a party on the island that night, find one particular fish he liked out of the school, and take her out on a date the next night. Fishing in the summers proved fortuitous for Will and the New Hanover fishing expedition. Rarely were there pictures to share, so quite often the fishing stories were embellished. However, like any good fishing trip, the stories that ensued from fishing with friends often lasted a lifetime.

If not for his summer job at the golf course, working at the Blockade Runner might have been a good choice of employment for Will, bringing him a little closer to fishing waters. Many of Will's friends worked at the resort during the busy summer season, some working inside the hotel as janitors cleaning restrooms. Others worked as waiters, while some worked as bus boys, cleaning tables in the banquet halls and hotel restaurant. The more tenured employees worked as front desk clerks. However, the most coveted summer jobs were outside on the beach or at the pool. Life-guarding was definitely one of the most coveted positions at the Blockade Runner, but managing the chaos of a crowded pool in the summertime took too much time away from socializing with friends or meeting new ones. However, the views behind the sunglasses were fabulous from the life-guard stands, according to Will's friends who had held these enviable positions.

The absolute best summer gig at the Blockade Runner was held by Will's friend, Ryan Fleming, a smooth-talking senior at New Hanover High, who lived near Will in Wilmington. Ryan worked in the Blockade Runner's tiki hut at poolside. Strategically positioned at poolside near the boardwalk leading to the beach, the tiki hut was like a mini Wal-Mart for the beach crowd, with T-shirts, sunglasses, floats, candy and beach towels packed inside this tiny commissary. While such necessities sold at a steady pace during the summers, the item garnering the most attention were the tanning oils. In addition to selling Mickey Mouse blow-up float-rings to toddlers, it was Ryan's duty to promote tanning products to the patrons at the Blockade Runner, and Ryan Fleming was the right man for the assignment.

Skilled in the art of salesmanship, Ryan enticed the female guests with free samples of tanning and after-sun products as they walked by the diminutive hut. Sensually rubbing the oils on the hands and arms of his potential customers, he sold bottles and bottles of suntan lotions and potions that Ryan convinced his female customer base were good for their skin. He had face crèmes, sun block, and after-sun aloe, but his big ticket item was coconut oil, the secret formula to a savage tan.

Sporting a healthy tan himself, Ryan used his charm and good looks to convince many a female guest at the Blockade Runner the benefits of purchasing a bottle of the tanning oil to generate the perfect tan. Ryan's customer base ranged from age nine to ninety, but most of the patrons were teenagers. One hundred percent were female.

Ryan became known as the snake oil salesman among the New Hanover locals that crashed the Blockade poolside. As they watched him operate from across the pool, bottle of oil in one hand, Ryan would stop the prospective client on the way to the beach with the offer of a free sample of the savage tanning product. From there, he would steer them toward his tiki hut and begin his pitch.

"Let me hold your hand, if you don't mind," Ryan would start, holding the prospect's left hand and applying a generous sample on her forearm. As he rubbed the oil on the full length of her arm, Ryan would explain the attributes of the product. His sale ratios appeared to be impressively high for those that observed his tactics from across the pool.

After watching Ryan on one particularly busy and balmy Saturday afternoon, Will and his friends decided to play a joke on Ryan. Soliciting the help from George Stratford, an old all-star baseball friend from Raleigh who stayed with his family at the Blockade Runner, the boys designed a perfect plan. Will commissioned George to play the part of an effeminate prospect in search of a tan like Ryan's. Ryan had no clue who George Stratford was. He appeared to be a typical guest at the Blockade Runner, except this afternoon, George was tapped to play the role of a male patron, interested in procuring a savage tan. Sporting a farmer's tan from his baseball uniform, George's lily-white torso was in desperate need of a more balanced tint. Acting the role of an effeminate customer at the tiki hut was not a part George was accustomed to playing, but he was always game for a good practical joke. Prancing to the other side of the pool, George approached Ryan, acting intrigued by the tanning products on display under the tiki hut's thatched roof.

"I've been watching you sell the tanning solutions from my chair across the pool. You have a wonderful tan. As you can tell, I need some help with my own tan. I'd like to learn more about what you have to sell," George inquired with enthusiasm to the unsuspecting Ryan.

Will and three of his friends discretely contained their laughter from across the pool. George extended his right arm in Ryan's direction, letting his hand bend at the wrist. The 'actor' then placed his left arm on his belt-line with his hip cocked in the direction of the pool.

"Can you apply some oil on my arm like you do for your customers, please? I've been watching you put that oil on the girls, and those girls have been buying these bottles like it's a secret potion. Tell me how it can make me have a tan like yours."

Ryan, visibly uncomfortable, squeezed a small portion of the oil on George's arm. Hesitantly, he looked George in the eye, unsure if he was serious.

"Aren't you going to rub it in?" George inquired in his manufactured sweet Southern voice.

"You go ahead," Ryan insisted, clearly uneasy when asked to apply tanning lotion on the arm of another male.

"Please, you rub it on my arm, like you do for the girls," George insisted.

By this time, Will and his buddies had conspicuously moved closer to the scene. Hesitant to comply with George's request, Ryan was uncertain as to how he should react. When it was obvious that the practical joke had worked flawlessly, Will and his sidekicks burst out in laughter, rushing the stage to applaud George's stellar performance. Ryan was the only one involved in the prank who was not laughing after the episode. George eventually introduced himself to Ryan with an extended hand. Reluctantly, Ryan shook the hand of the one who had shamed him.

"Before you take a swing at me, they put me up to it," George said, pointing at Will and his allies, the architects of the successful antic, now doubled over in laughter.

In addition to reconnecting with friends from his past, Will met many new friends during his summers at the Blockade Runner. Some female friendships lasted beyond their vacation week at Wrightsville Beach. Others lasted only one night, while some friendships were reinstituted in college when he recognized familiar faces attending the University of North Carolina, the melting pot of college students from the Tar Heel state.

As summers ended and the tourists left the Blockade Runner, Wrightsville Beach slowed to a quieter pace, leaving the restaurants, hotels, and summer rental cottages mostly vacant for the off-season. The buzz of activity and summer frolic ended with a whimper as another school year began. However, fall brought with it a new season of entertainment for the locals at New Hanover High.

After tourists departed Wrightsville Beach after Labor Day, the high school population at New Hanover High found refuge on the island for weekend fun and nighttime activity. Away from the Blockade Runner, the north end of Wrightsville Beach was the more desolate and undeveloped part of the island – a perfect venue for keg parties and other unwholesome activities. For years, the north end of the island had been known for its privacy. About twelve miles from the Blockade Runner, the pavement ended and became a network of dirt roads that led through palmetto bushes and sagging oak trees.

Motorcycles, jeeps, and dune buggies found the north end of Wrightsville Beach an optimal venue for a joy ride. It was also the ideal setting for a young couple to find solace at the end of a romantic evening. Some of the New Hanover crowd named the extreme north end of the island the "Petting Zoo" due to the nighttime follies that took place under the sprawling moss-laden oak trees.

On the road to the north end of the island, just before where the blacktop ends, maybe a half mile south of the Petting Zoo, visitors found a spacious parking lot off North Lumina Avenue, with easy beach access. Known in its day as Salisbury Park, it was the optimal location for a high school party. On any given Friday night, after a high school football game, the parking area at Salisbury Park overflowed with cars, jeeps, and pick-up trucks. By daylight, Salisbury Park was no more than a parking area for beach access during the warmer months. By night, Salisbury was favored over the Wal-Mart or mall parking lot for several reasons, not the least of which was direct access to the beach. Due to its remote location, the kids could hang out in the parking lot, make noise, smoke pot, and drink alcohol with little to no hassle from the island neighbors or the New Hanover County authorities.

With space for almost one hundred cars, the Park was the perfect meeting place for such parties. Just beyond the spacious parking lot, miles of dark and desolate sandy beaches called the crowds, and during Friday night parties, a few industrious attendees would build a bonfire on the beach, especially on the colder nights.

The carnage the morning after the colossal parties was widespread on the north end of the island. The aftermath soon became more than just a nuisance to the permanent residents of Wrightsville Beach as beer and liquor bottles littered the dunes, parking lot, and beaches. The locals began to complain to the authorities after the parties grew to enormous proportions by the time Will was a junior in high school, and the bonfires were the first of the night-time activities to be banned from Salisbury Beach.

Though the parking and beach areas were public, the authorities made an effort to close off the parking area after dark, but island merchants complained that their evening customers would stop patronizing the restaurants, gas stations, and shops if access to the public beaches was locked down at dark. Either way, residents continued to complain about the parties on the north end of Wrightsville Beach. It was no secret that more than underage drinking took place on the placid beaches of the north end of Wrightsville Beach. With no geographic barriers except the Atlantic Ocean, four miles of mostly private beach area, a blanket, and a moonlit night, the setting made for the perfect romantic encounter.

"I'm tired of walking my dog on the beach on Saturday and Sunday mornings and picking up trash," an older lady was quoted as saying during one of the public hearings on the efforts by the Wrightsville Beach residents to curb the weekend parties. "I don't mind picking up an occasional beer can, but I refuse to pick up condoms on the beach,"

Another resident, in an attempt at humor during the public hearings, but at the same time making his point, was on record for making the statement, "I'm afraid of walking barefoot on the beach these days, because I'm worried I'll step on a jellyfish. And I'm not talking about the marine life jellyfish that often wash up on the beach."

If the beaches and dunes could communicate, volumes could be written on the indiscretions that took place on Wrightsville Beach as night fell on the pristine island, but those depraved nighttime activities were soon to be curtailed. After heated debate, the New Hanover County Commission agreed to lock the gates to the public parks on Wrightsville Beach at 11:00 p.m., reaching a compromise with the residents, the merchants, and nighttime beachcombers.

The New Hanover Sheriff's Department was forced to take a different approach to the nighttime activities after the free rein the teenagers held in the mid-1980s. Finally, the residents of Wrightsville Beach demanded their island back. The bonfires were completely banned, the parking lots along North Lumina Street closed at 9:00 p.m. rather than 11:00 p.m., organized beach parties were shut down after dusk, and parked cars were checked more closely to moderate drinking, drugs, and other marginal activities that took place on the desolate north end of the island.

Will and his high school friends enjoyed an era of laissez-faire rule from the authorities, the police, and even their parents during their high school days. The students owned the beaches of Wrightsville Beach for too long before the residents fought and won control of the island again. Like an ocean breeze, the party era at Wrightsville Beach had blown into history and became just a high school memory etched in the minds of those who experienced those days gone by.

By the late 1980s, Wrightsville Beach returned to the family beach it had been in the 1960s. The Blockade Runner still exists today as one of the focal points of the island, and North Carolina families still visit the resort each summer, and some of the locals occasionally crash the pool and hang out at the beach in front of the hotel. The resort still hires teenagers from Wilmington to work as lifeguards, landscapers, janitors, and bus boys. At night, a small group of partiers might be heard on a weekend night on the beaches. One might still find a car on the far north end parked underneath one of the majestic oak trees on a moonlit night, but today, Wrightsville Beach has been restored to its original heritage, and returned to its residents.

The University

Chapter 5

The year was 1984, and a student athlete by the name of Michael Jordan had arrived on the UNC campus by way of Laney High School in Wilmington three years earlier. College basketball had reached its pinnacle in the state of North Carolina, and behind the talent of North Carolina basketball legends Jordan and Sam Perkins, the campus was electrified by a hoops team ranked number one in the national polls. Will Jordan took great pride in the fact that MJ was a product of his same hometown.

In addition to the basketball phenomenon on campus, UNC's academic rankings were one of the highest among the nation's public colleges. The campus population had risen to over 20,000 students, and Tar Heel pride was at an all-time high. Students from all over the country applied for admission to UNC, but only a few select applicants were accepted from out of state due to the strong demand from in-state students. In a state that stretched more than three hundred-fifty miles wide from the Smokey Mountains to the Atlantic, UNC served as the melting pot of college-aged students from the great state of North Carolina.

The University had six campuses around the state, but the main campus was in Chapel Hill, a classic college town of 50,000 residents nestled in the rolling hills of North Carolina's Piedmont region. The city of Chapel Hill rivaled any major college campus in America in terms of its poetic beauty, lavish history, storied traditions, classic architecture, superior athletics, unparalleled academics, and school pageantry. After all, UNC was "*The* University of North Carolina," and Chapel Hill *was* the University of North Carolina, and UNC was Chapel Hill. The words UNC, Chapel Hill, and the University of North Carolina, or simply "Carolina" were all used interchangeably, like the Father, Son, and the Holy Spirit, and with similar reverence among North Carolinians.

The sky blue school colors dominated the campus landscape and a popular bumper sticker boasted, *IF GOD IS NOT A TAR HEEL, THEN WHY DID HE MAKE THE SKY CAROLINA BLUE*? could be found on dorm room doors and car bumpers all over the UNC campus. Carolina blue was a distinctive color, just like the school itself.

The year 1984 was a great time to be a Tar Heel, and although just a freshman, Will lived and breathed the full experience, capturing all that UNC and Chapel Hill had to offer. His father and grandfather had both studied at Carolina. His mother and most of her siblings attended one of the UNC campuses. Will's blood bled Carolina blue.

Will discovered that the University of North Carolina offered a balance of challenging academics, a large campus in the classic college town of Chapel Hill, and endless extracurricular and social activities. It was the perfect fit for Will's college experience. Still, the biggest draw by far at Chapel Hill was the campus scenery. While the campus was known for its meticulous landscaping and historic architecture, the university's most treasured asset for natural beauty was its female population. Girls made up 57% of the student population at UNC in the eighties. With over 12,000 females on campus, Will made it his goal to date as many of them as possible. From Asheville to Winston-Salem and all parts in between, the Chapel Hill campus was a collage of the state's most attractive young women, all assembled in one college town.

Never one to settle for just one exclusive girlfriend, Will played the campus coeds like an attack covers the lacrosse field, darting in and out of traffic on the field, covering as much ground as needed to take as many shots on goal as possible. The ultimate challenge of the attack position was to avoid the competition and score, and score he did while on campus.

"It's like shooting fish in a barrel," Will often said, quoting a line from his Uncle John, describing the opportunities to meet women on the Carolina campus. Will's high school days of "fishing" at the Blockade Runner had served him well as an optimal training ground for his days of pursuing the fish in Chapel Hill. Will had learned the lines to use and not to use from his days of approaching a girl at poolside in those summers past. His friendly, yet humorous, approach to pursuing the female gender usually put the females at ease, and his brownish-blonde hair, sparkling blue eyes, and prevalent smile did not hurt his cause either. His training had transitioned well from Wrightsville Beach to the University of North Carolina campus, and although an independent operator at heart, Will learned early in his college career the value of working in teams when it came to meeting girls - just like in his high school days at the Blockade Runner. Girls on campus ran in packs, herds, cliques, and groups. Rarely did you see a girl alone on campus, unless she was on the way to class. However, when it came to parties, studying, bars, pool halls, and even going to the bathroom, girls stuck together.

While maintaining a 3.7 grade point average in his four years at UNC, Will was schooled in a few new things outside the classroom as well. Not good enough to play college baseball on the Division One level, Will learned the game of lacrosse, a popular sport at the time on the campuses of the mid-Atlantic states. With his baseball background, he was also a standout on the fraternity softball team. He was also a regular for a game of pool at Papa Jake's, a rustic bar and pool hall just off campus on West Franklin Street.

As a sophomore, Will discovered his love for the game of pool at Papa Jake's, famous for its four-dollar pitchers of draft beer on Monday nights. Jake's was not known for attracting many females, but as the men on campus soon discovered, the low priced beer and open pool tables generated a copious number of both beer drinkers and pool players - even on a Monday night.

"I think Jake needs a lesson in economics," Mark Coleman of Raleigh, the fraternity treasurer, once commented, making note of the fact that the beer might be priced *too* low. As the demand for beer at Jake's increased, the pricing structure stayed the same, defying Keynesian economic policy. In time, Will became far more intrigued with the pool tables at Jake's than the cheap beer, but despite his social interests, Will's studies always came first during his time at Carolina. Will was the guy who would spend two hours at the library on campus and stop by Jake's to shoot a game of pool on his way back home after the library closed.

Like his UNC classmates, following sports programs played a big role in Will's life on campus. In addition to consistent dominance in basketball, lacrosse was emerging as the new sport on campus at North Carolina, and the Tar Heels' lacrosse team had reached national notoriety. Like on any Division One campus in the South, football was a celebrated fall tradition at Chapel Hill. The Carolina baseball team was competitive with any team in the Atlantic Coast Conference, and as a high school baseball player, Will enjoyed attending Carolina home games at Boshamer Stadium in the spring.

During his first year at UNC, attending baseball games was often bittersweet for Will. Though he loved the game, watching the Tar Heels play from the stands created some heartache, since playing baseball for the Tar Heels had been his dream since he was six years old. Although Will was a stellar Little League and high school player, playing baseball at the collegiate level for a NCAA division I school was a dream that dissolved by the time Will was a junior at New Hanover High. Consequently, Will resolved that he would settle for stardom on the intramural fields and participate in UNC athletics from the stands.

Of all the sports at the University of North Carolina, basketball was by far the supreme spectator sport. There was no such thing as an empty seat at Rupp Arena for a home hoops game. The ACC had become the dominant basketball conference in the country, and UNC stood perennially at the top of the conference. Steeped in basketball tradition, North Carolina became the bedrock of the Atlantic Coast Conference's rise to domination in college basketball.

At the pinnacle of each basketball season was the matchup between the Tar Heels of North Carolina and the Blue Devils of Duke. With the campuses located just ten miles apart, the rivalry in college basketball matched no other in the country. Duke, the much smaller of the two schools, was known for its superior academics, but its basketball program consistently ranked among the top in the nation, and continues to do so today.

Hence, the two rival schools, along with neighboring Wake Forest and North Carolina State, adopted the name of

Tobacco Road to symbolize the corridor between these four academic institutions. Other smaller schools in the Piedmont region of Carolina, where the game of basketball got its start in the Tar Heel state in the early 1900s, dot the map along the undefined Tobacco Road.

Tobacco Road cannot be located on a map, although numerous Tobacco Roads exist throughout the state of North Carolina. Nevertheless, the mention of Tobacco Road symbolizes a region known for two North Carolina traditions: basketball and the tobacco industry. Running east and west, Interstate 40 serves as the linear link between the four major universities in the Piedmont region of North Carolina. Though the interstate signage does not reflect it, one might think that I-40 is the closest major road connecting its basketball schools.

However, even today, Tobacco Road is synonymous with the most prolific region of college basketball on the entire globe. Collectively, Carolina and Duke can boast thirty-three National Collegiate Basketball Championships, and the two schools are consistently ranked in the Top Ten each fall, so the tradition of more championships will certainly follow.

Durham, North Carolina, home to Duke University, was named for Washington Duke, a tobacco magnate who made the name Bull Durham famous from its brand of chewing tobacco. Duke's son and heir to the company endowed what was then Trinity College with a substantial gift to have the college renamed for his father in 1924. Today, the name Duke is associated with accomplished academics and exemplary basketball. Home to two of the largest tobacco companies in the world, the global headquarters for R.J. Reynolds and Lorillard are located along the Tobacco Road corridor in Winston-Salem and Greensboro, respectively. While the tobacco crop itself is grown in the less populous flatland region of North

Carolina, south of the Piedmont region, the corporate head-quarters are located in the metropolitan cities along Tobacco Road, just a two-hour drive north of the farmland of eastern Carolina's sprawling tobacco fields.

It is not uncommon for the Duke and UNC basketball teams to be ranked by the national pollsters as number one or two in any given year. The most heated rivalry in all of college sports occurs when the Duke Blue Devils and UNC Tar Heels basketball teams meet at center court each winter.

The Decision

Chapter 6

Will had enjoyed an impressive run at the University in his four years as an undergraduate. He had maintained an enviable regiment of good grades and on-campus activities, while making time to weave in a balanced dose of social activities. Well respected by his peers for his approach to college life, Will was elected president of his fraternity in the spring of his junior year. His presidential term culminated as the UNC basketball season came to an end in March of his senior year. During the second semester of his senior year at UNC, his run at Carolina was almost over, and Will knew it was time to make some decisions about his future, with graduation just three months away.

Several of his friends had already accepted jobs in accounting, banking, marketing, and engineering fields. A few seniors had been accepted to law school at UNC, a fortuitous opportunity to stay in Chapel Hill for another three years. Fraternity funny man Bart Rollins had accepted a job with one of the corporate food giants, selling potted meat to grocery stores. Jobs in the sales field with larger corporations paid well, but the applicant often had to accept the position in the city where the job was located. Bart's position started July 1 in Roanoke, Virginia. Moving to Roanoke was not Bart's first choice of places to live right out of college, but he was happy to have a job, even if it meant leaving his home state of North Carolina and selling potted meat.

With a high grade point average in the Kenan-Flagler business school, Will was an attractive candidate for potential work in Charlotte or Raleigh for one of the larger North Carolina banks. He had been offered invitations by two mega-banks to enter their training programs, to be followed by a job, during the summer following his graduation in May. The stock brokerage business had been an attractive option for graduates with finance degrees, but the stock market crash of 1987 had occurred just six months previously, so the money management business had less appeal to Will and other 1988 graduates.

However, job opportunities in the financial sector for graduates with good grades were limited, but available. After the Black Friday crash of the stock market in October of 1987, the economy began to teeter. Jobs were scarce for recent graduates, especially in financial services fields, and even those at the top of their classes academically had trouble finding jobs.

After several interviews with commercial insurance companies, money management firms, and large regional banks, Will was not enamored with any of the job opportunities. With his resume and grade point average, Will expected more. A few of his older friends with finance degrees had gone to work in New York, and while working on Wall Street had some appeal, living in New York City was not his first choice of places to live. Plus, the financial services world was still hung over from the events on Wall Street last fall.

Will's family began to weigh in on the decision. His parents leaned toward his going to work in Raleigh or coming home to Wilmington. "With your grades, Will, you should be going to law school," Uncle John suggested. Practicing law did not sound intriguing to Will, and neither did another three years of intense study. After all, Will was more of a numbers guy and less of the lawyer type.

Will had taken the GMAT for admission into business school, as UNC had an impressive graduate school program in finance. An MBA from Duke even sounded intriguing. Though bitter athletic rivals in the Tobacco Road consortium, most Tar Heels had respect for Duke's reputation as one of the top academic schools in the Southeast. Staying at Chapel Hill and entering the business graduate school was high on his list of options, but Will was ready to spread his wings and further his surroundings. After four good years at UNC, maybe it was time to move on to other turf.

At his father's suggestion, Will sent his GMAT scores, transcripts, and an application to several Ivy League schools to test his credentials against the academic elite. Maybe graduate school was a way to put off entering the job market in this feeble economy. The graduate school application process was a long and arduous task, and Ivy League grad school applications themselves were particularly time consuming. Will was certain that his applications to Yale, Harvard, and Princeton would end up in a huge dumpster outside the admissions office.

Will had visions of Ivy League school administrators sitting around a conference room table laughing at the dismal applications from all the Southerners who had pipe dreams of attending an Ivy League institution. He envisioned a consortium of education snobs passing the inferior applications around the table with comments like, "Hey, Arnold, get a load of this one. He was president of the Chess Club at No Name State College and has a 3.0 GPA. Are you kidding? Pass!" as the file that took the applicant hours to prepare was brushed off the table, dropped into a large rolling trash bin and as another applicant's dream fell into an unassuming dark grave among thousands of other rejected applications.

After the rigorous task of completing and mailing graduate school applications, Will was diligent in checking the mail each day for responses. By early February of his last semester at Carolina, Will had been accepted to UNC, Duke, and the University of Virginia, all highly respected business school programs in the Southeast. Still, the Ivy League schools were a different story. The rejection letters followed in sequence: Princeton, Harvard, Brown, Columbia, Cornell, and Penn. The acceptance rate for applicants at Ivy League schools ranged between eight to fifteen percent, depending on the level of prestige of each school at the time, and it was apparent that Will fell into the rejection majority.

One afternoon, while searching through the pile of mail at the fraternity house after class, Will noted a letter addressed to him. The top left corner sported a dark green logo. He inspected the crisp off-white envelope, and realized the letter was from Dartmouth College. He had heard from all the other Ivy League schools, except Dartmouth. He imagined that this was the last of the rejection letters. With little emotion, Will opened the envelope cautiously and meticulously, as though any letter from an Ivy League school had to be handled with special care. After six previous rejection letters, the anticipation of the contents was now far less suspenseful.

The letter started like the others. "*Thank you for applying for admission to Dartmouth's College of Business for entry into the fall class of 1988...*" The second sentence was different. It read, "*We would like to congratulate you for being accepted into the Dartmouth Graduate School of Business for the fall class of 1988. Please notify us of your intent to attend Dartmouth by*

May 15 as the applicant pool is competitive, and the number of available slots is limited."

"Wow," Will whispered, looking around the chapter room to see who else might be loafing in the spacious meeting room of the fraternity house. He was alone. He knew nothing about Dartmouth, only that his research had shown that it was one of the eight Ivy League schools in the northeastern United States.

Accepted. Will read the letter again to make sure he had read it correctly. Acting as though hiding a love letter from a secret admirer, Will slid the letter back into its envelope and placed it inside his corporate finance book for safe keeping. He pondered who to call first, wanting to share his good news with someone. Then, he laughed. "Dartmouth? Where the hell is Dartmouth anyway?" He walked down the tiled floor hallway toward his room and unlocked the door. His roommate was in class, so he put down his books on the desk in the corner of his room and picked up the phone.

"Dad, sorry to bother you at work, but I wanted to read you this letter I got in the mail," Will said, trying to contain his excitement. He skipped over the introductory comments of the letter, until he got to the paragraph that stated, "We are pleased to inform you that you have been accepted into the fall class of the Tuck School of Business."

"Congratulations, son!" his father exclaimed, his voice filled with pride.

"I thought you were crazy when you said I should apply to all of the Ivy League schools," Will admitted. "I would have never imagined. Still, I know nothing about Dartmouth. It's in New Hampshire, right? I'm sure the weather is bitter cold in the winter."

"We'll have to plan a trip up there for you to visit. It might not be the right fit, but you got in. That's great news. Have you heard from any other schools?" Mr. Jordan asked.

"Only Virginia's Commerce School, UNC, and Duke, but I got Dear John letters from all the other Ivy League schools," Will said, now unsure of whether a small school in New Hampshire was the right choice for him. "We need to see the campus, Dad."

"How about in the spring, when it warms up? When is spring break?" Mr. Jordan inquired.

"In about a month," Will responded, wondering if he wanted to spend spring break in New Hampshire rather than in the Outer Banks with his girlfriend's family. "We'll see, Dad," Will said. The reality of leaving North Carolina and being so far from home had stifled the excitement of attending an Ivy League school. Maybe it wasn't such a good idea after all. "It's a long drive, right?" Will asked.

"We'll look at the map. We might just fly since it will be a short trip," Mr. Jordan responded. "I hear it's a beautiful part of the country up there."

"I'm sure it's expensive, Dad. Can we afford it?"

"Don't worry about that. We'll figure a way to make it work. It's not every day that you get accepted to attend an Ivy League school."

"Thanks, Dad," Will said, now at an age where he appreciated the support his parents had given him through the years.

"I'm proud of you, son. This is great news, and I'm excited about seeing the campus."

"Me too," Will said half-heartedly, the enthusiasm waning somewhat as the reality of leaving familiar surroundings firmly entered his mind.

The Graduate

Chapter 7

The Tuck School of Business at ~~Dartmouth~~ in Hanover, New Hampshire was over six hundred miles away from the UNC campus at Chapel Hill, and worlds away in terms of the college experience Will left behind at the University of North Carolina. Founded in 1769, Dartmouth was rich in tradition like Will's alma mater at Carolina. Though known for its academics, Will was drawn to the school for its reputation, its campus setting in the hills of New England, and emphasis on collegiate sports.

After spending his first twenty-two years of life in North Carolina, Will realized that attending Dartmouth was an opportunity to see another part of the country, experience a different approach to education, and procure a MBA from a prestigious Ivy League institution. Not only was Dartmouth located in a completely different part of the country, the cultural differences were significant. As a son of the South, could Will handle the Northern ways of New England?

By Will's senior year at Carolina, the UNC-Chapel Hill campus had grown to over 22,000 students. The exclusive Tuck Program at Dartmouth had a total of five hundred students in its two MBA classes. Many of the MBA candidates at Dartmouth had already been in the workforce for two to four years before entering grad school, so the student population was also older. Known for its quality of Southern coeds, one UNC sorority alone had more attractive women than the entire Dartmouth campus, based on Will's early assessment on the initial visit.

However, despite its differences, one visit to Hanover in April was all it took to sway Will's decision that Dartmouth was the place for him to spend the next two years. Set along the Connecticut River separating New Hampshire and Vermont, the Dartmouth campus in springtime was picturesque. A regatta race took place on the river while Will and his dad visited the campus.

"I guess the school stages these regatta races for visitors like us that come here to see Dartmouth in the spring," Mr. Jordan joked.

For all its differences, the Dartmouth campus did resemble that of Chapel Hill, with its classic nineteenth century architectural academic buildings. Nestled in the foothills of the White Mountains, the city of Hanover, New Hampshire was a picturesque New England college town, also known for the fall foliage that covered the campus in the fall.

The winter months were brutal, however. "Though our winters are known to be cold here, the ski slopes of Vermont are only a twenty-minute car ride from campus," the campus tour guide explained to the group of prospective Dartmouth attendees. Will's snow- skiing experience had been limited to a few weekend trips to Asheville to visit his cousins as a middle school student, and he well knew that snow skiing in western North Carolina did not compare to the slopes and snow mass in the mountains of New England.

The list of notable Dartmouth alumni was also impressive to Will and Mr. Jordan, the number of governors and congressmen too numerous to list, yet Daniel Webster and John D. Rockefeller were among the most famous. The current U.S. Surgeon General at the time, C. Everett Koop, was also an alumnus. The most impressive graduate however, as far as Will was concerned, was Chris Miller, a screenwriter who wrote the popular *Animal House* movie about his own fraternity days at Dartmouth in the seventies. As president of his own fraternity, Will could appreciate and relate to the classic depiction of college fraternity life created by Miller.

Maybe it was the professional sales job of the admissions director and the campus guide, but the visit to Dartmouth convinced Will and his father that this was the right place for Will to get his MBA. "Impressive place," Will commented as they left the campus that Sunday afternoon, bound for Logan International in Boston to catch their flight back to North Carolina. "Can we afford it, Dad?"

"We'll make it work. You heard them mention about the loans and scholarships available through the school. We'll follow up on those opportunities right away. Don't worry about the money. You're going to Dartmouth! It's a great school. I wish I could go," Mr. Jordan said as the two drove the rental car through the hills of Vermont bound for Boston.

After spring break, Will was back on campus in Chapel Hill, unsure how to let his friends know about his decision to attend Dartmouth. Always the clandestine type, Will had kept the visit to Dartmouth to himself. Only his girlfriend and his roommate, Marshall, knew of the weekend visit to Dartmouth. Once Will finally told a few of his closer friends, word got out among the guys at the fraternity house. Will had always seen himself in graduate school. He was a good student, but he had never pictured himself as an Ivy Leaguer.

Now in his final quarter of undergraduate school, conversations abounded among the seniors about their plans after graduation.

"Where the hell is Dartmouth?" senior Andrew Lutz asked Will, while sharing a beer on the front porch of the fraternity house.

"I asked myself the same thing," Will replied. "It's in New Hampshire." He turned to his friend. "Do you know where New Hampshire is?"

"In France?" Andrew responded, playing stupid.

"That's great news, Wilbur, but I thought you were a Southern boy. That's a long haul from here."

"Yep, I'll miss it, but it's a two-year program, and I'm sure I'll end up back in Charlotte or Raleigh after I pay my dues up there. I just wasn't ready for the real world yet. College has been too much fun," Will confided, rationalizing his decision to leave North Carolina.

"I'm sure it's a good school. You'll probably end up making a million dollars a year on Wall Street after you get your MBA," Andrew said. "Plus, you're a lot smarter than the rest of us around here."

"Oh, I don't know about that. I think Dartmouth wanted some diversity in the MBA program. They needed a few token Southerners to balance out the class of Yankee liberals up there, but I won't be going to New York after grad school. That place is not for me."

"Well, congrats, Wilbur," Andrew commented. "That's great news. And what about you, Lush?" Will asked, using his friend's fraternity nickname. "You going back to Greensboro?"

"I'll probably work in the family real estate business this summer and see how I like it. I'll interview around Greensboro and Winston-Salem to see what opportunities are out there. This economy is not the best for graduates looking for work. You're making a good choice getting the MBA and waiting for the economy to improve," Andrew responded.

"I hope so," Will said, heading inside to find his cooler of beer. "Jobs are scarce out there. Good luck figuring it out."

The Campus

Chapter 8

As expected, winters in New Hampshire proved brutally cold. It was Will's first winter in Hanover, and the coldest days during the dead of winter felt like he lived in Russia or Alaska. After two months in Hanover, Will was convinced that winter semester at Dartmouth was good for only two indoor activities: studying and playing pool. Well, maybe a third, but in Will's limited time on campus, he was still working on the third indoor activity. "It's no wonder you guys are such good students up here," Will was known to say. "These winters drive everyone inside. It's so damned cold that no one has anything else to do except either drink or study." Will lived in a single room in Topliff Dorm on campus. The private room gave him the solitude to study, but after living in the fraternity house on campus at Carolina, the walls soon caved in around him and his room felt like solitary confinement. So, to maintain his sanity, Will spent most of his time during fall semester at one of two places: the campus library or the local pool hall in downtown Hanover.

When not studying, Will found his way to Salt Hill Pub for a beer and a game of pool. Shooting pool had become his passion during the winter months when outside activities were prohibitive. Comparatively, winters in Chapel Hill produced some low temperatures and a few snowfalls, and when it snowed heavily at UNC, classes were typically cancelled. Heavy snow days at Carolina meant snowball fights with the fraternity house next door or sledding down the hilly slopes of campus on dining hall trays.

The snow never stopped classes from being held at Dartmouth. At Carolina, the colder weather signaled the start of the Tar Heel basketball season. At Dartmouth, cold weather represented more time to stay inside and study. When the New England TV stations chose to cover ACC basketball, Will watched the Heels play on television, but it was difficult to follow UNC hoops like he once did. Catching the Dartmouth basketball games on campus offered a substitute to attending a game in Chapel Hill, but the experience was never the same. By the time March arrived, Will could be found at the pub, watching the Heels in the NCAA tournament.

While watching basketball and playing pool were Will's winter pastimes in Hanover, the one outdoor activity Will discovered that winter was skiing. In order to master the New England ski slopes, Will started practicing on the campus slope during his first winter at Dartmouth. Later in the season, Will and some of his classmates made the short trip to Killington, Vermont's largest ski resort. By Will's second year of grad school, he and a few fellow grad students discovered Magic Mountain, a low-key ski resort with smaller crowds and an easier strain on the wallet than Killington.

Like no other student on campus, Will longed for warmer weather to arrive. As a Southerner, winters in New Hampshire took their toll on Will's psyche. The days were short and the temperatures rarely rose above freezing for the winter. The bitter cold of the New England winters made him long for his home state, and spring could not come fast enough. He looked forward to the chance to travel to Wilmington over Spring Break, giving Will something to look forward to as he struggled through his first year at Dartmouth. Winters in New England lasted well into April, so by the time spring arrived in Hanover, Will's mind had thawed and he could enjoy watching the Dartmouth baseball team play various schools in the Ivy League conference. Dartmouth was known for its superior sports teams among the Ivy League, and the baseball program was no exception. Watching Dartmouth's Big Green baseball team brought back fond memories of his playing days in Little League and high school.

In the warmer months, Will took off by himself or with other grad students to the Green Mountains one Saturday, hiking until late afternoon and making it back to Hanover in time to enjoy a beer and shoot pool at Salt Hill Pub. As a flat-lander from the coast of North Carolina, Will did appreciate and was captivated by the picturesque views and colors the mountains of New England offered in spring, summer and fall, but for now, he longed for home.

As one of only a handful of Southerners, Will found himself outnumbered by Yanks on the Dartmouth campus, but he made fast friends with the students in his graduate school class. Though he had a good cross-section of friends at Dartmouth, the dating pool prospects were shallow. He met a few undergraduates that he dated on occasion, but Will had probably overestimated the talent of available women on campus. Indeed, Will found the women at Dartmouth to be very academic at first, but he eventually gained an appreciation for their intellect and ambition. He learned quickly that Ivy League girls were very different than the Southern girls at North Carolina. Maybe it was their rigorous Ivy League environment, but the girls in his MBA class were far more studious and driven, while the Carolina girls, at least the ones Will remembered, were more social and far more laid back, especially when it came to academics and ambition.

Always friendly, Will made friends with many, both male and female, in his MBA classes. As the only Tar Heel in the MBA program at Dartmouth, he stayed true to his roots and spoke often of the North Carolina traditions, like UNC basketball, which he followed closely in the winter. Not necessarily the smartest guy in the class, Will earned the respect of his classmates as a hard worker devoted to his studies. He learned to stay away from conversations about politics, as most of the MBA students were far more liberal than Will's conservative Southern viewpoints.

Frequently, Will questioned his decision to attend Dartmouth. Some days, he felt the academics were too challenging, and on other days, he felt like an alien in an academic environment among northerners with whom he shared little in common. Nevertheless, Will reminded himself that he was getting a MBA from an Ivy League school, and he would appreciate his education one day. He'd fight through these two years and reap the reward when he finished.

By his second year of grad school, Will had become good friends with three classmates from various parts of the northeastern United States. While he had little in common with his new friends, the four of them shared an interest in sports, skiing, and adventure. Each of them in the MBA program had ended up at Dartmouth for various reasons, and his new Yankee associates had their own stories.

Chris Cain was a blue blood from New York State, a man who aspired to become a U.S. Senator. Alan Story was a liberal from Boston who wanted to take over Wall Street, and Joel Kaplan was a New Jersey scholar who aspired to run his own hedge fund. When they asked Will what he wanted to do, he admitted that he was not as focused on the future as his class-mates. "Oh, I just want to graduate and start earning some money," Will responded, really unsure where his MBA from Dartmouth would lead him. "I've been working on a few things back home. Charlotte and Atlanta are great cities too, especially in the banking and financial arenas. I like finance, so we'll see where that takes me. I'm not ruling out anything at this point."

After interning at Merrill Lynch in Wilmington for the summer after his first year at Dartmouth, Will had become intrigued with the investment field. He enjoyed analyzing why a publicly traded company was profitable. For recent MBA graduates however, the best jobs in the financial analysis world were mostly based in New York.

"The four of us should all interview in New York, get jobs on Wall Street, and live in the city," Joel suggested. "We could all share a place in Manhattan and take over the Street."

Moving to New York City still did not sound particularly motivating to Will, although a large number of his Dart-mouth classmates were headed to jobs with Wall Street firms. Returning to the South had more appeal to Will, despite the impressive first year salaries the New York jobs offered.

Financial services companies from New York had begun visiting the Dartmouth campus during fall semester to assess which students were the brightest and best in the class of 1990. Though nowhere near the top of his class, Will knew the right job was out there, even in this challenging economy. He just had to get outside of New Hampshire and find the right opportunity.

The Boston Roadtrips

Chapter 9

By the spring semester of his second year of graduate school, Will discovered that New England had more to offer a twenty-four-year-old graduate student than shooting pool at the Salt Hill Pub in Hanover, New Hampshire, on a Saturday night. Classmate and Boston resident Alan Story invited Chris, Joel and Will to Bean Town in February, and the boys' eyes were opened to life beyond the foothills of the Dartmouth campus.

The two-hour road trip from Hanover to Boston soon became a weekend tradition for Will and his three classmates. Boston was steeped in United States history, though it was a place Will had never had the chance to visit. A part of him wanted to see some of the sites in Boston, like Fenway Park, but Alan had a different type of sightseeing in mind on those weekend trips.

On the first trip into Massachusetts, Will had a limited view of one of the country's greatest cities from the back seat of Alan's car, as the winter sun set early in Boston and the nightlife was calling.

"Boston is a great walking city, guys, but we're not here to walk," Alan explained to his passengers. "You can walk the historical Freedom Trail on your next trip, but we're here to make our own history, gentlemen," Alan proclaimed, as his Toyota Corolla made its entry into downtown Boston. "Let's move north to Cambridge and find us a tea party. But you guys won't find me drinking tea tonight," Alan laughed as the car crossed the Charles River and entered Cambridge by way of Beacon Street.

Resonant of the Revolutionary soldiers that had gone before them, these militiamen were on a mission to take Harvard Square by force if necessary. Though inexperienced in battle like the Minute Men of the revolution, these four Ivy Leaguers were ready for rapid deployment into Cambridge.

"I don't know all the hot spots in Cambridge, but we'll park the car here near the square and take the town by foot," Alan explained in his New England accent. The February sun had already begun its early descent over Massachusetts. "We'll meet back here at midnight if we get separated," Alan suggested. "If one of us hits gold and gets lucky, then we'll need to meet here at twelve and make arrangements. If we all hook up, then we'll meet back here at nine tomorrow morning," Alan said with an optimistic laugh. "But nobody better think about bringing a girl back to my parents' house. My mom has always slept with one eye open, and she is only expecting the four of us," Alan explained to his fellow Minutemen as they walked down Brattle Street, headed to the bar district in Harvard Square.

"I like the optimism, Story," Chris chimed in.

"So, can we expect the talent pool for these Harvard girls to be that much better than Dartmouth?" Will asked in anticipation of a Saturday night out in a college town again.

"Guys, you have to understand the dynamic here," Alan explained. "It's not just the Harvard chicks we're going to see tonight. There are girls that come in from all over the state to meet the Harvard guys. This place is a magnet for babes from Boston College, MIT, U-Mass, and all the other ten thousand schools in the Boston area. That's why we're here, boys."

"And Tar Heel, I'm following you," Joel interjected. "You're our lead man. I'm your wing man. You're the face guy. I'm just here for your left-overs, pal."

That first trip to Boston and Cambridge proved to be a success. The boys met some new friends, had a few laughs, and Will was able to see what life looked like on another Ivy League campus.

"We're coming back next weekend, right?" Chris inquired after meeting at the appointed time that night.

"Yeah, that was a good time, and the eye candy is so much better here in Boston compared to Hanover on any day of the week," Alan responded.

"I'll second that," Will said from his designated position in the back seat.

The weekend road trips to Cambridge became something to look forward to for Will, Alan, Chris, and Joel. The routine included a scheduled departure from the Dartmouth campus on Saturday afternoon, arrival in Boston by dusk, an early dinner at one of the pubs in Cambridge, and then shoot pool, drink beer, and meet girls until midnight. The guys would then drive to Alan's parents' home in Chelsea and be back on the road to Hanover by mid-morning on Sunday.

After learning the ropes and sticking to their weekend routine, the boys finally struck gold in Cambridge one night in late March. The piercing cold of the New England winter had begun to relent, though still considered winter by any Southerner's standard. Still, the night brought with it a hint of spring in Massachusetts and anticipation of warmer days ahead. It was another Saturday night in Cambridge, and the traveling Dartmouth Dodgers had made another road appearance at Shay's Pub on John F. Kennedy Street. The combination of the warmer weather and the end of another semester in sight seemed to have generated a larger than normal crowd in Harvard Square that night.

The Dartmouth travel team brought its A-game to Boston that night, ready for the best that Cambridge could offer this companionship of road warriors. The road-tested Saturday night system was now familiar to these four carpetbaggers from New Hampshire, and Will, Chris, Joel, and Alan had earned membership into this exclusive weekend social club in Harvard Square. They were not Harvard boys, but they all carried the Ivy League card, and that was enough to gain entry into the game.

When in Cambridge, Will was content to shoot pool, while his other three Dartmouth classmates preferred to walk through the crowds and sightsee. Typically, Will played pool until he grew bored, or got beat, and then he would meet up with the boys inside Shay's or another bar on JFK Street.

While shooting pool at Shay's early that night, Will noticed a particularly attractive college student who showed up during one of Will's successive games of eight-ball. She stood in the corner with two of her friends and observed the game like she was trying to learn the rules. She either had an interest in playing pool or she had a boyfriend playing in the next game, Will concluded. Discretely, Will admired her after each shot, and then, suddenly, winning this current game of eight-ball didn't seem to matter anymore. He would gladly give up the table in exchange for an opportunity to talk to the attractive spectator.

As his opponent lined up his final shot, Will calculated his approach and rehearsed his opening line, hoping the girls would stick around until the end of his game. Will watched the black eight ball disappear in the corner pocket. The game was over. After falling to the unknown, faceless, yet formidable opponent, Will approached the lean blonde and her two female bodyguards.

"Are you waiting on the next game?" Will asked, pool cue still in hand.

"No, I just like to watch," she responded with a slight smile.

"You should try to play. You could hold your own against these rookies," Will suggested.

"No, I'll watch," she said, with another smile.

During that short dialog, Will detected the sharp Boston accent that had become all too familiar to him over the last twenty months since he had moved to New England. "Are you in school here at Harvard?" Will inquired.

"No, I'm at Holy Cross. Do you know where that is?"

"Not really. I've heard of it, though," Will replied.

"You're not from here, are you?" she asked, taking a pronounced sip from her beer bottle. "Texas?"

He observed closely as she drank from the bottle, noting her choice of beer as he smiled. He had been branded as a Texan ever since he set foot on the Dartmouth campus, so the question was a familiar one to him. "No, I'm from North Carolina," he stated with pride. "Do you know where that is?" he joked. At first, she looked offended, but then she offered him a broad smile. "Sorry, I had to ask. You asked if I knew where Holy Cross was," Will stated, making an apology of sorts for his attempt at humor. "Seriously, I should know, but where *is* Holy Cross? I guess it's close to here, right?"

"It's on the west side of the city, about twenty minutes from here," she replied. "How about you? Do you go to Harvard?" she asked.

Will smiled before responding. "Are you kidding? I applied here, but I couldn't get in. Harvard rejected me. I go to Dartmouth." He hesitated. "Do you know where that is?"

She smiled back, seemingly enjoying the geographic bantering between them. Always attentive to his prime target's traveling companions, Will made an effort to interject the other two girls into the conversation. "Do you girls play pool?" Will asked the girls, standing just to the left of their friend.

"No, not really," one of the girls replied, leaning against the dark wall of the billiards room.

"My name is Will," he said, introducing himself to all three girls. "I'm from North Carolina, before you ask, and make fun of my accent." The girls introduced themselves one by one, but Will was only attentive enough to catch the name of Catherine, the girl that had captured his eye. "My guys are somewhere around here. The four of us come down a couple of times a month from Dartmouth. We're all in business school there. Have y'all ever been to Hanover?" The girls shook their heads, indicating that they had never been to the Dartmouth campus. "It's an awesome campus, but it's really quiet up there, so we try to get down here to the big city when we can," Will explained. "Okay, if you're not going to play pool, then who needs a beer? I know I need one," Will asked, looking in the direction of the bar.

"I'll take another," Catherine said, taking a final sip of her beer.

Amstel Light?" Will inquired, taking the empty bottle from her hand.

"Yes, thank you."

"Girls?" Will asked, looking toward Catherine's friends.

"No thanks," they responded.

Will looked around in search of his running mates. They were not in the vicinity. Surely, they hadn't left the bar, as this is where all the action was. Figures. He had a fish on the line and the guys were AWOL. He walked toward the bar, placed his order with the bartender, and looked in earnest for his

Dartmouth running mates. Where were those clowns, Will wondered, eager for them to meet Catherine and her friends.

He returned to the billiards room with a beer in one hand for Catherine and one for himself in the other. His eyes locked in on her from the time he paid for the beers and started walking toward her. Her off-white jeans fit tightly around her lean figure. She carried herself with a certain air of confidence and seemed to have a witty personality, which Will liked. This girl's a goddess, he thought, and repeated her name over and over in his mind. Catherine, Catherine, Catherine, so he would remember her name. Back in the poolroom, Will delivered the beer to Catherine and looked at her wing-women. "Are you sure I can't get you guys a beer?" Will asked, being sure to say you 'guys' rather than 'y'all'.

"No, we'll get one in a little while," one of the girls responded.

"Let's play some pool, the three of you against me," Will suggested. "We'll play on the empty table over there." He pointed to a second pool table in the room that got less use. "It'll be fun. The loser buys the next round of beer. What a deal! If I lose, I have to buy three beers, and if you lose, you split the cost of one beer by thirds. How do you not take that bet?" The girls looked at each other to arrive at a consensus. "Come on," Will urged. "I'll help you make some shots."

The girls followed Will toward the pool table in the corner of the room. He helped the girls choose a stick, showed them how to rack, and decided he should have the honor of the ceremonial break. Quickly, he gave them the highlights of the game. "I'll break." The clash began with an impressive break by Will as the pool balls spread over the expanse of the table.

The girls struggled, amidst their laughs, to make any shots. Will purposely missed several of his shots and even knocked in a few of the girls' balls in to keep the game close. Toward the end of the match, the rest of the Dartmouth travel team arrived at the pool table.

"Where have you guys been?" Will proclaimed, as if the boys had been missing for days.

"We went down the street to stalk out some other bars. We thought you were going to keep winning on the other table, so we checked out for a change of scenery. We knew you'd still be here if we left for a while," Chris explained.

"Well, it's good you came back, because I'm in an epic battle with these girls for a rather large wager. They may need some help though," Will explained. "These are my friends from Dartmouth - Joel, Chris, and Alan," Will said from the far side of the pool table. The boys proceeded to introduce themselves to Catherine and her friends, saving Will the embarrassment of having to make introductions without knowing two of his opponents' names. "We've got a game to finish, guys. You may be just in time to help these girls with some additional instruction. They're about to go down in defeat," Will announced.

Alan, Chris, and Joel were not quite the caliber of pool sharks as their friend Will, but the three added some valuable advice on each shot the girls took. The game ended abruptly as Catherine's friend, Lucy, inadvertently knocked the eight ball into one of the corner pockets.

"Too bad, and you girls were making a comeback," Will stated. He had won the bet, but he decided that cashing in might not be in his best interest. He attempted to offer a creative alternative to the girls buying him a beer for his victory on the pool table.

"So here was the bet, guys," Will explained to his Dartmouth allies. "If I won, the girls had to give me a tour of Holy Cross tonight. If they won, I had to buy them beers." The girls smiled at each other in disbelief, puzzled by the proposition Will just offered.

"Oh, so you guys all go to Holy Cross?" Joel asked.

"Yes," Catherine answered for all three girls. "But I don't think you guys would find Holy Cross all that exciting. It's a great place, but I think you guys would rather hang out in this part of Boston."

Will decided to take a chance and see if the girls wanted to spend more time with the boys from Dartmouth. "Okay, you've figured out that I'm a slow Southern boy. I don't get out to the big city much. So, if it's not Holy Cross, then let's go downtown and you locals show us what Boston at night looks like," Will suggested.

"Yeah, how about the Pearl?" Alan suggested, looking for approval from the girls.

"That place is cool ... if you like to dance," one of the girls said, giving the Pearl a partial endorsement.

"That place is wild, but it's fun," Catherine added.

"All right, let's do that. It sounds better than a campus tour of Holy Cross," Will said, trying to build momentum for a late night in downtown Boston.

The New England travel squad had now grown to a contingency of seven, and the assembly of thrill seekers set off for downtown Boston in Lucy's Jeep Cherokee. Alan, the local Bostonian, announced that he would drive, while Will and Catherine agreed to wedge themselves in the storage area behind the back seat for the voyage across the Charles River into the city of Boston.

Like the Tea Party activists of 1773, this gang of colonists took the Pearl by storm. The difference was that the seven rebels had no political agenda, but were just there to have a good time. The Pearl was a definite diversion from the bar scene in Cambridge in terms of the crowd, so the seven colonists banded together on the dance-floor for most of the night. By the time the crew left the Pearl shortly after 1:00 a.m., Will was determined to keep the Boston Tea Party movement alive. Jammed into the back of the Jeep with Catherine, Will started the slow chant, "Holy Cross, Holy Cross, Holy Cross!"

Once back in Cambridge, Will continued his push for a side-trip to the Holy Cross campus. "It's still early guys," he announced. "And these girls have a bet to repay. I'm dying to see Holy Cross."

Will's political activism paid off. Alan and the boys loaded into the Camry and followed the girls in the Jeep westward to Worcester, Massachusetts, home of the historic College of the Holy Cross. Once on campus, the contingency of seven reloaded into the Jeep, and the guided tour began.

Lucy started the driving tour in the heart of campus at Fenwick Hall. She then drove past the classic brick academic buildings in the center of the school, out to the lacrosse fields, through the residence halls where Catherine and her room-mates lived their freshman year, and down Linden Lane to the signature building on campus, O'Kane Hall, home to Fenwick Theater. The tour concluded at Fitton Football Stadium.

As the entourage made it to the stadium parking lot, Will requested that he and Catherine be released from the back of the Jeep. "It's time to let the dog out of cage. I need to stretch my legs and Catherine is tired of me kicking her every time I try to get comfortable."

Once out of captivity, Will insisted that the band of seven make its way inside Fitton Stadium and onto the football field. Will met some resistance from the girls. "What are they going to do, kick you off campus? You're all seniors and you graduate in two months. Come on, we're doing this!"

Joel and Chris made their way toward the stadium entrance and discovered the only barrier that prevented public access to the field to be a six-foot high fence.

"Oh, this is a piece of cake, even after a few drinks," Joel announced without hesitation. He scaled the fence like he was twelve years old again and made it to the field in a full sprint in a matter of seconds. Chris followed with little of the grace and skill that Joel had displayed on his way over the chain-link barrier.

"Girls, you ready?" Will asked, grasping Catherine's hand. "This looks easy enough. Are you with me?" he asked. She appeared athletic enough to scale the fence. "I'll help you get over," he offered. He looked at the other girls, anticipating an answer.

"Not me," Lucy stated.

"I'm out," Paige responded, shaking her head.

"Catherine, we're doing this," Will insisted.

Will and Alan helped Catherine to the top of the fence, and once there, she gracefully swung her legs over the top of the fence and slid down the inside of the fence with a drunken giggle. Alan and Will watched with great anticipation as Catherine's boots made a soft landing on the asphalt. She had made it to the other side. She yelled at her friends.

"Come on, you scaredy-cats, and get your asses over here. It's easy."

"We're here to help," Alan pleaded with Lucy and Paige.

"What the hell," Lucy said, heading toward the fence where Will and Alan stood like Marine guards ready to uphold the motto of "leave no one behind."

"Let me hold your purse," Paige insisted as Lucy prepared for her fence mount. "I'm not getting my fat ass over that fence, and I'm too drunk. I'll either embarrass myself or hurt myself, or both."

"You stay here and keep an eye out for the campus cops. We won't be out here long," Alan instructed.

"You'll hear no argument from me," Paige muttered.

Once Alan and Will were over the fence and on the field,

Will made a full sprint toward Catherine and tackled her play-fully to the turf. She let out a short scream as her lean physique fell near the forty yard-line. Using good sportsmanship, Will offered her a hand to help her off the damp surface from the night's dew that covered the field. As she stood up, the two remained alone in the night, face to face. They stared at each other, only long enough for Will to realize he had a choice. He had been with Catherine and her friends for the past five hours. He knew they had a connection. He did not hesitate any longer. He kissed her. As they unlocked from the lengthy embrace, Will felt that a whimsical spell had been cast over him. The two of them then slowly turned toward the others who had been watching the enraptured couple kiss at mid-field. It was Dartmouth versus Holy Cross, meeting on the Gridiron, while the fans watched the action from the sidelines.

Since he set foot on the Dartmouth campus eighteen months ago, Will's time in New England had been void of any romance – until tonight. Catherine was enchanting. He had not met anyone in New England previously whose beauty had even so much as turned his head.

The blustery New England wind blew her dirty blonde hair toward her winsome face, and he watched with intrigue as she whisked her shoulder length hair away from cheeks that the wind had kissed with a rosy red tint. "We better get out of here," Will said in a bit of a panic. "We're on borrowed time here. My guess is the campus police will be making the rounds any minute now."

"What makes you think that?" Catherine asked. "You're just paranoid. You were the big talker, coaxing us on the field, and now you're scared?"

"Ha, I just don't want to get you in any trouble. Come on, let's go," Will said, breaking into a trot while pulling Cath-erine by the hand.

"Let's go," Will yelled toward the others with a wave of his free arm. The four of them turned and walked toward the stadium entry. After a long night together, the spectators had bonded as well. Will saw the baseball field ahead of him, beyond the entry gate. Lucy's Jeep was parked between the football and baseball fields. "Maybe we should try to sneak on the baseball field next," Will joked.

"I'm game," Catherine responded with a laugh. "Let's go."

"Do you ever go to any of the baseball games here?" Will asked idly, his mind still fixated on their magical kiss just a few minutes earlier.

"I've been to a few games. It's fun to do when the weather warms up," Catherine responded.

"But I bet you're a Sox fan, right?"

"Oh yeah. My dad, my sister and I used to go to a lot of games when we were little."

"Oh, I'd love to go to Fenway. Maybe we can try to sneak into Fenway later tonight."

Suddenly, bright lights beamed directly in front of them.

"We're busted," Will exclaimed.

"Oh shit," Catherine muttered.

"I told you we were on borrowed time. I had a feeling we were about to get a visit from the cops," Will said.

The spectators merged toward Will and Catherine in the end zone until all six of the gatecrashers held their arms at eye level to shield their eyes from the bright lights of the car parked facing the entry gate.

"I got this, guys," Will said. "This was my idea. I'm sober enough to talk to the cops. He approached the campus cop. "Good evening sir," Will said politely. "We were just leaving."

"Not so fast, fellow. You realize you folks are trespassing on public property," the policeman affirmed. "There's a reason this gate stays locked."

"We apologize, sir," Will said, eyeing the officer's double chin. "We're here from out of town and are big Holy Cross fans. We wanted to see the stadium, it was my idea. We were just trying to have a little fun and weren't out there digging up the turf or destroying property."

"Do any of you attend Holy Cross?" the campus cop inquired, surveying the band of law-breakers.

Silence pierced the cool Massachusetts air for a matter of seconds. Alan spoke up. "The girls do, sir. It was not their idea though. We're from Dartmouth, in New Hampshire. We're here admiring the campus."

"You folks can admire the campus in the daylight. I ought to give every one of you a sobriety test, but it's late and you guys should be headed home. I don't want to see you anywhere near the public buildings on this campus again tonight. You understand?"

"Yes sir," the trespassers responded one by one.

"Consider yourselves lucky," the portly cop warned. "I've had guys locked up for lesser offenses. Now you folks be safe, and I don't want to see you anywhere else on campus again tonight. You got me?" He opened the gate and let the villains out.

"Yes sir," the boys responded, heads held low with embarrassment.

The campus police officer waddled back toward the patrol car, gave the trespassers a final look before climbing in, and then drove out of the parking area. The freed perpetrators watched as the car turned around and pulled away from the stadium.

"Let's go eat," Chris announced. "I'm hungry."

"Yeah, is there a waffle house near here?" Will asked.

"A waffle house? What's that?" Lucy asked.

"Oh, it's a southern thing. I guess you guys don't have waffle houses up here."

"There's Lucky's in downtown Worcester. It's awesome and stays open late," Catherine suggested.

"I'm done for the night," Paige stated. "When the cops showed up, I knew it was time for me to go home and get some sleep."

"It's not late," Alan proclaimed.

"Are you kidding? It's only two twenty-seven by my watch," Joel said, peaking at his wristwatch underneath his coat sleeve.

"Paige, you drive us back to the apartment," Catherine suggested. "We'll see who wants to go eat from there. Sound like a plan?"

By the time the nighttime voyagers got to Lucky's Cafe, it was Lucy and Catherine dining with the four Dartmouth boys in one large booth in the back of the restaurant. "How far is the drive to Dartmouth?" Catherine asked after the contingency was served its breakfast. "You guys aren't driving back tonight are you?"

"We could go back to Alan's parents' house in the city, but they wouldn't like us crashing in their house at five o'clock in the morning," Joel said, explaining their lodging dilemma.

"We could always sleep on the couch in one of the dorms. We did that on a few road-trips during basketball season at UNC," Will said.

"Are you kidding?" Lucy blurted. "Do you know what those dorm maggots do on those couches late at night? Those couches are beyond gross."

"Well, so much for that idea, Will," Joel commented, as he took another bite of eggs.

"Don't worry guys. We have plenty of floor space - and a couch that's actually pretty clean," Lucy offered.

The boys took care of the breakfast tab, and the six of them made their way out of downtown Worchester and back to the girls' apartment, located just off the Holy Cross campus.

A coin toss determined who got the couch in the two-bedroom unit, home to four Holy Cross seniors: Lucy, Paige, Catherine, and a fourth roommate, Kari, who had stayed behind at Holy Cross last night with her boyfriend. Alan won the lottery and got to sleep on the couch while the others were awarded blankets and a pillow, but left to procure floor-space on their own.

By ten o'clock the next morning, the hung-over crowd had begun moving around the apartment amidst moans and aching bodies from the previous night's activities.

"What time did you guys get home last night?" Kari asked as Catherine headed for the kitchen in search of a cup of coffee.

"I don't know," Catherine answered lethargically. "Ask these guys. I think it was some time after four,"

"You look like death, girl," Kari said, watching Catherine's feeble attempt to make a pot of coffee.

"Thank you. You look gorgeous this morning too," Catherine smiled.

"Who are these guys?" Kari whispered, surveying the carnage from the night before.

"They're from Dartmouth. We met them in Cambridge," Catherine explained. "We ended up going downtown to Pearl, drank too much there, and then these guys wanted to see Holy Cross. None of them had ever seen the campus, so we crashed the gate at the football field, and got busted by this heavy-weight cop for being on the field."

"Did you get arrested?" Kari asked, intrigued by the adventurous night her roommates had experienced.

"No, but almost. I think the cop knew we all had been drinking. He was pretty cool, but we were out there just running around on the field," Catherine explained as the coffee machine gurgled.

Faint moans from the den indicated that the after-effects of the alcohol, combined with a hard-carpeted surface for a bed, had severely affected the Dartmouth houseguests.

"Somebody just shoot me," Joel blurted out from the living room area within earshot of the kitchen where Catherine and Kari waited patiently for the coffee to brew.

Will was the first to gain vertical status. He made his way to the bathroom, wrapped in a down comforter that had served as his bed-sheet. Walking past his fallen comrades, Will resembled a monk who had escaped from a monastery, covered in the brown blanket he used to cover himself with as he passed by the kitchen. "Morning," he mumbled to Catherine and Kari as he passed by the kitchen in search of the bathroom.

"Good morning," the girls responded in unison.

Kari gave Catherine the look. "Wow, where did you find him? I'm impressed."

Catherine took a coffee cup off the shelf, and then looked at her roommate with raised eyebrows, acknowledging the endorsement. By the time the coffee finished brewing, the late-night ramblers were awake. Laughter and chatter from the night before had been silenced by the pain of alcohol-induced hangovers the next morning as the Dartmouth contingency moved slowly through the apartment. Other than an occasional moan, there were few words spoken among the group.

"Coffee anyone?" Lucy asked the houseguests.

"Sure."

"Please."

"I'll take a full pot," Chris requested.

After coffee was poured, Will broke the silence barrier. "Thank you for hosting us last night. We would have never made it back to Hanover if we had left here at four and tried to make the two-hour drive. None of us were in any condition to drive."

"You're welcome. I think we were all over-served last night," Lucy added.

"Well, it was fun. We'll do it again next Saturday, okay?" Will joked.

"You girls have put up with us for long enough. We appreciate the tour of campus last night," Alan said, bowing and honoring the memories of their night on campus. As he stood, he moved his right hand from his head down to his chest, forming the cross as a Catholic priest would perform after a prayer. "Holy Cross, I'll never forget you."

"You guys were awesome putting up with us," Joel said in his heavy New York accent. "You see, Dartmouth is up in the mountains. As you can tell, we don't get to the big city very often, and we don't know how to act once we get out of New Hampshire."

"Thanks for everything, especially a place on the floor last night," Alan said, holding his back and contorting his body in a way to dramatize the painful night's sleep.

Even after a rough night, Catherine looked stunning in her pajamas and robe, nursing a cup of coffee. Will knew he wanted to see Catherine again, but he wanted to be discrete about securing her number. He cast a glance at the phone mounted on the wall in the kitchen and memorized the seven-digit number written on the phone in his mind.

The Dartmouth crew gave the girls a good-bye hug and thanked them again for their hospitality. Will hugged Catherine a little longer than the other girls. He wanted to tell her that he would call her, but did not like making promises he might not keep. Plus, he preferred the surprise element of a follow-up phone call. The memory of the whimsical kiss on the field lingered in his mind as he tightly hugged her waist. "We had fun. Thank you," he whispered in her ear.

"It *was* fun," she replied as they broke from the hug. "You guys certainly aren't like the Ivy League guys we know."

By ten forty-five on Sunday morning, Alan's Camry was on the road, bound for New Hampshire. Will repeated the apartment phone number over and over in his head to insure he would not forget it.

"That was a good time last night, boys," Alan commented. "I'm feeling it right now, though."

"Did you get her number, Tar Heel? I assume you are going to call her, right?" Chris inquired.

"Maybe," Will shrugged, trying to appear nonchalant.

"Maybe? Are you kidding me? If you don't call her, then I want her number," Joel said from the back seat.

"She was certainly worth the price of admission," Alan added.

"Yeah, she was all right," Will replied with a subtle smile.

The Call

Chapter 10

By Thursday of the week following the Boston adventure, Will made his first attempt to reach Catherine by phone. He missed her once in the afternoon and again that night.

"Sorry, she's out tonight," Paige said after Will's second attempt to call her.

Will concluded that she was out on a date. After all, she was too hot not to have a boyfriend. He didn't call back until Sunday night.

Will wanted to hear her voice again. Was there really something here? Or was he just deprived of a decent supply of women here at Dartmouth? Still, she was gorgeous. The guys agreed she was a ten, even the next morning in her flannel pajamas, standing in the kitchen.

He needed an excuse to call her, but did not want to appear too eager. Remembering the kiss on the 50 yard-line, he knew there was a connection, but he wanted to secure some one-on-one time with her to see if he really liked what he saw last weekend.

"Hello, it's Will," he said when a girl answered the phone. "Who is this?"

"This is Lucy. Hi Will. Do you want Catherine?"

"No, I really wanted to talk to you," he jested. She acted like she took him seriously.

"Okay, what's up?" she asked, ready for a conversation. Will knew she knew he had called for Catherine, but he played along with his own joke. "How are you? Did you guys go back to Cambridge last night?"

"No, not after last weekend. We're still recovering," she said, laughing.

"Yeah, I'm with you on that."

"Catherine is actually here. I know you really called to talk to me, but you can talk to her if you want to," Lucy joked.

"She's actually there?" Will asked in disbelief. "I'm surprised. Yeah, I'll talk to her."

Within moments, Catherine was on the phone. "Hello?" she said.

"I wondered if I would ever be able to catch you at home," Will commented.

"Well, I've been at the library a lot this week," she responded.

"The library? Okay, I believe you," Will said.

"Really, I had some tests this week."

"Did you ace them?"

"Oh, yeah. All that studying really paid off," Catherine said, her voice only slightly sarcastic.

"Well, I thought for sure you were out drinking again this week," Will offered.

"Not this week," she replied. "Last weekend pretty much did me in. I usually don't go out much during the week.

"I know you probably think I talked too much about North Carolina when we were together in Boston last weekend, but I have another story about my last semester at UNC. Four of us decided to make a pact that we would go out every night in our last semester on campus. So, from January to May, we went out every night except Sundays. The rule was you had to drink at least one beer. Some nights, we stayed out for fifteen minutes, but we had to go to a bar or a party and drink one beer, even during exam week. We called it the 'streak'. We were all seniors, and three of the four of us kept the streak alive all spring semester. The fourth guy had a girlfriend, and he made it for maybe ten days, but then he folded like a cheap lawn chair."

"Maybe I should have set that as a goal for my last semester," Catherine responded, seemingly impressed with Will's story from his senior year of college.

"Listen, I'm a big baseball fan and after we talked the other night, I thought how incredible it would be to go to a Red Sox game. I was wondering how hard it is to get tickets to a game at Fenway."

"How many tickets do you need?" she inquired.

"I didn't realize I had reached the ticket broker's office. Let's see, uh, two. One for you, and one for me." He paused. "Maybe I didn't make myself clear. I wanted you and me to go to a game."

"Oh, are you asking me out?" she asked, feigning surprise.

"I guess I am. Are you accepting, or blowing me off?"

"And when did you want to go?" she asked, sounding now like the ticket broker he had accused her of being.

"I checked the home schedule and was hoping to go to the Sox-Indians game, but I know Fenway is a tough ticket. The series is in three weeks. I knew to ask you early as well, because I know what it takes to get on your social calendar. I don't know what's more difficult, getting tickets to a Red Sox game or getting you on the phone."

"Are you using me for my connections to Sox tickets?" Catherine asked.

Will hesitated, not knowing Catherine might truly have a way to get Red Sox tickets. "Yes, I guess I am. I'm a poor grad school student from the uneducated south, and I have never been to a place as magical as Fenway. I can pay up to ten dollars per ticket, if you know how to find us tickets," Will joked.

"*Ten dollars! I had you pegged as a big* spender, but I didn't know you'd be willing to pay *that* much for a Sox ticket," Catherine replied, her comebacks witty and amusing. "I might be able to get you tickets, but you'll pay dearly if you use me as your ticket broker. My finder's fees are pretty high."

"I'm sure they are. I have an idea then. Why don't you and I meet for dinner in Boston and discuss your fee structure and negotiate terms for seats behind home plate. Are you available next Saturday night?" Will asked.

"So where are we going? Back to Lucky's Café?"

"Only if you're lucky," Will replied. He cringed at the poor choice of play on words. "Sorry, bad joke. I'm usually better than that."

"That *was* bad," she agreed.

"Seriously, we can go into the city. You'll have to coach me on where we should go. When it comes to Boston, I only know Cambridge and now I know about the Pearl, but that's it," he admitted.

"I have a few places I like, but I want to be sensitive to your beer budget," she responded.

"Maybe some place near Fenway. I'm sure you're used to the finest in dining, so you pick your favorite place, and I'll borrow some money from my friends up here, and we'll tear through downtown Boston again, like last weekend."

"Oh, I don't think my body can take another night like last Saturday," she hedged.

"This Saturday will be a little more laid back. I promise,"

he said. "I'll plan to pick you up at your apartment around seven, if that's good."

"Sounds like a plan," she said in agreement.

"Okay, I'll try not to embarrass you in your home town," he said.

"Just don't plan on trying to break into Fenway on Saturday. We'll end up in jail for sure," Catherine advised.

"No worries there, I'll be on my best behavior," he replied. "I'll see you on Saturday."

"Sounds good," she agreed.

"Bye," Will said. He hung up the phone and pumped his fist into the air. "Yes!"

The Park

Chapter 11

The chill of the New England winter still lingered into spring. It was mid-April as Will and Catherine made their way down the aisle to their seats along the first base line only eleven rows behind the Red Sox dugout. Will was consumed in the history of Fenway Park and not paying attention to the numbers on the concrete steps indicating where the seats were located.

"Here we are, Will. Row eleven," Catherine motioned, tugging on the back of Will's jacket.

"These seats are amazing," Will said in awe. "I assume you've sat in these seats before?"

"A few times," Catherine responded casually, sweeping her blonde hair behind her back before sitting down.

"Incredible," Will commented as he settled into his seat. "Have you ever seen anyone hit one over the Green Monster?"

"I think so. I remember one time when I was in middle school, someone with the Sox hit one over the big wall, and the fans went crazy," Catherine recalled.

"I had no idea we'd be this close to the field," Will commented, still in awe of the surroundings. "I wish I had a camera. When was the last time you came to a Sox game?" he asked, curious to know her interest in the game of baseball.

"We came with my dad last summer," she answered. "Summer is the perfect time to come. April is still too cold for me."

"I agree, but this is Fenway! I can't believe it. "How many games do you make a year?" Will asked.

"One or two. Not many. Okay, now I get to ask a question, Mr. Inquisitive," she said, grinning. "What position did *you* play?"

"Shortstop. Do you know that position?"

"Of course, it's right there," she said with confidence, pointing toward the space between second and third base.

"So who is the Sox shortstop?" Will asked, pushing the limit on Catherine's baseball knowledge.

"We're not going to play that game. I have no clue. I don't know the players, unless they're really good looking," she explained.

"Okay, I get it," Will said, now comprehending her love for the game and knowledge of one of America's iconic teams in baseball. "Are these your dad's seats, or just seats he uses occasionally?"

"His company has seats somewhere else, but a friend of his has these seats, season tickets."

"So where are the company seats?" Will asked.

"Over there somewhere," she replied pointing toward the third base line. "That's where we usually sit when we come."

"Where does your dad work?" Will inquired.

"He's a money manager with an investment firm. He used to be with Fidelity, but he was part of a group that started their own firm around six years ago," Catherine responded, her tone growing more serious as she spoke about her father.

"How have they survived the downturn in the market?"

"I think they're fine. He doesn't talk about it. Plus, I was in school during the crash. I didn't hear much about it, except at Thanksgiving a little that year. He doesn't talk much about work, and I guess we don't ask either. Maybe if he had a son, he would talk more about business. He's surrounded by girls all the time. All we ever talk about are clothes and shoes, you know."

"So where did you get your sense of humor?" Will asked.

"Not from my mom. She calls it sarcasm, and says it's not very lady-like," Catherine explained, rolling her eyes.

"Well, I think you're funny. It puts people at ease."

"You don't know me. I'm really mean."

"I don't believe it. I'm sure it's a cultural thing. You girls in the northeast have a little different way about you than the southern girls," Will said, choosing his words carefully.

"I'm not really mean. I just don't like to be mistreated."

Will agreed with her statement, making note of her comments. He surmised that her statement about being mistreated must be a warning of sorts, possibly an open wound from a previous relationship. He appreciated her openness, however. He looked into her green eyes, searching to know more of who she was. "I won't mistreat you," he said. He placed his left hand over her right hand, on the armrest between their seats. It was only their second date, but Will felt compelled to let her know he was interested.

It was the Red Sox versus the Cleveland Indians in an American League match-up. The Sox won by a score of 5-2, the first win of the season. After a high-five from the fan in the seat next to his, Will hugged Catherine in celebration and conveyed his exuberance with a quick kiss on the cheek. As the two unlocked from their embrace after the excessive celebration, they looked into each other's eyes for no more than a second. It was clear that they both felt excitement beyond the fact that the Red Sox had just beat the Indians.

"How can I thank your dad for the tickets?" Will asked as they walked hand in hand down Commonwealth Avenue after leaving the jubilation inside the brick walls of Fenway.

"Well, what about this? I'll give you a chance to thank him personally next Sunday. I usually go home on Sundays, and we go out for lunch at the Ted. Can you come?"

"Sure, but what's the Ted?" Will asked, feeling a little uneasy about his lack of New England culture.

"It's my parents' country club Marblehead, the Tedesco," Catherine responded. "We call it the Ted in our family."

"Okay, sounds like fun. Can I wear shorts?" Will asked.

"No, and you'll need a sport coat. They'll throw you out on your head if you show up without a sport coat," she smiled.

"Is it really that stuffy?"

"No, not at all, but just don't forget your sport coat"

"Are your parents real formal? You clearly aren't," Will said. "But I mean that in a good way."

"My mom's a little on the snooty side, but you'll like my dad. I think you guys will get along well."

"So, who else will be there on Sunday?"

"Oh, only a couple hundred people," Catherine laughed. "No, seriously, just my sister, my parents, and sometimes my grandma comes. It's no big deal. It's something we do after mass on Sundays."

"Okay, as long as I don't have to go to mass beforehand. I have a hard time following the Catholic service. I feel like a major league catcher after all the up and down from kneeling, sitting, and standing up. I'm confused already just thinking about it."

Catherine laughed at Will's comments about the service. "Well, you would have never made it at Holy Cross," Catherine grinned. "But don't worry, I usually just meet them at the

Ted after mass. I'm not that industrious on a Sunday morning. It's usually a struggle for me to get there by lunch."

"Sounds fun," Will said. "I look forward to meeting your family."

The Advisor

Chapter 12

The afternoon breeze formed a ripple effect on the open waters of Boston Harbor as Will admired the view from the nineteenth floor of the High Street office tower.

"Have a seat," Mr. Key, Catherine's father, offered, directing Will toward one of chairs positioned in front of his neatly maintained desk.

After the Sunday visit with Catherine's family for lunch at Tedesco in Marblehead, Will found himself meeting with Richard Key, father of his love interest as well as a prominent second-generation money manager, for a mid-week meeting to discuss Will's career opportunities.

Mr. Key grew up in Wellesley, a south Boston suburb, and attended Boston College. He was a well-connected New Englander who certainly dressed the part as one of Boston's elite. Will had made a mental note of his stylish attire when they met at the country club for brunch just ten days ago. He wore white pocket-squares in his suit coat, dress-shoes with gold or silver implements, and a freshly starched white dress-shirt with stiff collar that stayed in place like children staged between their parents in a church pew on Sunday morning.

Like many New Englanders in his generation, Richard Key had grown up around Boston, attended college in the metro area, and took a white-collar job in Boston. For Mr. Key, the financial services industry was a natural career path since his father, Richard, Sr., was a pioneer in the stock market wealth management business, post 1927. Senior had formed a financial advisory firm in the 1940s that was sold to Merrill Lynch in the late fifties.

Richard II had risen through the ranks of Fidelity Investments in Boston to the prestigious position of fund manager. At the age of forty-six and near the top of his career, he decided that he had made his mark on the fund management world at Fidelity, so he joined forces with a group of wealth management advisors, who were also some of his best friends on a social basis. The firm advised sizable institutions like schools and endowments, as well as wealthy individuals in the New England area.

As Will and Catherine's fledgling dating relationship developed, Mr. Key thought his Rolodex might serve as a springboard for Will to interview with some of Boston's most renowned financial service companies. Impressive grades at UNC's business school, president of his social fraternity, high school athlete, and now a MBA from an Ivy League school made Will an easy sell to Mr. Key's influential friends in Boston.

Having spent the last two years in the quiet town of Hanover, New Hampshire, Will was enthralled with downtown Boston, including the city's history, architecture, and the vibrancy of cultural and commercial activity downtown. Downtown Boston was a true city within a city. Unlike many cities in the south, suburban sprawl had not occurred in Boston. People still worked in the city, lived in the city, and stayed in the city after dark. Downtown Boston supported a young and vibrant population of working professionals who lived downtown, despite a deflated economy in 1990.

As far as the financial sector, Boston was second only to New York in terms of the size and depth of career paths for financial and investment sectors. The job market, particularly in the investment world, had been rocked after the U.S. Stock Market correction in October of 1987. The U.S. economy was still reeling from the sting of a 22.6 percent one-day drop in the Dow Jones Industrials. By 1989, the American economy had started its downward spiral, with further gloom ahead in the next two years. Will's strategy of attending graduate school in hopes that the economy would be better by 1990 did not prove fortuitous. Most of the country was still in the middle of the post Black Friday recession.

"Have you interviewed with any firms here in Boston?" Mr. Key inquired.

"No, I haven't. I don't have any contacts here in the city and hadn't really considered Boston as a place to work, until recently. Most of my focus has been with firms in the southeast."

"What fields interest you the most, Will?" Mr. Key asked, placing his hands behind his head as he rocked back in his high-backed leather chair.

"I think my skills are in finance," Will answered. "I like numbers and am intrigued with how public and private companies are financed, but I also enjoy working with people. I'm not a total numbers geek." He smiled. " I like valuations and how a stock price is determined, but I don't see myself as a stockbroker, at least not right out of school. I could see working for a large financial institution, like a bank or an investment house, as an analyst reviewing loan packages or company valuations. The bank training programs are interesting." He paused. "I've had some interviews with the big banks in Charlotte and Raleigh, and I have an offer from

Nations Bank in Charlotte, with their management training program. I'm not necessarily enamored with banking, but I know the training programs have a lot to offer."

"I'm not sure banking is the way to go, at least not for you. If you had a degree in finance and no MBA, the bank training programs are almost like a mini-MBA. In my opinion, banks pay relatively poorly, and someone with your resume has a chance to make a whole lot more money in other areas of finance, at least from what I can tell."

Will nodded, acknowledging Mr. Key's assessment. He felt like it was time to interject a question. "What about on the wholesale side, working as an analyst for some of the big names like Mellon or your old employer, Fidelity?"

"It sounds like you have an interest in the analyst side of the business. I can set you up with some of my people at Fidelity and the other larger investment houses," Mr. Key responded, looking at the ceiling as he thought through different opportunities. "There's always the consulting side. I have a few friends at Boston Consulting Group. That's a good horse to ride if you can stay on until you make partner. Of course, I don't know who's actually hiring in this market, but you're in the right city - unless you want to go to New York."

"I don't think New York is for me," Will explained. "I wouldn't last more than a couple of years down there. I've been to the city for a weekend, and while I'd like the experience, I don't think I would enjoy the quality of life. I guess I've got too much small town Southerner in my blood."

"What about Boston? What's attractive about Boston?"

Your daughter is the most attractive thing about Boston right now, if you want to know the truth, Will thought before answering Mr. Key's question. He did not dare offer this same response to Mr. Key. Instead, he replied seriously. "I'm really looking for the best opportunity in this economy, where I can find a job in finance. If there was a job that was particularly attractive in North Carolina, then I would look hard in my home state. But maybe the better opportunities to advance my career are here in the northeast. Boston appears to be an epicenter of financial service firms, a smaller version of New York. I really like the energy of downtown Boston as well."

"With the number of good colleges in New England, Boston has benefited from that brainpower," Mr. Keys acknowledged. "I think Boston has much to offer someone like you coming out of school. It's a much better alternative than living in Manhattan in some twelve hundred dollar a month apartment you share with three other people you don't know. There is a reason so many people leave New York City on the weekends and come to places like Boston to get away. In my opinion, you can make an equally good living in Boston without having to pay your dues on Wall Street.

"So what field of finance would you look at if you were in my position, Mr. Key?"

Mr. Key thought about Will's question for a moment. "There are some guys I know who do quite well in the investment banking world. You hear all the investment bankers are in New York, but we have a few boutique firms in town that do *very* well. In fact, I should see if the firms I know would be interested in talking to someone like you. It's an analytical, banking, finance, and consulting job all rolled into one. I'll put that one on the list to contact as well."

"That would be great. I really appreciate the help," Will said.

"How about your grades, Will? How have you done in graduate school? These folks may or may not ask. As you will learn in life, no one asks about your grades in college the older you get," Mr. Key mentioned, coughing out a laugh at his comment.

"I'm not exactly at the top of my class. I struggled a little in my first year, but it wasn't for lack of effort. I had very good grades in undergrad, but I think I underestimated how smart the students were at Dartmouth. I've held my own and maintained a B average, but I made my share of Cs as well. Do you think that will hurt me?" Will asked.

"Not really. You have a lot to be proud of. Not many can say they have a MBA from an Ivy League school. Carry that confidence into your interviews."

"I really appreciate the advice, Mr. Key. I can't thank you enough for your help," Will stated, standing from the chair to shake Mr. Key's hand.

"We've got to help Cat get a job as well," Mr. Key commented, referring to his daughter's entry into the workforce. "All of a sudden, I've got too many graduates that want to find jobs in this economy."

"I thought Catherine had a job with the PR firm downtown," Will inquired.

"She has an offer, but I think she's overqualified to do what they want her to do," Mr. Key clarified. "That may ultimately be what she ends up doing, but I want her to interview some more before she accepts that position. She really hasn't interviewed enough, in my opinion."

"Well, I greatly appreciate your help. I'm a little behind in my interview process. Looking back, I should have looked at more opportunities here in Boston between my first and second year, but I wanted to spend the summer at home with my family, so I took a summer internship with BB&T working with a loan analyst."

"Did you enjoy that?" Mr. Key asked.

"Yes sir, I really did. As I mentioned, I like corporate finance and analyzing how a company is capitalized."

"Well, that's good experience," Mr. Key relayed. "Speaking of, let me get a few more of your resumes. I'll fax them to my contacts this afternoon. You could be hearing from Boston

Consulting Group, Fidelity, State Street Equities, a commercial real estate company based here, and a few other smaller financial firms, including the investment-banking group I mentioned. Do you have a car phone?"

"No, I don't. All I have is my phone in my apartment back in Hanover. That number is on the resume," Will said, retrieving additional resumes from his portfolio to hand off to Mr. Key.

Will glanced around the expansive corner office, but did not want to seem overly impressed. His eyes were drawn out the window, mesmerized by the view from the 19th floor of the downtown office tower. On the credenza, overlooking the harbor, were framed pictures of Catherine and her sister in their younger years. From what Will could tell, the Keys were a close family. "Thank you for your help, Mr. Key," he said, turning to leave. "I'm excited about meeting with these contacts."

"Glad to help. But hold on a minute." He lifted his hand. "I understand you've become a Sox fan after going to Fenway. It's good to see the Sox starting to win after a slow start this season," Mr. Key commented.

"Yes sir," Will said, smiling at Mr. Key from his place near the door. "I've always been a baseball fan, but North Carolina doesn't have a major league team, so it's been fun to follow the Red Sox."

"Well, we'll have to all go to another game as it gets warmer," Mr. Key suggested.

"Yes sir, I would enjoy that," Will replied, growing suddenly nervous with the change of subject and the venture into more personal territory.

"I hear you may be coming to the Cape with us for Memorial Day," Mr. Key said, moving around his desk and leaning against it, arms crossed over his chest.

"Yes, if I can make it work," Will nodded. "I was planning to go home to Wilmington, but Cape Cod sounds like fun."

"It will be a good place to celebrate your graduation and Catherine's," Mr. Key smiled.

Mr. Key extended his hand to Will again and Will shook it with confidence. His time here today was over. Will thanked him again for his time. The excitement of having this level of help from Mr. Key gave Will confidence that there was a job out there that fit his skills and talents. He was ready to take on the workforce.

The Transition

Chapter 13

Will drove his Cutlass Supreme out of the parking deck onto High Street, southbound through Chinatown toward the Mass Turnpike. The two-door Carolina-blue sedan then headed west toward Worcester, home to Holy Cross University. Navigating the streets and highways of Boston had become more familiar for Will after the weekend trips to Cambridge, and more recently the visits to see Catherine at school.

The Massachusetts Turnpike traffic had not started to build at 3:40 in the afternoon, so he knew he would have time to spend the afternoon with Catherine and take her to dinner before heading back to Hanover. The upcoming corporate finance test he had on Friday seemed less significant now. Finding a job took precedence. He was lagging behind his Dartmouth classmates in the process of interviewing, but with Mr. Key's help, Will felt he was headed in the right direction.

As the car built up speed on the interstate, Will's excitement for his future mounted. Boston seemed like the ideal city to launch a career in finance. The experience he would gain working for one of Boston's financial institutions would enable him to write his ticket once he decided it was time to move back to North Carolina. Many of his UNC friends had predicted he would finish Dartmouth and end up working on Wall Street, but Boston was a far better solution.

Mr. Key's connections by no means guaranteed him a job, but Will's confidence level of landing a position in Boston's financial arena was elevated after his meeting this afternoon. It was too early to celebrate, but the future looked promising and the excitement of working in a city like Boston was enough to stimulate Will's spirits this April afternoon.

With the Boston skyline behind him, his thoughts turned to Catherine. He was excited to see her this afternoon and convey the details of the meeting with her father. For the last month, the two of them had seen each other mainly on the weekends, so today's mid-week rendezvous was something to look forward to.

Arriving at her building, Will knocked on the apartment door. Catherine greeted him at the threshold with open arms and an enveloping hug. She was happy to see him, and Will could tell that she was eager to hear how the meeting with her father went. He appreciated the inviting welcome. She wore her running clothes, and her shorts revealed her long, shapely legs. "Are we going for a run this afternoon?" Will asked, loosening his tie while she led him inside her apartment.

"Well, I was thinking about it. What did you bring to wear in your bag?" Catherine asked, pointing to the small gym bag that Will carried with him into the living room.

"I have a pair of running shoes, but I'll have to borrow some of your short running shorts," he laughed.

"I don't see that happening, running around this campus," Catherine commented. "So tell me," she asked with a smile. "How did it go with my dad?"

She sat down on the couch, and suddenly Will felt like the family man who had just returned home from the office, dressed in his suit, now relaxing on the couch with his wife as she asks, "How was your day, honey?"

"Oh, it went great! He had some good ideas, and it looks like he'll put me in touch with several of his finance contacts. Who knows where it will lead, but he was extremely helpful," Will said as the two sat facing each other on the couch.

"That's exciting!"

"Your dad is really an impressive man. He's obviously very well respected in the industry, and extremely well connected in Boston. I need to send him a note to thank him for his help."

"Did he mention anything about an opportunity at his firm?"

"Oh no, that didn't come up. I don't think that was the intention of the meeting. He's helping me network with people he knows in finance. He thinks there are good opportunities to work as an analyst, crunching numbers for a corporate finance or real estate firm."

"So, are you excited?"

"Yeah, I really am. Boston seems like a great place to work, especially for someone with my background and interests. This city is full of financial service firms. I just don't know how to wade my way through the process of finding what's out there. I've been sheltered at Dartmouth in remote New Hampshire, and boxed out of the real world. It was good to get some help from someone as connected as your dad. He's a good man."

"Glad you like him," Catherine smiled. "I think he's pretty cool myself."

Will was impressed by the relationship Catherine seemed to have with her father. It was obvious that she came from a good family, and that was important to Will. It was also apparent to Will that the Key family came from money. After being in his office this afternoon, it was evident that Mr. Key was obviously very successful. Will found he was drawn to Boston's financial elite, and he envisioned himself sitting in one of downtown Boston's office towers like Mr. Key as a respected corporate financial manager. He was just learning about the jobs in New England's financial sector, but he was very interested in knowing more, and Mr. Key was his window inside this new world of opportunity. "Your dad kept calling you Cat. I like that name – Cat," Will smiled. "Can I call you Cat?"

"Only if you kiss me first," she grinned.

"Okay, Cat. I can do that. Do you want me to kiss you on the cheek, Cat?" Will asked, overusing the new nickname as he moved from the middle of the couch closer toward her.

They engaged in a long impassioned kiss. "Who's here?" he whispered, wondering if the two of them were alone in the apartment.

She answered by grabbing his tie with her right hand and pulling his face toward hers. Another long kiss ensued as they both stretched out on the couch. Thoughts of his meeting with Mr. Key danced in his head as he tried to stay focused on the duty that lay nearest him. He felt himself enflamed in a mental quandary, humbly appreciative of the help that Mr. Key had just offered, while engaged in a passionate embrace with his daughter.

"I like it when I get to see you in the middle of the week, Cat," Will remarked.

"Why don't you take your jacket off and stay a while?" Cat suggested.

"I think I will," he said as he rose to his knees and removed the suit coat. She watched as he removed the jacket, then his tie, and placed them on top of his bag that sat on the floor between the couch and the coffee table.

He snuggled next to Cat, face to face. The couch enveloped them as Will pulled her close.

"You comfortable?" she asked.

"Yes, Cat, very comfortable," he smiled. "Are we alone?" he asked for the second time.

She answered with a passionate kiss.

The Phone Call

Chapter 14

The home telephone rang three times. "Can someone check the caller ID to see if that's a real call?" he yelled from the kitchen. He was up to his elbows in hot, soapy water washing a stainless steel pot, performing his nightly duty of cleaning the kitchen after the girls had prepared dinner for the family.

"Don't answer it! It's long distance," came the voice of a teenaged girl upstairs.

A fourth ring. His youngest daughter's teenage voice activated after the fourth ring, requesting to leave a message after the prompt. He anticipated a click signaling a hang-up from the caller, but the caller persisted and left a message after the greeting. "Will," the unfamiliar Southern voice began. Will rarely got phone calls at home, particularly on the home phone in the evenings. "It's Farrell. Call me when you can tonight. Try me at home, on my mobile number, or at the office if you're traveling." He left all three numbers at the end of his message.

Will glanced at the clock on the stove. It was 8:13 p.m., wondering what Farrell wanted. Maybe he's coming to Boston for a conference and wants to come by for a visit. It seems a little odd that he didn't leave a message as to why he called, Will thought as he dried off his hands with a clean dishtowel from the drawer next to the sink.

"Who was that?" Cat asked from her small office off the kitchen, sitting in front of her laptop. "I couldn't hear the message."

"It was my cousin Farrell from Charlotte," Will explained. "He didn't leave any detail on the message, just said to call him. I'm curious what he wants. I hope no one's died. I'm going outside to call him back from my cell phone."

Cat was focused on her computer screen, so she didn't respond to Will's comments. Now that the family was fed, her work for the day was done. It was her time to relax and zone out the needs of her husband and two teenage daughters. The girls, ages seventeen and fourteen, were upstairs in their rooms doing what teenage girls do on a summer night with no homework.

Will walked upstairs to secure his mobile phone from the bureau in the walk-in closet off the master bedroom. He took the phone back downstairs with him, as his curiosity contemplated the purpose of the call from his cousin tonight. He entered the garage and grabbed a bottled beer from the old refrigerator that housed his supply of contraband. Farrell's number was not one he kept in his phone. While the cousins exchanged holiday cards during the Christmas season, since Will moved to Boston two decades ago, the two rarely saw each other. The last time Farrell and Will were together was at Will's mother's funeral in Wilmington more than four years ago.

Time and distance had a way of separating family, even families like the Winfield cousins who had grown up together in their formative years. The travel distance between Farrell's home in Charlotte and Will's residence in the northern suburbs of Boston had prevented the two of them from spending any time together since college. Will replayed the message from his cousin and retrieved his mobile number. He dialed the number, and Farrell picked up on the second ring.

"Hello, Will?"

"Yes, how are you, Farrell?"

"I'm pretty good," Farrell replied.

"How's the family?"

"Everyone's good."

"How are Catherine and the girls?"

"They're good, despite the fact that I live in a house full of hormones. Both the girls will be in high school this fall. We're in the home stretch," Will proselytized, stepping from the kitchen onto his back deck overlooking the 14th fairway of the Tedesco golf course. He took a seat on one of the teak chairs around the table where the family had just finished dinner on this pleasant June night in Marblehead, Massachusetts. Beer in his right hand, mobile phone in his left, with both feet propped on the chair next to him, Will asked the question. "So what's up, Farrell?"

"Well, I'm afraid I have some bad news," Farrell replied, his voice somber. "Uncle John died earlier today."

Will hesitated before responding. The news was profound, and he gathered his thoughts before speaking. "That's terrible news. I thought he was in remission," Will commented, carefully setting the beer down on the table.

"He was doing better, but the cancer weakened his body. One of the neighbors found him slumped over the wheel of his truck, pulled over on the side of the road a few miles from the farm. The reports are that he died of a heart attack, but no one knows for sure. There's speculation that he may have been trying to drive himself to the doctor or hospital in Elizabethtown," Farrell explained.

"That would be just like him, trying to drive himself to the hospital. He was one independent man," Will commented.

"He was the toughest of all them, outlived all his siblings. We thought he had beaten the throat cancer, but at his age, he couldn't go on but so long. The treatments over the last three years weakened his body, particularly his heart. That's the speculation from Henry," Farrell conveyed, referring to his brother's assessment.

"How old was he?" Will asked. "I lost count."

"Eighty-four. I talked to him on his birthday in March. He seemed to be doing better. Mentally, he was doing fine," Farrell explained.

"You're a better nephew than me. I haven't talked to him in years. It's sad. An entire generation has passed. So, what are the arrangements? Do we know anything yet?" Will inquired. He stood, took another sip of his beer, and tried to fight off feelings of regret, knowing what little effort he had made to stay in touch with his uncle since moving to Boston after graduate school. He pictured the last time he saw his uncle, at his mother's funeral, the same time he had last seen Farrell. He recalled the conversations he had with John at the funeral. Will had made some empty promises about bringing the family to the farm that summer, but an activity-filled life in Boston seemed to get in the way of visiting family so far away.

"The funeral is this Saturday in Elizabethtown. I don't know all the details, and there's really no one around to plan the funeral. When you think about it, we were his only family left," Farrell stated grimly.

"I've got to get down there. We were planning to go to Cape Cod this weekend, but I'll see who I can convince to come with me. So who from the family is planning the funeral?"

"I haven't talked with any of the other cousins about the news or the arrangements. Henry, since he lives the closest, got the call this afternoon. He asked me to reach out to you and Clay, so I said I'd get the word out. I would have called earlier, but I didn't have your work number or cell phone," Farrell explained.

Will contemplated how he could convince Cat and the girls to trade a weekend at Cape Cod for another funeral in North Carolina. The girls had unfavorable memories of family trips to Wilmington to see their North Carolina grandparents. The drive down and back between Marblehead and Wilmington was long and arduous, but the more menacing part was the boredom of being in Wilmington for a week between Christmas and New Year's. Though it seemed heartless, the annual pilgrimage from Boston to Wilmington each holiday season was a tradition that Cat was glad to see end after Will's parents died a few years ago.

"Well, thanks for the phone call," Will said. "Keep me posted on the details, but I'll start working on flights tonight. I'll do my best to get down there. I guess we'll see everyone on Saturday," Will finished, preparing to hang up the phone.

"All right, please let Clay know, and we'll be in touch via e-mail or text about the details of the funeral. I hope you can make it down this weekend, Will. It's been too long, and I need to catch up on what your girls are up to."

"Thanks, Farrell," Will said, his spirits low as he considered the somber realities of his uncle's death.

"Good-bye, hope to see you on Saturday," Farrell said.

After the call, Will dialed his brother's home phone in Raleigh, North Carolina. Will and Clay talked to each other every other week or so by phone, but Will had only seen his brother once over the last four years since their parents died. Just two years behind Will in school, the brothers stayed close, although the distance between their hometowns prevented them from seeing each other on a regular basis.

The brothers had followed similar paths after high school, both attending college in Chapel Hill. Clay studied accounting at UNC and had worked as a CPA for ten years in Washington, D.C. before moving to Raleigh nine years ago to work as controller for one of North Carolina's preeminent software companies. Clay's three children were all much younger than Will's teenage girls, ranging in age from six to eleven.

"I've got bad news, Clayton," Will said when his brother answered. "Uncle John died today. It sounds like it was a heart attack. The funeral is this Saturday. I'm going to try and get there, but I'm not counting on Cat and the girls to make the trek. I may need you pick me up at the airport, but I'll look into taking the train if the schedules work. I'll start working on travel plans tomorrow. Do you think you'll be able to make it?"

"Sure, I'll plan to go, although I'll need to rearrange some things in the schedule. Just let me know what you work out on your end. For a weekend trip, I'm guessing you'll want to fly. You need to come off the dime and tap into that war chest you've been building over the years."

"I'll check the flights and let you know, but with only three or four days' notice, the airlines will kill you on fares," Will stated.

"Okay, let me know what works out on the flights, and I'll pick you up. We can make the drive down on Saturday morning," Clay said.

The brothers said their good-byes and hung up. Now it was time to let Cat know about Uncle John's death. She had only been around Will's uncle a few times, and by the time Cat first met him, John was in his sixties and living alone on the farm. She saw him sparingly in Wilmington during the Christmas holidays when John made a point to visit while Will and his family were in town seeing Will's folks. It was always Cat's speculation that Uncle John was gay. Though Will tried to refute her, Cat was convinced that she knew the reason why John never married.

"Think about it, Will. Your uncle lived with his mother most of his life. That's pretty strong evidence that the man was gay." Cat had shared her views with Will on the long drives back from Wilmington after spending time with Will's family during the Christmas holidays.

"He did the honorable thing and took care of my grandmother after my granddad died," Will would retort.

"You have no idea what goes on that farm when he's there all alone," Cat told Will on more than one occasion when the topic arose.

"He's just very independent, that's all," Will replied. "He was a ladies' man back in his day and had a girlfriend who lived in Elizabethtown."

"That's what he had you and all your cousins believe all those years. The girl was just a plant, someone he was friends with to make it look like he had a girlfriend. Why didn't he ever marry her then? You mark my words, he was gay," Cat had stated with confidence.

Cat had retreated upstairs to her bedroom to start her nightly ritual before bedtime. While Will was on the phone with Farrell and Clay, the summer sun had set over New England and it was now after nine o'clock and Will approached his wife of nineteen years to let her know the news of John's passing. He had already prepared himself for Catherine's callous response to the news of John's death, and given the distance from Boston, anticipated that she would have no interest in attending the funeral. Still, Will had to let her know that his plans for the weekend would most likely change, as he felt obligated to attend his uncle's funeral and forego the family's weekend plans in Cape Cod.

"That was Farrell on the phone," he said. "He let me know that Uncle John died today."

"I'm sorry. What happened?" she asked, sitting up in bed and turning down the volume on the television with the remote.

"You remember that he had throat cancer and was undergoing treatment, but Farrell said someone found him slumped over the wheel of his truck on the side of the road not too far from the farm. They think it was most likely a heart attack."

"Are you guys sure he didn't have AIDS?" Cat asked.

"That's terrible, Cat!" Will replied. "You need to back off your theory that he was gay."

"I'm sorry, that was mean, but how do you guys know he was really sick from cancer? That could be a cover-up. I think he had AIDS and hid it from all of you cousins."

"I'm not buying it," Will said, shaking his head at Cat's line of thinking.

"And the poor guy had no family to look out for him while he was sick," Cat said. "But I guess he probably had a friend that cared for him, one who probably lived there on the farm with him."

"I don't think so, Cat," Will countered. He sometimes wondered if Cat's theory was possibly true. Could there have been another man who lived secretly on the farm with John? He wondered who took care of him while he was sick. Maybe he wasn't alone when trying to drive himself to the hospital? It's possible that John's boyfriend is the one who found him in the car. Who knows? "The funeral is this Saturday, and I know the girls have friends going to the Cape, but I feel I need to go to the funeral."

Cat hesitated, thinking through her response. "You go right ahead, just don't expect me to go," she said, then looked down at her iPhone on the bedside table.

"I didn't think you wanted to go, so I'll look into taking the train or check on flights tomorrow."

"You do what you think you need to do. I understand he's your uncle, but it's a long way to go for a funeral," Cat said.

"I *have* to go. I've told myself a hundred times over the last few years that I need to get down to the farm to see John, but I didn't even so much as pick up the phone to call him, even when he was sick," Will said, shaking his head.

"That's a long trip to take strictly out of guilt," Cat said, without looking up from her phone.

"He was my favorite uncle. It's the least I can do, and even if I have to drive down, I'm going," Will said. "Plus, I haven't seen Clay and the cousins in a while. It's the right thing to do."

The Funeral

Chapter 15

The piercing screech of the train's brakes signaled another wake-up call along the series of periodic stops in small towns he had never heard of along the Amtrak's route down the eastern seaboard. Just like the last few stops through the night, Will woke with a hollow stare, noting the name of another city marked on the train station wall. With his head resting on the interior glass of the coach seat, Will opened one eye to read the name of the city on the placard as the train came to a complete stop.

WILSON, NORTH CAROLINA

He neared his destination, with just one more stop on the overnight train ride from Boston to Fayetteville, North Carolina. He knew he should have taken the damned sleeper car when he booked the ticket. So much for the idea of seeing the countryside on the trip down, it's been dark most of the trip, Will thought after being awakened for the last time on the twelve hour train trip between downtown Boston and his former home state.

Though his body told him to sleep, the brightness of the morning sun let him know that it was time to wake up and prepare for his final stop in Fayetteville. Now that it was daylight, Will surveyed the passengers on the train. Though he had the row to himself, the railcar was scattered with passengers, many of them dressed in military fatigues, clearly destined for Fayetteville as well, home to Fort Bragg Army Reservation.

Will stretched his arms in front of him and released a faint morning moan. He longed for a cup of coffee to wake him up from a restless night of sleep sitting up in a chair. What a way to spend a Friday night, he thought. Thankfully, the train ride was almost over.

As the train retained its top speed again, Will peered out the window and observed the landscape of a new day. The rising sun illuminated the rolling hills of Carolina's Piedmont region, which soon gave way to the flat farmland in the coastal plains of southeast North Carolina. With such short notice, flights from Logan International to Raleigh-Durham had been excessively expensive, so the overnight train from downtown Boston to Fayetteville proved to be the most cost-effective and efficient form of transportation for Will to get to Uncle John's funeral in Elizabethtown. Clay planned to leave Raleigh around eight o'clock Saturday morning, in time to pick up his brother at the train station in downtown Fayetteville by ten in order to make the eleven o'clock funeral in Elizabethtown. Will's train arrived in Fayetteville around eight-fifteen, so his wait time on his brother in Fayetteville would be a little less than two hours.

The only challenge in the travel plans was the twelve-hour train ride Will had to endure through the night from Massachusetts to North Carolina. Still, the sacrifice of a poor night's sleep was the least Will could endure for the neglect toward his uncle over the last twenty years, he theorized. On the ride home, he'd definitely upgrade to the sleeper car, he thought, gazing out the train's window, glad to be back in the Tar Heel state.

His mind took him back to Boston, knowing that his family would soon be up and ready to leave for their weekend trip to Cape Cod. Maybe it's best that he was here and the girls can enjoy their time together with their friends. They would have been miserable on this trip, attending the funeral of a great-uncle they barely knew. Plus, Cat wouldn't be caught dead riding on an all-night Amtrak train, and she would convince the girls that it was beneath them to travel this far by train. While the train was an adventure for him, and the girls might have enjoyed it, Cat would rather sit in a dentist's chair for twelve hours than endure this ride.

Wilson, North Carolina was another hour and forty minutes to his final destination of Fayetteville. Will pulled out Friday's edition of the Wall Street Journal from his brief-case and continued reading a story on the future of the Euro, ready for the train ride to end.

Like clockwork, the train arrived at the Fayetteville station at eight-eleven, and the familiar sound of the train's screeching brakes sounded more tolerable on this stop. He had reached his destination. Before the train slowed to a complete start, Will had his suit-bag in one hand and briefcase in the other, headed to the front of the car and ready to disembark. He surveyed the waiting area inside the Fayetteville train station, the room mostly desolate, with one single Amtrak attendant standing behind a laminate counter. Two army soldiers clad in camouflage sat upright, sleeping on the dated red laminate chairs that lined the far wall, away from the ticket counter. The vinyl coated floor tiles were in definite need of a deep clean and a wax job.

Though the train station waiting room was quiet, Will dismissed the thought of spending the next two hours inside reading his book and newspaper, as the waiting area was undeniably uninviting. Instead, Will decided to march down

Martin Luther King, Jr. Avenue in search of a cup of coffee.

Surely, there's a coffee shop open at eight o'clock in downtown Fayetteville on a Saturday morning, he thought as he repositioned his luggage on his shoulder to prepare for the walk down unfamiliar MLK Avenue to locate a café.

The streets of downtown Fayetteville were mostly desolate early on a summer Saturday morning. Will stopped the first person he passed on the street and asked where he could find a cup of coffee. The man appeared to be homeless, maybe in his late fifties, dressed in a dirty sweatshirt, carrying a red Nike bag over his shoulder, and moving slowly up the sidewalk in Will's direction.

"Good morning, sir, do you know where I could find a good cup of coffee?" Will asked.

"You in luck today, my man. You headed in the right direction," the heavy-set gentleman said, slowly pointing over his right shoulder. "There's a coffee shop just two more blocks south on the corner. I can't tell you the name of it, but you can't miss it."

Will pulled a dollar bill from his wallet, gave it to the man, and thanked him for the directions. Friday's Wall Street Journal, his tablet, and Kindle would be enough reading material to keep him occupied before Clay picked him up at ten o'clock. A corner booth in a downtown coffee shop with wireless made for the ideal venue to burn the next hour or so.

Shortly after nine o'clock, Will's cell phone rang. As expected, it was Clay. "I'm ahead of schedule, bro. I'm probably only twenty minutes out," he announced.

"Imagine that," Will responded, acknowledging that Clay was due to arrive early. Unlike Will, his brother was early everywhere he went. Clay had been born two weeks before his due date, and he had been early to every event since. As a CPA, fashionably late was not part of his social skillset. Some things never change, Will thought, wishing at times he could be as prompt as his brother.

The brothers worked out the details of the pick-up at the coffee shop, and the two were headed south down Highway 53 toward Elizabethtown, on schedule to arrive at Trinity Methodist with plenty of time to spare before the funeral. By quarter past ten, Will and Clay pulled into the Melvin's parking lot, and Will changed into his suit inside the restaurant restroom.

"We're early," Will stated as he climbed back in the car, dressed in a light gray suit with a tie draped around his neck.

"Maybe we can catch up with the other cousins before the service," Clay suggested as they drove two blocks down Main Street to the church.

As expected, Will and Clay arrived at the church thirty-five minutes before the service was due to start. The brothers were the first of the cousins to arrive, while Henry, Farrell, and his family were next to show up at the church. Farrell brought his wife and three children from Charlotte. Henry and his wife walked in next. The cousins, spouses, and children greeted each other with hugs and handshakes.

"Do we know if Chuck and Owen are going to make it?" Henry asked family members who had assembled in the narthex, just inside the front doors of the church.

"It's still early," Clay commented. "I'm sure they'll be here."

Henry, the senior delegate of the cousin contingency, lived the closest to Elizabethtown and the farm. After living in Greensboro most of his working career, Henry and his wife had retired to Carolina Beach, located just south of Wilmington. Unlike the other cousins, Henry and Laura did not have children.

"Henry, thanks for coordinating the arrangements for the funeral," Will mentioned, once the cousins had all greeted each other in the narthex.

"Oh, I didn't do much at all. I just talked to the preacher once. I assume some of the ladies from the church took care of the details," Henry explained, a little surprised to get credit for the arrangements.

Will checked his watch. The service was still not due to start for another twenty minutes. He wandered a few steps away from the assembly of cousins and peered through the glass in the double doors leading into the sanctuary. He saw his uncle's casket centered in front of the pulpit, positioned at the end of the center aisle, waiting patiently for the service to start. The casket was open, a little to his surprise. Will pulled the door open slowly so as to not alert the funeral attendants or his cousins as he slipped inside the sanctuary.

Will walked quietly down the center aisle, as if his presence might disturb his sleeping uncle. The rays of the late morning sun pierced the stained glass windows, the beams of light resembling the fingers of God reaching toward the casket, preparing to take this fallen warrior home. Will searched the sanctuary as a series of memories flooded his mind. He was alone, just he and his uncle. Only the sound of Will's hard-sole shoes stepping on the venerable pine floors as he approached the casket from the center aisle broke the solemn quiet.

Trinity Methodist Church was built in 1834 and stood as the oldest structure in Elizabethtown. The Winfield family had been card-carrying members of Trinity Church since the late 1800s, but today marked the end of that era. Spanning across three centuries, the Winfield's association with Trinity Methodist would terminate at noon today when Uncle John's funeral service concluded. Will had been to this church countless times in his youth, but the last visit was for his grandmother's funeral twenty-four years ago. Will had been in college and drove down from Chapel Hill to attend the service.

He remembered sitting in these stark white wooden pews as a child with his cousins on Sunday mornings. The cousins would line up on one row, with the parents seated in the row behind them, pleading with the disruptive cousins to keep quiet. Still, Trinity Church was most remembered for the funerals he attended, and now, he was here for the last of the Winfield interments.

The most humorous family story recanted from this sanctuary dated back to his grandfather's funeral, when Will had been four years old and Clay was only two. Grandpa Winfield, John's father, died at the age of ninety-two. He had married for the first time in his mid-thirties, so he was an older groom, particularly in 1921. Affectionately known as Pop-Pop, he lived long enough to see all eight of his grandchildren born, but passed away soon after the last grandchild, Owen, was born. At the funeral, in this very sanctuary, the preacher did most of the talking that day, but young Clay stole the show with his comments during Pop-Pop's service.

Similar to today's funeral, the coffin was open, with Grandpa Winfield's face exposed to the attendees. In the quiet moments before the service commenced, young Clay loudly asked his mother a question. "Pop-Pop got tired and took a nap?" The attending mourners could barely contain their laughter. Later in the service, as the long-winded preacher took some liberties in his eulogy for Grandpa Winfield, little Clay, exasperated at the length of the service, shocked the crowd with another question. "Mommy, when's this show going to be over?"

Will smiled as he remembered the humorous stories from his childhood. When the cousins assembled later today at the farm after the funeral, Will was certain he would hear a numerous amusing chronicles from their time together, including Clay's commentary at Pop-Pop's funeral forty years ago. He sighed and then turned around to check the balcony to ensure he was alone as he approached the casket. He studied his uncle's ghostly white and hollow face. His features were still the same, but John had aged considerable in the four years since Will had last seen him.

A rush of despair came over Will, standing alone with his uncle, lying motionless in the casket. Were his emotions from the loss of his uncle or from the guilt of his neglect over the past two decades? Had he traveled so far for this very moment to be alone with his uncle? "I'm sorry," Will whispered, memorizing every feature on his uncle's face. "I left and never came back. I promised I would come back, but I didn't." Why hadn't he made more of an effort? Will thought. Tears welled in his eyes, longing for his endeared uncle to respond. He wanted John to say, "I forgive you," but he lay peacefully on the white satin lining of the casket, unable to respond.

Will studied his uncle's features, thinking that the grimace on his face now replaced the perpetual smile he remembered from years past. The pale color of his skin substituted his formerly sun-kissed tone. Today's events took him back four years earlier to his mother's funeral in Wilmington. In similar fashion, he had stared down at his mom's appearance for the last time as she lay motionless in her open casket. As he examined his uncle's face, he noted the similarities of his mother's features in John's. The way the corners of John's mouth met his cheeks resembled his mother's mouth. Suddenly, Will raised his head, realizing that he and his uncle were no longer alone.

"I don't mean to interrupt," a deep voice reverberated off the arched beamed ceilings. The middle-aged man was dressed in a black robe that covered his robust torso. He held a Bible tucked under his arm. He was obviously the preacher, preparing to start the service shortly. "Take your time, the service won't start for another few minutes," he said.

Will hesitated before he spoke, unsure what to say, thinking he should apologize for not being back in the narthex with his cousins. He felt it appropriate to introduce himself. "Hello, I'm Will Jordan. John is, or *was*, my uncle. I haven't seen him in a long time."

"I understand. It's important to grieve at this time. I'm Michael Watson, the pastor here. Your family has been a member of this church for too many years to count, long before me, even," the pastor said with a chuckle, demeaning his age. His resonant voice reflected off the hallowed walls of the sanctuary as he spoke.

Will felt compelled to let the preacher know more about his uncle, his character, and what his uncle personally meant to him. "I know you may not have seen my uncle here in the pews every Sunday, but I can vouch for the man he was. He was the greatest uncle a boy could ever hope to have. He taught us how to hunt and fish at the farm. He would hug and tickle us like we were his own. I never understood why he never wanted children of his own," Will said, a slight frown marring his brow. "He would have been a great father. He was a terrific teacher in everything he did, from farming, shooting a gun, driving a tractor, and down to the way he treated others. I could spend the next hour telling you what a wonderful uncle he was to my cousins and me. Forgive me for bragging on him, but these are times when you want the preacher to know the true character of the man he's about to eulogize."

"Oh, I understand," Pastor Watson smiled. "I visited your uncle a few times at the farm when he was sick last year. I know the man he was, and this community loved your uncle. He was well respected and admired by all. I don't think he had an enemy in this world." He glanced between Will and John, lying prostrate in the casket, as Will stood guard next to his uncle.

"Thank you for sharing that. I wasn't sure how well you knew my uncle. I moved away from here twenty years ago and live in Boston now. I neglected to come back to see him over the last several years. My daughters met Uncle John when they were little, but they don't know him and never got to experience life with him. I hate that they missed out on knowing such a good man."

"Your generation left the smaller communities and moved to big cities like Charlotte, Raleigh, Winston-Salem, Atlanta, Washington, and places like Boston," the pastor said. "Our community, like other small communities, needs good people in our schools, in leadership positions, and in our churches. I hope the trend will one day swing back to where kids in this next generation will realize the value of living in smaller communities, a better place to raise their families."

"I grew up in Wilmington, and I've been trying to recreate that smaller town environment for my girls. We live on the coast in a smaller township on the north side of Boston, but my girls have been raised in an urban setting for sure."

"Well, Wilmington is no longer a small coastal town. It's grown tremendously in the last twenty years since you've been gone."

"You're right. It was one of the fastest growing towns in America seven or eight years ago," Will relayed, displaying pride in his former home town. "I know you need to get ready for the service," Will said, looking at his watch. "I didn't mean to take up so much of your time."

"Not at all. In fact, you have given me some good information for my eulogy," the pastor responded. "Thank you for sharing what you did about your uncle. I'll see you this afternoon at the farm for the graveside service."

Will quickly shook the preacher's hand and scurried up the aisle toward the narthex where his cousins waited to enter the sanctuary. "I was visiting with the preacher," Will explained to Clay and his cousins, accounting for his absence, and covering the fact that he had engaged a tearful conversation with his uncle.

The remaining contingency of cousins had now arrived, and Will greeted his lone female cousin, Virginia, or Ginny, as she preferred to be called. She and her husband, Robert, had flown into Raleigh from south Florida the previous evening.

"We made it," Ginny said. "There is no easy way to get here by air, unless you own an airplane. We drove down from Raleigh this morning."

"Good morning Chuck," Will said to his other Florida cousin in attendance. "You couldn't get Owen to come?"

"He's in a fishing tournament this weekend in Sarasota. I couldn't convince him to come. He's passionate about his fishing."

"Let's get inside," Henry suggested. "I think we have reserved seating up front, fifty yard line seats."

The sanctuary was hardly full, but Will was pleased to see that seventy or eighty people had come to pay their final respects to John Winfield. Will expected mostly older members of the community to attend, but the church held a good cross-section of the community, young and old, Mexicans and African-Americans, farmers and bankers. John's life had evidently touched many in the community. After an obese sopranoist covered in a purple choir robe sang Amazing Grace from the pulpit, Pastor Watson stood, surveyed the attendees, and then began his eulogy.

"John Winfield was the consummate Southern gentleman. Born and raised right here in Bladen County, he was taught many skills. He learned to farm, shoot a gun, skin a rabbit, catch catfish, and probably most important, with six brothers and sisters, John learned to lead and get along with others. He carried those characteristics with him all the way through his life. I am reminded of the noble Roman general Cincinnatus, who lived five hundred years before Jesus. Cincinnatus was a soldier who became a general and a war hero, and, like so many in that time, the military leaders, not unlike our own Dwight Eisenhower, came home to become political leaders. But Cincinnatus was different. He was appointed dictator in 458 B.C. but gave up the office to return to life on his farm."

The pastor paused, warming up to his topic. "Like Cincinnatus, John Winfield served his country in the United States Army in World War Two. He left the family farm at age nineteen, and one of his first tours was at Normandy on D-Day in 1944. John served in the Army for four years and lived the life of a patriot until he died this past Tuesday. After his discharge from the army, John returned to the farm, just like Cincinnatus, and then went on to receive his accounting degree from East Carolina University. After college, he returned to the farm and practiced public accounting for several years right here in Elizabethtown, but he never left his first love —farming."

Will was enjoying the eulogy so far, and settled back in his seat, listening with fond memories of his uncle.

"As his father aged, John took over the farm and dedicated his life to farming full time. John was not only a farmer, but also a businessman, and he ran Winfield Farm like a business. Always a tobacco farmer, John was forced to diversify the Winfield farming operation as the tobacco industry changed in the eighties. John diversified from tobacco and planted more corn, sorghum, soybeans, vegetables, planted pine, and began to raise cattle. A bachelor for eighty-four years, John did not lack for family. He remained close to his six siblings and outlived all of them. He was like a father to his seven nephews and niece. He loved children, even those that were not his own. Quietly, he met the needs of those in this community. If there was an employee at the farm in need of a hand, John was there to provide. If a family in our community fell on hard times, John would privately provide financial assistance."

Will listened with tears in his eyes as Reverend Watson told the story of Uncle John's life. It was as though the preacher had walked through life side-by-side with him. Will was pleased that the pastor had shared so much detail on John's life in his tribute.

"John grew up in this church, as did his father before him. John was here in this sanctuary as a teenager when the service was held for his younger brother who died of pneumonia at age eleven. His aunt, mother, father, another brother, and sister were all eulogized here in this church before being buried in the Winfield family burial plot on the farm. John is the last of his generation of Winfields. He leaves a legacy in this community and a lasting impact and memory among his niece and nephews, the next generation of Winfields. We will all miss John Winfield - a patriot, a farmer, a gentleman, a man of honor who was respected by his fellow farmers and this community, revered by his family, and a friend to all."

Will was moved to tears by the preacher's reflection of John's life. He stared at the casket as it was closed and draped with the American flag. *A life well lived,* Will thought as the pastor concluded his comments.

"Now please join me in reciting the Twenty-Third Psalm found on the back of the program," the pastor concluded.

The service ended and the cousins lined up in front of the casket to greet the attendees. The conversations were short, but many of the older residents wanted to know which cousin belonged to John's various siblings.

"Now whose child are you?" Mrs. Carolyn Walker asked each cousin as she went through the line to greet the Winfield cousins. Will and Clay stood next to each other at the end of the receiving line and relished in the esteemed comments each resident offered about their uncle.

"I used to work in tobacco with your mother in the summers," Lucinda Warren told Will and Clay as she walked through the line with her cane. "That was some hard work, boys. Picking tobacco taught you how to work, and was it hot working in those open fields, but I remember your mama was a worker. She could sure work that tobacco."

"Thank you for coming today," was the general response Will and Clay offered those that came through the line.

Soon, a familiar face appeared toward the end of the line. Will recognized Martha Joiner, Uncle John's long-time girl-friend from Elizabethtown. "Here comes Martha," Will whispered to his brother. "She still looks hot."

"I wouldn't go that far," Clay shot back. "She is in her eighties, after all."

"Wonder why they never got married?" Will whispered, waiting for the next guest to make it through the line.

"I think Uncle John was too independent, or maybe he liked playing the field," Clay jested.

"You know Cat's theory on why John never married, right?" Will whispered.

"Yeah, but I'm not buying it," Clay commented quietly as the brothers waited for Martha to speak to each of the other cousins. "Cat never cared much for our side of the family. Plus, she didn't know Uncle John in his younger days like we did."

"You're probably right," Will agreed, with only an inkling of doubt as Martha finally made her way to the end of the receiving line.

"Now you must be Rachael's boys. All of you and your cousins are all grown up now. I haven't seen any of you since you were teenagers," Martha said.

"Yes, ma'am," Clay responded.

"Are you going to come to the gravesite with us after the service?" Clay asked Martha, after she hugged both Clay and Will's neck.

"Oh, I don't think so. I wasn't invited," she responded.

"Well, you're invited now. You can ride with us," Will suggested.

"Thank you boys, but I haven't been to the farm in many years. I don't think so," she replied.

"But you're like family. We'd love to have you," Clay said.

Again, she responded with a shake of her head. "Oh, I don't think so, but thank you. That's a nice offer, but I don't think I should go."

She walked away gracefully in her black knee-length dress and low heels. She had always dressed with style and class. Mentally, she appeared to be as sharp as she looked, even in her eighties.

"Their relationship must not have ended well," Will commented quietly to his brother as Martha walked up the center aisle of the sanctuary.

"Wonder what happened?" Clay asked.

"My guess is she probably wanted to get married, and he wouldn't marry her. He probably made up his mind up thirty years ago that he wouldn't get married. Maybe she just got tired of waiting and moved on," Will surmised.

"I guess it's something we'll never know, and we can't go ask John what happened," Clay joked. "Who knows? Maybe Cat's speculation *was* true, and Martha was just a friend of the family."

The Burial

Chapter 16

The mid-day June sun beat down on the black asphalt in the church parking lot. With temperatures in the low nineties, it was no day to be standing outside, particularly wearing a suit and tie. Will surveyed the small church from the parking lot to the narrow steeple that stood above the other structures in downtown Elizabethtown. He remembered the church as much larger from his childhood, but all buildings seem more substantial from the eyes of a child.

The cousins stood next to the hearse, making plans to eat before proceeding to the farm for the graveside ceremony at the Winfield cemetery.

"We don't have much time, so let's go by Melvin's in honor of Uncle John and pick up some burgers. We can eat at the house before the graveside service," Henry suggested.

The group agreed and made the short trip down West Broad Street from the church to Melvin's before congregating at the farm. Will ordered an extra burger and fries for the preacher and purchased a Melvin's hat especially for Uncle John. He planned to put the hat on top of the casket at the graveside service.

The hasty detour to Melvin's had the cousins back on US 701 headed north in the direction of the farm in time to meet Reverend Watson at the house by one o'clock. Through the gate and down the long dirt road, the cousins' convoy arrived at the two-story structure in time to meet the preacher, already there waiting for them. The farmhouse looked just like Will remembered it, though it had been twenty-four years since his last visit. The home's nineteenth century federal-style architecture had stood the test of time, but the paint on the columns and shutters had begun to chip, showing signs of the home's age.

Memories of simpler times with his cousins flooded Will's mind as Clay pulled the car behind the others in the dirt driveway. In many ways, it was like old times from their child-hood. The cousins were all here, gathered together at the farm, though today was different. Instead of a greeting from Nanny and Uncle John on the front porch, a hearse was parked in the driveway beside the house.

Will refused to look at the black hearse as he walked toward the porch. As far as he was concerned. Will held firm to the premise that he was still eleven years old, and he was here to visit Uncle John and his cousins. He imagined him and Clay walking into the house, and Uncle John, flanked by their cousins, would acknowledge their arrival with a big bear hug. Then, Nanny would emerge from the kitchen into the living room and welcome her grandchildren with hugs and kisses.

Instead, Will and Clay were greeted today by the preacher, some neighbors, and two bags of hamburgers from Melvin's.

"Hello again," the pastor said, with a slight bow as Clay and Will entered the living room. "Do you remember Eileen Saxon from down the street?"

Will remembered the family who lived on the edge of the Winfield property, but did not recall any of their names, except an elderly Miss Sarah, who often brought eggs to his grandmother. Will assumed that Eileen must be Sarah's daughter.

"Yes, I remember," Will hedged. "I'm Will, and this is my brother Clay. We're Rachael's boys." He took a step toward Eileen hand extended.

"Oh, I know who you are," Eileen said with a gentle handshake. "I would have recognized you boys without you needin' to tell me your names."

Eileen was probably in her late fifties, maybe sixty, based on the lines on her face. From the looks of her, it appeared that life for Eileen had not been easy, and her face showed a lifetime of struggles. Her wiry hair was mostly gray and unkempt, and she wore a black dress that looked as if she might have worn it to his grandmother's funeral over two decades ago.

Will knew that Eileen and her family had lived in the small tenant house about a half mile down the main road from the home-place for three generations. He remembered visiting Eileen's house as a child with his mother. His memory could not recall the individuals in the family, but he did have vivid memories of the wooden frame house they called home. The house had been aged and decrepit when Will was in grade school, so he wondered about its condition today. From what he remembered, the house was, for all intents and purposes, a shack. He knew that Miss Eileen and her family were people that the Winfield's revered and cared for like their own, so he understood why they were here today to honor John Winfield.

"Meet my children," Eileen said, as she stepped aside to make the introduction. "This is my oldest, Brooke, and my son, Wyn." Eileen's children appeared to be in their late twenties. They stood in the back corner of the living room on the other side of the fireplace, away from the crowd. Given the choice, it was evident that Brooke and Wyn preferred not to be here today. Both were quiet and unengaged with the crowd. Brooke wore a dress that could have been worn by her mother to a prom in the 1950s, and Wyn wore jeans, cowboy boots, and a short-sleeve checked plaid shirt worn over a black t-shirt. The collared shirt was faded and un-tucked. Will and Clay greeted Wyn and Brooke with a handshake and a smile.

The cousins turned their focus to eating their hamburgers as the pastor announced that the processional would leave in five minutes for the graveside service. He expressed his gratitude that the cousins had thought of him when they ordered hamburgers from Melvin's.

"Eileen, we didn't expect you guys for lunch, but we may have enough to share," Henry offered, waving Eileen's family toward the dining room. "Why don't you come in here and have you a hamburger?"

"No thank ya," Eileen responded. "We've done ate, but thank you anyhow."

As the crowd of mourners left the house, Virginia spoke. "Henry, should we lock up?"

"No, don't worry about it. We won't be gone long," Henry replied as he stepped off the front porch. "Eileen, do you have a key or do you know where John kept a key?"

"I keep a key, but I am not sure where it is," she said. "John didn't never lock the house, unless he was leavin' to go on a trip."

"I guess we'll need someone to watch over the house for the next few weeks," Henry said. "Eileen, we might need your help looking over things for a while, until we get someone here to oversee the farm. I'll try to come when I can, but I won't be able to get over here that often."

"Can someone give us a ride to the cemetery?" Eileen asked.

"Sure, it's just Laura and me, so you guys ride with us," Henry offered.

"We ain't got a car right now, so we wasn't able to get to the funeral. That's why we showed up today for the graveside service. We hope y'all don't mind. I know it's supposed to be just family at the cemetery, but we wanted to pay our respects. Your family has been good to us through the years, especially John and your grandmother," Eileen explained.

"We're glad you're here. I'm sorry you missed the funeral service. Pastor Mike did a fine job," Henry said, as he opened the back door of his BMW sedan for Eileen, Brooke and Wyn. "It'll be a little tight back there, but we don't have far to go. The cemetery is only a mile down the road."

"Oh, I know right where it's at," Eileen pronounced.

"That's right, I forget, you probably know the farm better than we do," Henry commented.

The funeral director and his two employees waited by the burial plot at Winfield Cemetery for the procession to arrive. The Winfield cousins and their families gathered around the freshly dug plot while the attendants placed John's coffin on the bier. Eileen, Brooke, and Wyn stood on the periphery, just behind the family. Pastor Mike stood in his black full-length robe with his back to the planted pine trees that guarded the half-acre burial plot.

"Family and friends, we are gathered this afternoon to say good-bye to an uncle and a friend, a man who lived life to the fullest even until his last days. Though he traveled the world, he stayed true to his roots and devoted most of his eighty-four years of life to Winfield Farm. So, it is fitting that John be laid to rest here with his parents, grandparents, a few siblings, and aunts and uncles here at Winfield Cemetery, on the land that he loved so dearly." He paused.

"Blessed are they that mourn, for they shall be comforted. Dust to dust, ashes to ashes. Now, let us pray."

The small crowd bowed their heads as the pastor said the

final prayer before John Winfield was laid to rest in the sacred grounds of Winfield Farm. "We thank you, Heavenly Father, for a life well lived. God, may our brother John rest in your arms in eternal peace. Amen."

As the assemblage raised their heads from the prayer, the casket was lowered into the East Carolina sandy soil. The American flag no longer draped the coffin, but a hat from Melvin's perched on top of the mahogany coffin. The family watched in silence as the casket slowly disappeared into the ground. The shade of the loblolly pines sheltered the heat from the bewailing gathering, but the afternoon sun was intense for an outside service in late June.

Will and the cousins felt emotionally drained, and the North Carolina humidity had further reduced their energy. It had already been a long Saturday, but the activities were not over yet. Cousin Henry had called a meeting of the cousins at the house after the graveside service to discuss the future of the farm.

"Eileen, why don't you ride back with us?" Clay offered. "We'll take you home. Henry, we'll give Eileen a ride back to her house if you can take Brooke and Wyn. That'll give them more room in the back seat."

The dry soil from the dirt road leading out of Winfield Cemetery created a cloud of dust as the entourage of cars left the gravesite. The dusty road led the processional through a forest of planted pine and back to the front entry gate into Winfield Farm. Eileen's house was another two minutes past the home-place on the main highway.

Eileen remained quiet on the short ride back to her house, and as Clay's car rolled past the entry gate, all four passengers turned to observe the Winfield house. Sitting maybe three hundred yards off the paved road, the white square columns of the house could be seen in full view from Highway 701, the white two-story structure standing majestically as the center-piece of Winfield Farm.

"Do you have anything at the house you left behind, Eileen?" Will asked to break the silence as the car passed by the front gate.

"No, I have everything," she responded.

"I'm sure Henry would be fine with you using John's truck when you need it," Will offered. "I know it must be tough to be without a car."

"The neighbors have been helpin' me get to work, but I need to get me a new car. Wyn went off and wrecked the last car we had," she explained as they pulled into the dirt driveway of Eileen's home.

Will vividly remembered the small house Eileen and her family called home. The house and the dirt yard looked much the same as Will recalled from his childhood - a wooden four-room structure on a cinder block foundation. The house still looked uninhabitable by Will's standards. As Clay drove into Eileen's dirt driveway, he stared, reminiscing children chasing loose chickens around the small front yard. The first time Will's mother brought Will and Clay to visit Eileen and her mother, provoked the first memory Will had of seeing real poverty up close. He recalled riding by the housing projects in downtown Wilmington on his way to elementary school, but the Stratford's home provided a ground-level view of what it meant to be poor. He recalled asking his mother after they left the shack that day, "Mom, do they really live there?"

"Yes, so that's why you need to study hard and make good grades in school." To a child in elementary school, Mrs. Jordan's response seemed like the right answer a mother would give her child when asked such a question.

Clay and Will bid Eileen good-bye. She thanked them for the ride as Henry and Laura pulled up behind Clay's car to drop off Brooke and Wyn.

"Do you remember seeing this place when we were kids?" Will asked as Clay turned around in Eileen's front yard. "It sure hasn't changed much. Do you remember the chickens that used to run around the yard here? It's sad, but I guess their family is a lot like Uncle John. They've stayed here in this house because that's what their parents before them did. I guess the farms around here have a way of keeping people employed and in the same place for generations," Will theorized. "What makes people live in poverty for generations?"

"It all goes back to education," Clay conjectured.

"Yep, I guess it does. It makes you thankful for being born in the family we're in. I mean, why didn't we grow up in this house?" Will speculated.

"Because our parents finished high school and went to college. I know what you're thinking, Will. Are you getting brainwashed by those Massachusetts liberals again?" Clay joked.

"Not really. It just makes you wonder why there's such a divide between those that have and those that don't," Will said, shaking his head as he studied the conditions around him.

The Plan

Chapter 17

The cousins gathered in the dining room of the Winfield homeplace. The antique oak table was ample enough to seat the six cousins who had made it to Bladen County for the funeral. The spouses and children who accompanied the cousins to the funeral were either outside on the porch or exploring the uninhabited rooms of the spacious house, leaving the six cousins in the dining room to contemplate the future of Winfield farm.

"It's been a long time since we were all here together, almost twenty five years, if my math is right," Henry began. "I was thinking that since there are eight of us, we could call the assembly of cousins the C-8 rather than the G-8 Summit, but there are only six of us here today." As the oldest cousin, Henry was typically the one to take the lead on family matters and always inserted some of his creative humor into their time together. He sighed. "Well, it looks like it's just us now. A full generation of Winfields has passed on, so the next generation is officially charged with contemplating what happens to the farm. It's sad, and we've buried a fallen hero today, so I wanted to get all of us together while we're here to talk about what happens now. This farm can't run itself, so I've been thinking about several scenarios. I don't have an opinion either way, but we need to get them on the table and develop a plan of action." He paused a moment, gathering his thoughts. "Here are my ideas. One, we can sell the farm, which seems like the more logical alternative, in my opinion. Second, we can hire a manager or a farm management company. Third, we lease out the land to tenant farmers and continue to own the farm, but then, what do we do with the house? There are a number of scenarios to consider."

"Forgive me for being presumptuous, Henry, but what about you running the farm?" Clay suggested. "We probably can't afford you, but we'll compensate you for your time. Or better yet, why don't you just buy the farm?"

"Well, I thought that might be a suggestion from one of you today, so this is probably the time to let the rest of you know what's going on in my world," Henry said, looking at each face at the table.

"I'm sure you guys see me as the likely candidate to either purchase or run the farm, but I just learned that I'm sick. I told Gin and Farrell a few weeks ago that I have been diagnosed with a form of leukemia, which thankfully, is very curable. This past spring, when Laura and I would take our daily walk on the beach, I noticed that I was getting tired and winded. I wrote it off as a sign of old age, but then I decided I should go to the doctor, which resulted in a number of tests. The diagnosis looks good, so don't worry, but I'll have to go through treatments, starting next month."

Will looked around the table at the cousins. Each cousin seated at the table had lost both parents over the span of the last twenty years, and today, they gathered here to mourn the death of their affable uncle. Now, the news that one of their own was facing a threatening illness overshadowed the purpose of why the cousins were meeting this afternoon. Somehow, the business of addressing the future of Winfield Farm took a back seat to dealing with the medical challenges that lay ahead for a family member in their own generation.

Now in his fifties, Henry had lived a good life. He had enjoyed a successful run in the computer software business and recently sold his company to North Carolina-based global software icon Red Hat. The sale had enabled Henry to retire to Carolina Beach at age fifty-two just last year. Financially, Henry was in a good position to buy the farm from the family. He lived close enough, about ninety miles away, but this news of his illness took Henry out of the running. Henry's announcement was a game-changer for the Winfield cousins and, potentially, for the future of the family farm. The concern of those at the table turned toward Henry's health and the treatments he faced in the next few months.

"Tell us more detail about the cancer, Henry. What are your doctors telling you?" Chuck asked.

"I'll be fine," he said, waving a hand. "I'm told that the doctors caught this early, and the chances of survival are very much in my favor. I appreciate your concern and comments, but Laura and I are going to beat this thing. Don't y'all worry. I may be a little weak right now, but we're going to do the right thing for Winfield Farm. I'm confident of that, so let's talk about the business at hand. Let me propose that we get some ideas on the value of the property, and then contact an auction company. I've been doing some research on auctions. I've come to learn that many family farms are put up for auction, especially when there are multiple heirs, like in our situation. Fortunately for us, the transfer of title will be pretty simple." He glanced around the table. "After our parents passed away, the attorneys and CPAs recommended that we name Uncle John as the sole owner of Winfield Farm in a limited liability company for tax purposes," Henry explained. "That way, we would all own an equal portion of the farm upon John's death, and we would all share in the estate tax burden equally." He gestured toward his two siblings. "As an example, the three of us would not own diluted shares just because there were three of us, as compared to Will and Clay, or Chuck and Owen, who would own a slightly larger percentage of the farm because there were only two siblings, rather than three, in their family. I have to give the previous generation and the estate planner credit, not because it benefits me, but because this is a much cleaner distribution. This way, we all get one vote each. Since there are eight of us, we could find ourselves in a four-to-four tie if there is some issue that we can't agree on, but I don't see that happening. In fact, I think Farrell has the file with him." He turned toward Farrell. "Read what the will says about the transfer, just so we're all reading off the same sheet of music."

"Sure," Farrell said, opening a manila file folder from which he produced a will and some of the other legal documents associated with John's estate. He skimmed the paragraph with the language that addressed the transfer of the estate, mumbling a few sentences until he located the exact language he wanted. "Here we go. The surviving heirs of the deceased will share equally the assets of the deceased, including but not limited to the farm, its equipment, assets, and proceeds. Further, any liabilities, including but not limited to, federal, estate, state, inventory, or property taxes will be shared equally among the surviving heirs of the deceased."

"Fortunately, this is very straightforward and should simplify the sale," Henry summarized.

"Speaking of a sale, should we engage a local realtor and have him list the property?" Clay asked. "It seems like that might yield a better price than an auction."

"That was my first thought," Henry responded. "However, in this economy, the chances for a quick sale are pretty improbable. If it takes us a year or more to sell, then we've got to hire a local farmer to oversee the farm in the interim. This farm is still operating, and that's another reason our parents wanted John to own the farm outright. Uncle John made decisions based on what he thought was right for the farm. That way, he could run the farm without the varied opinions of the eight of us."

"The farm is profitable," Farrell agreed. "John made sure of that, and he deserved to own the entire enterprise and reap those profits without having to write disproportionate distribution checks to each of us. Unfortunately for us, Henry is not in a position to oversee the farm and its operations, so we'll need to make some alternative decisions."

"That all makes sense, but what makes you guys feel we can get our price in an auction?" Will asked. "The auction process seems like somewhat of a fire-sale to me." He looked at the others. "I sure wish we could hire a local farmer for two years until this economy turns around, and then put the property on the market. I think we'd drive up our value based on that approach."

"I agree, but I don't think we have that luxury," Farrell explained. "I don't know if there is a farmer who can devote the time to run our farm while he runs his own, but I'm certainly not the one to ask."

"Maybe there's a farmer who lost his own farm in this downturn and might be looking for an opportunity like this," Will suggested. "We would pay him a salary, and he runs the farm, but without the risk. He might even share in the profits."

"I just don't know how we'd go about trying to find that individual," Henry inserted. "I like the concept, but I think our best alternative is to look into the auction process. That's our second option. Let me give you some detail on my research. There are two kinds of auctions. One is an absolute auction where the farm sells at whatever price is offered by the highest bidder. The second, which seems to fit our profile, is where the auction company sets a minimum price the sellers would take. If the minimum is not met, then the property doesn't sell."

"Henry, you've done your homework," Virginia piped into the discussion.

"The internet is a wonderful thing," Henry laughed.

"Let me suggest this," Clay offered. "Will and I have a friend from UNC that's in the auction business. They're a pretty good sized auction company in the southeast from what I've seen, but they're based here in North Carolina. I can contact Ben Holcomb to see if he could send us more information about the various types of auctions and the costs."

"That would be great," Henry said. "I didn't make any direct contacts. I just read a few websites and tried to better understand the auction process."

"Farrell, what other assets did John have? Is there a list of his financial statements or cash?" Chuck asked.

"Not as much as you might think. Most of his estate is held in the farm, including the equipment and cattle. There's a reasonable amount of cash in the farm account, but my guess is John didn't make too many distributions to himself, particularly later in life. He holds a couple hundred thousand dollars in equities in one account that could be construed as a retirement account," Farrell conveyed, flipping through the pages of the file.

"What about life insurance?" Virginia asked.

"Very little, not even enough to settle the taxes due on the estate. Truth is, with no wife and children, he didn't need much in the way of life insurance," Farrell said.

"So, get ready gang, we're going to owe Uncle Sam some money for estate taxes," Henry said. "As Farrell explained, there is not much liquidity in the estate. The farm is the largest asset by far. I'm afraid we'll either have to come out of pocket or sell the farm to raise money for the taxes."

"Maybe we could sell a portion of the farm considered more valuable to raise enough money for the death taxes," Clay, the CPA, suggested. "Estate taxes are a bitch, especially in a situation like ours. We're inheriting a relatively large estate, but there is very little liquidity to pay the estate taxes. That's why the auction might make the most sense. Either way, we'll need to raise enough cash for the eight of us to pay the estate taxes that are due. We have nine months to pay the estate taxes, but as a closely held businesses and farm, that may allow us a longer pay-out period."

"You guys probably know this since we've all lost our parents, but the IRS will determine a fair market value of the estate at the time of John's death." Farrell explained. "It's called a stepped-up basis, so there should be no capital gains taxes after the sale of the farm. However, it's the estate taxes that will hammer us, because the value of the farm is over the exemption amount the IRS has in place."

"Good point, Farrell," Will said. "I vote we set up a conference call toward the end of next week with the accountant, and Clay can update us on the auction process after connecting with our friend in the business. I want to learn what our tax liabilities are. We went through this with our parents, and it was complicated, but there was life insurance and liquidity in their estates to pay the taxes. From what I'm hearing, we don't have enough liquidity in the estate to pay the estate taxes." Will looked toward Farrell and Clay for verification. Both shook their heads, confirming Will's statement. He continued. "I have a conference call number at my office that we all can dial into. Maybe we can plan to talk with the accountant and get Ben on another call the following week, after Clay speaks with him. We've got some work to do. We have some serious decisions to make."

"Sounds good," Henry agreed. "We'll get it figured out. The auction is sounding more and more like the way to go. Well, all of you have a lot further to travel than I do, so let's get on the road. Is anyone staying here tonight?"

"We are," Virginia smiled. "We drive back to Raleigh in the morning to catch our flight."

The chairs slid on pine flooring away from the dining room table, signifying that the meeting was over. After handshakes and hugs between the cousins, spouses, and children, followed by questions for Henry about how he felt and what the doctors had told him about his treatments, the gathering broke up. It had been too many years since they were together, but the bonds from their childhood were still strong.

They were family. They were Winfields.

The Wait

Chapter 18

Clay drove the Volvo sedan down the long dirt driveway with the Winfield home place in the rear-view mirror the entire way. Will stared out the passenger-side window, observing the cows that seemed oblivious to the day's activity. The wooden fencepost came to an end, and Clay turned right out of the front gate onto Highway 701, headed west. The brothers were bound for the train station in Fayetteville.

Will had made this drive off the property a hundred times, leaving the farm after a weekend with his grandparents, aunts, uncles, and cousins. As a child, he had always been a bit glum after leaving the farm, and with each departure, a part of him did not want to leave his cousins and the fun they had together at the farm. Today was no exception. Each time he left Winfield Farm as a child, he had left a part of his heart there on the property. Today had been like one of those days from his youth, but this time he was leaving a larger part of his heart behind, as the cousins had buried their beloved uncle today.

"What a day!" Will commented to his brother as they passed the nondescript entry to Eileen's house on the right side of the two-lane highway. "An entire generation has passed, and it makes me wonder what will happen to this place. We had some great times here."

"We did," Clay agreed as the car sped past the bright green corn crop at the end of the Winfield Farm property line.

Will wondered if Clay was experiencing the same nostalgic thoughts. As a child, Clay had always been more stoic, showing less emotion. He was passionate about many things, like his family, the South, UNC basketball, even his work as an accountant, but Will wondered if Clay felt the same emotion toward their childhood memories of the farm.

As the brothers grew older and only gathered around each other for holidays, Clay had always been quick to remember stories from their summers at Winfield Farm and White Lake. He had an uncanny ability to recall names and events from that era that Will had forgotten. Therefore, it was evident that Clay did have fond memories of the times they spent in Bladen County as youngsters.

"Do you ever regret not bringing your crowd down here more often to show them the farm?" Will asked, referring to the limited number of times Clay had brought his wife and three children down to the farm from Raleigh.

"No, because I'm not sure my kids would appreciate it. It wouldn't be like the times we all had here with all the cousins around. I think doing so would have been more for my benefit. Without other kids around, they wouldn't have the same memories that we had. Sadly, I think my kids might find it kind of boring."

"I'd love to bring my girls again, if I lived as close as you, but I can identify with what you're saying," Will said. "My girls and Cat have such negative memories of North Carolina after all the trips we made every Christmas. They always enjoyed being around your kids, but being around Mom and Dad when they were old and sick was not fun for my girls.

"I didn't do a very good job of getting down here to see Uncle John in his later years," Clay confessed. "Raising a family seemed to get in the way."

"It's hard not to feel a little guilt today for not being around for John in his later years," Will agreed. "He was so good to us, and after all, we were the only family he had. Today brought back the same feelings of guilt that I felt after we buried Mom and Dad, particularly Mom. I think it's the family that are left alone, like Mom, after Dad died, that you feel the most guilty about, and John was the same way, except I guess he was used to being alone."

"You're right," Clay said, his gaze focused on the two-lane highway as the North Carolina afternoon heat reflected off the asphalt.

Will was momentarily lost momentarily in thoughts of his mother's last days, alone at home in Wilmington while Will went about his ways in Boston.

"Yeah, that was a lot to absorb in one day, and the day's not over. I have a two-hour drive back to Raleigh, and you have an all night train ride to Boston," Clay reminded his brother.

"I don't mind the train ride," Will said. "I think the wait in that train station in Fayetteville is the most depressing part. I think I'll get you to drop me off at the coffee house downtown. It has wireless, and I was able to log in and get some work done and read this morning. He idly noticed the sign that informed them they had crossed the county line, leaving Bladen County behind.

"What time does the train leave Fayetteville?" Clay asked.

"Not until after eight, like 8:22, and arrives in Boston around 8:30 or so in the morning, with a number of stops in between. The train ride was not that bad, actually. It was kind of fun, and I slept most of the way. It was all the stops throughout the night that took away from the experience. I'm definitely booking a sleeper car for the ride back," Will explained. "I thought I'd tough it out on the way down and see some of the countryside, but that scenic part was over-rated. Plus, it was dark outside most of the trip."

"Maybe we'll look into taking the train the next time we come visit you in Boston," Clay suggested.

"I'd recommend it, and your kids would enjoy it," Will smiled. "Sounds like a good idea for summer vacation. The train is a whole lot better than paying up for the cost of flying five of you to Boston. We'll get you guys back out to Cape Cod."

"That'd be fun. It's been too long since we've seen Sarah and Lauren," Clay commented.

"So, I guess you'll be home in time to go out to dinner with the family?" Will asked, looking at his watch.

"Yes, but I missed a soccer game today. Claire's on a summer travel team. That's part of the reason Sherri and the kids didn't come today," Clay said. "She's in a tourna-ment in Durham this weekend. Sherri just let me know that the team won, so we'll drive back up there tomorrow for an afternoon game."

"That's good you'll get to see her play tomorrow," Will mentioned. Will loathed the fact that he had not known that Clay's daughter was on a summer soccer team. Being on a summer team meant she was a good player. Will had never seen her play, and that bothered him. "I'm sure your crew would have been really bored here today, what with an early departure from home, a funeral, a graveside service, and then a boring family meeting. Sounds like a blast for the kids," Will said. "You did the right thing, letting them stay at home, espe-cially since Claire had the tournament."

"Truth is, I probably would have blown off the funeral myself if you hadn't decided to come," Clay admitted. "That was motivation for me to go. I don't miss many of the kid's games, but I'm glad we went today. There're some pretty big decisions facing the family, and after hearing Henry's news today, I'm glad you convinced me to go."

Well, I gotta' tell you," Will said, shaking his head in disappointment. "My reasons for coming today were more inspired out of guilt. I hadn't talked to Uncle John since Mom's funeral. I told him four years ago that I would make plans to get the girls down to the farm to see him, but I didn't exactly make good on that promise."

"Look, Wilbur, don't beat yourself up. You live a thousand miles away. I live two hours away. Based on the number of trips I made to see Uncle John, I haven't exactly won any medals for being the model nephew. Let's face it, we've both had our hands full the last few years."

"I know it's tough to stay in touch, even with family. So speaking of, is Carson still playing lacrosse?" Will asked, trying to change the subject and stay updated on his brother's three children.

"He played in the spring and might play in a rec league this fall, but he's not playing now. He's on a swim team this summer, but hates it. He'd much rather be playing lacrosse," Clay explained.

"Have you taken Carson to see a lacrosse game in Chapel Hill?" Will inquired.

"Oh yeah, one time, and that's all it took. Now, he's all about playing lacrosse in college for the Tar Heels. It's a lofty goal for a twelve-year-old, but it gives him a reason to practice, and keeps him off the streets at night," Clay grinned.

"I'd love to see him play. It's criminal that I don't get down here more often. I'm going to plan a trip this fall to visit. Our schedule gets so damned busy when school starts, and it's hard to break away," Will said, frustrated.

"I can't believe Sarah will be a senior. Is she leaning toward Holy Cross?" Clay inquired about Will's oldest child.

"Maybe, but there are so many other good choices right there in Boston. She's interested in going to a school in New York. It seems like all teenage girls have this fantasy about living in New York," Will shared.

"I can see her at Holy Cross. With two generations of history there, I can see the path is paved for her. Not that you have to worry about it, but what's the tuition at Holy Cross? I need to start preparing myself mentally for the cost of college," Clay inquired.

"You don't want to know, but it's a little over fifty thousand dollars a year, including room and board, if you can believe that."

"Do you remember what it costs us to go to Carolina? I think it was fifteen hundred dollars a semester - maybe," Clay said, shaking his head.

"Those were the days!" Will smiled. The drive along State Highway 210 turned from farmland to suburbia as the brothers crossed the Cape Fear River just east of Fayetteville. The east side of Fayetteville resembled the suburbs of Wilmington when Clay and Will had grown up there. "Well, I guess we'll talk about the sale of the farm next week. Personally, I favor the auction process. Do you keep up with Ben Holcomb, the master auctioneer?" Will asked.

"No, not at all. I hear his company has done well though, especially since the real estate crash. They handle a number of foreclosed properties, so while the rest of us are losing our ass in this economy, he's making money," Clay laughed.

"So, Ben's company does more than just auction off farms?" Will asked.

"Oh yeah, they do it all — farms, homes, even some commercial auctions," Clay responded.

"I'm sure we'd make out much better if we could sell the farm to one of those wealthy hog farmers in the area, rather than go through the auction process," Will proclaimed.

"That's an oxymoron, I think," Clay turned to look at Will with a smile. "Is there such a thing as a wealthy farmer?"

"You may be surprised, after hearing Henry and Farrell talk about the hog farmers in Bladen and Sampson Counties that they went to high school with," Will shared.

"I guess if one of the hog farmers really wanted the property, he could buy it at auction," Clay suggested.

"Guess so," Will agreed. "Part of me wishes we really didn't have to sell, but the death taxes are huge. I guess the farms really get hit because all the assets and value is tied up in the land. What family is liquid enough to pay the taxes due after an inheritance? The tax laws today almost force a sale of a family farm in circumstances like ours."

The forty-minute drive from Winfield Farm to downtown Fayetteville had passed rapidly, but the next leg of the trip would not pass so quickly for Will. Now in front of the coffee shop, he turned to bid his brother good-bye.

"Thanks for the ride. You should look into the train trip to Boston later this summer. I think your kids would enjoy the train ride," Will suggested. He opened the car door and reached in to grab his travel bag and briefcase before offering a final wave to his brother. Then, with a sigh, he mentally prepared for the two-hour wait on the train at the coffee shop.

Will stood on the curb and watched Clay drive away. Besides Catherine and his daughters, his brother was the only immediate family he had left. *Why do we have to live so far apart?* he wondered. Will's girls didn't really know Clay's children, and his and Clay's children would never be able to experience the bond that the Winfield cousins had. As far as Will's two girls were concerned, they had two cousins who lived near them in Boston - Catherine's sister's children. Based on how little they saw each other, Sarah and Lauren's cousins in North Carolina might as well live in China.

The steady activity of the day's events ended abruptly as Will prepared to enter the coffee shop. The emotional build-up of the funeral, the graveside service, the memory of his own parents' death, the decisions surrounding the future of the farm, estate taxes, and the news that Henry was facing a life-threatening battle with cancer all proved mentally exhausting. The thought of calling home to Boston had hardly crossed his mind all day. Cat and the girls were at Cape Cod, staying at his in-laws house for the weekend, so they probably didn't even expect to hear from him. They probably haven't given him two thoughts all day. They're caught up in their own world, having fun at the beach. He dialed Cat's mobile number. "Hey, how's it going?" he asked when she answered.

"We're having fun. I ended up inviting Nicole to join us, so I would have someone to play with," Cat said in an upbeat voice.

"Good, I'm sure you guys are having fun," Will said, kicking a cigarette butt across the sidewalk away from the coffee shop entrance.

"So how was the funeral?" Cat asked.

"It was good, as far as funerals go. I'm glad I decided to make the trip, though."

"Did anyone ask why I wasn't there?"

"No, but they all asked how you were doing. They under-stood why you couldn't make it. Farrell brought his whole family. Only half the cousins brought their spouses, so you're fine."

"I know they all think I'm the Yankee bitch that never visits North Carolina," Cat commented.

"That's not true," Will replied, though Cat's description of herself was an accurate depiction in his mind. "Clay's wife didn't come either. Everyone understands and no one cares. "The big news is that Henry has a form of leukemia and will be starting treatments next month," Will said, as though conveying news about a neighbor, rather than a family member. Cat hardly knew Henry. She had been around him only a few times at the funerals for Will's parents. She knew him more from the stories Will told about Henry and the other cousins from their childhood.

"That's sad," Cat responded. "Are you tired?"

"Not as much tired as I am emotionally drained, but I'm glad I decided to come. It was the right thing to do. It's been a long day, and I've got a few hours before the train leaves," Will said, looking inside the coffee shop to make sure it was still open.

"How was the train ride? I still can't believe you rode that damn train. Do you still have your wallet?" she asked.

"Ha," Will laughed, placating her attempt at humor. "It was a good experience. We should all take a trip down here this summer on the train. It would be fun."

"Don't even think about it, Buster. You won't catch me on a train trip, especially to Nowhere, North Carolina."

"Is Nicole having fun?" Will asked, changing the subject.

"Oh yeah! You know, she loves it here," Cat responded.

"Weather good?" Will asked, now looking through the store window to see if other patrons were seated inside.

"Yes, perfect. We're going to the Lobster Pot tonight, since you're not here to cook out."

"Well, sorry about that, but you guys have fun," Will said, ending the conversation. "Tell the girls and Nicole hello, and I'll see you some time tomorrow afternoon when you guys get back."

Will clicked off and walked inside the coffee shop, the bells on the doors signaling the arrival of another customer. With his coat draped over his right arm and tied loosened, Will surveyed the menu of items located on the wall above the counter. The North Carolina heat left him sweaty and parched.

"Can I get you some coffee?" the attendant asked.

"I'd prefer a beer, but I think I'm at the wrong place," Will smiled.

"Believe me, I'd like one too," the attendant replied.

"What time do you close?" Will asked, noticing that there was only one couple seated at a small table in the back corner of the store.

"Not until ten tonight," she answered.

"Oh, good. It feels great in here. Your electric bill must be enormous to keep it this cool in here," Will commented, glad to be out of the heat.

"These coffee machines put off a lot of heat, so we gotta' keep the air cranked up," she said, offering a friendly smile in return.

"Well, if you don't serve beer, then I'll take a bottled water and one of your cookies," Will requested. He stood facing the cash register, still glancing at the menu above the attendant's head. The attendant moved to fill Will's order, and he checked out her attire, a white apron over a green t-shirt and a pair of tight fitting jeans. Her ponytail bounced as she moved behind the counter from the cooler to the glass enclosure that held the cookies. He was intrigued by courteous smile and service, not to mention her attractive figure.

The attendant was probably in her mid-thirties, but her attire and ponytail made her appear much younger. She had a certain spring in her step that indicated that she was more than just an employee punching a time clock. She was either the Employee of the Year or had a significant stake in the business. Will's guess was that she owned the shop and spent a significant part of her life running the business. He was intrigued to find out more about her.

"So how's business?" he inquired, gazing around the small shop, conscious of the fact that he was most likely out of place wearing a suit on a balmy day in mid-June.

"Not bad," she responded, as she dried her hands on a white hand-towel. "It's been kinda' slow today, but that's to be expected on a Saturday,"

"I was in here this morning and had one of your blueberry muffins, so I had to come back and see what you had besides coffee for an afternoon snack," Will said, letting her know he had patronized the shop twice in one day.

"I'm impressed you came back. We'll have to give you one of our Java Joe's coffee cards if you plan on coming back twice a day," she laughed.

Will smiled back at her as she handed him cold bottled water.

"Where are you visiting from?" she asked.

Will hesitated before answering. Was he a visitor from Boston or somewhat of a local from eastern North Carolina? "It's a long story. I grew up in Wilmington, and am here today for my uncle's funeral. I didn't put on this suit just to come downtown to Java Joe's." She was just being nice to an out-of-town customer, but he found her attractive and was drawn to her friendly personality.

"No offense, but you sound like you're from the northeast. Are you sure you live in Wilmington?" she asked, brows lifted with curiosity.

"Do I really sound like a Yankee?" he asked, somewhat surprised, even embarrassed, by the fact that she was able to detect his Boston accent.

"Yep, you do. So where are you really from?" she asked.

"Well, that's the rest of the story. I moved to New England to go to school and never left. I used to catch hell up there about my southern accent, but now I guess I sound more like a Yankee, according to you. No one down here has challenged me on my accent for a long time. That's very perceptive."

"I used to work on the base, so I hear a lot of accents," she confessed.

"So, I have to ask, do you own this shop?" Will asked.

"I do," she nodded, again with a smile. "I opened it after I got divorced two years ago. I needed something to keep me sane, but I think owning a coffee shop has made me more insane."

"I take it you work pretty long hours."

"Oh, yes. I guess I picked the wrong business, if I was looking for normal hours. But the way I look at it, if you're paying rent, you might as well stay open as many hours in the month as you can to get your money's worth."

"I get that," Will said, nodded in agreement. "I guess people drink coffee nowadays any time of the day, so you better generate the revenue to justify the overhead. Speaking of overhead, how many employees do you have?"

"Just two, both part time. I'm here most of the time," she replied.

"Yeah, I don't think you were here this morning when I came in for a cup of coffee," Will offered.

"I was home sleeping. Saturday is my one day to sleep."

"Forgive me for asking so many questions," Will said. "I analyze and value businesses for a living. I'm intrigued by the way people operate their businesses, small and large. I wasn't trying to be nosey."

"I'm impressed that you would ask," she responded. "No one ever asks about the business. They typically just want coffee or something to eat. The locals like to talk, but mainly about the weather or what's going on in town or at the base."

"My name is Will, by the way," he said, extending his hand across the counter to formalize the introduction.

"I'm Rebecca," she said with a sheepish smile. "Nice to meet 'cha."

"I'm getting on a train in a couple of hours, going back to Boston. I don't know if you've spent much time in the waiting room at the train station, but it's not exactly like hanging out in the Crown Room at the airport. So I hope you don't mind if I hang around for a little while until my train gets here." He motioned toward one of the booths on the storefront glass.

"That's why we're here. Make yourself at home," she said in her hospitable Southern voice.

Will reached for his wallet and paid for his cookies and bottled water. "I'll try one of your coffees a little later. I'm sure I'll need some caffeine in a little while," he said, moving toward a booth. He removed his coat, placed it neatly on the seat, settled comfortably into the booth, and pulled out his tablet. He stared out the window, observing the lack of activity on the streets of downtown Fayetteville late on a Saturday afternoon. Other than a few retailers, very few businesses appeared to be open, as far as Will could tell. He was content to be in this roomy booth in a quiet, air-conditioned shop for the next two hours. He logged in to his e-mail. Not much going on there, he thought, so he started reading a book he had programmed into his tablet. Covertly, he peered beyond his tablet to watch Rebecca while she worked. He looked for a reason to talk to her again, but did not want to distract her from working, so he attempted to stay focused on his book.

A few customers came in, ordered coffee, and left. By 6:15 or so, the lone couple in the corner also left the shop. Will nodded at them as they walked past him on their way out the door, and they called Rebecca by name as they exited. Suddenly, Will felt a different dynamic as he realized he was alone with Rebecca in the shop. He tried reading his book again, but it was not holding his attention. To prevent from being seen as some train-traveling stalker from New England, he decided to let some time pass before he re-engaged in a conversation with her.

Finally, he had to look, and glanced up from his tablet to watch her. Her back was to the counter while she busied herself restocking the shelves over the coffee makers and espresso machines. He checked his watch, realizing he still had an hour to kill before the train left the station. He decided to scan through some old e-mails on his tablet. Finally, complete boredom overtook him. He should walk around. He'd be on that train for the next twelve hours, and thought he'd better stretch his legs for a while.

"Rebecca," he said as he slid out of the booth. "Will my things be okay here for a little while? I'm going outside for a walk. My train doesn't get here for another hour."

"Sure, I'll watch it. It'll be just fine there in the booth," Rebecca obliged.

"I won't be gone long. I'm in search of that beer I mentioned when I walked in," Will laughed as he headed toward the door.

"I can send you toward a liquor store, but it's a pretty long walk. I'm pretty sure that's your best place to find a beer, unless you want to go in one of the bars downtown," Rebecca suggested.

"That's okay. I don't have much time, although a beer sounds good right now," he conceded as he pushed open the door and stepped into sweltering summer humidity. The concept of a cold beer sounded inviting now. With no purpose to his direction, Will turned to the left once outside the coffee shop, only because it was a part of downtown Fayetteville he had not seen. He was just killing time.

North Carolina heat in the early evening was dramatically different than New England temperatures. The southern humidity, combined with ninety-degree temperature, scorched the downtown concrete. By this time of the day, the temperatures on Cape Cod would drop comfortably into the high seventies. The southern humidity was Mother Nature's way of equalizing the playing field for the mild winters the South enjoyed compared to the ferocious winter months in the Northeast.

The heat and humidity in North Carolina brought back memories of playing Little League baseball in Wilmington. Spring baseball temperatures were tolerable, but the summer tournaments, especially the afternoon games, had been punishing to the players. Will remembered wiping the perspiration quickly off his brow with the left sleeve of his jersey after each pitch to prepare for a ground ball hit in his direction as shortstop. The indignant heat had never bothered Will, however. He played his best baseball in the torrid heat of summer.

Downtown Fayetteville was desolate as the early evening sun began its descent to the west of the city, and his thoughts shifted from baseball to his newfound infatuation with Rebecca. He deliberated how she was able to generate enough business to stay open on a Saturday night with the lack of activity in downtown Fayetteville. He wanted to help her business, but in his lustful mind, he also wanted to collect his consulting fees in a non-customary fashion, not with a traditional payment plan.

Will's fantasies for other women had been fairly regular since his marriage started to sputter fifteen years ago. Despite his wandering eye, he had managed to stay faithful to Cat over the last nineteen years. He had lived by the motto of, "Look at the menu, but just don't order." He had some tempting offers along the way, but he had never physically crossed the line — only in his mind.

As his relationship with Cat encountered periods of trial, Will found that his wandering eye symptom ventured farther from center. The marital strain started two years into their marriage, soon after Sarah was born. The pressures of stay-at-home motherhood and a father working long hours to build an investment banking practice collided. Two and a half years later, Lauren's arrival doubled the duties at home, while Will felt compelled to work that much harder to provide for his family. Though justified in his own mind, Will found the responsibilities of raising a family subordinate to the pressures of generating income in a commission-based investment banking career.

Simultaneously, Cat discovered the pressure of mothering two small children to be taxing. She loved the girls dearly and was considered by her friends, and Will, to be a dedicated caregiver. Given Will's income, it made sense for Cat to stay home with the children, but the benefits of a stay-at-home mother came with a price. Though she would not have chosen any other path, Cat learned early on that being a stay-at-home mom was the most thankless job on the planet.

By the time Sarah and Lauren were out of diapers and ready to attend preschool, Will and Cat agreed that they should move from the city to the suburbs. Marblehead, where Cat had grown up, seemed like the logical choice. Marblehead city schools were known for their academic excellence, and having Cat's parents in close proximity would help with the daunting duties of raising two toddlers.

The move to Marblehead settled a number of issues in their complex lives offering a support system for raising children from Cat's parents, the Keys. Better schools, safer neighborhoods, more community, and a larger home were all reasons that justified the move north. The only downside was Will's thirty-five mile daily commute between Marblehead and his office in downtown Boston.

Always one to work late, Will rarely left the office before seven o'clock at night, his late departure from the office, a strategy to minimize the time he spent in traffic on the way home at nights. Still, the late departures from the office made for late arrivals at home, leaving little time to spend with the family in the evenings. Particularly when the girls were younger, Will usually arrived at home to find his daughters fed and bathed, just in time for Daddy to read them a story before bed. Will became the consummate weekend dad, devoting himself to work during the week. Eventually, Cat resented Will's long work hours and pleaded with him to work less, but Will justified the long hours in order to perform the noble task of providing for his family.

From the outside, it looked like Will and Cat had it all, but inside the four walls of their home, paradise was amiss. Will's long work hours and Cat's retaliation for his absence created a vicious cycle of unrest at the Jordan home. The conflicts continued, even as the girls grew older. By the time the girls entered their teen years, the damage was done and a cavernous divide existed between Will and Cat. Despite the frequent conflicts between their parents, Sarah and Lauren had grown into relatively well-adjusted teenagers. They were both good students, had plenty of friends, played lacrosse and soccer, and other than the normal teenage hormonal imbalances, were mostly respectful to their parents. Though he rarely voiced it, Will was convinced that both girls had been spoiled unmercifully throughout their lives - similar to their mother.

The fights, it seemed, typically stemmed from Will's work hours or his alleged lack of commitment to the family. To be honest, Will had never been able to fully appreciate the job and commitment of a full-time mother, and in his mind, he was the provider and Cat was the caretaker. In the early years of parenting, Cat would have gladly re-entered the workforce.

"Raising children with very little help and no appreciation is *much* harder than any job than I could find in Boston," Cat told Will on a number of occasions through the years.

Due to Will's long hours and lack of balance with work and family, she had withdrawn from Will as he focused on his successful investment banking career at Liberty Capital. Summers at Cape Cod seemed to be the best times for the Jordan family, providing a reprieve from the pressures of homework, soccer practice, lacrosse games, and other activities during the school year. The family spent most weekends at the Cape, and Cat and the girls established a tradition of staying the entire month of July at the Key family cottage. Will commuted from the Cape into the central business district most every day during the month of July. Family stress levels dropped dramatically when the family lived at the beach for a month.

Admittedly, Will realized he was far better at making money than at being an attentive husband. The more she complained, the more he worked. The more Will worked, the more she resented it. The office became Will's hiding place, sheltered from the duties of parenthood and a safe haven from a crumbling marriage. The marriage never healed, even after the girls had entered grade school and motherhood was supposed to get easier. Will continued to work long hours and left most of the parenting and household duties to his wife. Understandably, Cat resented Will's love affair with Liberty Capital.

"You don't love me. You're in love with that damn job," Cat reminded Will regularly.

Will continued to ask himself what life would be like had he not met Cat that night in Cambridge. What if Mr. Key had not helped him get his job at Liberty Capital? Where would he be? Although he had made a good living in Boston and created a good life for himself and his family, what if he had taken a banking job in Charlotte? What if he had made more of an effort to stop Kaitlyn that day on Wrightsville Beach before he moved to Boston, prior to starting the job at Liberty Capital? Tonight, the questions raced through his head. Did he take these major life decisions lightly? Was he captivated by Cat's family and their lifestyle? Was he really in love with Cat or was he just enamored by her good looks and family? Did the country club in Marblehead, house at Cape Cod, and Red Sox tickets blind him into making a bad decision when it came to asking Cat to marry him? Maybe the Liberty Trust job was the right job, but did he feel an obligation to Cat and her family to keep dating her because her dad had hooked him up with this great job? Such thoughts kept him occupied as the evening sun set over the down streets of Fayetteville. That was over twenty years ago. He'd never dated anyone else in Boston. Maybe at twenty-four, he was too young to get married. They were both young, maybe too young, to make such big decisions, decisions that were supposed to last a life-time. What happened to them? They were crazy about each other when they dated. They couldn't stand to be away from each other. Maybe it was fate that Cat and he met that night. Maybe they were supposed to be together. Who knows where he might be if they had never met? He doubted he would have moved to Boston. He wouldn't have found the job at Liberty Capital, that's for sure. What if he was like Uncle John and never married or had a family? Well, he'd made his bed, so now he had to sleep in it.

The evening walk through downtown Fayetteville gave Will the opportunity to reflect on the day's activities. He was able to relive the good memories he had growing up with his

Winfield cousins and honor his uncle by being there for his funeral. He had the chance to spend time with his brother, time that he hadn't spent in years. Though the travel was taxing, attending the funeral had been the right thing to do.

His evening walk ended as he found his way back to Rebecca's coffee shop. He gazed inside the windows to see if any patrons inside the shop. Actually, he hoped to see the shop full of customers. He wanted to see Rebecca and Java Joe's succeed. He felt compelled to help her. That was his nature.

"Empty," Will mumbled as he surveyed the shop from the sidewalk through the storefront glass. He was disappointed for Rebecca. As he pushed open the door, the bells on the door announced Will's return with a faint jingle.

"Hello, I'll be right with you," came a familiar voice from the stock room behind the coffee and espresso machines.

Will heard her, but could not see her. Her voice was distinctly Southern, but not to the extent of the rural dialects in nearby Bladen County. There was Southern, and then there was *rural Southern*, like he had been around in Bladen County at the funeral earlier today. Will felt a certain bond with her, due merely to the lilt of her voice. Perhaps it was the fact that he was over eight hundred miles from Catherine. Maybe it was because he had compassion for Rebecca, as a sole proprietor in a small business. Maybe he was attracted to her work ethic and entrepreneurial efforts. Maybe he just liked her ponytail and the way it bounced with each step she took. For whatever reason, Will was excited to have a little more time with Rebecca before he left for Boston.

"It's just me again, Rebecca, the Southern Yankee," Will announced, as he headed toward 'his' booth. Before sitting down, he checked his watch. Seven-ten, he thought. Still plenty of time to hang out here with Rebecca for a little while longer. Then she appeared, walking his way. He stood by the booth and watched with intrigue as the ponytail bounced toward him.

"It's been deathly quiet in here tonight. When it's slow like this, it gives me time to restock the shelves and get ready for the start of a new week," Rebecca explained.

"Why don't you sit down for a minute," Will suggested, motioning toward the booth. "You've been working way too hard tonight."

"I believe I will, if you don't mind," Rebecca sighed.

Will felt like he was inviting a guest to sit down in his office back in Boston. He watched with intrigue as her shapely frame slid between the table and the seat cushion. After she sat down, he spoke. "Can I get you anything?" as though the roles were temporarily reversed.

"No thanks," she laughed.

Will sat down in the booth across the table from her and looked into her almond colored eyes. "I know you think I ask too many questions, but I wanted to ask you about the name of your place. Java Joe's ... I really like the name. It's catchy."

"You know, with the military influence here in Fayette-ville, the name sorta' sounds like G.I. Joe, so it had a good ring to it," she answered with a smile.

"Did you come up with the name?" he asked.

"I did," she nodded. "It took a while to come up with the right name, but I think it works. I just wish the clever name would draw more customers ... like tonight. This is what I call the dead zone. If people are downtown on a Saturday night, they're at dinner. I'll have a few folks come in after dinner or for a late night coffee, but people drink less coffee when it's hot outside. It's been particularly slow tonight."

"So I guess you're open seven days a week?" he asked.

"Oh, yes," she said, letting out another sigh.

"What's your busiest time?" Will asked.

"Most weekday mornings are pretty good," Rebecca responded.

He wondered if he made her feel like she was in an interview seated across the table from him. "Maybe you should close one day a week, or at least close on Saturday and Sunday nights. Give yourself a little break," Will offered. "Focus on the prime time people drink coffee and offer some promotions or special offers, like 'Buy one, get the second for half price'. Do you ever offer any promotions or advertising?"

"No, I really don't," she said, seemingly not bothered by his continuous line of questions. "You really *are* some kind of consultant? Did someone send you here undercover to help me with my business?"

He shook his head and smiled. "Like I said earlier, I actually *am* somewhat of a consultant. I sell businesses and help people buy companies, so I guess that's why I'm intrigued by your business. I can't help myself. You'll really get nervous when my next question is to see your cash register receipts," he laughed.

"You do ask lots of questions," she observed, staring at him.

"Oh, I'm just getting warmed up. Do you have any partners in the business?" Will continued.

"No, why? Do you want to invest?" she responded.

"I might. Let me see your cash register receipts," Will joked.

"What time does your train leave?" she asked, somewhat hesitantly.

"Eight twenty-two, to be exact," he replied. "Why, you trying to get rid of me already?"

She laughed. "So, tell me about your uncle," Rebecca inquired. "Were you close to him?"

For a brief moment, Will forgot about the fact that he had a train to catch. Not since Uncle John died four days ago had anyone inquired about his uncle and their relationship. No one at Liberty Capital or at home had shown much interest in his uncle. No one, not even Catherine, really seemed to care, yet now, an outsider, someone he hardly knew, wanted to know about his relationship with his uncle. He hesitated before answering. Her question had pierced right through his chest to his heart. He had to look away momentarily to regain his composure, and his thoughts took him back momentarily to the church in Elizabethtown and the five minute conversation he had with Uncle John in the coffin just before the funeral started.

"It could take a little while to answer your question," he said, serious now. "Thank you for asking. You're the first person to ask about him. Well, first he was a soldier. He was in World War Two, at Normandy in fact. He enlisted when he was nineteen, and fought in Europe. He returned to North Carolina and went to college in East Carolina, but his first love was our family's farm in Bladen County, about forty minutes east of here. He was born there, raised there, and really never left after his time in the war and at college." He continued to tell her about his uncle, smiling fondly at the memories. "He lived on the family farm until he died, just this week, at eighty-four years of age. He had battled lung cancer for a long time. Growing up around tobacco all his life, he had been a smoker for sixty-five years. So, to answer your question, yes, we were close, very close when I was younger, but I neglected to come visit him while he was sick. Truth is, I had not even seen him or kept up with him since my parents died four or five years ago."

"He sounded like a wonderful man," Rebecca said. "I'm sorry for your loss. I can tell you loved him very much."

Will felt her sincerity, and the tears returned to his eyes. He fought back the emotion, generated by Rebecca asking the simple question about his uncle. "Words can't describe what a good man he was and how special he was to all of us," Will said, his voice cracking slightly. He cleared his throat. "Are *your* parents still alive?" he asked, shifting the focus of the conversation back to Rebecca.

"Yes, but they're divorced," Rebecca replied. "They're in pretty good health."

"Do you see them much?" Will asked.

"Not really, they live in South Carolina, where I grew up."

"Well, take it from me, from someone who lived *too far away*, go visit any chance you get. I live with that regret every day. First with my parents, and now with my uncle. As your parents get older, they'll really need you. Don't find yourself in my position of not spending time with the ones most important to you because you're working too much and have built a life in another state," Will shared.

She nodded her head in agreement.

"Close the shop next weekend and drive down to South Carolina and surprise your parents," he suggested with a somber smile.

She looked at him for several moments, and then slowly nodded. "I might just do that. You've given me some things to think about. For now, I want to hear more about your uncle's farm. What did he farm?"

"Now you're the one with all the questions," Will joked. "We had cattle, used to farm mostly tobacco, but now we have corn, some acreage in soybeans, and grow some vegetables, like sweet potatoes".

"How many acres? It sounds huge," she asked.

"It's pretty good size, around eleven hundred acres, but a good bit is in planted pine. It was a lot for my uncle to manage at his age, but he kept the farm operational, even when he was sick."

The bell on the front door jingled, notifying Rebecca that the evening rush was about to commence. She moved quickly from the booth toward the counter and greeted the patrons as they surveyed the chalkboard menu, located high above the sales counter. Will fixated his eyes on the way her jeans hugged her backside as she scurried away from the booth to greet her customers. Finally, he checked his watch. Though he wanted to engage in more conversation with Rebecca, he knew his time with her had come to an end. He watched her every move as she handled the customers with service and a smile. He knew Java Joe's would succeed, based solely on her ability to connect with her customers.

With a sigh, he packed up his belongings, wedging his tablet into the packed briefcase, a faded brown leather case that Cat had given him for Christmas twelve years ago. He made his way out of the booth and draped his suit coat over his arm, leaving a folded ten-dollar bill on the table under his empty water bottle. As he stood, a part of him did not want to leave, but his time in Fayetteville was drawing to a close. Will stood by the door and waited until the customers were served their coffee. He could have left with a quick good-bye, but he felt compelled to at least give her a hug her after their time together. "Thank you Rebecca," he said as he approached the counter.

"Wait, I have some treats for your train trip," she offered, placing a muffin and a cookie in a small white paper bag.

"That would be great," he said, reaching for his wallet.

"No, it's on me. I appreciate your advice," she said.

"Advice? Don't you mean my excessive interrogation? I'm sorry about all my questions," Will stated. "You were a terrific listener to the stories about my uncle. I hope I didn't bore you."

She stepped from behind the counter with the white bag in hand. He placed his briefcase and overnight bag on the hardwood floor and opened his arms to signify he wanted a good-bye hug. She obliged, set the bag on the counter, and stepped toward him.

"I really enjoyed talking to you. Thank you for letting me hang out while I waited on my train," he said as they hugged.

"My pleasure," she said. "Please come back."

"If I'm ever in town again, I will," he said, knowing he would most likely never see Rebecca again.

The Disposition Plan

Chapter 19

The conference call with the Winfield cousins was scheduled for 5:30 in the evening on the Thursday following the funeral. All eight cousins dialed in to the teleconference line at Liberty Trust. Will had organized the call, but Henry, as the executor of Uncle John's estate, was the facilitator.

"Is everyone on?" Will asked. One by one, the cousins identified themselves by name, except Virginia, the only female, who merely had to say, "I'm here."

"Well, for those who were able to attend the funeral last Saturday, I would say it was a fine tribute to Uncle John," Henry stated. "For those unable to make it, I understand that distance played a part in not being able to get there. We told some old stories, laughed, and cried a little. It was a little like old times, except we're all old now. Will, thanks for getting us set up on this high tech conference call, but I was expecting video-conferencing so we could all see each other. Next time, you make that happen, okay?"

"We'll get everyone set up for a video conference on the next call," Will promised in response to Henry's attempt at amusement.

Henry continued. "I think Clay and Farrell have done some research over the last few days on the most fortuitous way to sell the farm in a timely manner. I'm going to let Farrell tell us about his conversation with the local land and timber broker in Bladen County, and Clay will follow with his knowledge of the auction process. Then, we'll take a vote on how we proceed. "Farrell," Henry said to his younger brother. "You're up. Tell us what you found out."

"First, can everyone hear me okay?" Farrell asked. The response was a harmonious affirmative, so he continued. "I had the chance to speak with Everett Hughes a couple of days ago. He's a realtor and timber specialist in Bladen, Sampson, Wayne, and Duplin counties. He knows the buyers of farm land in the area and can also help us determine the value of the timber on the farm," Farrell started. "Everett knows his stuff, but he said the demand on larger farms, like ours, has been slow, and the price of farm land is down twenty-five to forty percent. Timber prices are not any better. He's been telling tree farmers to hold off cutting timber until prices get better." He paused, as if consulting notes, and then pushed on. "He's helped Uncle John in the past, so he has a pretty good idea of how much of our land is in planted pine. He is working on a price to value the timber on the property and a price per acre we could expect on a sale. He also said we most likely need to thin some of the acreage and do some burning. The land that we used to hunt with Uncle John has grown up with scrub bushes and some smaller natural pine, according to Everett. It's not critical, but something we need to have done or wait on a buyer to take care of. They'll be some up-front cost for us, but thinning the pine could yield us some revenue near-term."

"What range did he give you on a price per acre?" Owen, the youngest of the cousins, asked.

"As far as pricing, it's all over the board, and some of it depends on how the crops do this year and the leases we have in place. He said five years ago, prices were as high as four thousand per acre, but now we'd be fortunate if we got twenty-five hundred, but two thousand is more realistic," Farrell replied.

"And what about the house and the farm equipment?" Clay asked. "What's that worth?"

"The home-place is worth some, but it has a lot of deferred maintenance. Sadly, the house is valued with the land, but if he had to put a price on it, Everett said it was worth around eighty to one hundred thousand dollars."

"That's disappointing," Chuck, Owen's brother, inserted.

"And how long should we expect to have the property on the market?" Virginia inquired.

"I asked that question myself," Farrell replied. "He said not much has sold recently, particularly in the larger tracts, so he can't tell. If we price the farm low, around twenty-five hundred an acre, we'll get more traction. Let's put it this way … he wants a twelve-month listing agreement with two six-month renewable extensions, if that tells you anything. It's not unreasonable to think we could still be trying to sell eighteen months from now," Farrell explained.

"That's not exactly the news any of us wanted to hear," Henry announced. "Clay, can you give us anything more positive on the auction process?"

"I hope so," Clay replied. From his office building in downtown Raleigh, Clay gave his cousins the recap of his conversation with Ben Holcomb, a second-generation owner of Holcomb and Massey, one of the premier auction companies in North Carolina.

"Basically, there are two kinds of auctions, as Henry explained to us at our meeting last weekend. One is an absolute auction, where the property sells at no matter what price, and the other is an auction where the sellers set a minimum price. If the minimum price is not met, then the property doesn't sell." He paused. "There is an argument that we could sell at an absolute auction price since there is no debt on the property, but I think, in this economy, we need to set a minimum. Ben said that in this economy, and with the limited pool of buyers for large tracts of farmland, that if we don't set a minimum, then the farm could potentially sell at a fraction of what it's really worth. There are some sharks out there that are looking to prey on desperate sellers with financial issues. We don't fit that model, so we're what I would call motivated, but not desperate. Our minimum should be around two thousand an acre, based on what Ben said."

He paused again, and then, when no questions were broached, continued. "With mid to larger size tracts like ours, the auction company divides the parcels into more afford-able portions. As an example, the timber tracts might be sold in two parcels. The house, barns, and pastureland might be sold as one parcel, and the cropland might be divided into one hundred to two hundred-acre parcels. Ben suggested that we divide the farm into eight or more parcels to capture the buyers that may be interested in just owning timberland, or a farmer who wants two to four hundred acres of corn. Once the prices are bid on the smaller tracts, then the auctioneer opens the final bid to one potential buyer who would buy the entire tract."

"And how is the auction company compensated?" Will asked as he sat on the twelfth floor of his office on State Street in Boston's central business district.

"There is a ten percent buyer's premium that each purchaser pays over the bid price, plus a fee paid to the auction company, but only if the property sells," Clay replied. "So, if the property minimum is not met, are we obligated to pay the auctioneer?"

Owen inquired, calling in from his home in Fort Lauderdale.

"Not as far as I can tell," Clay said. "Which reminds me of one more thing. This is a live auction that occurs on site at the farm. There are no internet bids."

"That seems to limit the number of buyers if you have to be at the auction to bid," Henry commented.

"I agree, especially in this day and time of internet commerce, but that's the way these live auctions work," Clay responded.

"Well, let's vote on this," Henry announced. "I think I'm pretty clear on what makes the most sense for us to do as a family, but I want to hear from y'all. Are there any questions or further discussion about the auction versus the traditional sale with a realtor?"

There was periodic silence on the line, until Virginia spoke up. "Let's vote. I think we know what seems most practical at this point."

"Okay, let's go down the list, youngest to oldest. Speak up if you want auction or realtor. Owen?"

"Auction, unless there's another option out there," Owen replied.

"Chuck?" Henry inquired.

"Auction," Chuck piped in from Asheville, North Carolina.

"I think I'm next," Clay said. "I'm for the auction. It will yield us proceeds a whole lot faster than waiting on a buyer and dealing with the long process of listing the property."

"Agreed, I vote auction," Farrell responded quickly in order to move the voting process along.

"Auction," Will stated firmly.

"Auction," Virginia said from poolside at her home in central Florida.

"America has spoken, and auction it is," Henry announced. "We'll need to discuss among ourselves where we should set the minimum, but this seems to be the route we should go. It's what's best for all of us and the farm. Clay, can you get a call scheduled with Ben early next week, so we can better understand all the ins and outs of an auction? I also want to ask him what he thinks our chances are of attracting a good pool of buyers in this economic climate."

"We'll make it happen," Clay responded.

"Okay, I guess we're finished for today. Look for an e-mail sometime next week with details on the auction. Thanks everyone," Henry said, finalizing the afternoon call.

The Auction

Chapter 20

The morning sun glowed radiantly over Winfield Farm. August was considered by most to be the hottest month of the year in North Carolina, and today's temperatures were projected to be in the mid-nineties by the afternoon. For the second time in as many months, a covey of Winfield cousins had returned to Bladen County. Today's purpose was to oversee the sale of the farm through to completion. This time, however, only four of the eight cousins had made the trip to the farm to attend today's auction.

"It's a perfect day for an auction," Ben Holcomb announced. "But it's already hot as hell out here. That's why we schedule these auctions as early in the day as possible, to beat the heat, and also give folks enough time to get here."

"How long does the auction itself last, Ben?" Clay asked.

"Oh, we'll start a few minutes after ten, and we should be wrapped up easily before eleven. The process goes pretty quick. You know, we auctioneers talk pretty fast," Ben responded with a laugh.

Winfield Farm had sat dormant for the last five weeks, but this Saturday represented a flurry of activity as Holcomb and Massey prepared for the day's event. It was shortly after 9:00 a.m. and Ben's auction crew was busy nailing the support stakes in the ground to secure the large auction tent that would shield the morning sun from the attendees. The white tent sat in the open field to the right of the old Winfield home-place, guarded by one of the farm's massive oak trees to block the sun's heat. Dressed casually in khaki pants and a polo shirt, Henry and Farrell walked out the side door of the Winfield house and approached Ben Holcomb and the Jordan brothers.

Ben extended his hand toward Henry. "Ben Holcomb," he said, introducing himself to Henry and Farrell. Nothing shy about Ben. Even in college, he never met a stranger. Always confident and personable, the affable Ben was well known at UNC and had a certain charisma with the women on campus. Now, though a little stockier, he was still capable of charming a crowd, both male and female. Today, Ben was in his element, confident of what today's auction might bring. Ben had grown up in the auction business. His dad, Big Ben, and partner, Harvey Massey, started Holcomb & Massey in 1971 in Hickory, North Carolina, as cattle auctioneers. The company had grown over the last four decades to one of the state's premier auction companies, while still maintaining its rural roots. Auctioning family farmland was a specialty of the firm, and, as an avid outdoorsman, Ben was particularly drawn to land transactions over the residential auctions.

"You Jordan boys better be glad that I have work to do, or I'd start telling stories to your cousins about Will and Clay and their days at Carolina. We'll tell a few stories over a beer, after we sell the farm, and you guys are on your way to the bank," Ben grinned. "I'd like to hear some stories about these two from their college days," Henry said. "The way we always heard was that all the brothers did was study while they were at Carolina."

"We *were* in the library most of the time, but it was guys like Ben who kept organizing these parties at our fraternity house. It was a major distraction. Library or party? Study or girls? Beer or books?" Clay joked, as he held his open palms in front of him, balancing the scales of justice.

"We had some good times," Ben laughed. "Those were the good ole' days. Not a worry in the world, and now I'm here on a Saturday, working my ass off in this Carolina heat." He turned toward Henry and Farrell. "Where did you guys go to school?"

"We both went to East Carolina. We grew up in Sampson County, just north of here, and stayed in this part of the state. Our parents didn't want us go to Carolina. All they ever heard was how wild it was up there," Farrell explained. "We grew up Tar Heel fans and still are, though."

"Hell, we're all Tar Heels, and proud of it, except Will here. He abandoned Carolina for the big bucks in Boston," Ben joked.

"I feel like a resident again after two trips back here this summer," Will said, defending himself.

"Well, I'd like to stay and visit, boys, but I better get over there and help my guys get set up," Ben said, looking at his watch.

"Ben, real quick, how many folks do you expect to be here today?" Farrell inquired.

"Actual buyers? Well, like we say, we're just looking for that *one*. Liars, they'll be a few. Tire kickers and nosey neighbors who are looking to see what the pricing brings, there will be several. It's hard to tell in this economic environment, but we've had as few as ten and as many as fifty lately, but all we need is that one," Ben explained, walking away from the four cousins toward the auction tent.

"Looks like it's just the four of us today, gentlemen," Henry said as the two sets of brothers stood on the dirt driveway between the farmhouse and the auction tent.

"Something about that tent just doesn't look right being set up here," Will commented, gazing at the tent that stood motionless in the field that once was Nanny's garden. "I don't know about you guys, but it hit me on the train ride down this morning, that this is the end of an era. If the farm sells today, there's no turning back, boys. We'll realize a nice payday when the property sells, but I can't help but feel a little regret about being here today. You know, we're selling off a piece of our childhood. Maybe I had too much time alone on that train to think about it, but it's sad in a way to let this property go."

"I agree," Henry replied. "I've had the same thoughts over the last few weeks. I've been over here a few times since the funeral to check on things, and I ask myself, 'Are we doing the right thing?' as I walked around the property. You're right, Will, that tent just doesn't look like it belongs here, but this is a passing of an era. I guess it's time to move on."

Will could not help but to think about Henry's health each time he spoke, especially when he made comments like "time to move on." He wondered. Was Henry really sicker than he's letting on? Was his diagnosis more serious than what he told them at the funeral? Concerned, Will had to ask. "Henry, how are you feeling?"

"Not too bad, a little weak most days. The treatments aren't any fun, but I'm doing okay," Henry responded, adjusting his hat that covered his once full head of hair. "In fact, let's go over to the tent. I wouldn't mind sitting down for a while after we check out the set-up."

Once under the tent, it was like stepping into an outdoor courtroom. Chairs were lined meticulously in three neat rows to seat up to thirty attendees. In front of the chairs stood a folding table with a portable lectern and microphone positioned in the center. Flanked on each side of the auctioneer's table stood two mounted marketing boards held upright by metal tripods. Professionally prepared, the boards held blown up photographs that provided an aerial overview of the farm. One board showed the farm divided by red lines into different parcels, while the other identified the different crops planted in each section of the farm.

"These are impressive," Henry commented, as he leaned over to inspect both laminated boards.

"I think we've got a good separation of the parcels," Ben chimed in, as he looked up from the lectern and removed the reading glasses perched on the end of his nose. "We divided the property into eight different tracts. As you can see, we have the timber in one large tract and the row crops in several parcels based on what was planted. The home-place and the surrounding pastureland is the smallest tract. The thought there is the local farmer or timber speculator is more interested in the land itself and might feel he's paying extra for the house. If someone is into restoring old homes and wants some pasture land for horses or a few head of cattle, then we've got the house and pasture to offer to a different type of buyer."

"Makes sense," Farrell said, as he and Henry studied the rendering of the separated parcels, while Clay and Will stared at the aerial on the opposing side of the table. "What about the tractors, the truck, and other farm equipment? Does that get auctioned as well?"

"We'll auction the equipment off after the parcels. If we don't meet the minimum, then we don't have to sell the tractors and implements. No need to sell the equipment if you still own the land," Ben explained.

"Okay, I get it," Farrell noted.

"The waiting is almost over," Ben stated. "The anticipation on auction day is the worst for the owners. You don't know how many folks will show up, who has money to bid on the property, if the price minimum will be met, and in this economy, we want to make sure we've identified a buyer with money, but you guys have set a reasonable minimum. Call me overly optimistic, but I think we'll find us a buyer today."

"One buyer or multiple?" Henry asked, looking up from the marketing board.

"Hard to tell. It's a big parcel, so my guess is we'll get a few buyers who want the farm land and maybe someone who'll take the timber. It's been a while since your uncle cut any timber, so there's immediate value for someone who wants to harvest the timber, although market prices are still down. Foresters are telling me that folks are holding off cutting timber until prices increase," Ben explained.

"Ben, let us get out of your way, so you can get ready. It's almost show-time," Will commented, noting that Ben appeared to have some work to complete before the auction began.

"I'm studying the order we'll offer the parcels. I'm actually going to call this auction today since you guys are friends. I don't call auctions like I used to. I'm a little out of practice, but I've still got it. We hope to get a bidding war started among these buyers."

By 9:45, a few vehicles pulled up to the designated parking area that the auction company had staked out with orange cones. "That's Lucius Cody who just got out of the truck," Henry stated. "He's a long-time hog farmer in Bladen County. Those are his two sons. He and Uncle John were good friends back in the day. From what I understand, he's done very well in the hog farming business. He was at the funeral six weeks ago, but I didn't get a chance to speak with him."

Mr. Cody was dressed in an old pair of faded denim overalls. He was a large man, probably in his late sixties, and he walked deliberately toward the cousins in a side to side motion, as if his legs were stiff from a long car ride. His sons walked just behind him, forming a triangular procession as they moved toward the tent. All three wore caps, and the boys were dressed in t-shirts, jeans, and rancher-style boots.

"Morning," Mr. Cody called as he got close enough to greet the cousins.

"Good morning, Mr. Cody," Henry responded. He stepped in front of the cousins to greet the Cody contingency. "I'm Henry Winfield."

"Yes sir, I know who you are," Mr. Cody replied. "These are my boys, Luther and Cy."

"And this is my brother Farrell and my cousins, Will and Clay," Henry said, motioning toward the three cousins standing behind him.

"Welcome," Farrell said to the Cody family.

"We wanted to see what you all had to offer today. This farm ran like a clock under your uncle's watch. It's been well maintained and produced some good tobacco and corn through the years. It's a shame at least one of you boys can't stay 'round here and run the farm," Mr. Cody suggested, shifting his weight from side to side, a sign of weakening hips or a bad leg.

"We were just talking about what a special place Winfield Farm is to all of us," Henry explained. "We have some great memories of our time spent here. It's hard to think about letting it go. Today is bittersweet, knowing there won't be a fourth generation of Winfield's to farm this land."

"I been farmin' my whole life, and all I know is farmin', but I can tell you that this farm is more than a farm. It's an enterprise ... meaning that your uncle was a smart business man and a helluva farmer. When tobacco demand started to slow down, he rotated into other crops, like corn and cattle. You also have timber that brings in a windfall every fifteen to twenty years. I don't have the diversity like John had here. He did it right."

The cousins and his sons listened like students in a classroom.

"Is this a property you would buy to diversify your farming operation, Mr. Cody?" Farrell asked, trying to determine if the Cody's were candidates to buy Winfield Farm.

"Most likely not, son," Mr. Cody replied. "My knowledge of farmin' is hogs. It's been a good living for my family, but that's all I know. That's why I respected your uncle so much. He had cattle, row crops, and timber, but I never could convince him to get into hog farmin'. I've been able to buy my land for a whole lot less than what this farm is worth. Hogs is known to tear up the land, so we own land that might be in the hundred year flood plain or considered to be poor farm land. Plus, I'm too old to learn how to farm row crops. Now, these boys might want to try their hand at a different kinda' farmin,' but not me. I doubt we're you're right buyer today, but you never know. It all depends on the price. That's what I tell these boys all the time. It all depends on the price."

Will stood between Farrell and Clay, observing the interaction between the Winfield and Cody men. He had been in meetings between buyers and sellers for the last twenty years in the investment banking business, but most of the time, the discussions took place in someone's office around a conference table. If Will's intuition was correct today, Lucius and his sons were not buyers. They were just window-shopping. If the Cody men could steal the Winfield property, then they would suddenly become buyers, but by Will's assessment, they were here to see what price a neighbor's farm might bring in today's environment.

Clay looked at his watch. "Well, we better get inside the tent. It's about that time."

Precisely at 10:00, the cousins made their way to their seats in the back row. The attendance this morning was much lower than expected, and Will counted only twelve attendees, outside of Ben's staff and the four cousins. Surveying the crowd, Will did not have a good feeling about the outcome. The cousins sat in silence behind the potential bidders, who had mainly congregated in the first and second rows. A local farmer, who looked to be in his late fifties, and his wife sat at the far end of the third row, alone.

Just before 10:15, Ben began the auction. First he welcomed the guests, made mention of the four members of the Winfield family in attendance today, and outlined the rules of engagement on how the auction process works. Ben resembled a judge standing behind the podium, preparing to hold court.

"We have eight parcels to auction today. We'll start with Tract A on your sheet," Ben explained to the crowd. He went on to describe the size and crop yield on the first parcel of land, then started his chant, an auctioneer's language that sounded more like a song than a plea for bids.

"Who'll gimme twenty-five hundred?" Ben crooned. "Twenty-five hundred for this fine parcel of land with corn that will yield at least a hundred and sixty bushels of corn this fall."

No takers responded at twenty-five hundred per acre. No bids at twenty-two hundred. Still no action after Ben lowered the starting bid at two thousand dollars an acre. Will glanced down the aisle at Clay and his cousins to gauge their reaction. On this particular parcel, the minimum price the cousins set had not been met. Henry raised an eyebrow toward Will and Clay, signifying that the bidding would have to pick up in order to meet their minimum price of two thousand per acre.

Ben solicited bids on the other parcels, starting at sixteen hundred dollars an acre. As he sang to the crowd in his auctioneer's tone, bids were offered on the other parcels, but the minimums were never met. The home-place and the surrounding pastureland was the last individual parcel to be bid on, before the aggregate parcels would be offered in the final auction of the day. A single bid on the home-place and surrounding pastureland was also well below the set minimum. Will felt a hollow pit deep in his stomach. It was like watching a losing baseball game in the final inning from the dugout. All he, Clay, Henry, and Farrell could do was wait until the game ended.

The 2.2 million dollar total price that the cousins had spent so much time discussing over the phone over the last few weeks would not be met today. In a final plea, Ben offered all eight parcels to the crowd. The day's momentum was waning. The end was near. Ben called for starting bids at 2.2 million dollars, but the crowd sat in silence. Again, Ben glanced toward the back of the tent where the cousins sat, the look on his face summarized the morning's effort. Finally, he banged the gavel on the top of the lectern and announced, "The auction is over. Unfortunately, the sellers' minimums were not met. The property will not be sold today. Thank you for attending."

Just like that, the auction ended, and the crowd stood up from the folding chairs and began to exit. Will likened the ending to a final strikeout by the home team to end the game. It was over, and just like at a baseball game, the crowd stood and left in silence.

Ben greeted the attendees with a head nod and quiet comments. "Thanks for coming," he said as each attendee walked past the lectern. His otherwise upbeat spirit was broken, and his expression mimicked the look of a losing coach. After the crowds dispersed, Ben would take the blame for the loss in the locker room. After the attendees exited the tent, Ben made his way to the back row, where the cousins stood waiting. "We gave it our best," Ben said, head down and shoulders hunched.

"No worries, Ben," Clay clapped him on the back. "It's not your fault. Maybe our expectations were too high."

"You guys did what you came to do," Henry commented. "You led the horse to water. The horse just didn't want to drink. Ben, you were very up-front with us about the market conditions. It's a tough time to be selling farmland, even good farmland. There's a buyer out there somewhere. We just have to find him."

"Let's hope so," Farrell said, dejected. "We need to let the others know what the results were today. We can make some phone calls on the way into town to get some lunch."

"Ben, can you join us?" Will asked.

"No, but thank you. I need to help the guys pack up, and you four have some family business to discuss. I know you have some decisions to make." He paused. "I'm really sorry guys." He shook the cousins' hands and bid them good-bye.

All four cousins thanked Ben with a handshake and let him know they would be back after lunch. On the way to the parking area, the cousins noticed Mr. Cody and his sons standing next to their four-door pick-up truck, as they walked toward Clay's car.

"Mr. Cody, thanks for coming," Henry said, stepping through the long grass toward the Cody's truck.

"Gentlemen, we just couldn't make the numbers work on your farm," Mr. Cody explained. "It's a beautiful piece of property. You folks will sell it. It may just take some time, but let us know if we can help you while you have it on the market."

"We appreciate that, Mr. Cody," Henry responded as the cousins walked away.

The tandem team of brothers drove down the dirt drive toward the front gate, bound for Elizabethtown. The cows behind the wooden fence looked up from their grazing to acknowledge another car leaving the premises. The cattle had not seen this much activity at Winfield Farm since Uncle John's funeral two months ago. The cousins watched in silence as a cloud of dust settled over the cow pasture.

"I guess we should let the others know the outcome," Will suggested as the car left the front gate. "I can call Owen. He was eager to know the results as soon as the auction was over."

"He'll be disappointed," Farrell commented. "Hell, we're all frustrated."

"Guys, I think we gotta' long road ahead of us," Clay offered.

"Yep, I agree," Henry said, noting to Clay that the left turn on to Highway 701 was just ahead. "I'll send out a text to the others letting them know how things turned out today and see if everyone can get on another conference call next week."

"Melvin's suit you guys again?" Clay inquired, heading south on the desolate two-lane road into Elizabethtown.

"Yeah," Will responded from the back seat.

"Suits me," Farrell replied, sitting next to Will.

The four contemplated the prospect of listing the farm with Everett Hughes, the land broker. Decisions about the next plan of action would be made over a hamburger at Melvin's. Meanwhile, the fate of Winfield Farm waited in the balance.

The Contemplation

Chapter 21

The hazy late afternoon August sun reflected off the pavement, creating a glare off the glass storefronts in downtown Fayetteville. Will was back in town, under similar circumstances, driving with Clay down Martin Luther King, Jr. Boulevard, headed toward Java Joe's, his afternoon drop-off before the northbound Amtrak train arrived. His mind was focused on Rebecca.

Though exhausted from another full day with Clay and his cousins at Winfield farm, his heart raced with anticipation of seeing Rebecca again. Since the auction was held at 10:00 a.m., Clay had picked Will up at the train station just after the train arrived, leaving no time for a walk to Java Joe's that morning. This afternoon was different. He had three hours to kill before the train arrived. He looked forward to surprising Rebecca. She had no idea he was in town again, and as far as she knew, the Southern Yankee left Fayetteville on a train bound for Boston six weeks ago and was never coming back.

Rebecca was not drop-dead gorgeous by Will's standards, but she was attractive in her own way. Her beauty was natural, so she needed very little make-up. She wore hardly any jewelry.

Her spirited personality magnified the attraction Will felt toward her. Rebecca was not the young twenty-something that Will typically found himself attracted to, and she certainly in no way resembled Cat. Will was usually attracted to blondes, like Cat, but Rebecca's long auburn hair tied in a ponytail had captivated him.

She appeared to be in her mid-thirties, was originally from South Carolina, recently divorced, but otherwise, Will knew very little about her. He didn't even know her last name. He speculated that all her hard work and stress from the business must keep her in good shape, because her figure resembled that of a fitness instructor. Perhaps it was her independent and entrepreneurial mindset that Will found attractive. It could have been the kind manner in which she spoke to her customers, combined with her humility, that Will was drawn to. On the other hand, maybe Rebecca was one of the few Southern women Will had been around over the last twenty-two years. Could it be the southern accent alone that had him captivated, he wondered. Or was it the fact that Will was twelve hundred miles away from Cat, and the mystique of being alone in another city, away from his wife, had a way of pushing a man into a mindset of infidelity? In any event, no matter what the reason, the chance to see Becca again had permeated his thoughts since he left downtown Boston last night.

"Are you on the same train home as last time?" Clay asked as he navigated the streets of downtown Fayetteville.

"Yeah, the eight twenty-two. Those trains run like clock-work," Will replied. "I'm almost getting used to the overnight train trip. I actually slept like a baby on the way down, now that I've figured out that the sleeper car is the way to go on these long trips."

"I know you have a few hours before your train arrives. I'd hang out with you for a while longer, but we've got a dinner to go to tonight in Millbrook, so I need to get back home at a reasonable hour," Clay explained.

"Don't worry. I've gotten used to waiting for the train. Plus, hanging out in the coffee shop makes the time go faster. It sure beats waiting around inside that train station. I had a good conversation with the owner when we were here for the funeral. We talked about her business and how it survives on the weekends in downtown Fayetteville."

"Some things never change," Clay laughed. "The women are still falling at your feet."

"Really, it's not like that. This girl's fairly attractive, but I'm not interested," he lied. "She's just a good conversationalist. If you've got steak waiting at home, why eat a hamburger?"

"So, how *are* things with the Cat?" Clay asked.

"I tried to convince her to come down here with me this trip. I told her we would fly into Raleigh, spend a few days with you guys before school starts, but she wanted no part of it. Not that she wouldn't have enjoyed spending some time with you guys, but the thought of attending an auction at the farm was not her idea of fun. Then she challenged me a little on why I had to come back down here again. I explained how Ben was doing the auction, and I felt like I needed to be here to see how things go. Based on how things went today, maybe I *should* have stayed home."

"I think it's good you came. Selling this farm is going to take some time and effort, and one of us is going to need to take the lead in dealing with the realtor and figuring out how we run the farm for the next six months to a year. Like we keep saying, the farm can't run itself," Clay theorized.

"I learn more and more about the farm and the crops we have planted each time I come," Will stated. "I couldn't have told you the acreage of Winfield Farm two months ago when we were here for the funeral. I wish I wasn't so damned far away, or I'd figure out a way to buy the farm or a portion of it."

"After Henry, you're the next family member with the resources to buy it, but I don't see you leaving that gold mine in New England to become a farmer," Clay commented.

"That gold mine you are referring to is starting to run a little dry these days. It's not like it used to be, and it's harder and harder to find M & A work in this economy. Plus, I've burned out. I don't work like I once did. I've lost a little of my steam in my older age," Will explained.

"You're probably hitting that mid-life career crisis, combined with an economy that's not as favorable to your business as it once was. With your resume, maybe it's time for you to come to Raleigh and find an investment banking job. I'm sure it would be a big haircut in compensation, but maybe you need a change from Liberty. What's it been? Twenty-three years?"

"Not quite. Next July will be twenty-two. It's been a good run, but maybe I *am* ready for a change. I'll let you be the one to tell Catherine that we're pulling the girls out of high school and moving to Raleigh, okay? She would think I was asking her to move to Alaska or a third world country," Will exclaimed. "You know, I'd like to somehow figure a way to get back down here at some point. I think about it all the time, but now my roots are so deep up there. It would take Massachusetts falling into the Atlantic Ocean to convince Cat and the girls to move anywhere else but Boston." He paused. "So, what are *your* thoughts on what we do with the farm?" Will asked his brother in an effort to shift the conversation away from him and back to the sale of the farm.

"The farm is a key part of our inheritance. It may be a small part of your net worth, but I need all the help I can get with three young kids. The previous generation went to great lengths to make sure that the farm was passed on to us in a way that minimized the tax implications and would preserve the farm's value. We don't want to flock it up," Clay shared.

"Maybe Uncle John is looking down on us and is mad as hell that we're trying to sell the property, particularly at prices below two thousand an acre," Will said. "I really did get a little emotional when we drove up this morning and the tent was there on the property, signifying the beginning of the end."

"It's a shame that Henry is not in a position to run the farm or buy us out," Clay reasoned. "That would have been the logical solution and enable us to keep the farm in the family."

"I certainly thought that would be the way things played out," Will said as he stared out the car window, looking for a familiar street sign that would lead them to Java Joe's. It felt good to be back in his home state again for the second time this summer. Will had been able to spend more time with his brother in these two trips to the farm than he had over the last twenty-two years. It was days like this that he asked himself, 'What have I done?' when contemplating his life in New England. His thoughts took him back to his destination - Java Joe's. Would Rebecca even be there tonight? Maybe she's taken my advice and closed the shop on Saturday night. She might be visiting her parents in South Carolina, like I'd recommended. The anticipation of seeing Rebecca again superseded his anguish of waiting three hours for the train to leave Fayetteville. He instructed his brother where to park for the curbside drop-off. He felt his heart give a little leap of excitement when he saw the lights on inside the shop. Java Joe's was open for business.

The brothers shook hands through the passenger side window of Clay's Volvo sedan. "We'll talk soon, thanks for the ride," Will said, and then stood to watch the car pull away from the curb. As Clay drove out of sight, Will wondered when he would see his brother again. He stepped toward the storefront of Java Joe's and gently pushed open the front door. The bells jingled, just like he remembered, announcing his arrival. With the ring of the bells, the scene felt déjà vu. He surveyed the store, looking for Rebecca. Two patrons sat in the far corner, away from the front door, but otherwise the shop was desolate. Then, she appeared from the storeroom.

"You did come back!" she exclaimed with a look of complete surprise. "But no business suit this time."

"I had to get my coffee and full dose of Southern hospitality before I leave town again," Will explained.

"You've come to the right place, but I thought I'd never see you again," she said, smiling.

Could she really be so happy to see him? "I couldn't stay away. I told you North Carolina was home."

"So, are you here to stay this time?"

"I wish. I'm back on the train for Bean Town tonight," Will said as he glanced at his watch.

"Yes, the eight-twenty-two," she stated.

"How did you remember that?" he wondered.

"I remembered more than you think that night," she said, glancing quickly at him, and then away.

"I don't know about that, because you're here, and the shop's still open. It's Saturday at five forty-seven and the shop is still open," he proclaimed. "I thought we talked about this six weeks ago. You were supposed to close the shop this morning at ten, right?"

"I'm working on that, but look, you showed up, didn't you? I have two other customers here now, and I'll have a few others come in tonight. Business has been okay, but you know what they say about old dogs and new tricks," she said with a grimace.

"I didn't exactly have you in the dog category," Will grinned.

"I'll take that as a compliment," she grinned back.

"You should, I meant it from the bottom of my heart," he flirted.

"Then by all means, thank you. You Yanks have a unique way of complimenting us women," she commented.

"Oh, I've got plenty more where that came from," he bantered.

"I can't wait," she said.

Will was out of one-liners, so he took the easy way out. "Do you, by chance, know where a Yankee could find a good cup of coffee in this town?"

"We actually serve coffee here, sir," she said, playing the game. "Best coffee in town."

"Perfect, then I guess I've come to the right place," Will said.

"Well, it depends on what you really came for," she said, her eyes riveted on his. Clearly, a door had cracked open, and it was not the door he entered just five minutes ago, accompanied by dainty jingle bells. He decided to play along and see where the pathway might lead. "Here's my story. I was here six weeks ago, and I met this very intriguing and attractive owner of this coffee shop. We had a conversation about her business. She thought I was some salesman with a funny accent dressed in a suit that was sent from New England to buy her business," he began. She placed her elbows on the bar and rested her cheeks in the palms of her hands, listening steadfast as this out of town customer recanted his experience of his first visit to Java Joe's. "I was impressed with the way she ran her business. Her work ethic and dedication to her customers had me captivated, so I knew I had to make another trip south to see if she had taken any of my recommendations. Well, it's obvious that my recommendations didn't really mean shit, so I guess I'm here to see if she might be hiring part-time help on the Saturday night shift." He shrugged, and then gave her a smile waiting for her response, impressed with himself and his ability to still talk a little trash to girls he found attractive. He felt like he was back on campus at UNC, telling a story to a young sorority co-ed. "Am I at the right place?" he added.

"I think so, but I'm not sure I could find work for someone like you. We have some very high standards for the people we hire at Java Joe's. You appear to be someone that is educated, but I have to ask, did you finish high school?" she asked, playing right along with his bantering.

"Yes ma'am. New Hanover High in Wilmington, North Carolina," he responded, thrusting out his chest with pride.

"Any technical school?" she asked hesitantly.

"If you're asking if I have any technical skills, the answer is no, but I did attend a small school in Chapel Hill, North Carolina and took a few college courses."

"I think I've heard of it, but I can't say I've been there," she said, as if deep in thought. "It must be a community college. I've heard Chapel Hill is a neat place. I need to put it on my list of places to visit, if I can ever get my hard-ass boss to give me a day off."

"It's a wonderful place," Will said, nodding. "Best four years of my life. Not sure why I left."

"And why *did* you leave?" she asked curiously.

"Something called graduation. They make you leave after you graduate, but I guess I could have stayed and kept going to graduate school. Instead, I moved to New Hampshire. Great place to live in the spring and summer - or if you're an Eskimo. I came back home to Wilmington for a month, but I went back, and never left ... until now." Will's diatribe turned from humorous to serious in one long breath. "So, here I am, and now you know my whole life story, but you don't even remember my name," he said, looking down at her.

"Of course I do," she said, straightening as she struggled to remember. "You're Will. Will ... Will something."

"Yes, Will Something is correct. I'm impressed. It's Will Jordan, and you are Rebecca," he smiled. "But I won't even attempt a guess at your last name.

"Becca ... my friends call me Becca. Becca Callahan," she smiled back.

"I'd be honored to call you Becca," he said chivalrously.

"Seriously, Mr. Jordan, I know we have the best coffee in town, but I know you didn't travel this far for a cup of coffee, so what brings you back to town?" she inquired.

He laughed at her confidence. "It's the coffee. It really is just the coffee," he explained. "But seriously, the truth is my cousins and I have been trying to decide what to do with the family farm I mentioned when I was here before. Today, we tried to auction off the farm, but there was not a buyer out there who was willing to pay our price. So, after the auction was a bust this morning, my brother and two of my cousins met with a timber consultant and a land broker to see what our next steps are in trying to sell the property."

"So, why would you want to sell the farm?" she asked.

"Funny you would ask. That's what I've been asking myself all day," Will replied.

"When you were here last time, at first, I thought you were bullshittin' me about a farm not too far from here," she shared. "This farm is not just some story you came up with."

"No, there really is a farm about forty miles from here in Bladen County. So, I'm sure you have plenty of customers that come in here and feed you lines, trying to hit on you," Will commented.

"It happens every now and again," she grinned. "But I can fend off the locals. It's the out of towners that I really have a hard time with."

"You have to watch out for those carpetbaggers, those guys from out of state who are just passing through with nothing to do except harass business owners like you," Will said, making a humorous reference to himself. She smiled at his efforts to humor her.

"Let me check on these customers, and I'll be right back," she stated, looking in the direction of the booth at the far end of the café.

"Sure, I'm going to put my things in a booth," Will said, turning toward the same booth he had sat in on his last visit to Java Joe's. He watched as she stepped from behind the counter and walked briskly toward the couple in a booth at the far end of the shop. Once again, he was impressed with the attentiveness she showed to her customers. He turned his head discretely to watch her walk, her ponytail swaying from side to side across her shoulders as she passed by his booth. Where was this headed, he wondered, his mind filled with impure thoughts toward Rebecca. *He had better stop gawking at her. The customers were going to wonder who the stalker is, hitting on the owner.*

He sat down in the booth with his back to other customers and took a deep breath, trying to get his mind off Becca. He pulled his cellphone from his shirt pocket and attempted to remember the names of friends from his era at UNC that were from Fayetteville. He typed the name Jack Peeples. *No Matches Found*, his Google search indicated. No other names came to mind, so he reasoned that if he knew no one else in town, Java Joe's might just be the best place to spend a Saturday evening while waiting on the train.

"Checking in with headquarters?" she asked as she brushed past him on her way back behind the counter.

"Yes, headquarters is asking what kind of progress I've made in convincing you to change your weekend hours," he said in a playful yet serious tone. "I told them your case was hopeless."

"Well, thank you," she replied, with faux sarcasm.

"Seriously, I was checking to see if any of my UNC friends still lived here in Fayetteville. I only remembered one name from here, and I couldn't find him. Peeples was his last name. Do you know any Peeples here in town?"

"Can't say I do," she responded. "Hey, I never did get you that cup of coffee, did I? You came in here harassing me about being open on Saturday afternoon, and I just forgot about serving you."

"Thanks for offering, but I have a better idea," Will stated. "Not that I don't think you brew an incredible cup of coffee, but what if I walked down the street and got us a couple of beers? I like coffee, but I like beer a whole lot more, especially on a Saturday night. Can I convince you to drink one beer on the job?" She didn't answer, but looked at him with a hesitant stare, though he could tell she was somewhat tempted by his offer. "Well, I'm going either way," Will quipped. "If you give me directions on how to find the nearest convenience store, I'll bring you a cold beer - just one. I know there has to be a place open within walking distance. So, what's your poison?"

"I prefer wine, but I can't handle wine and function for the rest of the night. I'll drink most any domestic beer, so bring me one, just one. There's a beer and wine shop on Hay Street. It's just a few blocks from here."

"All right, here's the plan then," Will said, clasping his hands together like a quarterback in a huddle. "I'm going to walk to the liquor store after getting the best directions possible, so I don't get lost. Then you and I are going to enjoy a beer together. Just one!" He could still sense her hesitance, but he persisted. "Now, which way to the liquor store? I'm not one to drink alone, so point me in the direction of Hay Street.

One beer and you can keep the shop open," Will whispered as he stood and looked toward the customers still seated at the booth. "Come on, you deserve this. It's after five o'clock on a Saturday night. You work all the time. It's your slowest time of the week. I'm bringing you one beer. It's the weekend, and we're going to have a beer!"

She finally relented and gave him directions. With a sense of urgency, Will stormed out of the coffee shop and took off like a kid with permission to ride his bike to his best friend's house down the street. Once out of sight of the coffee shop, Will realized he had not called home all day. He pulled his phone from his pocket and dialed Cat's mobile phone. The call was more of an obligation than a desire to call his wife. Plus, he didn't want her calling when he and Rebecca were enjoying a beer. She answered. "Hi Cat," he said. "What's going on there?"

"Not much. The girls rode over to Sandwich to see some friends, and I'm trying to make plans for dinner tonight, since my husband is away again for the weekend," she replied, her tone slightly sarcastic, linked with a faint laugh. "How's everything down south?"

"Oh, it's wonderful. I'm killing time in downtown Fayetteville, waiting on the train. I'm trying to find a place to have a beer. I need to drink away my disappointment. The property didn't sell today."

"What does that mean?" Cat asked.

"It means I'm going to have to move down here until it sells," he said, testing her reaction. Nothing for several seconds, and then she responded. "You *are* kidding, right?"

"Sort of, but I think I'll need to be down here to help find a caretaker and facilitate a sale. It's not fair to leave Henry and Clay with all the work we need to do to get the farm sold. We've all got to help out until the farm sells."

"I thought it was supposed to sell today," she said.

"It was, but we didn't get our minimum price in the auction. It wasn't even close. There was not a serious buyer at the auction, just a bunch of tire kickers, as I call them."

"You're starting to sound like them again."

"What does that mean?" Will asked, walking briskly toward Hay Street.

"Like a southern redneck," she responded. "I can tell you've been around Clay and your cousins all day, because you start talking like them."

"So, are the girls having fun?" Will asked, refusing to acknowledge her comments about his accent.

"Yes, it's been one of those perfect days at the beach. Elizabeth and Thomas decided to drive down, so we're having fun," Cat said, referring to her sister and brother-in-law .

"I got bored waiting at the train station, so I'm walking into this package store to buy a beer. I'll call you when I'm on the way to the Cape tomorrow morning. I should be there by ten, I guess," Will said, now standing outside the front door of Bob and Sheree's Beer and Wine Shoppe. The call ended as he walked through the front door. Will greeted the attendant and walked to the back of the store where the beer coolers were located. He inhaled the cold blast of Freon as he opened the cooler door. Quickly, he procured a six-pack of Budweiser, paid cash to the attendant, and watched as she placed the bottled beer into a brown paper bag. Within moments, he was back on the streets in the summer heat, bound for Java Joe's.

The disappointment of the auction earlier that morning now seemed like a distant memory as Will walked quickly up Green Street and burst through the front door of Java Joe's. With the bag tucked securely under his arm, he broke through the door's threshold like a fullback hitting his designated hole in the offensive line, the bells on the door signifying his return.

"Anyone else here?" he asked, surveying the coffee shop, hoping that he and Rebecca were alone to enjoy a beer or two.

"No, but how is this going to work?" she asked with a reluctant smile. "Are we going to sit here in the front of the store and get drunk?"

"No, we'll offer your customers a beer when they walk in. Beer or coffee? You have choice today, you'll say," Will jested. "In fact, I had an idea while I was walking back. You should start serving beer and wine on the weekends. It can't be that hard to get a license to serve alcohol in this town. That would be the perfect complement to your dilemma of how to drive revenue on the weekends. Plus, this place looks like it was probably a bar at some point in its history," Will said, looking around the shop.

"You have some crazy ideas, Will," she said, shaking her head.

"I'm just here to help," he shrugged.

"Let's open those in the back," she said, motioning for Will to step behind the counter.

"Isn't that what you typically do every afternoon, step in back in the stock-room to have a drink?" Will laughed.

"Maybe some of my employees have a few on the job, but let me assure you, this is a first for me," she replied.

She led him past the counter into a small room behind the coffee machines. It was dark and filled with boxes of what appeared to be coffee and supplies for the shop. In the back corner of the room stood a desk, littered with receipts, an adding machine, and stacks of mail. Will looked around the room and wondered about her revenues. The retail business is a tough way to make a living. He wondered how many of the bills in that stack of mail were bills she's struggling to pay. "Smells good in here," he commented, inhaling deeply. He loved the smell of coffee.

"I apologize, the light in here is terrible, and forgive

my mess," she said as she moved a box on the floor to create enough room for Will to sit down in a metal folding chair positioned next to the desk.

"We could go outside," Will suggested. "It's hot out there, but that gives me another idea. Why don't you buy some small metal tables and set them up outside for your customers? There's room out there for at least two tables and chairs."

"I've thought about it, but I just haven't gotten around to it," she said.

"I could see some nice metal tables and chairs out front with a planter between the tables. This could be a draw for people walking by, especially in the spring and fall when it's not so hot," Will suggested, feeling good about his recommendation. "Let's look online and see what we can find, but first things first. Now, we drink!"

"You're serious about this, aren't you?"

"Oh yeah, you're going to have some chairs and tables out front by Labor Day." Will removed two beers from the carton and opened them. "A toast," he said, lifting his beer with his right hand. "To the success of Java Joe's."

"I'll drink to that," she agreed.

Their bottles pinged as Will leaned forward to tap the base of her beer bottle, signifying collaboration on the toast. He never got tired of hearing the cling of two bottles colliding in a toast before consuming a cold beer. "How long have you owned the store?" Will asked after taking his first long sip.

"A little less than two years," she replied.

Will stood up and situated the four remaining beers in her upright cooler, positioned on the floor next to Becca's desk. "Tell me more about how you came to open the store," Will asked.

"I told you a little about my story when you were here last time," she said. She shrugged. "I had always wanted to run a restaurant, but you always hear how hard it is to make money in the restaurant business. So, I started thinking about a coffee shop. I went through this ugly divorce, and I needed something to take my mind off that, so one day I saw this building was available. After driving by over and over, I said, 'what the hell, I'm going to do this.' So I scraped together all the money I could and took an equity loan out on my house, and here I am. I run it on a shoestring budget. That's why I'm here all the time."

"Do you have any partners?" Will asked.

"No, just me and the bank," she smiled.

"You've done a good job with it. Forgive me for asking, but how is the business doing? Is it profitable? I know nothing about the retail business." He felt somewhat guilty for being so direct with his questions.

"I haven't missed a meal, as you can tell," she said, patting her stomach. "But it's hard to tell if I'm making money. I'll put it this way ... there's not a lot left over at the end of each month, once I pay my employees and the rent and utilities on the building."

"I'm sure the location is limiting. You only get so much traffic here during the week, and weekends are slow," Will commented. "I still think you should cut back your weekend hours."

She shrugged again. "If I'm paying rent, I need to be open. Plus, now you're a regular here on the weekends."

"I assume you don't have any children as hard as you work," Will asked, and then drained the rest of his beer.

"No children of my own. My ex had two, but we never had any. I wanted children, but he said two was enough for him. I'm sure if we had children of our own, things could have been different for us, but now, I'm sure glad we didn't have any ourselves."

"How long were you married?"

"Too long," she laughed. "Six years."

Will did the math in his head, calculating how old she might be. He guessed mid-thirties. "What did you do before you opened Java Joe's?"

"Damn, there you go again, asking all the questions," she said, exasperated. Still, she answered him. "I worked on the base, not as an enlisted, but as a civil servant. I worked for a group of colonels who were pretty high up in the pecking order over there," she shared, pointing with her beer toward the west in the direction of Fort Bragg.

"I'm going to have another beer. Are you ready?" Will inquired as he stepped outside the storeroom and reached for the cooler.

"Not yet. I can't keep up with you," she laughed as she took another swallow in an effort to keep pace.

"I've been out in the heat most of the day without much to drink. That's my excuse," Will explained..

"You're pretty good at asking all the questions. Now I get to ask you some things about you," Becca stated.

"That's actually not the way it works. See, I get to ask all the questions. I'm the consultant," Will jested. "No seriously, ask away. Shoot, I know I asked you some personal questions, but this is strictly business. You can only ask questions about *my* business. In fact, let me give you my business card," he said, reaching for his wallet in the back pocket of his khaki pants. He handed her the card and let her inspect it. "You ever been to Boston?" he asked as she examined the card.

"Just once, a long time ago," Becca replied. "See, there you go again. You're asking all the questions. Not fair."

"You have to be quick at this game," Will said. "So go ahead. Ask away."

"Okay ... do you have children?"

"Yes, two teenage girls," he replied. "I live in a house full of hormones most of the time."

"You're too young to have teenagers," she said.

"I'll take that as a compliment," he replied. "But I did get started sorta' early, maybe too early."

"Happily married?"

"Wow! That got personal real fast. You're supposed to ease into questions like that."

"You have a train to catch. I don't have you here much longer. Maybe I'm not so good at the question game. I guess you could call me direct."

"It's us Yankees that are supposed to be direct, so how about asking first: Are you married?" he suggested, still startled by her question. "Then you could progress with other questions from there."

"That's too easy. You're wearing a wedding ring, so I assumed you're married. I thought my question was a good one, but I think you're avoiding my question." She stared at him, waiting for a response.

"I *am* avoiding your question," he admitted. "I plead the fifth."

"I shouldn't have asked," she said sheepishly.

"No, I've been asking you all the questions, up until now. It was a fair question," Will stated, as he put his left hand behind his back, as he often did, in a half-hearted way to hide the gold wedding band when he was in a conversation with a girl he found attractive. There was a short moment of awkward silence, so Will decided to change the subject. "Next time I'm here, if I ever get back, I should let you drive me from the train station to the farm. It's a beautiful property. If you like wide open spaces, you would like our place," Will offered.

"How far is it from here?"

"Only about forty-five minutes, southeast of here," Will

said, pointing toward the partially opened door that led back into the shop.

"I'd love that. I like riding horses, but I doubt you have horses. It's not that kind of farm, I'm guessing."

"We have cattle and a pasture, but no horses," Will responded. "I sorta' had you figured for a horse girl."

"I rode horses growing up, but I haven't been riding in a long time. Horses were big where I'm from in South Carolina, near Aiken."

"I wish my girls had learned to ride, but they're city girls." Will watched her as she turned the bottle up in what appeared to be her last sip. He looked deep in her eyes. She peered back at him as she held the bottle to her lips and took a substantial swallow. Words were not needed. There was a definite connection between the two of them. Will took the final sip of his second beer as he leaned back in the metal chair. She sat across from him with the back of her chair against her desk so she could keep an eye on the door in case a customer entered the shop. "I'm having another beer, and you've got some catching up to do. I've had two, and you're way behind," Will announced. He stood and stepped toward the doorway.

"I thought we talked about just one beer," she said. "You're very persistent. I'll have another, but two is my limit, especially since I'm on duty."

He opened the bottle with the opener and stepped toward her. As he leaned in Rebecca's direction, Will felt a sudden urge to kiss her. His intuition told him that she would respond favorably to his advance, but felt it was too soon and maybe not the right place. His conscious got the better of him, though it was clear to him that sparks would fly, if he chose to step across the line and kiss her. Though tempted in the past, Will had never pursued any type of affair, a fling, much less a kiss, up to this point in his marriage. Why now? he wondered.

Though his relationship with Cat had been strained for years, he had elected to stay faithful to her for twenty years. He made a conscious decision to forgo any physical advances today. "Let's go outside and look at where we want to put your tables," Will suggested, thinking a walk outside would clear his head from lustful thoughts about her.

"But I just started my second beer. You sure are antsy," she stated.

"Bring it with you," Will suggested.

"I'd rather not," she responded. "A customer might come by."

Will watched again as she turned the bottle up toward the ceiling. She knew he was watching her. Beer bottle up to her lips, she cut her eyes his way. Both of them knew there was a connection between the two of them, but where would it lead?

He extended his left hand in her direction, in a chivalrous gesture to help her up from the chair. She stood, offering another opportunity for him to kiss her. After a short debate in his head, Will elected to pass. In his mind, he blamed the decision on the fact that he hadn't had a shower since yesterday morning, and he had a train to catch. The fact that he was married played into the decision as well, but the marital deterrent was secondary in his thought process. Becca hid the beer behind the counter as she walked out of the storeroom and toward the front door. "Bring the beer," Will suggested. "Don't worry about it. If a customer shows up, they'll appreciate the fact that you're enjoying a cold beer. It *is* Saturday night, after all."

"Okay, there you go again, convincing me to do something I don't want to do. I can tell you're a salesman," she smiled as she turned his way before pushing the front door open with her hips.

"Remember, I'm a consultant, not a salesman," Will replied. "I'm just trying to make sure you and I both have some fun while I'm here. I may not be back again," he commented. Was this really the person he wanted to risk my marriage for, he asked himself as he followed her outside the shop. His eyes stayed fixated on the back pockets of her jeans. He was a million and a half miles away from home. No one would ever know.

As Will and Becca discussed table and chair configurations, a customer arrived. Becca greeted her by name, discretely handed Will the partially consumed beer bottle, and led the patron inside the store. Will felt it was his place to stay outside and wait until the customer left. He watched the interaction between Becca and the customer for a while, and then checked his watch. It was just past 7:30 and the North Carolina heat had finally dissipated, making for a pleasant night in downtown Fayetteville. He turned toward Green Street and sat down on the ledge of the storefront window with his back to Becca and the customer.

He held the two beer bottles side by side, like two toy soldiers facing each other, and then began gently tapped the tops of the bottles together, creating a harmonious ping. He crossed his sockless feet together at his ankles and took a deep breath, his thoughts carrying him back to the farm and the events of the day. What will happen to the farm? How long will it take to sell it? How low will we have to reduce the price before it sells? How ugly will the negotiations get? Will we be back here in a year, begging Ben to auction the property again with a take price of sixteen hundred dollars an acre?

The streets of downtown Fayetteville were almost empty. A few residents walked the streets at a leisurely pace, unlike the flurry of activity in downtown Boston. There were no tourists here, no crowds, no kiosks, no stores, no traffic, no business suits, and no one walking by in a rush. Time seemed to stand still. The only noise on the street in front of Java Joe's was the sound of Will clinging the two empty bottles together. Suddenly, he asked himself, *What am I doing here?* He felt out of his element. He was in a town where he had no ties, having a beer with a woman he was mildly attracted to, and was over a thousand miles from home. Though he was enjoying himself and the time he spent with Becca, Will suddenly felt awkwardly out of place, and the urge to get home came over him. He was distracting Becca from doing her work, and he couldn't miss this train. He better get going. He stood and began to pace the sidewalk in front of the shop. It was time for him to leave. Becca and the customer interacted while Will waited impatiently. Finally, the customer left the shop with a to-go cup in each hand.

Will greeted the customer with a nod and a quick smile as she left the store and walked down the street in the direction of the train station. Quickly, Will went back inside the shop.

"Well, it's about that time," he said. "The train will be here soon. He picked up his briefcase from the booth. "I think I'll take a beer for the road and leave you one to enjoy when you close shop."

She was silent for a moment, then spoke. "Let me give you a to-go cup for your beer. Are you sure you don't want the last one? I'm not one to drink a beer by myself. A glass of wine, yes, but not a beer. So why don't you take the extra one? You might need it for that long train ride."

"You're probably right, I could use it. It'll help me sleep on the train ride. Can you put one in a to-go cup, and I'll put the other in my briefcase?" he asked, standing behind the counter, ready to leave. He watched her as she poured the contents of the beer into a large Styrofoam coffee cup. With her back to him, she looked like a bartender pouring Will a draft beer from a pub in downtown Boston. She turned and placed the beer on the counter. Slowly, he put the briefcase down and walked toward her. He opened his arms to give her a hug, and she stepped from behind the counter in his direction. "Thank you for letting me hang out here again," Will said as he wrapped his arm around her waist and pulled her torso toward him.

"It was my pleasure. Believe me, this was one of the more exciting Saturday nights I've had around here in a while."

"Two beers? That's not exactly a throw-down," Will laughed.

"Will you be back?" Becca asked

He thought he caught hope in her voice. "I'm sure I'll be back at some point," he said, still in the prolonged embrace. "I just don't know when."

"Well, I'll be here," she said. "You know that's for sure."

He kissed her gently on the left cheek and thanked her again. With his briefcase in one hand and the Styrofoam cup in the other, he made his way out the door. The bells on the door jingled as he stepped outside, facing the setting sun.

The Ride Home

Chapter 22

The sun began its slow descent over Fayetteville as the skies turned from Carolina blue to shades of subtle violet. Daylight prepared to yield its way to darkness as Will boarded the Amtrak train. He walked forward through two cars until he found an unoccupied row, placed his briefcase in the middle seat and positioned himself next to the window on the right side of the passenger car. As the train's engine idled, preparing to pull away from the station, Will made an attempt to read a book on his tablet, but lascivious thoughts of Becca once again distracted his ability to concentrate on reading.

He stretched his legs straight ahead, sliding his Ferragamo brown suede loafers under the seat in front of him. Stretching his upper torso, he lifted the tablet high above his head with both arms. Mentally, he prepared himself for the long train ride ahead of him, but his devious side wondered if he should be staying an extra night in Fayetteville. Fantasies about spending the night with Becca clouded his mind. He even went so far as to contemplate the details of a cover-up to Catherine. She would never know, he thought to himself. He could easily justify to Cat why he needed to stay an extra night in North Carolina. After all, it was a long trip to make in one day, and there was work to do at the farm in order to list the property for sale. For all Catherine would know, Will had decided to spend the night at the farm or in Raleigh with Clay and his family.

His demented mind played out the details of a one-night affair with Becca. Detailed visions of riding in Becca's car past the military base to her house in the Fayetteville suburbs clouded his head: her car, her house, the décor, the shower, her bed. Though he had never been anywhere near Becca's house, Will had every detail of the affair recorded in his thoughts.

The train's doors still stood open, waiting for final passengers to board, still time for him to delay his return to Boston and surprise Becca with a consternation of surprising proportions. It would be an easy coup to pull off, and Cat would ever know. If Will was inclined to carry out his game plan, an 8:40 a.m. northbound train out of Fayetteville would have him back in Cape Cod by 10:00 on Sunday night.

Suddenly, Will's fantasy was interrupted by the abrupt sound of the railcar doors closing. Wanton thoughts of Rebecca were soon replaced with the reality of spending time at Cape Cod with the family on Sunday afternoon. Again, he made an effort to focus on his book as the train began to build momentum northbound out of the Fayetteville station.

The speeding train crossed the Cape Fear River as the landscape outside Will's window changed from apartment buildings and retail centers to open countryside. The panoramic views of boundless farmland over his right shoulder passed like pages in a magazine. He closed his tablet and placed it on the empty seat next to him. His eyes fixated out the window, Will felt captivated by the stretch of open land dotting the landscape. He looked east as far as his eyes could take him with unrealistic hopes of capturing a glimpse of Winfield Farm. The farm lay a distant forty miles from the railroad tracks. Seeing it from an airplane would have been plausible, but a view of the farm from the train was only a vision Will could create in his mind.

He wondered when he might be back, or if he would ever return to his beloved state of North Carolina. He looked in earnest in the direction of the farm, picturing the farm in his head. As the train moved to its top speed of eighty miles an hour, headed to the Piedmont region of the state, Will realized he was leaving a part of himself behind in North Carolina - again. Why was he leaving, he wondered. This is where his heart was. It was the same story every time he came here. He always tried to figure out a way to move back, but where would he live? What would he do to make a living?

In a little more than eleven hours, Will would be back in Massachusetts, and by Monday morning, North Carolina would be a distant memory once again. Any hopes of moving home to Carolina would soon be replaced with the pressures of making a living in Boston and providing for his family. Suddenly, the thought occurred to him. Why didn't he buy the farm? He could find someone to run it. He could come down by train every other week and spend two or three days overseeing the operation. That's not illogical. They couldn't let this farm get sold to some pirate who buys it for fifty cents on the dollar. He wouldn't let that happen. Maybe Clay could help him run it, or maybe he might be interested in a partnership. The thought of actually operating the farm was less appealing than the desire to spend more time in Carolina. However, the excitement perpetuated as Will derived ways to make his new idea a reality. Maybe he should call Clay and run the idea by him, he pondered, but his mind was moving in too many directions in an effort to justify why buying the farm would be a good idea. It's still too early to run this idea by him, and he's out with the family tonight. He'd call him Monday morning on the drive to the office from Cape Cod.

The excitement of owning the farm and keeping it in the Winfield family occupied his mind as the blanket of darkness began to shroud the railcar. In his head, he calculated various price-per-acre scenarios and contemplated his financial liquidity in various investment accounts. His brain eventually hit overload calculating pricing alternatives, a total purchase price, a significant down payment, and an amount he could comfortably finance. So, he quickly snatched his tablet from the adjacent seat and began to input numbers on an excel spreadsheet.

It all came down to what number the cousins would accept on a final purchase price. How desperate are they to sell? Would the cousins sell to him for less than what they would on the open market? Is there value to them to sell now versus a year from now? Sure! Before they got the realtors involved, what's the bottom number they'd take? Twelve hundred an acre? Probably not. Fifteen hundred? Maybe.

Then, Will began to consider the revenue side of Winfield Farm. It was still uncertain what this year's crops would yield on an annual basis. He had never had any reason to see the farm's financials. He assumed Uncle John had kept the books all these years. Were the farm revenues enough to sustain the same level of income he'd enjoyed over the last ten years? Probably not, but was that okay? He was okay with less income to replace the stress he was under now in this economy. He felt ready to trade in the pressure of producing a certain level of fees in the investment banking business every year for something he enjoyed, but is farming something he would enjoy? Could he somehow do both for a period of time? He was sure he could set up an office at the farm and still run his business from both places, at least for a while. Maybe he could spend half his time in Boston and half down here?

Will was committed to make his new plan work. He had built a sizable nest egg of savings in hopes of finding a business to buy one day. After evaluating businesses for others to buy or sell for over twenty years, he had aspirations of one day buying a business of his own. After all, he was exposed to opportunities every day. Three years ago, he had looked seriously at investing in a lumber business in New Hampshire, only a thirty-minute drive north of Marblehead, but he decided to pass on the purchase for a number of reasons. His main aversion was the uncertainty of sustained growth in the housing industry. His theory on the collapse of the housing construction market had proven correct, and foregoing the purchase at the top of the market played out to be a sound business decision.

Now, the financial markets had tumbled, the housing sector in all regions of America had tanked, and values of companies, both public and private, had plummeted, stalling the sales of privately held businesses, which directly impacted Will's income. With values of companies, particularly the private firms, cut by twenty-five to fifty percent in some cases, business owners were not motivated to sell in a down market, unless they absolutely had to unload their business. The fire sales did not bode well for the sellers or the investment bankers.

Will had built his career on the small to mid-sized business owners in New England. The business owners in the closely held private enterprise had seen a significant run-up in values during the mid-1990s through 2007, and selling or merging the business had proven to be lucrative for those who took advantage of the market during this era. Larger companies and eager entrepreneurs with capital were paying a premium to buy profitable privately held American companies in growth markets like New England, so Will rode that wave for the better part of his career. By the third quarter of 2008, as the U.S. economy started its slide, Will's ability to generate considerable fees stagnated, as merger and acquisition activity hit a wall.

After a successful 15-year run, the investment banking business became almost oppressive, particularly in Will's sector. If not for a few fire sales, where fees were often arduous to collect, the M & A business at Liberty Capital had shifted from robust to lethargic. The firm itself was still in good financial shape, but fee income on sales was down substantially over the past three years. Liberty had been forced to lay off three analysts and two administrative assistants in 2009 due to the slow-down, but no partners had left the firm during the recent downturn. The lay-offs were the first in the fifty-six-year history of the firm. Long hours, late nights, and weekend work during the height of the M & A era were now just a memory, as Liberty Capital entered a period of survival - a mode it had avoided over the last half a century. Annual partner distribution checks ceased for two years to build reserves to weather the prolonged downturn. Bonuses to salaried employees were either eliminated or curtailed to a fraction of the peak levels in 2005. If there was ever a time to buy a business, it's now," Will recalled telling his buyers over the last two years. Would Will take his own recommendation to heart and put his money where his mouth was? He had accumulated the liquidity, so was it time to take action? Even if it were, was the acquisition of the farm the right business choice for Will?

As the train moved northward into the darkness, Will sent Cousins Henry and Farrell an e-mail from his tablet, requesting the farm revenues and expenses over the past three years, but he did not disclose why he wanted the numbers. It was too early to reveal any interest he had in purchasing the farm. He had far too much due diligence ahead of him, on a personal and professional level. Will's request for the financial statements should not raise any suspicion among the cousins as to his newly contrived purchase plan. He was determined to treat this potential acquisition as he would for a client on the buyer side. He would take an objective view and try to keep the emotion out of his assessment. However, his emotions were already running high. He knew the excitement of this potential acquisition would prevent him from a decent night's sleep on the train.

Will pulled his financial calculator from his briefcase and began plugging in numbers based on projected purchase price scenarios. As a seller, he already had equity in the deal. As a buyer, he could apply his portion of ownership to potential purchase price. In a realistic, conservative scenario, Will calculated that he could buy the farm for one point six million, apply his two-hundred thousand portion toward equity, put six-hundred thousand of his own cash in the deal, and finance an even eight-hundred thousand. One point six million seemed like a good number, and those numbers played out to just under fifteen hundred per acre and made for an easy calculation when evaluating the windfall that each cousin would realize in the sale.

The thought of carrying debt of eight hundred thousand on an enterprise he knew very little about was daunting, but he knew the farm was moderately profitable. With his business background, he could grow the farm revenues, sell the existing timber, and pay off the debt over the next ten years. In advising his investment banking buyers, Will was not a proponent of recommending that his clients carrying massive debt to finance an acquisition. Heavy debt to equity ratios, even in a good acquisition, was never a good idea, Will always cautioned. Will lived by the same rule with his personal finances. The only personal debt he carried was on his home. His house in Marblehead was worth just over a million dollars, but his principal balance was less than two hundred thousand.

Paying cash for the farm was not a financial option, but neither was maintaining sizable debt. Will was liquid, but not solvent to the point of writing a check for over a million dollars, much less one point six million, less his inherited portion of two-hundred thousand. Interest rates were at historic lows, but how would the conservative bankers in Boston feel about loaning eight hundred grand to a white-collar investment banker turned farmer, even with eight hundred thousand in equity? Maybe a good local bank in Bladen County would better understand farm loans and willingly lend him the money, he thought. In fact, there are probably some low interest government-backed farm loans, even for inexperienced farmers like Will.

Will wanted answers to make a full assessment of the farm purchase, but the financial information would most likely have to wait until Monday. In the meantime, he tried to envision himself as a farmer, working on the farm, learning the trade, and growing old on the farm. He saw himself back in the stands at Rupp Arena, watching his alma mater play basketball in Chapel Hill. He visualized weekends and holidays with Clay and his family in Raleigh and beach trips with the family to Wrightsville Beach in the summer. Will already had his new life back in North Carolina planned out in his mind, but then it hit him. What would Cat say when he dropped this bomb on her, he wondered. He couldn't tell her anything until this was a done deal. Suddenly, his excitement for the farm purchase dissipated. Cat would never go for it. Never! But she knows what's going on in his business. She knew he was frustrated with work. She'd seen the tax returns and known they were not making the kind of money they used to. She got the fact that income was down. Surely, she would support him in this venture. But she would *never* move down here. It would be a stretch for her to even visit. Still, they would have horses and an old home to restore. It would be fun, but he didn't see her wanting anything to do with the farm. As for the idea of reinventing himself, from an investment banker to a farmer, she'd never go for it. And the girls, surely they would appreciate the opportunity to spend some time on a farm, maybe spend the summers there. In three years, they'd both be in college. There is no way he could ask Cat and the girls to move down here. The girls were happy in Marblehead. How could he leave the girls every week and commute each way?

The excitement of buying the farm faded with each turn of the train's wheels as Will faced the reality of leaving a family he loved to buy a business he knew so little about. The hum of the steel wheels rolling over the train-track began to lull Will into a light sleep, but the bellow of the train's brakes soon woke him.

The sign on the brick wall of the station read LYNCH-BURG, VIRGINIA. As Will peered out the window with one eye open, still in a daze, he placed the tablet and HP calculator back inside his briefcase and prepared to retire to the sleep-car. Briefcase in hand, he passed through to the next railcar, which looked similar to the one he had just left. The faceless riders resembled the passengers in the previous car. Some appeared to be asleep while others stared aimlessly ahead, waiting for the train to depart from the Lynchburg station.

Will showed his ticket to the sleeper car attendant, dressed in a black uniform and matching hat, hardly a fashion state-ment, but perfectly suited for the job. He pointed Will to an empty bunk behind a black curtain. He stepped inside, dropped his bags, kicked off his loafers, and wedged his way on to the lower bunk bed. Within minutes, he was prostate with his head on a flat meager pillow, his bare feet crossed at the ankles, hoping to sleep until daylight. He lay on the lower bunk motionless and thought about his time with Becca. Was she that attractive or was she merely the only Southern female he had a conversation with on this trip?

Will began making comparisons in his mind between Southern girls and females in New England. Clearly, he was biased toward Southern women. He thought about Cat and how attracted he was to her in those early days while they were dating. She was as pretty as any girl at UNC, and Chapel Hill was known for its deep supply of Southern talent. So, what happened? Why was he no longer attracted to Cat? Will wondered. He believed that her constant berating had finally gotten to him. He couldn't see past the way she rode him. Her demeanor clouded his ability to see her the way he used to.

As he lay in the bunk unable to fall asleep, his mind started to play the "what if" game again, and his thoughts took him back to the last time he saw Kaitlyn Gerrard at Wrightsville Beach. It was the summer before he left North Carolina for graduate school. What had he been thinking that day?

Kaitlyn was the girl he had always admired but never pursued. She attended the main private school in Wilmington while Will was at New Hanover High. Kaitlyn, or Kate as some people at home called her, was three years younger than Will. He'd met her at a camp in high school when he was a senior and she a freshman. Though they grew up within three miles of each other, Will and Kate rarely saw each other. Attending different schools, Will was busy playing baseball, while Kaitlyn was occupied pursuing her interest in acting. An only child, Kate kept to herself. She was confident, but shy. She was not one to attend the boisterous parties on the north end of Wrightsville Beach, but she would frequent the Blockade Runner pool on occasion, sometime with a girl-friend, and other times by herself. Most of her time during summers was spent performing at Thalian Hall in Wilmington with the North Carolina Theater Company.

On one occasion, when Will was home for the summer working at the Pine Valley Country Club golf course between his sophomore and junior year at Carolina, Will and Clay were convinced to attend a play with their parents at Thalian Hall. Out of respect for their parents, the boys attended. The musical was entertaining, but the real entertainment for Will was seeing Kaitlyn perform on stage. In many ways, Kaitlyn represented everything Cat was not. At 5'7", Cat was tall and athletic, while Kaitlyn was average height and more academic, although she played volleyball in high school. Cat was more outspoken, and Kate was more reserved and shy. Cat was a natural dirty blonde, and Kaitlyn's hair was jet black – the color of coal. Cat would be considered more striking in her looks, while Kate was less assuming, but naturally attractive. Cat was social, Kaitlyn more of a loner. Then, there were the cultural differences. Cat came from a wealthy New England family, while Kate was from the South and grew up in a small home in an upper middle-class neighborhood near the Pine Valley Country Club.

Though Will never dated Kaitlyn, he tried to keep up with her whereabouts after he graduated from high school. It was no surprise to anyone, including Will, when Kate chose not to attend the University of North Carolina. UNC had an excellent theatre program, but Kate's personality was more suited to a smaller, more academic environment. She had far less concern about the social aspect of college, so Kate shunned the larger in-state schools like UNC and chose to attend New York University to pursue her acting interests. Once she left Wilmington to attend NYU, she only returned in the summers to spend time performing with the North Carolina Theater Company.

"Out of sight, out of mind" was Will's excuse as to why he never pursued his interest in Kaitlyn. While Will was enjoying himself at UNC, Kate was in high school, until she left for NYU during Will's senior year of college. While Will was at Dartmouth, Kate was in New York. Never once did their paths cross, until that fateful day at the Blockade Runner on Wrightsville Beach after Will's graduation from Dartmouth.

It was late June, soon after Will's graduation from Dartmouth. Will had come home to Wilmington for a few weeks before starting work at Liberty Capital in Boston. He and Catherine had been dating steadily for almost three months, marking the longest stretch in their short dating relationship that they had not seen each other at least once a week. Will thought about inviting Catherine down to Wilmington for a few days, but he calculated that it was a little early in their developing romance to meet the family. Plus, the Key family had planned a two-week trip to England and France for Catherine's graduation. They would return to Boston toward the end of June.

Will planned to move to Boston the first week of July and spend the Fourth of July on Cape Cod with Catherine and the Key family. He was due to start work at Liberty on July 15th, so he had some time to relax before starting his job as a financial analyst in downtown Boston.

To pass some time in Wilmington before his July departure for Boston, Will spent time with his family, played golf with Clay, saw some old high school friends, hung out at the bars at night on the Wilmington waterfront, and learned to surf at the beach in front of the Blockade Runner. At the end of June, Will invited his Dartmouth road-trip confidants to Wilmington for some sun and fun. Joel, Chris, and Alan all met in New York City and drove south to the Carolina Coast for a long weekend before the band of road warriors started their respective jobs in the Northeast.

Will had set the expectations low prior to the visitors' arrival, explaining that Wilmington had its beaches, bars, and girls, but it was by no means as lively as South Beach in Florida. Nonetheless, the guys were ecstatic about another road-trip together, especially for the chance to see some of the South's natural beauty. Will was determined to show the guys a good time, so he mapped out a good balance of beach and pool time during the day, and touring Wilmington's finest waterfront taverns by night. He anticipated a slight culture clash between his brash Dartmouth-educated Yankee friends and the gentile Southerners in Wilmington, but it was a weekend to look forward to while passing time between graduation and work.

The visit from the Dartmouth trio included an introduction to Southern food, which included Carolina barbeque at Jackson's Big Oak Barbeque and grits at the Waffle House. The food was palatable, but the Northerners were more interested in Coastal Carolina's preeminent natural resource, the bikini-clad beachcombers at Wrightsville Beach. Naturally, Will took his grad school accomplices to the Blockade Runner for sightseeing. The beach and pool at the Blockade Runner swarmed with guests that early summer weekend, and the boys found no shortage of eye-candy as they split time between the pool and the surf. Late in the afternoon on Saturday, as the summer heat began to dissipate, the four Dartmouth amigos walked along the boardwalk that connected the pool and the beach at the Blockade Runner, destined for another jaunt to the surf. As the boys walked single file on a beeline toward the beach, Will spied Kaitlyn walking toward him, apparently headed to the pool area. Wearing a black one-piece bathing suit, Kaitlyn moved rapidly from the shoreline along the sunbaked boardwalk, drenched from head to toe and appeared to be in search of a towel, from what Will concluded.

Except for a few performances on stage, Will had not seen Kaitlyn since they were together at camp during Will's senior year in high school. He was once again captivated by her looks as she approached him. She appeared taller now than he remembered from high school, and her wet black hair clung to her shoulders. As her slender frame moved in the direction of the boys, Will noted the distinctive olive tone of her skin that matched the color of her piercing brown eyes. He prepared to speak to her as their eyes met. Never short on words when it came to approaching a female, Will suddenly searched for the right words to say. He wanted to stop her and ask where she was in school and hear about her acting pursuits. She was approaching quickly, so if he wanted to talk to her, he knew he would need to stop her from her apparent mission to locate a towel.

The Dartmouth boys followed in single file behind Will as he advanced toward the beach on the boardwalk. Then, a thought entered his mind. What would these guys think if he stopped to talk to Kaitlyn? They knew he was dating Cat. These guys were there the night Cat and he had met. Would they think he was hitting on Kate if he stopped to talk to her? Surely, it's harmless to talk to her and see how things are going, right? As Kaitlyn got closer, Will decided he could stop her and chat for a moment. He greeted her with a smile as she passed, and Kaitlyn responded with only a quick hello and kept walking. As he turned to stop her, he hesitated. Just let her pass, he told himself. She's in a hurry. She apparently didn't want to stop and talk.

Joel, Chris, and Alan suspected nothing of his brief encounter with Kate. She passed like an ocean breeze, and Will never saw her again. All he had left of Kate was the brief memory of her passing him by and regrets of not stopping her that day. Why didn't he stop her? He could have introduced her to the guys. That was innocent enough. One of them could have hit it off with her. You never know. Maybe she was in a hurry to go meet her boyfriend at the pool, or it could be that she needed to get to the restroom and was in a rush. Possibly she was mad at him for never asking her out all those years ago.

Will had several theories that day of what transpired in those limited seconds as Kaitlyn passed by him. With the theories came several regrets as well. He wrote off the incident to fate, fate that he and Kaitlyn were not meant to be, and so the door was open to pursue Cat. It was his destiny to marry Cat. Kaitlyn was apparently not meant to be. It's as simple as that, Will speculated after the Kaitlyn sighting that afternoon at Wrightsville Beach. Other than being from the same hometown, Kate and he didn't have much else in common. After the encounter that afternoon, Will wrote off any further thoughts of pursuing Kaitlyn, and his relationship with Cat flourished after his move to Boston. He didn't think much about Kate again — until now.

Why was he suddenly so determined to harvest Kaitlyn's memory? It had been twenty-one years since the Blockade Runner sighting of Kaitlyn. Why the recall? He concluded that two trips to North Carolina this summer had him thinking more about his past. As his and Cat's relationship started to demise over the years, Will found himself wondering what life would have been like had he married someone else. So, his mind led him to ponder who that *someone else* might have been. After suppressing any thoughts of her for two decades, Kaitlyn's name kept surfacing in his mind this summer. Maybe it was the mystery and the unknown of what might have been if he had dated Kate just one time — once to determine if a spark existed between them. Of Will's numerous girlfriends from high school and UNC in that era, none of those names emerged as girls he saw himself marrying. All of his old girlfriends had various issues or baggage, Will concluded. Maybe Kaitlyn had issues as well, but he never even gave her a chance to expose her shortcomings. As far as he knew, she had no shortcomings. Who knows, maybe there were some real skeletons in Kate's closet? It's possible that he had dodged a bullet, but her reputation and her family's good name were known to be stellar. She certainly had a far better reputation than every other girl he had dated in high school, that's for sure.

As Will lay in the sleeper car trying to fall asleep, his thoughts bounced back and forth between the farm purchase and the various females in his life. He weighed the merits of living in Boston versus North Carolina, the decision to invest in the farm, or put the property on the market. When not debating the choices he faced with buying the farm, his mind ricocheted between Cat, Kaitlyn, and Becca. Cat, he knew all too well, the other two he knew to a limited degree. Becca represented the one he had erotic thoughts of, while Kaitlyn was the girl he positioned on a pedestal. As the train rocked along the railroad tracks through the night, the decisions clouding his mind subsided, and Will finally drifted off to sleep.

The Decision

Chapter 23

The sun's warm rays formed a mirage in the distance toward Sandy Neck on Cape Cod. The incoming waves crashed along the Massachusetts coast, signaling that the afternoon tide had reached its high point along the coarse sand of East Sandwich Beach. Sunday temperatures had peaked at 84 degrees on this lazy August Sunday in New England.

"When will the girls get back?" Will asked Cat as he looked up from his Sunday edition of the Wall Street Journal. They sat side-by-side in beach chairs facing the surf.

"Oh, it could be another hour or so," Cat said. "When they get around their friends, I don't know when to expect them. As long as they're home before five or so, I'm usually not worried about them."

"I haven't seen them since Thursday night, so I might text them and see when they plan to get back here," Will mentioned, sitting straighter in his chair.

"I would, if I were you," Cat suggested. "I'm sure they want to see you too."

"Can you text them? I forgot, my phone's dead from yesterday. I didn't have a place to charge it."

"Oh, that's right. I remember now that the farm house doesn't have electricity," Cat joked.

He smiled at her jab, stopping short of a laugh. He put down the newspaper and picked up his tablet, eager to see if Henry had responded to his inquiry about the farm's finances.

"What are you working on today?" Cat asked, frustrated by Will's inability to relax. "I thought you would be sleeping this afternoon after your long train trip, but you sure are busy for a man whose business is supposed to be slow these days."

"I'm looking for some financial documents from Henry and Farrell for the farm," he responded.

"You seem enamored with that farm all of a sudden," she murmured. "I can't believe the auction was a total bust. You went all the way down there for nothing."

"It wasn't a bust by any stretch," Will replied. "Making the trip was the right thing to do. We made some progress, although the auction didn't go as planned. I learn more about the farm every time I go. It's really a profitable business, and at these low prices, someone is going to make a really good buy on it. Part of me wishes there was a way to keep it in the family."

"As long as you can help your cousins analyze the value from up here and not keep making these weekend trips down there, then I'm fine with you running your spreadsheets as much as you like," Cat commented, adjusting her sunglasses and returning her attention to her novel.

This was going to be a tougher sell than he thought, Will thought. She'll blow a gasket once he told her of his plans to buy the farm. "I'm sure I'll need to make another trip or two down there before it's all over, but this is important. The farm has been in our family now for three generations. Uncle John made sure the farm ran profitably, and we want to make sure we don't lose any value just because he's no longer around.

It'll take some effort from all of us to put the right people in place and make sure the farm maintains its viability and profitability. Since Henry's sick, I'm willing to step in and help, particularly since things have slowed down at work for me."

"How *is* Henry doing?" Cat asked, turning toward him. "Was he there at the auction yesterday?"

"Yes, he was there," Will nodded. "He seems to be okay. You can tell he's lost some of his stamina and he's wearing a hat, so I think he's lost some hair from the chemo. He and Farrell were both there. Henry's still the guy on the front line as far as decisions and overseeing things on the farm, but he's not in a position to be there consistently. That's why I'm trying to help out where I can. If Henry had children, they might have been the ideal choice to run the farm," he hypothesized. "But the right buyer will surface soon, I think."

* * *

On his drive into the office from the Cape on Monday morning Will called Clay in Raleigh. "Sorry to catch you so early, but do you have a few minutes to talk?" he asked.

"Yeah, what's up?" Clay asked.

"I've come up with a crazy idea on the farm, and I wanted to run it by you."

"Okay," Clay responded, without much enthusiasm.

"I'm seriously thinking about making an offer to the cousins to buy the farm," Will stated. A moment of silence followed his announcement.

"I think it's a great idea. Would you move the family down here?" Clay asked.

"Eventually, I guess, but it would be just me at first. I haven't thought through all of the details, but it's all I've been able to think about since the idea hit me on the train ride home Saturday night."

"What does Cat say about the whole idea?"

"I've made some hints about it, but I haven't told her yet. You're actually the first person I've mentioned it to."

"I never thought about you as the buyer, but I've been wondering who's going to step up and keep the farm operating while we try to sell it. I think it makes perfect sense, the more I think about it. You've got the resources, and the mergers and acquisitions world is not exactly clicking like it once was. This may be a good side business for you."

"Well, I've looked at the numbers that Farrell sent me late yesterday, and with a little boost in revenue, the farm could be quite profitable. It won't yield a seven figure profit every year, but in a good year, the farm could generate a quarter of mil or so in profit, if it's run efficiently."

"That all sounds positive ... and exiting," Clay offered. "It's certainly a radical change from where you are in life, but you've been able to generate a good income for a number of years, so you're probably in a pretty good position to pull this off."

"I know it's radical, to use your word, but like I shared, I've been burned out in my career for the last two or three years. Like we talked about this weekend, I've been at the same company for more than twenty years, and the work, particularly the prospecting part, is not getting any easier. It's been a good run at Liberty, but I find myself looking at all these companies I'm evaluating and wondering if I shouldn't be the guy buying the business. I know Cat is going to flip when I tell her my plans, though."

"Trust me, you better get her on board before you get too deep into this," Clay recommended.

"I know, but it's still a pipe-dream at this point. I won't tell her until I've solidified a price and have a loan in place. Based on what I want to pay for the farm, I'm not sure you guys will agree to the sale."

"The way I see it, this farm sale is found money for me and the other cousins. There's some emotion to selling the farm at a certain price, but it's more about making a deal, taking the cash, and moving on. That's why the auction made so much sense. The auction was supposed to be a way to sell the farm quickly at a slight discount. I think I speak for the cousins in saying that if your price is reasonable, and even slightly unreasonable, we'll sell. I don't think any of us want to go through the agony of waiting up to two years for the right buyer. Plus, if we know someone in the family still owns the property and gives us visiting privileges, then that's even more motivation. I know that's my position. I think the others will feel the same way."

"Maybe I'm more attached to the property from a senti-mental standpoint than you are, or maybe I'm in this phase of life where the thought of letting go of the farm means more than what it might have three years ago," Will theorized.

"I'm not at the same stage as you," Clay offered. "You're in the home stretch, as far as raising your kids. You've made your mark on the finance world and banked more money at forty-four years of age than most sixty-year-olds. So, you're clearly in a different position than me. I've got three kids to feed, so the cash sounds more appealing than the thought of keeping the farm in the family. You've crossed a different threshold than me. Hell, I'm still in survival mode."

"I've been there," Will responded. "I guess it's my mid-life crises, but I don't want to make some stupid decision and blow my life savings on an idea that sounds real sexy right now. I know one thing, though. Being back in North Carolina these last two times has made me realize how much I miss it. I've got a good life here in Boston, but I guess my heart is still in Caro-lina. But I don't want this purchase to be a rash emotional decision. That's why I wanted to run the idea by you first."

"I like the idea," Clay said. "You left a lot behind when you made the decision to stay up north. Like Dad used to always tell his friends in Wilmington, 'Will fell in love with a Boston girl and left his North Carolina roots.' But you had a good opportunity with a great firm in Boston, and you've done well. Let's face it though, your roots are still down here in Carolina."

"You're not doing a very good job of talking me out of this purchase," Will laughed.

"I think buying the farm makes a lot of sense for you, given where you are in life, and selfishly, we'd love to have you closer to us. We don't get to see you anymore, except when someone in the family dies."

"I think that's a big part of it," Will shared. "I look at where I am in life, and maybe I've accomplished a few things, but I've moved a thousand miles from home to get there. Is it really worth it? I've abandoned my Southern roots and become one of 'them'. I have a wonderful family and great in-laws, so I don't have any intentions of leaving them, but I see this as an opportunity to reconnect with you and your family." He paused. "We spend every holiday and summer with Catherine's family, which is fine, but it's been a one-way street. As I've thought through the practicalities of buying the farm, I've realized that I can work in one place and live in another. People do it all the time. The girls are older now, and I'm not needed at home as much anymore. Maybe three or four years from now would be the ideal time to make this purchase, but with both girls in high school this year, I think they can survive without me during the week."

"It sounds like you've put a lot of thought into the plan and are committed to moving forward. The only challenge I see is the distance between the farm and Boston. It'll be a big sacrifice for the family. You'll probably miss a few lacrosse and soccer games during the week, but you sound committed to make this work," Clay commented.

"You're right about the distance, but I've got this train thing between Boston and Fayetteville pretty well figured out. It's really an efficient way to travel, especially when I can sleep on the train. It's not Delta or Continental, but it works pretty well, and it's a whole lot easier on the wallet than flying. I can get back to Boston on the overnight train, make homecoming or a lacrosse game, and spend some time working in Boston if I want to."

"I didn't think about your folks at Liberty. I'm sure you'll send shockwaves through the firm if you leave," Clay mentioned.

"I've thought about that as well. It will take some time to completely get out of the investment-banking world, so I'll work out an arrangement with the partners to keep my ties with the firm, at least for a period of time. Who knows? I may be able to operate a satellite office from North Carolina. Raleigh sounds like a good spot. It'll be tough to just completely cut the cord from Liberty. This whole farm enterprise could go bust one day, and I might need a place to start over again," Will admitted.

"I think you're ready. I'm excited for you," Clay said. "Just don't beat us up too bad on the price."

"Like I always tell my clients, the numbers have to pencil out on both sides for it to make sense," Will said as he finished his last sip of coffee from his to-go cup.

"So, what's your time-line, Wilbur?" Clay asked, using his brother's nickname from their high school and college days.

"I think it makes sense to move pretty fast before we list the property with Hughes, the land and timber guy we met," Will responded. "If we can't come to terms on a price in a couple of weeks, then the logical thing to do is list the property with the realtor."

"I'm sure we'll be able to work out a deal, as long as your price is more than fifteen hundred an acre," Clay commented.

"I'll be north of fifteen hundred, but less than eighteen," Will suggested. "I hope that will get it done."

"I'm sure it will, as far as I'm concerned," Clay revealed.

"I plan on sending an e-mail to all the cousins in the next couple of days after I talk to some lenders. I hope I can find some favorable low-interest farm loans to finance the purchase. I'm not real sure how good I feel about carrying a million-dollar note, but I guess that's what it takes to buy a business these days."

"Welcome to the big leagues. Keep me posted. I'm pumped," Clay said.

"All right, I've taken up enough of your time with this idea," Will said, as he made his way north past Plymouth toward downtown Boston. "Thanks for your input. I guess it's time for the games to begin."

The Offer

Chapter 24

Will had walked the halls of Liberty Capital Trust with a different perspective this past week. He was more perceptive of the comfortable surroundings he had called home for the second half of his life. The artwork, the lavish reception area with the hardwood floor covering, the spacious plush private offices, the panoramic views of downtown Boston from the twelfth floor of the office tower, and particularly the people in the firm were all reminders of what he might let go of if he moved forward with the purchase of Winfield Farm.

Twenty-two years? Maybe it was time to move on. He'd had a good run here, but was this really where he saw himself for another twenty-two years? It's been a great place to work, but maybe he'd reached his peak here. He was not in a position to one day be the managing partner. He'd been too busy with his head down, trying to make money as a producer, that he'd shunned any potential leadership opportunities. Plus, he hadn't kissed the right rings to be the man in charge here one day. He wasn't sure that's really what he wanted, either. Perhaps it was time for him to return to his roots and start something new. The investment business has become stale and not near as much fun as it used to be. It would be tough to leave, but twenty-two years is a long time to be with the same firm. Will continued to debate with himself as he stood in his office staring out the window into Boston Harbor. He'd miss this view, and he knew that he'd miss the city, but he'd still have Cape Cod and Marblehead to come home to.

Will sat down at his desk. It was a few minutes after six. He drafted an e-mail to his cousins and brother. He started by summarizing the results of the auction that had been held five days ago. The inability to reach the minimum price per acre, coupled with the uncertainty of how long it would take to sell the property after listing the property with a real estate firm, was the ideal preemptive into Will's next paragraph:

AFTER MUCH THOUGHT ABOUT HOW WE CAN ACHIEVE A SALE IN A TIMELY MANNER, I HAVE DECIDED TO MAKE AN OFFER TO PURCHASE THE FARM BASED ON THE TERMS I HAVE OUTLINED IN THE ATTACHED LETTER OF INTENT.

I HAVE OFFERED A FAIR PRICE AND DO NOT WANT TO SPEND YOUR TIME OR MINE NEGOTI- ATING THE PRICE. BASED ON THE UNCERTAINTY OF A SALE IN THE NEAR FUTURE AND THE UNKNOWN OF WHAT PRICE THE PROPERTY MAY BRING, I AM WILLING TO CLOSE IN THE NEXT 30 DAYS.

A TIMELY SALE WILL AVOID THE BURDEN OF HAVING TO WRITE A CHECK TO COVER THE PENDING ESTATE TAX OBLIGATIONS WE ALL HAVE TO FACE. I HOPE YOU FIND THESE TERMS ACCEPTABLE SO WE CAN MOVE FORWARD WITH A CONTRACT.

WILL

Will attached the letter of intent he had prepared earlier in the day to the e-mail, read the wording again, and hesitated. He took a deep breath and stretched his arms behind his back. "Here it goes," he whispered. He tapped the send button on his laptop. This was the start of the second half of his life. He stood and looked out the window in his office.

He tried to focus on his next task at hand, but it was difficult. He had an uneasy feeling inside, but it soon passed, and he felt no remorse. The cousins could always say no, Will reasoned. He sat back down at his computer and pulled up a spreadsheet outlining the last three years of financial data on a biotech firm located in the Quincy area of south Boston. Time to get back to work. Within minutes of starting the analysis of the revenues on the Excel spreadsheet, his cell phone rang. It was Henry.

Henry did not identify himself or even say hello. As soon as Will answered, his cousin bellowed, "You sneaky bastard! You should have saved us the agony of the auction and just made your intentions known when we all met after the funeral."

Will walked around his desk and quietly closed the office door. Rarely did he close his office door, but this conversation was definitely one he did not want heard around the office. Though it was after six o'clock, plenty of Liberty personnel were still working or might walk by Will's office on their way home.

"Honestly, it was the farthest thing from my mind at the time," he explained. "I was, and still am for that matter, the least likely candidate of the cousins to buy the farm. The idea hit me when the train left Fayetteville just last Saturday night." Henry laughed in the same way Will remembered from his cousin's teenage years. The familiar sound of his distinctive laugh took Will back to his childhood days.

"You may be the least likely of us to buy the farm, with one exception," Henry said. "You have the resources to buy it."

"We'll see about that. It all depends on the price," Will proclaimed, now taking himself out of the role of Henry's cousin and placing himself in the negotiating position as a buyer.

"What if we say yes?" Henry asked. "Are you prepared to close quickly?"

"Oh yeah, I've already talked to a few banks. I'll be in debt up to my eye-balls, but I'll be ready," Will replied. Henry laughed again, and Will sensed his cousin's excitement. The enthusiasm stemmed from the fact that someone in the Winfield family might buy and keep the farm in the family. Henry, like Will, seemed to have more sentimental attachments to the farm than the other cousins. Or, maybe, as the oldest cousin, Henry was just more vocal about his love for the farm.

"This is exciting," Henry said in his eastern North Carolina accent. "I gotta tell you though, I'm a little jealous. I wish I was in a little better health to be in your shoes."

"There is still a chance for you to partner with me. You and I could own it together. You know a whole lot more about farming than I do," Will offered. "Think about it."

"That's a tempting offer, but I don't think I'd be a good partner, certainly not an equal partner."

"Well, I'm serious about some ownership, if you're interested. Either way, I'll need your help and advice running the farm. You know a whole lot more about farming than I do," Will offered. He stood with his back to the closed office door, watching a cargo ship slowly make its way toward the shipping docks.

"I can't commit to invest, but I'll be over there as much as you need me. You might get tired of seeing me over there, if I feel up to making the trip," Henry shared. "So, tell me, do you plan to hire someone to run the farm and still live in Boston, or will you be moving the family down here to the farm?"

"I'm still trying to figure that part out. One thing's for sure, there's no way in hell I'll convince Cat to move to the farm. Right now, my thoughts are to spend most of the week on the farm and take the train home on the weekends. I'd like to keep an office at Liberty and continue working in the investment banking business part-time, if I can make it work. The reality is that I'm sure I'll be at the farm most of the time, especially during the first six months during the harvest season, and to learn the business."

"This is really exciting!" Henry commented, exhilaration in his voice. "Part of me can't believe it. I'm excited for you, and for the Winfield family. Young Wilbur is coming home!"

"I'm excited as well, but nervous at the same time."

"It's a huge lifestyle change," Will conveyed.

"So, what *does* Catherine have to say about all this?"

Will hesitated. "I haven't told her yet. I don't want to say anything until the details are final. Shoot, I'm not sure the sellers will accept my offer. They can be pretty stubborn, I'm told," Will said with a nervous laugh.

"We'll work something out." Henry said with confidence. "Let me assure you that we'll find some middle ground on the price you've offered. You're stealing it from us, but I think I speak for the seven of us, that we don't want to drag out the sale. This property could sit on the market for eighteen months ... easy. So, you better get home and tell your wife to start packing her things. She's gonna be a farmer's wife."

Will winced at the words. Cat as the wife of a farmer represented an oxymoron of extreme degrees. "You guys go easy on me. If you'll agree to my price, I'll make sure all of the cousins still have visiting privileges at the farm," Will joked. Henry laughed.

"You get ready, 'cause I'm going to start working on the others right away," Henry said. "Give us the weekend to discuss the offer, but his is an opportunity we can't afford to miss."

The two said their good-byes, and Will clicked off and placed his cell phone on the desk beside his briefcase. He stood next to the credenza positioned against the exterior glass, overlooking the harbor. Reviewing the spreadsheet on his computer screen was now the farthest thing from his mind. He wondered if his offer price of fifteen hundred an acre was too high. Henry made it sound like this transaction was already done. Though the price was significantly lower than the auction minimum the cousins had set, it seemed all too easy so far. Mentally, Will was prepared to go as high as seventeen hundred per acre or around $1.8 million in total, but how would the cousins respond?

The wait had officially started. Will checked his e-mail to see if any of the other cousins had responded to his offer. Farrell, Owen, and Virginia had all sent him e-mail messages. The responses were for the most part positive. Farrell was the only one to make a comment on the pricing.

"THIS IS EXCITING AND INTERESTING. NOT SURE IF WE CAN SELL AT THIS PRICE, BUT WE'LL TALK TONIGHT AMONG OURSELVES AND GET BACK TO YOU AS SOON AS WE CAN."

Will called Clay on his cell phone to discuss Will's offer.

"Taking your portion out of the total price makes sense to me," Clay said. "Showing a lower sales price by reducing your percentage helps us on the capital gains for tax purposes. That's real money to the seven of us. You know I'll do what I can to help facilitate the sale. I'm in a slightly conflicted position, you know, wanting to bolster the price, but also hoping you get favorable terms."

"If this thing's meant to be, it'll happen, and we'll agree on a fair price," Will stated.

"Fair is a relative term. You are definitely positioned to buy the farm at a deep discount from where pricing was three years ago, according to what Ben and the realtors told us."

"I've been overpaying for everything I own for the last twenty years. Stocks, furniture, my house, jewelry, you name it. It's time for me to make a value play. I'm due."

"Well, I'm sure you knocked a few of our cousins off their chairs today when you sent out the e-mail," Clay commented. "Personally, I think the sale to you makes sense for all of us on a number of levels. We could all be here next August after paying the estate taxes and without an offer, asking ourselves why we didn't take your offer when we had the chance."

"Maybe I should wait a year and offer you guys twelve hundred an acre," Will joked. After the call, Will sat down at his desk, reading other e-mails that had hit his computer since he sent out the offer letter. Until the official response came from the cousins, it would be difficult to concentrate on work and make any new calls on prospects, but Will's diligence took over, and he went back to work on his spreadsheet.

By 7:10 that night, Will decided it was time to go home. The waiting game would continue. Mentioning anything about today's offer to Cat and the girls was not going to happen. As far as the family was concerned, it would be another typical Thursday night at the Jordan house.

Will left the office, torn between his excitement at the chance to buy the farm and the uncertainty how his offer would be received by the cousins. The next few days would require an exercise in patience.

The Negotiation

Chapter 25

Henry's call came to Will's cell phone four days after he had sent the offer letter to buy the farm from the Winfield cousins. It was Monday evening, shortly after six o'clock. Will sat in his office, responding to e-mails. "I was wondering if I was going to hear back from you," he joked. "I thought maybe you guys had decided to list the property with the realtor."

"Believe me, this is harder than I thought, coordinating seven different opinions and schedules to come up with a consensus. Wilbur, we're all family here, so we're not going to respond to your offer in writing," Henry started the conversation.

Will's heart skipped a beat but sat up straight in his chair and listened as Henry continued.

"I'm going to tell you verbally what we can do. We had some varying opinions between the seven of us, but I think your brother and I convinced everyone to respond with one number, so we don't have to negotiate back and forth for the next two weeks. We're probably crazy, but because it's you and not some random buyer, we are willing to let the farm go for sixteen-fifty per acre. You think about that, or let me know right now if you think that amount is acceptable."

Will pulled the calculator from his desk drawer and began punching in numbers after Henry conveyed the counter-offer. "Sixteen hundred is as high as I'll go," Will responded. Silence lingered on both ends of the phone. Will had learned different styles of negotiating in his years of working for buyers and sellers of various sized businesses. *State your price and don't apologize or try to explain it.* He held firm to this premise of negotiating. In his mind, he had prepared himself to pay up to sixteen-fifty per acre, even as high as seventeen hundred, but he thought he would have a little fun with Henry and test his negotiating skills. He waited for a response.

Henry finally broke the silence. "Damn, Wilbur. This is your cousin you're talking to, not some hot-shot New England businessman with a multi-billion dollar company he's trying to sell. Go easy on us."

"At sixteen hundred an acre, that yields each cousin an even two hundred and twenty thousand," Will commented. "This is a strong offer, so that's my final number."

"Let me get back in touch with the others and see if they'll agree. You drive a hard bargain, Will. I guess you know too much about our position," Henry stated in a frustrated tone, now anything but his usual jovial self. "You know how desperate we are to sell. This just isn't a fair negotiation."

"Okay, you guys let me know. I can close in less than thirty days," Will said casually as the call came to an end. *Thirty days?* That's daunting. He was telling Henry that he could close in less than thirty days, and he hadn't even told Cat that he was considering this purchase! On the ride home from the office that night, Will contemplated a course of action. When would be the right time to tell Cat and the girls about this acquisition? How would they respond, particularly Cat? Should he tell them each individually or when we're all together? How would he spin it? Was this simply an investment he could oversee from Boston or was this purchase a permanent move that would require him to be on the farm seven days a week? Maybe Cat would like the idea of him being gone during the week and home on the weekends. Maybe the separation during the week could possibly help the marriage. Does absence really make the heart grow fonder? He was convinced that Sarah and Lauren would take the news just fine. It was Cat's anticipated response that caused him anxiety.

As Will approached Marblehead on his northbound drive on Highway 1-A, he made the decision to set up a family dinner on Friday night at Tedesco and break the news then. Their weekend plans were to go to Cape Cod on Saturday, so a Friday night dinner would be the perfect place to drop the news on the family. He couldn't allow his excitement for this acquisition be tempered by Cat's response. She knew he'd been unsettled for a while with work. Surely she would understand and support his decision, he theorized. Will's phone rang. He was sure it was Catherine calling to ask when he would be home. However, it was Henry. "Tell me we've got a deal, Henry."

"We do ... I think. We've got everyone on board but Owen. He wants to hold out for sixteen twenty-five an acre," Henry explained, appearing exhausted from his efforts to garner a consensus from the other six cousins.

"You've got the votes to sell at sixteen hundred, so outvote him," Will stated. "My position hasn't changed. I'm holding firm at sixteen hundred. That's as much as I'll pay." The phone went silent for three seconds, which felt like three minutes.

"Okay, you stubborn son of a bitch," Henry remarked in frustration. "We'll sell at sixteen hundred an acre, but we want assurances you'll close. You could change your mind next week. We can see Catherine convincing you this is not a good idea. It's no secret how strong-willed she is."

"Don't worry, Henry. I'm committed. I'll draw up a purchase contract for one million five hundred and forty thousand. I've already committed that amount to memory based on a sales price of sixteen hundred an acre, less my portion. I've got a lot of work to do, including the financing part, but I'm not going to bail out. I've talked to several lenders here in Boston that I have relationships with, but I'm going to do some research on low interest farm loans with banks in Bladen County as well."

"Well, keep us posted, and we'll look out for the contract early next week," Henry requested.

"Will do," Will said. "I appreciate your hard work in coordinating the sales price with the cousins. I know some of them can be stubborn, like the Winfield's. After all, I'm one of them!" Will laughed.

"I'm just glad we got it done," he sighed. "Now it's up to you to perform. Your brother says you've got the resources to pull this off. I hope that's the case. We're counting on you."

"Let me assure you, I've been saving for this day for a long time. As Clay may have told you, I've looked at a number of businesses to buy over the last few years, but I never found the right one. Although the farm's a long way from here, it's the perfect combination of a business I know a little bit about and a way to reconnect with my home state. Believe me when I tell you, I'm pumped about this opportunity."

"This is exciting for all of us. Keeping the farm in the family for another generation is something you can't put a price-tag on, but this sale feels a little like the Louisiana Purchase. Remember the French sold the United States all that land along the Mississippi River for pennies on the dollar. Well, this is the Winfield version of the Louisiana Purchase," Henry laughed. "But seriously, I'll help you any way I can, especially in the transition."

"I appreciate that," Will said, feeling a little guilty for driving such a hard bargain with Henry and the other cousins. Before the two hung up, he inquired about Henry's health. Henry shared with Will details of his upcoming treatments. The timing of this move may be ideal, Will thought, knowing he would be able to visit Henry on occasion, with the farm and Carolina Beach being a little more than an hour's drive apart. It would be good to be around him to offer support while he and Laura are dealing with all this.

The plans were set. The negotiations with the cousins were behind him, and he felt ecstatic about the purchase price. Now, he had so much to do, so much to contemplate, plans to make, lenders to contact, and so many people to tell. Most of Will's friends and colleagues would be excited for a new chapter in his life, but telling Cat was the one person who would receive the news less than favorably.

The Announcement

Chapter 26

Will went to work immediately on the sales contract from his home office in Marblehead. On Tuesday morning, he sent the documents for review to Sam Andrews, a Boston attorney that he used frequently for M & A transactions. Sam was instructed to keep this acquisition quiet until Will made his announcements to Catherine, her family, and Will's co-workers at Liberty Capital Trust.

As the sales contract was being finalized, Will's excitement built. Focusing on his deals at Liberty became more difficult as he made plans to close on the purchase of the farm in mid-September. He thought of ways to balance his work life between two jobs in different regions of the country. More importantly, he struggled with maintaining his familial obligations in Boston while living twelve hundred miles away during the week. He reasoned in his mind that the girls were at the age where they did not need their dad's influence and presence like they had in their younger years. After all, Sara and Lauren would both be in high school next month. The girls didn't need him around the house any more, except to feed their bank accounts, he reasoned. The contracts were sent via overnight mail to Henry on Thursday, with instructions to sign the documents and ship the contracts to the next cousin for signature.

Finally Friday arrived. Will had prepared a speech in his head over and over throughout the week in anticipation of the dinner at Tedesco in Marblehead. Conveying his news to his partners at Liberty would be easy compared to the backlash he anticipated from his wife. So, before he left the office to get home for tonight's dinner with the family, Will decided to meet with Liberty Trust's managing partner, Stuart Peterson. He wanted to let him know his plans, and still maintain his ties with Liberty. Was he kidding himself? Was he really going to be able to keep working for Liberty while he ran the farm? Would the partners let him keep an office here? Maybe they'd let him open a southeast regional office in North Carolina.

He walked down the hall and spoke with Emily, Stuart Peterson's personal assistant, to make sure Stuart would be in the office later this afternoon for a short meeting. Emily indicated he was available around four o'clock. On the way back down the hall, he stopped in to speak to Martin Sanders, one of Will's contemporaries at Liberty Capital.

"Hey, Sandbag, you got plans for lunch today?" Will asked as he stuck his head in the threshold of Martin's office door. Martin's office was four doors down from Will's office, and based on their mutual love for sports, the two had become fast friends when Martin had joined the firm seven years earlier. Martin was a hard-charging investment banker who focused his practice on buying and selling financial advisory and insurance firms. He had grown up outside of Boston in the western part of Massachusetts, attended Colgate University in Hamilton, New York, on a lacrosse scholarship, and returned to Boston to get his MBA from Harvard Business School. He was in his late thirties, and although six or seven years younger, Will considered Martin one of his closest friends in the firm.

"Yeah, I'm open. You wanna' walk down to the deli?" Martin replied to Will's offer for lunch. "I think you owe me lunch from the bet we had on the Sox-Yanks game."

"Oh really?" Will replied. "I didn't know we actually had a bet. I just said the Yankees would win the series. I know we didn't shake on it."

"Never bet against the home team," Martin warned. "I keep tellin' you that, Tar Heel."

"Yeah, yeah. I'll walk down a little before twelve and we'll go," Will said, turning away from Martin's office.

"Sounds good," Martin confirmed.

As he sat back down at his desk, Will found it difficult to concentrate on his current M & A projects. He looked over his list of prospects and active deals that he kept on his computer. He calculated in his head the time-line it would take to close some of the business he had in his pipeline, but his focus today was clearly on starting a new career in farming. He felt confident that his business-minded approach and hard work would help grow the farm's revenues. He clicked from his valuation spreadsheet for the sale of an automotive supply business in Maine to a Google search for articles on cattle farming. While on the internet, he subscribed to an online farm publication, joined the North Carolina Farm Bureau, and ordered two books on soybean and cattle farming, determined to get his hands on any reading material that would help him learn his new trade and maintain a successful farm operation. Before lunch, he studied the tax credits offered by the State of North Carolina for a possible solar installation in one of the idle fields at Winfield Farm. Based on his research, the opportunities in farming today were endless, and Will's excitement built with each new piece of information he attained. He had not generated this kind of excitement working on an investment-banking project in years. The purchase of Winfield Farm is just what he'd needed for the last few years to generate some excitement in his professional life. It was going to be awesome! Why should he be timid about telling anyone about what his plans were.

The lunch hour arrived and Will walked toward Martin's office with a new spring in his step. "Let's go, Sandbag," Will said, sticking his head in the door. Will had labeled Martin with the nickname, "Sandbag" two years ago after Martin became notorious for under-estimating his production numbers year after year. Every year, Martin poor-mouthed his pipeline until the fourth quarter arrived. After Peterson ranked the company's producers for fee income generated at the end of the year, Martin's commissions positioned him among the top producers in the company for a string of successive years. For his annual bemoaning, Will appropriately tagged him Sandbag, and the nickname stuck among the Liberty Capital hallways.

Now face to face with Martin at the deli, Will turned the conversation from sports and sales transactions to a more serious tone. "Sandbag, I haven't told anyone at the firm yet, but I wanted to let you know that it looks like I'll be leaving Liberty next month."

"What?" Martin stared at him, dumbfounded. "Did another shop give you one of those massive signing bonuses?"

"Not hardly," Will said, shaking his head. "I'm getting out of the business altogether. I've had a chance to buy my family's farm in North Carolina. It's a great opportunity, and it's no secret that I've been burned out of the M & A world for the last three years. "

"You're freakin' kidding me, right?" Martin replied, placing his roast beef sandwich down on the plate. "That's awesome news! You're headed home, Tar Heel. I had you pegged as a lifer here at Liberty, but that North Carolina noose you had around your neck was always tugging at you. I can't believe it. I'm happy for you, bro."

"Thanks, I'm fired up about it," Will admitted. "It's what I need at this stage of my life. I kept asking myself if I saw myself sticking around Liberty like some of the long-termers, and I just didn't see it. I haven't been having as much fun in the business over the last two to three years. Maybe I'm selling out, but this opportunity to buy the farm at a discount from my cousins just fell in my lap. I never saw myself doing something like this. Guess I'm not exactly the farming type, but I looked at the numbers, and the farm is already profitable, and has some real upside. Plus, I'll be the fourth generation family member to run the farm, and keeping it in the family had a big part to do with the decision as well."

"So, what's Cat got to say about all this?" Martin asked. "I can't see her moving to North Carolina, much less to live on a farm."

"You're right. She won't move. I plan to commute by train every week. It'll be hell, but I've thought it all through. I'll make it work."

"So, what did Catherine say when you dropped the atom bomb on her?"

Will looked his friend and hesitated before giving Martin an answer. "I'm telling Cat and the girls tonight. This news is brand new. I just finalized the sales contract last night. I didn't want to tell her before I knew we had a deal."

"Damn, you made a decision like that without even consulting with her? I'm sure you're dropping a big part of your nut on buying this place. Man, I can't even buy ticket to a Pats' game without at least talking it over with Diana."

"I know, but Cat would shut down the idea at the first mention of investing in a farm. She only knows Boston and the financial world. That's all she's ever known, with her dad being in the business, and me working here for the last twenty-two years. With her, it's all about me working at the right place, bringing in a good income, and not rocking her world. I'm not looking forward to breaking the news tonight, but I'm sure she'll support me. She knows I've been frustrated with work for quite a while now."

"I'm sure she'll understand," Martin empathized. "Hell, look at the consulting guys we know. They're on the road all week. They show up with a suitcase full of dirty underwear on Friday night and pack the same bag for a flight out on Sunday or Monday. You'll make it work."

"She won't like it, but she probably won't mind me being gone. A little time away won't be a bad thing for us. We've been raising kids for the last eighteen years. She'll probably like the fact that I'm gone during the week. Truthfully, her only concern will be how we're going to maintain our lifestyle on a farmer's income," Will laughed without humor.

"I know her roots are deep up there in Marblehead. You guys have a good life up there. You got the in-laws' place at the Cape and access to her old man's Sox tickets. You got a helluva set-up. I'm sure she doesn't want to leave all that and move her ass to rural North Carolina."

"You're right," Will agreed. "I do have a good life in Marblehead and two girls that mean the world to me. I don't want to uproot their lives. I look at it like having the best of both worlds. I get to make a living in my home state, but I can still call Marblehead home."

"How far will you be from Chapel Hill? I guess you'll get to see your Heels play hoops all the time," Martin smiled.

"The farm is a good three hours from campus, but I've already thought that through," Will grinned. "I can drive up there for a few Wednesday night games when the basketball season starts."

"Yeah, so let's talk about those tickets to the Sox games your father-in-law sets you up with. Don't forget about your buddy, Sandbag, busting ass here at Liberty without you around to harass me," Martin joked.

"Those Sox tickets aren't going anywhere, unless Cat decides to divorce me over this decision. You and I can still make some games on the weekends when I'm in town. I promise you that! Next spring, we'll pick one of the good home stands, maybe with the Yankees. I'll make that happen."

"Now you're talking, Tar Heel. Hey, seriously, I can help you with some of your deals to get them to the closing table. You were always the independent son of a bitch that never needed any help on your deals, but I'm here for you."

"That's part of why I wanted you to buy me lunch today," Will explained. "I'm sure I'll need some help getting what little I have in my pipeline closed. I'm not going to be able to turn off the spigot cold turkey. I'll hopefully be able to keep my e-mail up for a while and stay in the business in some part-time capacity. I'm still trying to figure all that out, but my first priority will be to learn all I can about this farm and push revenues there where it's possible."

"You know I'd be honored to help you. I'll even pay you five percent of everything I close," Martin explained with a serious look on his face.

"That's what I was afraid of, you selfish son of a bitch," Will responded, laughing at Martin's unjust offer. "Let's walk back. I have a lot to take care of with the purchase, and I'm supposed to talk to Peterson at four this afternoon."

"How do you think Peterson is going to take it? He may drop a loaf right there on the thick carpet after hearing he's losing his star twenty-year veteran," Martin commented.

"At least I'm not going to work for a competitor," Will replied. "He doesn't take too well to losing producers to the competition."

The two left the deli and walked back toward State Street. The mid-day August sun forced its way through the towering downtown office buildings, where Boston's central business district was filled with tourists and business people moving like ants through the downtown streets. Will paused to imagine where he might be a month from now. A move to the farm would mean no more long commutes, no more crowds in the central business district, and no more lunches with his associates like Martin. Life as he knew it was about to take a dramatic turn. Was he really prepared to leave this life in Boston, a place he had spent his entire working career? Only time would tell.

Once back in his office, Will rehearsed the pitch he had prepared to give Mr. Peterson this afternoon. Anticipating Peterson's question about his departure date, Will contemplated the time-line of when he would leave Liberty and start his new career in North Carolina. He had thirty days to close on the purchase of the farm, so the financing was the last major hurdle to jump. Henry and the other cousins all agreed that Will had forty-four years to inspect the property, so the Inspection Period in the contract was factored into the thirty-day closing period. A title search was under way but almost unnecessary, given that the property had been in the Winfield family over a hundred and twenty years and touched a span of three centuries.

At a few minutes before 4:00, Will walked down the hall to Mr. Peterson's office. Emily sat outside the office in a desk positioned between Peterson's door and the seating area. Peterson's door was open, so Will could see that the managing partner of the firm was on the phone.

Will took a seat in front of Emily's desk and watched Emily as she typed frantically on her keyboard. She was the quintessential twenty-something that had come to Liberty right out of college as a marketing assistant. Though she had never worked directly with Will, Emily had been an assistant preparing marketing and presentation packages for a group of four or five producers on the IPO underwriting team, until that financial sector wilted. Several moments later, Peterson walked out of his corner office, greeting Will with a smile and a look of apology.

"Sorry Will," he said. "I couldn't shake that guy off the phone. Come on in." He turned to his secretary. "Emily, you can take off when you need to. I know you're trying to get out of town this afternoon." He closed the door as Will settled into one of two chairs positioned in front of Peterson's desk.

"So, how are you seeing things out there, Will?" Peterson asked. "Are the markets improving?"

"It's not bad, maybe slowly getting better," Will replied. "At least people will talk to you now, and the distress sales seem to be dissipating somewhat. Still, the pricing expectations of the buyers are still unrealistic. There's still a big disconnect in price between the buyers and the sellers today."

"That's what I hear," Peterson offered.

"It's late on a Friday, so I'll jump right in as to why I wanted to see you," Will said with a nervous smile. He paused to capture his thoughts, and then began with his well-rehearsed lead-in sentence. "I have a business opportunity to purchase my family's farm in North Carolina. I've negotiated terms with my cousins to buy out their interests. As the new owner, I could hire someone locally and run the farm from up here, but I think it's in my best interest to move down there and oversee the full-time operations of the farm. I'm struggling with leaving the M & A business cold turkey, but I'm committed to make this new venture work. I'll have a large part of my personal resources invested in the farm and also a lot to learn about farming, so I see myself in North Carolina pretty much full time once I close. My family is not going to leave Boston, so I'll be here on weekends, holidays, and for special events for my girls."

Peterson stared at him and he plunged on. "I've had a good run here. It's the only job I've had since leaving business school. Part of me doesn't want to let it go, but I've also hit a wall in my career. I guess I've burned out somewhat, especially in this economy. I love chasing deals. It's in my blood, so I want to leave the door open to come back or work part-time from North Carolina. I've got so many ideas in my head right now, but I'm excited about this new opportunity. It's given me something new to look forward to."

Peterson appeared to collect his thoughts. Finally, he spoke. "Wow, that's a shocker for one, but congratulations on this new venture. So many investment bankers find companies they want to own and run, so they go from the financial advisor to the buyer and operator. We've lost several producers as a result of that formula, but you're taking a different path and pursuing a family business."

Peterson leaned back in his chair. "Let me say this: of all the partners that have sat in the seat you're sitting in now, that have decided to leave the firm, I can only think of one who decided to come back. Still, he left to start his own practice, and then he came back to the firm. It's hard to run your own business and try to generate business for Liberty at the same time. You can't serve two masters. I think you'll find that your new venture needs both hands on the tiller. And in your case, that's *literally* the case," Peterson said, smiling. "But secondly, let me tell you that there will always be a place for you here. You've been a proven and consistent producer for a long time, but more importantly, you represent what this firm has been all about in its sixty-three years of existence - hard work, a good name, doing the right thing, day in and day out. Liberty has prided itself on maintaining a good name in the market, and we've been able to do that with people of your caliber and character."

"Well, thank you," Will said, seriously touched. " These are tough decisions, and leaving Liberty won't be easy. That's why I'm trying to figure out a way to keep a big toe in the water. It's tough to walk away from something you've always known."

"And an income you've become accustom to," Peterson said with a wry smile. "We'll miss you greatly. I wish I could talk you out of it, but it's not like you're leaving to go to work with a competitor. This sounds like a really neat opportunity, and it gets you back home. We'll have to find us another token Southerner to take your place around here. So, tell me, what's your timing?"

"This deal is progressing pretty fast. As you can imagine, my cousins are eager for me to close on the sale as soon as possible. They want their money," Will admitted. "It could be three weeks, no more than a month, so I have some time to close out what I'm doing here and hand off some of the deals I'm pursuing or have in my pipeline. If it's okay, I'd like to keep my e-mail here for an extra thirty days just to stay on top of what I'm trying to finish."

"Absolutely, that's perfectly fine. Whatever you need, Will. So, tell me more about your farm. What crops do you grow?"

"There's quite a long history associated with our farm. My grandfather purchased the farm in the late 1800s and grew corn and tobacco. It was primarily a tobacco farm for sixty or seventy years. My mother grew up on the farm, and my uncle has been running it for the last fifty years. He just died last month. That's what predicated all this. My uncle was never married and left the farm to my cousins and me. I'm taking my percentage and putting it toward my equity in the purchase. That's what makes it financially feasible. My uncle, to his credit, saw that tobacco was falling out of favor several years back, so he diversified the crop rotation. We're heavy in corn right now, which is good, given the demand for corn as an alternative fuel source. We also have a few hundred acres in soybeans, planted pine, and about fifty head of cattle."

"That's quite a large operation, from what little I know about farming, but it sounds like you've been doing your homework. If you approach farming the way you did the M & A business, then you'll be the wealthiest farmer in the state. Tell me, what part of North Carolina is the farm in?"

"Oh, it's very rural. We're in eastern North Carolina, east of I-95, about an hour inland from my hometown of Wilmington."

"A long way from here," Peterson said with a wide grin.

"I've been down a couple of times this summer, once for my uncle's funeral, and the second time to try and auction the farm."

"Sounds like you have your plan in place," Peterson stated. "I'll need to make a formal announcement at some point?"

"I want to make the rounds and let folks here and outside the firm know my plans," Will requested. "So I wouldn't make any announcements for another week or ten days. I also have some loose ends to tie up with the farm purchase before I go public with the news."

"Well, this sounds like a good opportunity, especially since it involves family, and I'm not one to stand in the way of a well thought out plan."

"It'll be a far cry from what I've been doing here for the last twenty-two years," Will stated. "I expect quite an adjustment, both personally and professionally."

"We'll miss you on a number of levels. I hate losing good people, but sometimes it becomes apparent when it's time to move on, especially when opportunity stares you in the face," Peterson said as he stood.

Will followed Peterson's lead and stood as well. He extended his hand as he took a step toward the firm's managing partner.

"You know, Will, it's been said that you can't go home, but for you, this seems like a good move. North Carolina's always been home for you, but you've made a good life for yourself here in New England. It's those damned pretty Yankee girls like Catherine that can change our course," Peterson said with a chuckle. "You'll be a success in whatever you do. I'm certain of that."

"Thank you for taking the time. I knew you would understand. It was not an easy decision, leaving a place where you've spent half your life."

"So, how *is* Catherine with this decision?" Peterson asked, as the two stood behind the close door as Will prepared to exit the office.

Will felt the blood rush to his head. He wasn't prepared for the question, so he decided to convey what he anticipated Cat's thoughts would be in three hours when he gave her the news about the farm purchase. "Oh, she's not really on board with the idea just yet. She and I have been talking about a career move for the last two years, but she loves everyone here at the firm, so she doesn't want me to leave. She's still trying to figure out how I'll go from investment banker to farmer overnight. I've been asking myself the same question."

"Will she eventually move down to North Carolina with you once the girls are out of the nest?" Peterson asked.

Will laughed. "Oh, I don't think so. She and the girls will come down and visit during the holidays, and hopefully they'll spend a good bit of next summer there, but I don't see my girls or Cat spending too much time there permanently," Will lied, making it sound like plans had already been discussed with the family.

"From what I know about Catherine, I don't see her living on a farm. Her roots are pretty deep up here, and her father wouldn't want her to stray too far from home."

"You're right about that, Stuart."

"Well, keep me posted on your time-line, and we'll plan a nice send-off for you one afternoon before you leave," Peterson said, extending his hand for a final handshake.

Will opened the door leading out of Peterson's office. Emily had taken the bait and checked out early to start her weekend. He walked down the hall toward his office. Time to make a list of individuals in the firm that he wanted to personally talk to before the word got out about his departure.

The talk with Peterson had gone well, yet it was only a trial run before conveying the news to Cat, Sarah, and Lauren in just a few hours. From a strategic standpoint, Will thought it would be prudent to have his daughters at dinner tonight as a shield to temper Cat's response, especially if she became hostile to the news about the farm purchase. He was ready. He knew the decision to move to the farm would not go over well with Cat, but his excitement over the new venture overshadowed even the most beleaguered response she could possibly contrive.

The Dinner

Chapter 27

The glow of the full moon shed its shadow on the placid blue water of the still surface of the Olympic size swimming pool. A warm summer night served as the sublime backdrop for a family dinner on the deck overlooking the Tedesco Country Club pool. While Sarah and Lauren sipped on soft drinks, Cat enjoyed her favorite summer vodka drink, mixed with cranberry juice and pink lemonade. Sitting on Cat's right flank, Will drained his first glass of beer in an effort to quench his thirst and, more intently, to prepare himself for the rehearsed speech he was prepared to deliver tonight.

He contemplated at what point during the meal he should break the news. He figured early in the evening, before the food was served, was the most prudent time to convey his plans. He leaned forward and looked squarely at Lauren first. "I have some big news I want to share with you guys tonight." His eyes darted quickly toward Cat, who sat to his left. He paused momentarily and looked at Sarah, his oldest, as he continued. "I've worked at the same place for the last twenty-two years, which is rare for anyone my age. We've been fortunate as a family. Many of my friends have been laid off or lost their jobs in the last few years. However, the last few years have been challenging in my industry, and I have struggled, not so much financially, but with what I want to do with the rest of my life. It's a lot like school. If you went to the same school since kindergarten, you'd eventually get tired of it. It might be the best school in New England, but at some point, it's time to go off to college or do something else. Move to a different school, even move to a different state, like Sarah is considering."

He looked at Sarah and Lauren as he spoke, hoping that his school metaphor would resonate with the girls. The girls could tell he was serious and hung on every word. "As you guys know, I've been to North Carolina twice now this summer. Once for my uncle's funeral, and the second time to try to sell the family farm at auction. The farm didn't sell, so I started thinking about buying it myself." There, it was out. He now focused more on Cat and her reaction. He had seen that look on Cat's face too many times to count, a look of fear, preparing herself for news she did not want to hear. Her mouth moved from a neutral response to a frown, and her brow began to furrow. Her green eyes widened with curiosity. He plunged on. "I know sometimes you guys get tired of hearing about it, but that farm represents everything about my childhood and my roots in North Carolina. I compare the farm to our family's place at Cape Cod. The farm is where my cousins and I spent our summers together. It's where my mom's side of the family got together for holidays, and where my grandmother raised a huge family. My grandparents, aunts, uncles, and cousins would all meet there, just like we do at the Cape. We had great memories of that place." His voice softened. "*I* have great memories of that place. Since I've been back, I've realized what a big part of me I left behind there." He leaned back in his chair. "So, forgive me for making this so dramatic," he continued, emphasizing the word *dramatic* so the girls could relate, "but I didn't want to let our farm get sold to just anyone, so I've made plans to buy the farm and run it."

He darted a glance at his wife. Her countenance had now turned from fear to shock. Before Cat or the girls could interject, he continued. "So what does this mean for all of you? First, let me assure you, we're not moving, but I'll spend most of my time down there during the weekdays. I want to be home on the weekends to be with you guys. I'll be home for soccer and lacrosse tournaments when I can, but I won't be around much during the week. I'd love it if you guys would spend some time down there in the summer and around the holidays."

His family sat speechless and he rushed on. "Let me just say this ... your life will not change, and I'm going to make the extra effort to be here in Marblehead as much as I possibly can." He sat upright in his chair and took a deep breath. He felt he had done a good job of conveying his thoughts about his current job, what the farm represented in his own life, and how this news affected the family. He looked at Cat.

"When is this all supposed to happen?" she asked, her tone conveying displeasure.

"Pretty quick, like next month," he responded.

She lifted a brow and grimaced. "I had no idea this was something you were even thinking about. You haven't mentioned any of this to us!"

"I know, but I didn't want you to get worked up about it, if it didn't happen. I *just* worked out the final terms with the cousins a few nights ago. It wasn't an easy decision, but you knew there was a change coming at some point with my job."

"A change maybe, but I didn't see a tsunami coming," she snapped. "You're dropping a bomb on us, Will. This is a shocker, to say the least."

"Maybe it was a mistake telling all of you at the same time, but we're a family, and I wanted to tell you while we're all together."

"I think it's neat, Dad," Lauren interjected. "You have to do what makes you happy." Will wanted to reach across the table and kiss his youngest daughter on the cheek. At least one of his three girls was supportive of his decision. "Sarah, any thoughts?"

"No, not really," she shrugged. "I guess we should be happy for you, but we'll miss you not being here all the time. You work a lot now, but this will be like you're on a business trip every week. I guess I'm the least impacted, since I'll be off at school a year from now. I'm excited for you, if this is something that you really want to do." She nodded, glancing back and forth between her parents.

"Yes, this is what I really want to do, for now. I may find that it's too far away, and the train trips back and forth might get old. I might realize that I miss the investment banking business and could find someone to run the farm. I could be back here in Boston working for Liberty again in twelve months. Who knows? It may turn out that I don't like farming. I could always sell the farm, if things don't work out. Part of the reason I decided to buy it was the price. Uncle Clay and my cousins were eager to sell, so they gave me a good price. Owning the farm could be permanent, or maybe not. Either way, it's an investment I feel really good about."

"A farm?" Cat gasped. "Of all things you could have invested in, I can't imagine a farm as a great investment. I thought farmers were struggling these days ... going broke." She lifted her glass and finished off her Pink Drink, the name the family called her vodka drinks.

"Let me assure you, the farm is profitable," Will stated confidently. "I've seen the numbers, and this farm is not going broke."

The waiter appeared. "You folks ready to order?" he asked.

"For starters, Mike, I'll have another vodka and pink lemonade with a splash of cranberry, please," Cat requested. "And tell Herman to make this next one a little bit stronger."

"Anybody else for drinks?" Mike inquired.

"I'll have another beer," Will said, raising his empty bottle to identify the brand. "And I think we better go ahead and order our food as well."

Mike took the family's food order and collected the menus, and Will decided it was time to change the subject. He asked Sarah about taking a few more college visits before her last semester of school started in three weeks. Keeping Lauren engaged in the conversation about colleges as well, Will asked her opinion of possible schools she'd like to attend after high school. Cat offered nothing to the conversation, but ate her salad and ordered a third Pink Drink, seething in silence. *The worst is yet to come,* Will thought, preparing himself for the tongue-lashing he would receive when they got home. Cat was not one to cause a scene in public, but once the bedroom door closed, her fury would unleash.

Unleash it did. After the silent treatment had continued on the short car-ride home from the club, Cat's censorship erupted as she got ready for bed. On most nights when she was angry, Cat donned her pajamas, climbed into bed with her iPhone, and turned on the television, zoning Will out completely. Tonight, rage rained like a violent thunderstorm. Her silence broke like a massive dam holding back water from the hundred-year flood plain.

"I don't really care that you're leaving," she hissed. "In fact, I want you to go. I've been raising these girls for the most part on my own for the last eighteen years. I can handle it from here. So, you go on down to your redneck farm. You *need* to be back in North Carolina. You've always put North Carolina above any place on earth and talk about that place like it's heaven on earth. In your mind, Boston never measured up to North Carolina, so that's where you need to live. The thing that pisses me off the most about you, Will, is the fact that you can make a major decision like this, and spend who knows how much, buying a farm in Podunk, North Carolina, without even running the idea by me first. That's why I'm blowing steam out of my ears right now."

"Not telling you earlier was a mistake," Will ceded. "I should have talked to you about it beforehand, but I knew you wouldn't like the idea. I should have at least told you the plan before I told the girls. It was a big decision for me and for the family. I thought I would tell you all at the same time."

"I'm your wife, for God's sake," she shouted. "At least for now. Of *course*, you should have told me first! You go on and leave as soon as you can. We'll be fine." Her chest heaved with anger. "This decision is probably for the best anyway. You and I were not going to make it past the next four years. This just confirms what you and I have known for a long time, but we just never talk about it. You go on down to that fricking farm and sit around by yourself. I'm sure you'll be real happy down there all alone. That's fine with us. I'm sure this will be the end of us. It was just a matter of time, Will." She refused to look at him, staring instead at the TV mounted on the bedroom wall.

While Will had certainly felt the wrath of Cat many times before, her anger had vented in massive proportions tonight. He knew all too well that her anger magnified when she was drunk, and the alcohol had fueled her anger. He understood her anger, even expected it. What he had not foreseen was her wrath being this extreme.

Asking Will to leave home now was her defense mechanism to the hurt and rejection she felt, he reasoned. She would still be fiery mad tomorrow morning, but much calmer and less direct. Vodka sometimes made her happy, but it also made her venomous, especially when provoked by adverse news from her husband. At Cat's suggestion, maybe he *should* go ahead and leave now. That idea was not practical, but it did cross his mind.

To break the tension, he left the bedroom and retreated to his home office on the main floor off the living room. He often spent hours alone here after Cat and the girls retired to their rooms at night. The library, as the family called Will's office, was his hiding place from the Household Hormone, a man-eating condition that even New England's best exterminator could not eradicate.

Is she really mad about the fact he hadn't told her any earlier about the decision to buy the farm, or was she mad about the fact that he was taking a different career path that doesn't really include her? Was she worried that he wouldn't keep up my end of the bargain in raising the girls? Was she worried that the move would impact their income and the lifestyle they'd enjoyed for the last fifteen years? If he really boiled it all down, he believed she was really concerned that he was leaving a job that carried a certain amount of prestige, and she didn't want to have to tell her friends that he was leaving Boston to become a farmer. Maybe she'd settle down by tomorrow and realize that this move could be positive on a number of levels. Then again, maybe she saw this decision as the beginning of the end for them. Who knows? Maybe the distance apart would be good for them, but he definitely should have clued her in first before breaking the news to Sarah and Lauren. That was definitely a big mistake.

Will kept his distance from Cat for the rest of the night. As her anger simmered, the vodka induced her into a comatose state and a restful night's sleep. Plans to drive to Cape

Cod tomorrow morning with the family were probably at risk, but Will was determined to keep life on a normal course until he closed on the farm in the middle of next month.

The Cape

Chapter 28

Within a week of the announcement that he was buying a farm, word of his plans began to leak among Cat's friends and family. Simultaneously, Will made a point to tell the associates at Liberty Capital his plans. Some were shocked after Will's two-decade tenure with Liberty Capital, but overall, his co-workers seemed supportive. Cat's parents and sister appeared less enthused and were curious about what would push Will to make such a dramatic career change. When discussing his decision among friends, co-workers, and family, he joked that the job change was the result of a mid-life crisis. Outside of work, his friends seemed to understand the move, but a few questioned how long he could lead two lives in different states and still keep things at home on an even keel.

Aside from the comments and feedback he received after announcing his plans, Will's excitement continued to build while he made the mental transformation from New England investment banker to a rural Southern farmer. He allowed himself ample time to make a smooth transition. He consulted every source he could think of to learn about farming, new trends in agriculture, profitable crops to plant in the future, the challenges that came with planting row-crops, current-day timber prices, possibilities in solar and wind farming, corn by-products like ethanol, and keys to successful cattle farming. Given his financial investment, failure was not an option.

As the start of a new school year approached, Will wanted to ensure that their traditional Labor Day weekend at Cape Cod with Cat's parents and her sister's family was as normal as possible. Early September would mark a dawning of a new era for the Jordan family. Sarah would start her senior year in high school, and Lauren would enter Marblehead High School as a freshman. Will would soon start a new job out of town, and Cat would be left behind in Marblehead to run the Jordan household during the week without her husband.

Cat stayed angry at Will for a solid two weeks leading up to the annual Labor Day weekend at the Key's beach house on Cape Cod. Keeping the peace among her side of the family was Will's only goal as the holiday weekend arrived. "Promise me one thing this weekend, please, Cat," he said. "Let's stay positive about the purchase of the farm. I know you don't agree with the decision, but I need your support. Please be positive for the girls' sake. I don't want them to turn against me as well, based solely on *your* opinion."

"How do you expect me to keep silent about this decision of yours?" she'd argued. "You're right, I don't agree with it. I think it's stupid and was not well thought out. You're running from something, Will, and it's hard for me to support a rash decision on your part, without taking my opinion into account."

"I know how easy it'll be to bash the decision and make me look bad in front of your family, but can we just give it a rest for the weekend and try to enjoy the time off?" he asked.

"Don't worry about that," she responded. "I won't have to say anything to make you look bad in front of my family this weekend. You've lost all credibility with them at this point with this boneheaded move to buy that damn farm. If you want to know the truth, they think you've lost your freaking mind."

"Oh really? That's not exactly the response I got when I talked to your dad. He certainly understood the logic behind the purchase of the farm. He seemed supportive, from what I could tell," Will said, his tone defensive.

"Well, I'm sure he's telling you his business opinion and probably not telling you how he really feels about the decision on a personal level. You don't just leave town like this on a whim without thinking through the consequences and how it impacts those around you, especially those that are supposed to be the closest to you."

"So, is that *your* opinion or his?"

"He's my dad. I know what he thinks," Cat replied snippily.

"I know this is a big decision and a major blow to the life we've been used to, but we'll make it through these next four years," Will said.

"The next four years! You make it sound like the next four weeks when you talk about it. Yeah, and then what happens after the four years is up? We lead separate lives for four years, and then what? You can bet the farm, excuse the pun, that I'm not moving down there with you. You can keep your ass down south, but Boston is my home, and I'm not leaving. You've made it clear how you feel about us, about me, and about the life you're leaving here. I think I'm beginning to get the picture now. This is your exit strategy." Her voice rose as they stood on opposite sides of the kitchen counter that Thursday evening before Labor Day weekend.

"Okay, let's drop it," he suggested. "I know you're not happy about this decision. If I had known it would have caused this much conflict, I might have reconsidered and maybe done things differently. But please, I don't want the girls to hear us arguing about it again."

"It's not going to go away, Will. The girls know my thoughts. They're not little girls anymore. They know what's going on here!"

"They both seemed fine when I talked to them individually earlier this week," Will said.

"Of course they seem okay. They're teenagers, Will! They're into their own lives. What are they really going to tell you? Oh, Dad, please don't go? Plus, you have them pretty well snowed that things will be normal around here, except that you won't be around during the week. You've convinced them that this commute thing is going to work flawlessly, but I can see how it's going to play out. You'll come back the first few weekends, then that long train ride will get to you, and you'll devote yourself to the farm the same way you did to your investment business, except now you'll be ten thousand miles away." She paused, glowering. "The trips home will become less and less frequent, and then you'll miss a few of the girls' events, and that will become the norm. Then, it won't matter, and you would have missed their high school years all together."

"It won't be like that," Will disagreed. "I plan to be back every weekend and leave on the Sunday night train from here every week. I may miss a sporting event or two, but I'll be back for the major things, and I'm counting on you guys coming down to the farm for Thanksgiving."

"You know we spend Thanksgiving with my parents every year," Cat argued.

"I was planning for *everyone* to come down for Thanksgiving. Your parents, sister, and whoever else wants to come. It'll be a fun way to spend Thanksgiving, and good time for them to see the farm, and the kids would love it. Clay and his family can come down from Raleigh. I've already mentioned it to him and to your parents as well."

"Not so fast, farm boy," Cat snapped. "Don't go making plans again without consulting me. You see where that got us before. I'm not real sure that run-down animal house can accommodate all of us, so before you start inviting my family, let's make sure this is something they want to do. It's hard to break family traditions just to accommodate you. That kitchen was ancient and gross when I saw it ten years ago. I can't imagine what kind of shape it's in now," she said, shaking her head in disgust.

"What about starting a new family tradition down south?" Will tried. "We don't have to cook a huge meal like your parents do every year. We can go to the Front Porch restaurant in downtown Elizabethtown or have them cater Thanksgiving at the farm. It's less about the meal and more about the time together with family. Don't you see that this whole move is partially about me trying to stay as connected with *my* family as we are with yours? Clay is the only family I have, besides you and the girls," he argued, trying to appeal to the fact that he rarely saw his brother because of all the time they spent with her family.

"Just keep making plans, but you may be down there all by yourself, so make sure everyone's on board first, including me, before you start making too many plans," Cat suggested.

"I'm not making plans. These are just ideas I thought would be fun. Ideas that keep families together, not destroy them—"

She interrupted. "Let's don't get started with this notion of destroying the family. You've done a pretty damn good job of that already when you decided to buy that farm. I know you're trying to come up with all these ideas to get us to travel to North Carolina out of guilt, but I'm not buying it. You're the one who's destroying our family, not me."

"Okay, I'm not going to win this argument," he sighed. "All I asked for, at the start of this conversation, was that we keep the peace this weekend and enjoy ourselves as a family. Let's don't dwell on the move until we see how it goes. You might just enjoy the fact that I'm out of your hair for most of the week. You can see that tennis pro that you like so much during the week, and I can be your weekend man," he attempted a joke.

"Don't be thinking you can come home on the weekends and jump in the sheets with me. In fact, if you haven't already noticed, you're officially cut off until further notice, maybe forever. I know how you like your Saturday night shag at the beach, but don't come pawing on me this weekend. You're *done* in that department, buster. You made your decision, so I've made mine. You need to get used to that!"

She did something Will had not seen from her in a while – she smiled. She took great pleasure in controlling the physical part of their relationship, and when she made her decision to cut him off for a period of time, she stuck with it for the duration. However, this dispute over the purchase of the farm was of an epic proportion. This was not about him forgetting to take the trash out or coming home late from the office. This was not about him being late for an appointment or forgetting to pick up the girls from soccer practice. This was not a feud over tempers or harsh words. This melee was a battle of the decade for Cat and Will, one that would take more than a week or ten days to heal.

Will resolved that once he left for North Carolina and got into a routine of returning on weekends that the perpetual conflict would ease, and Cat might actually enjoy her time alone without having him around invading her space. As far as the sex part, he would just have to prepare himself for a forty-day drought, maybe longer.

* * *

The heated discussions over the purchase of the farm continued right up to the time the Jordan family arrived on Cape Cod for Labor Day weekend.

"Are you guys arguing about Dad's move again?" Lauren inquired as the family traveled east on Route 6 toward the main bridge leading on to Cape Cod.

"We're not arguing," Cat explained. "We are having a discussion. No one is yelling."

It was Saturday morning of Labor Day weekend and the Jordan's were prepared to join the Key family and Catherine's sister and her family at the Key's beach house in Sandy Neck on Cape Cod. Will and Catherine had learned to avoid the heavy traffic on Fridays in the summertime by driving from Marblehead on Saturday mornings.

"I'm resolved to not talk about the move all weekend," Will stated. "We're here to have fun, so we're going to table any discussions about North Carolina for the rest of the weekend, okay?"

"But, I'm sure Nana will bring it up when we're all sitting down at dinner tonight," Lauren offered. "You know how she likes to ask questions that create conflict."

"And I'll answer their questions, but Mom and I are going to give it a rest for the next three days. Right, Mom?"

"Yes, I'm fine not to talk about it," Cat agreed. "I wish I could ignore it, but have you ever heard the expression, 'there's an elephant in the room'?"

"Okay, but let's ignore the elephant for the weekend," Sarah said, offering her opinion on the subject. "We don't like to see you guys keep arguing about Dad's move. Can we please give it a rest?"

"I'll agree to the truce, but when you're being abandoned, it's hard to stay quiet," Cat remarked, adding fuel to the fire.

"Abandoned?" Will exclaimed. "Abandoned is when you leave your family with nothing and never come back. Abandoned is a little extreme, don't you think?"

"Well, that's the word that keeps going through my head," Cat snipped.

"It's nothing like abandonment, but remember, we're not talking about it, right?" Will stated conclusively as the Jordan family arrived at the beach house. "I'm sure we'll take this abandonment issue up again on Tuesday."

The Jordan's were greeted by Catherine's sister, Elizabeth, and her family, and Cat's parents as they entered the Key family beach house around eleven on Saturday morning. Elizabeth's children, already dressed in their swimsuits, embraced Sarah and Lauren as they came through the front door.

The sun was shining. The beach was calling. The extended family was now assembled. It was the ideal setting for a fun and relaxing Labor Day weekend at Cape Cod, which marked the end of the summer in New England and the rite of passage to a new season of life. In the Northeastern United States, school typically started right after Labor Day. The Key family shut down the old house in East Sandwich after the long weekend, marking the end of one season and the beginning of another.

The old two-story frame house had been built in the 1940s and had been in the Key family since 1957. The beach house had served as a place for the entire family to congregate in the summers. The two-story structure had four bedrooms and a bunkroom in the attic for the younger children. The sleeping arrangements were tight, but the old structure was just big enough to house the ten members of the extended Key family.

Most of Cat's family seemed outwardly supportive of Will's decision, except for Cat's mother. While most on Cat's side of the family understood the logic behind the decision, her mother was rather overt about her disapproval. She had already been influenced by Cat, convinced that the purchase was a bad idea. The thought of leaving Boston for any reason was ludicrous in her mind, but particularly in order to purchase and operate a farm in North Carolina.

Charlotte Key, Will's mother in law, was a Bostonian blue blood from Wakefield, Massachusetts, a smaller town north of Boston and just west of Marblehead. She had been raised in a life of privilege, attended Amherst College, and lived in the northern suburbs of Boston all her life. It was Will's opinion that Mrs. Key did not acknowledge that the United States had forty-nine other states in the union, all with their own attributes. The world, according to Mrs. Key, revolved around the state of Massachusetts. Therefore, Will elected to keep his distance from his mother-in-law during the weekend following a few of her snide remarks about being away from the family during this "critical" time in the girls' lives.

As the family unpacked the Range Rover, Will envisioned what life next Labor Day might be like. The Jordan family had made this Labor Day trip to Cape Cod together for the last eighteen years. There was no reason to believe that all four of them wouldn't be back here next Labor Day weekend. Sarah would be in her first semester of college. Will would make the trip from North Carolina. Lauren would have completed her first year of high school, and Cat would still be mad as hell about the purchase of Winfield Farm. Will was determined to keep the family traditions intact, even though change was imminent over the next twelve months.

With a sigh, he realized that it would take a gallant effort on his part to stay engaged with the family and maintain the traditions the Jordan family had come to enjoy. He equated his new job to that of a soldier on deployment for an overseas tour of duty. Like the soldier, he would leave his home and family to support a cause he believed to be honorable. In his case, the battlefields were the soybean and cornfields, the planted pine, and the cow pastures. The cause was to keep the farm in the Winfield family for another generation, an honorable call, but not without sacrifice.

The Send-Off

Chapter 29

The weekend at Cape Cod had gone as well as could be expected between Will and Cat. Their pledge not to talk about Will's upcoming move had been broken a few times, but Cat's family had an endless array of questions for Will about the farm: his travel schedule between Boston and North Carolina, the crops, the town, and people of Elizabethtown and Bladen County, the timing of his departure, and how the associates at Liberty Capital had reacted to his decision. He was happy to answer all the questions about his new life as a farmer.

At least publicly, Mrs. Key and Cat appeared to be the only dissenting exceptions regarding Will's decision to leave Liberty Capital and pursue the family farming business. At dinner one night over that Labor Day weekend, Mrs. Key made a snide remark about Will being away from the family all week. He dismissed the comment, noting how much Cat and her mother had in common now that Cat had reached her forties. Unless the skeptics were saying something entirely different behind his back, Will's community of friends in Marblehead and his associates at Liberty seemed supportive of his career change.

Friends and business associates in Will's life all seemed to understand his need for a change at this stage of his career. Some even displayed a hint of envy in their voices as Will described his new venture, something entirely different from the daily grind of the investment banking world.

In his last two weeks at Liberty following the Labor Day weekend, questions about the farm came in droves from partners, assistants, producers, and analysts at work.

"Are you going to miss the chase and the deal, Will?"

"Won't you be bored all alone down there by yourself?"

"Do you have employees at the farm?"

"Do you have chickens on your farm?"

"How far is your farm from Chapel Hill?"

Will enjoyed answering the questions and telling his work associates and friends in Marblehead about the farm. As the day of departure approached, the partners and Liberty's office manager planned an afternoon party to allow the firm to honor Will's twenty-two years of service to the company, scheduled for the afternoon before his final day at Liberty. The entire staff of fifty-two was invited.

Will closed on the purchase of the farm on Tuesday, the 11th of September. His last scheduled day at Liberty was to be Friday, the 14th and the send-off event was planned for Thursday, the 13th. Most of the week leading up to his last day at Liberty was spent updating his clients of his plans and sending the word out among the investment banking community of his departure from Liberty. As he surveyed his existing pipeline of business deals, Will carefully assessed where he needed assistance from producers in the firm in closing the sales in progress.

Through the years, Will had forged friendships with many of the principals and dealmakers of New England's private equity firms. He had as much in common with the private equity guys as he did in his own firm. The private equity crowd lived to pursue deals, just like Will. The private equity dealmakers had similar educational backgrounds to Will, and many had MBAs and had started their careers as analysts, assessing company financials, and then evolved into deal junkies - like Will.

The send-off reception for Will was held in the Liberty conference room, but spilled over into the spacious reception area on the twelfth floor of the high-rise office tower on State Street in downtown Boston. Wine, beer, snacks, and finger foods were set up. Hugs and handshakes were the order of day as Will made his way through the crowd, doing his best to speak to every attendee. The event gave Will the chance to say his good-byes, and let the staff know how much he would miss them. The send-off also gave the partners a chance to tell a few funny stories that had taken place in the halls of Liberty Capital over the last twenty-two years. At a few minutes before five o'clock, managing partner Stuart Peterson tapped his wine glass with his wedding ring to get the attention of the crowd. After several pings on the glass, the crowd quieted.

"I need to start by saying that these are not the events we like to host here at Liberty Capital. Some associates here are *asked* to leave, and some leave us to join competing firms. We typically don't have a reception and drink beer and wine when we fire someone or when one of our own decides that there are better places to work here in town. But today, we are here to toast a man that has been with our firm since some of you were in diapers. People leave Liberty for different reasons, but I feel confident in saying that Will Jordan will go down in the history of our company as being the first one to leave us to become a farmer."

His comment elicited a few laughs from the crowd. "When Will approached me about a month ago about his decision, I was crushed because we hate to lose good producers, but more importantly, we hate to lose good people." He stood in front of the crowd of well-wishers gathered to bid Will farewell. "I think we all have dreams. Some have dreams of becoming a partner at Liberty. Others want to retire here. I'm sure many of you have aspirations of taking *my* job," he joked. Again, he received laughter from the crowd. "There are many days I would gladly hand over this position to you. Will has achieved great things in his twenty-two year career at Liberty. He started as an analyst and moved into a producer role within three years. He's been one of our most steady producers for the last fifteen years in a very challenging business. Yes, he's generated an impressive amount of fees for the firm ... and for himself. But I support his decision to leave. Of all the things Will's been able to achieve at Liberty, the most important of all is the good name he built for himself, and his own good name carries over into the reputation Will has helped this firm build in the investment banking space. It's no secret that Will loves his native state of North Carolina. Just walk in his office, and you'll see it's full of UNC paraphernalia. I understand his decision to return to North Carolina to run a business that's been in his family for over a hundred years. That's honorable, and I respect his calling to leave Boston and Liberty Capital to follow that dream."

Will found himself squirming a bit at Peterson's comments, but he hung on every word. He wished Cat could hear these comments. Maybe it was a mistake not to invite her.

"Will, I know you will be successful in your new endeavor, and I know I speak for everyone here in saying we'll miss you, we wish you the best, and there will always be a place for you and your UNC fanfare back here at Liberty, if you ever decide to come back. So, I offer a toast to someone who has made tremendous contributions to the culture of this firm over a span of two decades, and we wish you the best as you head down south!" Peterson lifted his glass of wine.

Will acknowledged Peterson with a tip of his head as murmurs rippled through the crowd in agreement with Peterson's words. Will felt humbled, and at the same time slightly uncomfortable with all the attention directed his way. He looked up to see plastic cups and beer bottles raised toward the ceiling. Peterson's eloquence in the short toast to Will confirmed why he had been tapped as the firm's managing partner nine years ago.

As the toast ended, the crowd looked toward Will. He felt warm tears welling in his eyes. The nostalgia of the moment, the thought of leaving a company he had come to love, floods of favorable memories over a period of two decades, combined with Peterson's kind words, had definitely touched him this afternoon. Peterson nodded toward Will, indicating that it was his turn to say a few words. Will stepped out of the crowd toward the reception desk and joined Mr. Peterson to address the crowd. Beer in hand, Will smiled as he faced the assembly of co-workers that had gathered in his honor.

"First, let me say, thank you for being here today. It means a lot to me. Second, I wish that I was as skilled at speaking as Stuart, but I speak from the heart when I say that I've had a great run here at Liberty. Leaving a place like this is not easy. There is a reason that this firm has enjoyed a strong reputation in the New England market for nearly sixty years. It's the people, and there is a reason people like me stay here as long as I did. It's a great place to work, with a tremendous culture. I've enjoyed the business, and my association with the company, but most of all I've enjoyed the people I've been able to work with here at Liberty over the years. Because this is a local company, we've been able to hire good people, people that respect each other, and get along with each other. We don't have people who are here to advance their own agenda. Liberty has built a company based on solid, hard-working people. That's why the company thrived, and that's why I stayed at Liberty for twenty-two years."

He paused. "I can't say I'll miss the work, but I *will* miss working with all of you. I think Stuart said it well. I'm not leaving here for any reason other than I feel compelled to carry on a family legacy, an opportunity for me to do something different before it's too late. I don't want to look back and regret not taking this chance. Like one of the former partners here told me a few years ago, sometimes the biggest risk in life is not taking a risk at all. I don't want to look back ten years from now and be that guy who wasn't willing to take a risk." Will paused momentarily to survey the crowd. So many faces that represented years of memories for Will looked back at him. "Thank you all. I'd like to give a special thank-you to George, the man who trained me as a green associate and taught me the investment banking business. He taught it to me the right way, the Paulson way," Will said, raising his beer toward his mentor, George Paulson, a career Liberty producer now in his mid-sixties.

Will stepped aside, shook Peterson's hand, and the two embraced after the handshake. Immediately, Will faced a swarm of well-wishers who had lined up to greet him. Was he doing the right thing, leaving this place, he wondered, facing a line of well-wishers.

Within twenty minutes, the crowd had dwindled down to fifteen or twenty attendees. The conversation among those still in attendance had shifted from Will and his departure to discussions about the Red Sox and the Patriots. Will stepped in the conference room in search of something to eat, and noticed two administrative staff members grazing at the conference room table, engaged in a conversation.

"You two aren't back at the desk working again?" Will joked.

"No, we're not going back to work until all the wine is gone," Meghan, one of the assistants, laughed.

"I don't think I'll be staying around for more wine or more work tonight," Cheryl, the senior staff accountant, commented.

Cheryl gave Will a hug. "We'll miss you around here. You brought a level of class to our company. You were well respected for your hard work. I have to admit, I'm a little envious of your situation. I've been working in accounting for so long that I can't get out. We all burn out, even in jobs we're good at. All the best to you, Will."

"Thank you, Cheryl, it's a tough place to leave. The culture here is so good. There are days I wonder if I'm doing the right thing, but like you say, we all burn out at some point. I feel fortunate to have something new to fall back on." He secured a carrot stick from the food tray on the conference room table.

Cheryl walked out of the conference room, leaving Will and Meghan alone. Will and Meghan had not worked together directly, so he searched for words to start a conversation with her. Like Emily, Peterson's assistant, Meghan had survived the lay-offs Liberty had been forced to implement in 2009. She had avoided the round of lay-offs because she was energetic, outgoing, and not afraid to learn new skills within the firm. She was humorous and appeared confident in her interaction with her peers and the partners at Liberty alike. Unlike many of the other young support staff at Liberty, Meghan was not a New England native, but attended college at one of the schools in the Boston area. She had come to Liberty after a two-year stint at Crawford Investments, another investment banking firm, as an administrative assistant for a group of traders, so she had been in the financial services industry all of her short working career.

"You sure shocked some people around here with your decision to leave," Megan said, leaning casually against the grand mahogany conference room table.

"Oh really?" Will remarked, glancing down at the way her boney hips protruded from the gray striped light wool pants she wore.

"Yeah, I think this crowd had you pegged to stay here for the long-haul. The guys around here forget that Boston is not the center of the universe. It's a great city and a nice place to live, but some people *do* have ties to other parts of the world," Meghan said, brushing her dark brown hair away from her face.

"I know you didn't grow up here, but went to school at Babson or one of the local colleges in Boston, right? You don't have the thick accent like the rest of them," Will said, noting the way she sipped wine from the clear plastic cup she held with her long fingers.

"You're right, I went to Babson. Very observant, and you are correct, I'm not from here. I don't tell too many people this, but I'm actually from Nebraska. That's where most of my family still lives."

"Oh, a Cornhusker?"

"Not exactly, at least not me. I had to get out of Nebraska after high school. Dallas and Houston were too close. Denver was cool, and I thought about L.A., but the northeast seemed like more my style, so I came here. I really wanted to go to school in New York, but my dad nixed that idea. He couldn't see sending his only daughter to New York City at eighteen, so we settled on Boston."

"I can relate," Will commented. "I'm going through the same thing with my oldest daughter. She's dying to go to school in New York." Will contemplated why he had never had a more in-depth conversation with Meghan in the past.

She was tall and attractive, but he was drawn more to her uninhibited ability to communicate. She was open and non-threatening, nothing shy about her. "Do you see yourself staying in Boston? It's such a great city."

"For a while. It's not like I've got that many ties to the city. I just broke up with this guy a few months ago, so I'm not tied down, except to my job here, which I really like, but I don't see myself in the corporate world forever," Meghan explained.

Will was amazed at her openness. Maybe she felt compelled to talk more openly since he was leaving. "Do you still want to move to New York?"

She smiled. "I'm not sure. I like going down there for the weekends. It's fun, but I'm not sure I'd want to live there. It's pretty wild."

"So moving back to Nebraska is not an option, I guess?"

"I miss my family, so I go back at least twice a year. It's a little slow for me back home, but it's still home. In fact, my uncle owns a ranch in Oklahoma. I miss going there."

"Cattle, I assume."

"Yep, it's a pretty big ranch. He's kind of like you. He has a day job in Oklahoma City, but the farm is his thing. I think he'd rather be on the farm full-time." She paused and looked straight at him. "So, I want to hear more about *your* farm. I think it's awesome that you're leaving the corporate world to buy a farm, especially a farm that's been in your family so long."

"Really? I thought anyone from your generation would think the idea of moving to a rural part of the world as insane."

"No! I love the idea. I get it. I grew up around wide-open spaces. I miss it. In fact, I'd love to see your farm. It seems like a neat place."

Will couldn't believe she just made the statement about visiting the farm. "You're kidding, right?"

"No, I'm dead serious. I told you I grew up around my uncle's place. I love being out in the open fields. I really do miss it," Meghan said, her tone sincere.

"Do you want a job down there?" he joked. "I may need some help. You probably know as much about farming as I do, especially cattle farming." He looked over his shoulder to insure they were alone in the conference room.

"Don't worry. I'm watching the door. I wouldn't make a statement about visiting the farm in front of the entire firm. In fact, if you're serious about having me, I'll keep it between you and me." Meghan smiled at Will.

Will grew flustered. He was flattered by her interest, but also astounded by her forward statements. Was this her way of baiting him because she was attracted to him, or was she really just interested in the farm? Suddenly, he found himself drawn to her, bonded by a mutual interest in farming, and intrigued by her offer. "Let me tell you, I'd love to have visitors at the farm. I want people to see it. It's a neat place. For someone who likes the outdoors, it's paradise on earth. If you're serious, we'll schedule some time for you to visit. I've got a brother down there who lives two hours away and a cousin who lives on the coast close by, but other than them, I don't know a soul down there, so visitors will be a good thing. It'll really be just me and the cows," Will said, choosing his words carefully.

"I don't want it to be uncomfortable for you, and forgive me for being so forward and inviting myself, but I am really interested ... just to see the farm," Meghan smiled again.

Will sensed nothing suggestive about her comments, although his willful and seductive mind couldn't help contemplating a few days alone with Meghan on his secluded farm in Bladen County, North Carolina. "It's a helluva long haul down there, but we should plan some time for you to come down later in the fall. I've got some work to do on the house, but there's plenty of room in the old farmhouse. You can even bring some of your friends, if you want. It has six bedrooms, but only one bathroom, a typical old farmhouse."

"I'll ask around, but I don't know how many of my friends up here would be interested in visiting a farm in North Carolina, but that's a thought. My crowd here in Boston is a little more into the urban thing, like going to clubs in New York City," Meghan laughed.

"There you are!" Bill Felton, one of the Liberty partners, commented as he pushed his head through the glass door leading into the conference room. "We were wondering if you had already slipped out, Will."

"No, I'm still here, talking a little farming with Meghan," Will responded. "She's telling me about her uncle's farm in Oklahoma. People start telling you all kinds of covert stuff about their lives once you announce you're leaving the company." He turned toward the door and moved in Felton's direction, feeling self-conscious about being caught alone with Meghan in the conference room.

"No worries," Felton replied. "We were just making sure you hadn't already left for North Carolina."

"I'm not *that* eager to leave," Will laughed. "We were just talking shop. Who's left hanging around?"

"A few folks," Felton answered. "In fact, we wanted to keep the party going and take this show on the road downstairs to Houston's or over to Julep Bar."

"Sounds great," Will said. "I'm available." He turned to Meghan. "Meghan, you in?" "Sure," she shrugged.

Meghan's heels clicked along the hardwood floors of the reception area as she followed Will and Felton out of the conference room. A dozen attendees, mostly partners, were left conversing around the reception desk.

"We're headed to Julep Bar for dinner and a few more cocktails, if anyone wants to join us," Felton announced.

Meghan was one of only two females still left at the function. Will checked his watch. It was a little before six o'clock. He had told Cat that he would most likely be out late tonight and not to expect him home for dinner. As the lingering contingency made its way through the double glass doors into the elevator lobby, he fantasized about hanging out with Meghan for the night.

His wish came true as he, Meghan, and five of Liberty's partners left the building and walked to Julep Bar in the Boston financial district for a few more drinks and a light dinner.

By 9:20, the nightcap portion of the send-off was over, and Will was greeted with more departing handshakes and hugs. He made sure that Meghan made it back to the train station safely, then thanked her for joining the contingency for drinks and dinner.

"I'm serious about what we talked about earlier," Meghan said, as she turned to walk down the stairs to catch the T home.

"I'm serious too," Will yelled back to Meghan as she struggled down the stairs in her heels, hampered by too many glasses of white wine. "Be careful. I'll see you tomorrow."

The following day would be spent packing the rest of his office into boxes, cleaning out his desk, and loading his pictures of family and UNC paraphernalia into his Range Rover for transport to North Carolina on Sunday. Tomorrow represented the end of an era for Will at Liberty Capital Trust and a twenty-two year investment-banking career in the history books. It also meant another round of final good-byes, and a chance to see Meghan again before his final departure. Will's mind swarmed with conversations he had with various Liberty associates as he drove home to Marblehead that night.

Everyone had been so gracious, but the conversation he could not get out of his head was the one he had with Meghan.

Was she really serious about visiting the farm? He wondered. What were her real motives? He'd had so little interaction with her in the four years she'd worked at Liberty, but for her to unload that statement on him was unthinkable. Maybe she had a thing for older guys. Don't flatter yourself, he scolded. Her motives are probably just what she portrayed. She has good memories of her own family farm and just wants to spend time on a farm again. That makes sense. Too wired and stimulated after the night's events, Will had trouble falling asleep, so he quietly made his way downstairs, secured a beer from his refrigerator in the garage, and sat in his home office to search the internet for information on his new career — farming. Still, he couldn't get Meghan off his mind.

Packing his office was relatively painless the next morning. He met with Martin, Mr. Sandbag, to talk about his sales pipeline and had lunch at the Harvard Club with Peterson and a handful of Liberty partners. He then made one final walk through the office on Friday afternoon, making it a point to pass Meghan's desk as he left the office. "Were you serious last night when we talked about visiting the farm?" he whispered, making sure no one within an earshot's distance of her workstation.

"Yes, I'm serious, if I'm invited," Meghan replied.

"Okay, we'll have to figure out a time to have you come down. The train is a pretty easy way to get there. It's a long ride, but the key is to book a sleeper car and sleep through the middle of the night."

"You let me know once you get settled. I would love to see what you've traded in for all this fame and fortune here," Meghan joked, referring to the office and the people he was leaving.

Will hugged her good-bye, wondering if he would really see her again.

The Departure

Chapter 30

Sunday morning marked the beginning of the end and the end of the beginning, the point in time that separated the end of Will's working career in Boston and the beginning of his life at Winfield Farm. He'd planned a family brunch at Tedesco at 10:00 for his send-off, after spending the early morning hours packing his Range Rover. Was he really doing this, thinking through what he might need in the way of clothes for the next week. What does a farmer wear to work? That was just one of the many questions he asked himself as he packed his suitcase.

The last four weeks had been filled with the excitement of pursuing something new: a new start, a new career, a new city, a chance to reconnect with his past, and the opportunity to be closer to his brother and cousins. However, today possessed a different feel. He was leaving behind the certainty and comfort of Old in exchange for the anticipation of New. Today, he faced the reality of his decision and the uncertainty of what lay ahead. It was also the day to say good-bye to Cat, Sarah, and Lauren. Though he would return home on Saturday morning, less than a week from today, the breakfast at Tedesco was best described as melancholy as he tried to keep the conversation somewhat lively, asking his usual spattering of questions.

"You better eat a good meal this morning, Will," Cat commented. "I can't imagine you'll be eating much of anything healthy all week. You'll eat those nasty chicken pot pies like your uncle used to fix himself."

Will laughed. "I forgot about those chicken pot pies. Funny what *you* remember about Uncle John."

"The freezer was full of them. I can see it. You'll be just like him, a single man, all alone, eating chicken pot pies every night for dinner," Cat jabbed.

"You're right, I'm sure I won't eat too well, so I'm counting on going out as a family every Sunday night before I catch the train back to the farm. Is that a deal?" he asked as the family finished eating brunch in the formal dining area at Tedesco. Sarah and Lauren nodded in agreement.

The Range Rover was packed and loaded with a full tank of gas. Cat and the girls were dressed for 11:00 mass, and Will was prepared for the eight-hundred-mile drive southbound down Interstate 95. As they said their good-byes in the Tedesco parking lot, Will hugged his girls and gave Cat a kiss on the cheek. The tension between him and his wife had eased slightly over the last few weeks, but she was still anything but supportive of his decision.

"I'll miss you guys," Will called out as he stepped into his vehicle and waved. He would have over ten hours of road-time to prepare himself for the mental transition from investment banker to farmer.

* * *

The sun had set over Winfield farm more than two hours ago. Will pulled the Range Rover into the dirt driveway and pressed the four-digit code at the front entry to the farm. The gate opened slowly as he squinted to find his way down the dark, desolate drive leading to the house. The house sat two hundred yards off the two-lane road and was not visible in the darkness. Other than the star-lit September night, darkness covered the eleven hundred acre farm. Maybe some lights out here would be a good investment, for starters, he thought as he flashed on his high beams to mark his way towards the house.

He had spent the last five hours of the trip in the car without a stop, so he welcomed the chance to put his feet on the ground. Once out of the car, he bent over to stretch the tightness in his legs and let out a faint moan, signifying to the cattle at Winfield Farm that he had arrived. "Home at last," he whispered. The key was exactly where Henry said it would be, under the empty planter on the brick steps leading to the porch that stretched along the front of the house. The wooden porch welcomed him with a quiet creak as he stepped toward the front door.

Once inside, Will fumbled through the dark living room for a lamp or a light switch. Captured in the darkness, he felt like a trespasser. Then the familiar smell welcomed him, an indescribable smell of Old, the Old that permeated venerable houses like the Winfield home. Old wasn't a particularly good smell or a bad smell, but it was the one essence Will remembered from this house, the aroma that brought back memories of his past, his childhood, his grandparents, his cousins, his uncle.

"*Finally,*" he sighed, locating a lamp next to the couch in the living room. He placed his suitcase next to the closed bedroom door off the living room and began his inaugural walk through his new home. With each deliberate step on the pine floors, he grew more aware of the reality of his decision.

He was no longer just a visitor here. The domain was now all his now.

While one part of him beamed with the excitement of an eighteen year old who had just bought his first car, another part of him felt unsettled. The uncertainty and unknown of the purchase still loomed in his head. He walked from the living room through the cased opening into the dining room. The vintage clock on the buffet ticked in sequence with each step he took as he swept his hand along the surface of the twin pedestal mahogany table where he and his cousins had met three months ago after Uncle John's funeral. So much had transpired since that day.

The kitchen floor sloped slightly away from the dining room, just as Will remembered. The laminate floor covering was aged and buckled, starting to curl in the corners like shoes on an elf. The archaic refrigerator was barren, except for an opened box of baking soda. For the time being, the freezer was void of any chicken pot pies. All the appliances were dated, showing signs of rust on the exterior, a far cry from what he was accustomed to in his contemporary kitchen back in Marblehead.

Will walked from the kitchen to the rear entry hall. Uncle John's gun case was positioned by the back door in the rear entry hall at the foot of the stairwell. The guns stood upright like uniformed soldiers in the open case. He pulled the twelve-gauge shotgun out of the rack and slowly raised it to the socket of his right shoulder, aiming the gun at the clapboard ceiling. With the shooting instructions of his uncle bantering in his head, he looked forward to shooting the shotguns again. Before heading upstairs, he carefully put the twelve gauge next to the other guns in its designated place on the rack.

Next to the stairs was the one bathroom in the house. His grandparents' bedroom and a guest bedroom flanked the stairwell and bathroom. He slowly made his way up the dark stairwell. The house felt so old, yet so new again to him. The tight stairwell was tucked into the back of the house, and led to three more bedrooms upstairs. Different memories of his childhood flooded his mind as he climbed each step. The upstairs bedrooms were just as he remembered them from thirty-five years ago. Each room had a designated name, depending on which family member usually slept there. The smallest bedroom at the top of the steps was Aunt Ruby's room, Will's great aunt. The middle room was the cousins' room, because it had two double beds and could sleep multiple younger guests. Will recounted the summers from his Little League baseball seasons, when the entire team of twelve was able to sleep in these two rooms during the White Lake tournaments.

The last room on the hall was Aunt Elizabeth's bedroom. It was by far the most palatial room in the otherwise modest house. The spacious room provided a panoramic view of the farm from the large hung-sash windows on the front and backsides of the house. The fireplace from the living room below ran along the east wall of the bedroom. The room was furnished with a four-poster bed and English antique furniture. The pine floors gave the room an added look of distinction. Elizabeth's room looked just like he remembered, though he had never slept in this room. It had always been reserved for adults.

He envisioned Elizabeth's room for his own guests, and wondered who would really come to visit. It was a really nice room, even suitable for Cat, her parents, or anyone else, like Meghan. Above the bed hung a portrait of his Aunt Elizabeth from her wedding, dating back to the 1950s. He glanced at a painting that hung on the opposite wall over the fireplace mantle, depicting a hunting scene with birddogs.

He left the room and walked back downstairs, unloaded his SUV, and locked himself in the house once all his belongings were put away. Had Uncle John ever locked the doors out here? Probably not. No one in the country locks their doors, right? He entered his uncle's small bedroom, off the living room. The room was even smaller than he remembered. He had six bedrooms to choose from in the capacious house, all much larger than his uncle's room, but he chose Uncle John's bedroom as his own. John had slept in this room over eighty years, as far as Will knew. If it was good enough for Uncle John, then it was good enough for Will.

He turned on the lamp, put his suitcase on the floor, stripped the linens from the bed, and threw the sheets on the floor outside the bedroom door. He then sat down on the bed and looked around. There were no windows, so it was easy to see how Uncle John was able to sleep so notoriously late in this dark alcove. This would be Will's bedroom for the foreseeable future, which suited him just fine. He was here to follow in his uncle's footsteps, so it was only fitting that he should select John's bedroom as his home away from home.

Will rose from the bed and walked toward the chest of drawers. He pulled open the top drawer, wondering if he would find any of the gold dollars that John collected. Instead, Will found a small wooden box. He opened it slowly. Laid flat on top of several layers of gold coins, he found a metal from John's service in the U.S. Army. Will picked up the metal and read its inscription:

MEDAL OF HONOR

Will beamed with pride. He had never seen the medal before today. In his humble way, John had never told his niece and nephews about the medal or the background of how he had received this honor. He carefully laid the medal on the surface of the chest, but it deserved a more prominent place in the house and he'd make sure it got properly framed.

He plundered deeper into the drawer, underneath a layer of various colors of socks. The smell of the cedar drawers permeated his nose as he searched through his uncle's past. Excavating below the socks, he came upon a large manila envelope. The tattered envelope was unsealed, with no markings on the outside. Will emptied the contents on the unmade bed and found at least twenty-five letters, all addressed to John Winfield. All were hand-written. He shifted through the envelopes, searching for a letter that looked interesting. It appeared that several of the letters might be from the women in his uncle's life, so Will considered those sacred and elected to save those for another time. Then he came upon several letters that were obviously from children, based on the handwriting. Among these envelopes, Will recognized one that appeared to be in his own writing from his elementary school days.

> *Dear Uncle John,*
>
> *We miss you and hope to see you soon. I like my school. I like my teacher. I like seeing you at the farm. We can play baseball and ride on the tractor when we come to see you next time. I love you.*
>
> *Will*

He opened a few more of the letters that he had written to his uncle. Among his own letters, there were also notes from Clay and the other cousins in the envelope. Will chose not to read any more of the letters, particularly the ones that appeared to be from John's girlfriends.

It was well past midnight before he made it to bed. He lay on his back in the darkness with his hands behind his head, too excited to fall asleep. Tomorrow was his first day on the new job. He had plenty to learn and a list of tasks to address. He felt ready. There would be no commute to the city in the morning. No tie or suit to wear. No parking deck or downtown traffic to navigate. He was elated to start his new life as a farmer.

It all began tomorrow.

The Land

Chapter 31

Even in his later years, Uncle John had been able to keep up with the advances and trends in efficient farming. Over the last fifteen years, farming had made significant strides in the use of biotechnology for farming practices. Since making his initial offer on the farm, Will had been studying the latest uses of technology in farming, pest management practices, reduction in pesticide use, and how to increase crop yields.

Corn and soybeans had emerged as the main row-crops planted on Winfield Farm since the decline of tobacco farming in North Carolina two decades ago. To his uncle's credit, John had been advised to boost Winfield's corn production eight years ago, before the demand for ethanol production surged in the United States. With corn prices exceeding $6.00 per bushel, the corn farmers profited from the demand for ethanol, an additive in gasoline.

Will's research during his due diligence period before buying the farm revealed several ways to cut costs and boost his commodity prices. First, by storing the corn in silos this fall, Will could time the sale of the corn crop with the fluctuation in the commodities market and wait for higher prices as the supply and demand varied during the buying season. Second, selling the corn, soybeans, and cattle directly to the buyers, rather than relying on brokers and middlemen, would generate a boost in farm revenues under Will's watch.

In recent years, Uncle John had relied on a crop broker from nearby Cumberland County to sell the corn harvest in one large block on a single day. Will figured that John left some money on the table by selling the corn without timing the commodities market. In his younger days, John had made the extra effort to store processed corn in silos and wait to sell when corn commodity prices peaked. However, as John grew older, selling the crops in one block to a broker seemed more efficient and much easier, but not necessarily more profitable.

As far as Will knew, the silos on Winfield Farm had not been used in decades. Given his financial background, Will was excited to try his hand at the commodities market and use the existing silos on the property to store corn in order to time the markets. The commodities markets moved like the stock market, and Will was now in an ideal place to track daily corn, beef, and soybean prices. To start his first day on the job, Will spent a few minutes on his laptop before the sun rose, with a cup of coffee, researching current commodity prices. He made a list of other farmers in the area he wanted to meet and learn more about how to make Winfield Farm more productive. While in Boston last week, Will had set up an appointment with the Bladen County extension agent to visit Winfield Farm, another resource to educate Will on farming trends, pesticides, and how to market his crops and cattle.

At dawn, Will laced up his running shoes and stepped out the back door just as the sun began its ascent over the cornfields behind the house. A short run to the river and back would energize him for his first day on the job. The dirt road behind the house wound through the towering corn crop, which was now over seven feet tall and almost ready for harvest. The morning dew kissed the bright green leaves of the corn stalks. It looked like a good crop to Will, but what did he know? He was a rookie farmer and a neophyte when it came to assessing what a healthy field of corn looked like.

The winding track took him past the dilapidated tobacco barn, through the first plot of cornfields, and into the planted pine forest. The massive loblolly pine shielded the sun's morning rays, letting in only beams of sunlight to illuminate Will's running path. The sunbeams resembled lasers shot from the sky down to the dirt pathway. The mighty pine trees blocked the view of the sunrise until Will reached the South River, the dark body of water that defined the northern boundary of Winfield Farm. The river also marked the dividing line between Bladen and Samson Counties. Though it was just over a mile from the farmhouse to the river, Will interrupted his morning jog to momentarily observe the still dark waters of the river.

The crisp morning temperatures formed a light fog over the murky waters of South River. Will recalled the times he had spent fishing with his uncle and cousins on the banks of this river that was no more than thirty feet across. He was eager to try his hand at fishing in the dark waters of the river again. Surely, there was an old fishing pole in the house or in the barn somewhere. He might come back tonight if he could find a pole and dig up a few worms.

He turned and resumed his run back to the house down the same dirt road and felt a new energy come over him. This vast and diverse landscape of Winfield Farm was now his. He was no longer just a visitor here to see his uncle, grandmother, and cousins. The farm was now his livelihood. So far, though the first day had barely begun, life on the farm felt pretty good.

He increased his pace as the dirt road led him past the

hay fields beyond tobacco barn and into the final stretch of his morning jog. Before going inside for a shower, he opened the barn doors to inspect the farm equipment his uncle kept inside. He was curious to see if Uncle John's old pick-up truck and the tractor would crank. As far as he knew, the old orange truck had not been started since John died back in June. The truck keys were still in the ignition and with one turn of the key, the 1978 Silverado fired up. The truck would serve as Will's primary mode of transportation on the farm and driving into town. Except for his drive back and forth to the train station, Will decided to park his Range Rover in the barn during the week. The Range Rover didn't exactly fit the profile of a rural farmer, and he preferred not to be the farmer in Bladen County who drove the fancy car. Plus, given the choice, he preferred the novelty of driving the truck around the farm and into Elizabethtown.

Will cut the truck's engine and decided to test the tractor's readiness next. The Chevy pick-up truck was dated, but the tractor itself was an antique. The 1952 Ford 8N tractor had been around Winfield Farm since his grandfather farmed tobacco. To Will's surprise, the old diesel engine fired without hesitation. It sputtered a few times in the cool mid-September morning temperature, but the engine droned within moments, signifying the tractor was ready to ride the open fields. Now seemed like a good time as any to test his tractor driving skills. Will moved the gearshift from side to side and over to the far right until he found what appeared to be reverse. Slowly, he let his foot off the clutch and tapped the accelerator. The vintage red and gray Ford tractor eased out of the open barn doors and backed on to the dirt driveway that circled the house. After a short test-ride through the pasture to introduce himself to the cows, Will circled the house and parked the tractor back in its designated parking place in the barn.

* * *

The first week on the job at Winfield Farm proved productive, educational, and fun. With no outside distractions, except a few e-mails and phone calls with clients and co-workers back in Boston, Will found that he could perform his farming duties during the day and research farming material on the internet at night. The only downside, Will concluded after the first week, was how quiet and lonely over one thousand acres could be, particularly after the sun set over Winfield Farm. To minimize the effect of secluded nights, he called Boston each night when he knew he could catch Cat, Sarah, and Lauren at home.

Within the first week, Will realized that he had a steep learning curve when it came to running the farm. Unlike other farmers in the area, Will had not grown up working on Winfield Farm. He had only seen the fun part of farming as a child. He and his cousins had been shielded from the hard work that came with farming. Fortunately, he was used to working hard and had prepared himself for the effort it took to operate a prosperous farm. However, he learned quickly that farming required far more manual labor and much less work behind the desk.

Time at Winfield Farm was not all about work. For entertainment, Will bought a new fishing pole and fished in the South River. Late one afternoon, he hunted the pine plantation for wild quail. Will recognized in his first week on the farm the value of seeking assistance from other farmers in the area. He was not shy about introducing himself and letting the other farmers know he was new at this profession and coveted their help. Based on the other farmers' affection for Uncle John, they were glad to offer recommendations and provide assistance to the rookie farmer. Will enjoyed being outside all day, and the research at night was motivating because he had so much to learn. If only his uncle was here to give him advice or to ask pertinent questions about the farm. Information was available from other farmers, the Bladen County extension agent, the internet, from books and trade magazines, but those resources paled in comparison to the void of not having a farming veteran in the office right next door. *If I could have one person here, even over my own family, it would be Uncle John,* Will thought on numerous occasions during his first week at the farm.

The Train Trip Home

Chapter 32

An 825-mile commute between Boston and the farm required transportation coordination on both ends of the train trip. Cat and Sarah were both available to pick Will up from the Amtrak station in Lynn, Massachusetts on Saturday mornings. Lynn was a fifteen-minute drive from Marblehead and eleven miles north of downtown Boston. Leaving his Range Rover parked in downtown Fayetteville for three nights over the weekend was a risk Will elected not to take. So, he devised an idea to identify a safe haven for his car during the weekends. His plan for the car involved his friend Becca, the owner of Java Joe's in downtown Fayetteville. She was the ideal person to keep an eye on Will's Range Rover over the weekends while he traveled back to Boston, but first, he had to get her buy-in on the plan. Will had not seen or spoken to Rebecca since he kissed her on the cheek at Java Joe's after the auction over a month ago in early August.

Will called the coffee shop from the farm on Wednesday morning. "Becca, I'll be back in town on Friday night, and I was hoping you could break away for an early dinner. I have a business proposition for you." He caught her slight hesitation.

"I'd love to go, but tell me what's up?" she asked. "You can't leave me hanging like that. What kind of business proposition do you have in mind? You've piqued my interest."

"I can't tell you," he said. "It's a surprise. You'll have to wait until Friday night, but I think you'll like my idea."

"You and your ideas," she commented. "I didn't think I would ever hear from you again. I figured you must have sold your farm and were never coming back."

"Well, there have been some changes at the farm, and that's part of what I wanted to talk to you about. I'll meet you at Java Joe's around 6:15 on Friday, if that's good for you."

"That's fine, but I wish you'd tell me what's up. I'll be here at the shop on Friday. I'll make sure I have someone around to cover the store for an hour or so. There are a couple of good restaurants within walking distance of here. I like this one Italian restaurant that's close by, if that's good for you."

"That's perfect," Will said. "See you at six fifteen."

He wanted to hang up before she asked more questions. As far as he could tell, Becca had no idea why he was in town, and she certainly had no clue that he had purchased Winfield Farm. At 5:30 Friday afternoon, Will secured the barn doors behind the house and drove out the front gate, leaving his new love, Winfield Farm, for the next three nights. His first five days on the farm had gone well. The workweek was so vastly different from his job in Boston, but he was adjusting to the transition. A part of him did not want to leave the farm this afternoon, but knowing that he would be back Monday morning was a motivation as he drove away, bound for Fayetteville to meet Becca for dinner.

Since his discovery of Java Joe's the weekend of Uncle John's funeral in June, the coffee shop had become Will's holding tank in Fayetteville before being sentenced to ride the overnight train back to Boston. Instituting Java Joe's into part of his weekly routine seemed like the practical thing to do. His excitement heightened as he drove northwest on Highway 210 toward Fayetteville, eager to surprise Becca with the news about his purchase of the farm.

Will parked his car on Green Street, a city block from Java Joe's, far enough away so Becca would think he had walked from the Amtrak station and made his customary entry on foot. As he had imagined, the crowd at Java Joe's was characteristically light for 6:15 on a Friday night. Two customers sat across from each other in one of the booths near the front door along the glass storefront, the only patrons in the quaint shop this evening.

Becca was dressed distinctly different tonight. She wore a pair of tight fitting jeans and cowboy boots. Her Irish green Java Joe's apron was tied tightly over a white, ruffled, long-sleeve blouse. Her long auburn hair was no longer tied in a ponytail on the top of her head, but worn down in dainty curls, pinned back to stay out of her face while she worked. With her hair down, she looked like she was seventeen again - ready to go to a movie with her high school boyfriend.

"You look like you are going out on the town after work tonight," Will exclaimed, greeting Becca with a hug. "You look great!"

"Thank you," she said, glancing quickly toward her customers. "Can you get away for a little while?" he asked, still dazzled by her striking appearance.

"I got Taylor to come in for a few hours, so I'm good to go," she responded. She untied the apron from her waist and tossed it under the counter.

"I'm serious as a Yankee can be. Let's go as soon as you're ready, 'cause my train leaves in a couple of hours."

"Oh yes, I remember, the eight twenty-two," she smiled. "I'm ready. " She turned to speak over her shoulder. "Taylor, can you come up front and watch the store for the next hour or so?"

An attractive teen-age girl, who appeared to be the age of Will's oldest daughter, appeared from the storeroom where Will and Becca had bonded over their first beer six weeks ago.

"Taylor, this is Will, the business consultant I was telling you about. He and I will be out for an hour or so. He's got a train to catch for Boston, so we won't be gone long," she explained in her introduction.

"Hi, Taylor," Will smiled. "Nice to meet you."

The bells jingled as Will and Becca exited Java Joe's. The sun was starting to set as the two walked up Worth Street toward the restaurant. "Business consultant?" Will asked. "Is that the way you describe me to your employees?"

"Well, she's my niece for one. I don't want her to think I called her in to work on a Friday night just so I could go out to dinner with some guy in from out of town. And you *are* a business consultant, right?" Becca asked.

"Well, I used to be, and that's what I wanted to talk to you about tonight. I have some big news to share. I didn't want to tell you on the phone because I wanted to see you first hand. I've bought my uncle's farm. After the auction didn't go like we planned last month, I started thinking about buying the farm myself, and I did."

"That's exciting! Congratulations! So that explains why you're in town again?"

"I've actually been here all week. I'm headed back to Boston for the weekend and will be back on Monday morning."

"That *is* big news," Becca said, happy for him. "Did you quit your job in Boston?"

"More or less," Will nodded.

"When you called on Wednesday and said you wanted to run a few ideas by me, I thought you were in Boston. I figured

you were coming through town to talk to me about selling
Java Joe's or give me more advice."

"Well, the offer to help still stands. I'll give you as much
advice as you can handle. And if you're a candidate to sell your
shop, I can put you in touch with a good investment banking
firm back in Boston," Will said, not quite joking.

Becca smiled back at him. "Wow, I can't believe you're
here. Are you going to keep riding the train back and forth
every week? That's going to get old, don't you think?"

"Yeah, probably, but that's what I've signed up for, at least
for the next few years. I need to be home for my daughters
until they graduate," Will explained.

"So, you don't think you'll move your family down here?"

Will laughed. "No, definitely not. My girls are in high
school, and I'm not about to rock their world with a move,
and my wife has lived in Boston all her life, so she's not
moving. Like I told you, she's really not a fan of rural life. She's
more of a big city girl."

The two approached the Italian restaurant located two
blocks from the coffee shop.

"This place is not real fancy," Rebecca said. "But I know
the owner pretty well. He lets me put my business cards next
to his cash register. It's good advertising for my shop. The hope
is that people will eat a good meal at Vito's and then walk
down to Java Joe's for a cup of coffee."

After Will and Rebecca were seated in a booth toward the
back of the restaurant, Will uncovered his plan for the car.
"I do have a business proposition for you. I was hoping you
could help me while I'm in Boston for the weekends. I have my
uncle's old truck that I keep at the farm. I don't think the truck
will make it back and forth between here and the farm every
weekend, so I feel better about driving my SUV. However, I
don't feel good about leaving the car in the parking lot at the

train station over the weekend. So, here's what I was thinking. You can drive my car on the weekends or park it somewhere safe. I'll buy you a twelve-pack of Papst Blue Ribbon every Friday for the inconvenience. You know better than me, but would you leave your car parked in that lot next to the train station for any length of time, especially over a weekend?"

"Probably not," Becca responded. "So, is *that* the business proposition you had for me that you mentioned on the phone? Taking care of your car?"

"You sound thrilled," Will said. "Sorry to disappoint you."

"I guess I didn't know what to expect. You were so coy on the phone when you called on Wednesday," Becca said, staring at him.

For a moment, Will lost himself in her hazel-colored eyes. "Okay, sorry I disappointed you, but I do have another offer," he grinned.

"Well, we haven't shaken hands on your last big offer. I may drive a hard bargain. You don't know what my fee is to babysit your car. A twelve-pack of cheap beer probably won't get it done," Becca said, smiling back at him.

"Okay, since you are such a hard-ass negotiator, here's my offer. I'll throw in an all-expense paid trip to Winfield Farm," Will offered before taking a sip of his beer.

"And where the hell is Winfield Farm?" Becca asked as she sipped her red wine.

"Now you've really insulted me," Will groused. "Winfield Farm is this pristine farm about forty-five minutes east of here. It's run by this Yankee who left his family and business to take over the farm."

"Oh, I'm really sorry, but I didn't realize your farm actually had a name. It must be some sort of huge plantation."

"Not hardly," he chuckled. "It's a pretty awesome place, but it's by no means a plantation. Winfield was my mother's maiden name. John Winfield was my uncle, that one that died this past summer."

"Well, if it means getting to go to Winfield Farm, then I'm game to take care of your car. With all this hype, you make it sound like you're driving a Rolls Royce, though. What kind of car is it?"

"A Range Rover," Will replied. "I'm not that particular about my car, but I'd rather have it here waiting on me when I get back on Monday mornings. I think this is a fair deal. You get to drive my Range Rover all weekend, and I don't come back to find the car stolen and on some joy ride in Mexico."

"Range Rover?" she stated with a raised eyebrow. "I see now why you're so protective of your car. I think I might drive that car down to Mexico myself for the weekend."

"That's fine with me. Drive it wherever you like. That's part of the deal. Just make sure it's back here on Monday morning at eight o'clock. But I'm serious about you coming to see the farm, if that's something of interest to you."

"Sure, you just let me know when, and I'll get someone scheduled to watch the shop."

"I still have some things I need to do around the farm, so I was thinking in two or three weeks. I want you to see the farm during the day, so you'll have to come over one afternoon and then I'll cook you a Winfield grass-fed steak."

"That sounds good. Now I'm really curious to see this farm, if you have your own brand of steaks," Becca commented.

"Remember, this is an old tobacco farm. Don't be fooled, we don't have that many cows."

After dinner, Will and Becca discussed the details of the car arrangement as they strolled back toward Java Joe's. "Here's an extra key," he said, handing it to her. "I'll call you Monday morning to confirm that the car will be here or another place behind the coffee shop."

Will hugged Becca and thanked her as they stood next to Will's car, parked on the street near the coffee shop. He trusted her and knew she was responsible, given the way she ran her coffee shop. "Thank you," Will called out, as Becca walked in the direction of Java Joe's, while he crossed the street in the direction of the train station.

Was he really interested in her or just drawn to her effervescent personality? He wondered what she thought he was doing, inviting her to the farm and leaving his car with her for the weekend. She probably thinks he was infatuated with her. He hoped she didn't think he was using her to keep his car on the weekends. He wondered if she'd even drive it. What would she tell her friends when they ask whose car she was driving?

It was a few minutes past eight o'clock, and the train for Boston would be arriving soon. All he carried with him on this trip was his briefcase. Traveling light was the key to making the long commute more manageable. He called the home phone in Marblehead and left a message. "I'm sure you guys are out. I'm at the train station in Fayetteville and am headed home."

Sitting alone in the desolate train station waiting area, Will wondered. Was he really headed home or was he leaving home? That question would continue to linger in his mind for a while.

The Visitor

Chapter 33

By late September, the foliage at Winfield Farm signaled that the sweltering summer heat in eastern North Carolina had yielded to fall's cooler temperatures. The green needles on the planted pine turned to golden brown. The majestic oak trees bordering the soybean fields and open pastures dropped acorns on the hallowed grounds, signaling further signs of autumn's arrival.

Now in his third week on the new job, Will prepared to have guests visit the farm. For starters, Cat and the girls had finally acquiesced to Will's pleas and agreed to fly into Raleigh on Thanksgiving Day, have lunch with Clay's family, and spend the rest of the holiday weekend at the farm. Privately, Will communicated with Meghan from the office for a visit in October. Will's in-laws had been invited to visit the week of Christmas, and Clay and his family were booked for a weekend in early November.

Henry was due to visit the farm the week in two weeks, and Will had invited some of his old high school friends to drive over for the day later in the fall, but the first official guest would be Becca. She was slated to come next Thursday. The scheduled visits gave Will something to look forward to and were a motivation to complete some overdue improvements to the Winfield home-place. The corn harvest was projected to be one of best on record at Winfield Farm, according to the county agent and neighboring farmers who casually surveyed the crop. The cattle were healthy and Will spent a number of hours on the tractor cutting grass in the hay fields to insure the barns were stocked for the winter. The soybean crop looked favorable for harvest in early October. Life on the farm seemed to be going as well as could be expected for Will, the neophyte farmer.

It was late morning on a Tuesday, the start of Will's third week on the job at Winfield Farm. Having just finished another cut in the hay pasture behind the old tobacco barn, Will drove the tractor with the mowing implement back to the barn behind the house. As the barn came into view, Will noticed a young male standing next to the barn, dressed casually in baggy blue-jeans, amber-colored rancher's boots, a long-sleeve black t-shirt, and a red cap.

As the tractor motored closer, it appeared to be someone waiting to see him, possibly looking for work. Will didn't recognize the fellow at first, but then it became apparent that the man was Wyn, Eileen's son. Seeing no signs of transportation, Will assumed Wyn had walked over from the tenement house down the road. He felt sure the imbecile was here looking for work. Will had figured he'd be down here at some point begging for a job. He'd like to help him, but was not sure he could find anything for him to do. He would never hire this guy off the street, though. He seemed like bad news, and made a terrible first impression. He would see if his second impression was any better.

Will stopped the tractor a few feet in front of where Wyn stood. The Ford's diesel engine sputtered as Will turned the key to the off position. He watched while Wyn nervously shuffled his tattered boots across the sandy surface in front of the tractor barn. "Good morning," Will said as he jumped off the tractor, staring at the emblem on the front of Wyn's long-sleeve t-shirt, the logo of some metallic band that Will did not recognize. From under his red Farmall hat, Will made note of Wyn's oily, dark hair, hanging in an unkempt manner over his ears. His face apparently hadn't seen a razor in at least three or four days. Will removed his work gloves and extended his right hand to Wyn's, who responded with a half-hearted handshake that Will thought resembled a greeting from a ten-year-old girl. Wyn kept his head down, his eyes fixated on the ground.

Will viewed Wyn's visit today as a distraction and was not prepared to waste much time talking to the visitor this morning. He decided to get right to the point. "What can I help you with today, Wyn?"

Will fully expected Wyn to ask about any work he could do around the farm, but his question was met with silence. Though frustrated with Wyn's lack of social skills for a man in his twenties, he stared at Wyn in an attempt to find compassion toward the wayward young man. His patience waned as he waited for a response to his simple question, and he concluded that Wyn must be mentally challenged in some way.

Finally, Wyn looked up from the dirt he was moving with his boots. "There's somethin' you should know about me."

Immediately, Will thought Wyn might be confirming the fact that he was somehow deranged or had some sort of debilitating disease.

"Your uncle was my dad," Wyn blurted awkwardly.

"My Uncle John, you mean?" Will asked, stunned. He stared at Wyn in disbelief, frustrated by his inability to communicate, waiting again for an answer to his question.

After what seemed like a lifetime, Wyn finally replied. "Yeah."

A plethora of thoughts entered Will's mind. His first thought was to deny the remark, but he figured it was best to find out what Wyn intended to do with this information. "So what does that mean?" He began to quickly process his uncle's will. What might this mean to the estate and the ownership of the farm? Could the misfit have any claim to Winfield Farm?

"Well, since you asked, I think you know what that means," Wyn replied. "It means you and I both own this farm together."

"Really?" Will responded, inwardly seething over Wyn's attitude and allegations. "That's funny. I didn't remember seeing you at the closing, when I signed a loan document that says I owe eight hundred thousand dollars, not to mention the six hundred thousand dollars I put down to buy this place. Do those numbers make any sense to you?"

"Don't try to throw a bunch of big numbers at me," Wyn grumbled. "I just know that he was my father."

"How can you prove he was your father?" Will demanded.

"It's on the birth certificate. I seen it myself. You want me to go get it and show it to you?"

"Yeah, I want to see it," Will said. "So, what took you so long to tell anyone? Why are you just letting us know this news now?" Will took two steps back and put his hand on the tractor's steering wheel, afraid of what Wyn might do if he stepped closer.

"I dunno," Wyn shrugged. "I didn't know how to get in touch with any of you. None of you were ever here … until now."

"I've been here two weeks, and I was here for the auction last month. We were all here for the funeral. You were here at the house and at the graveside service. We gave you a ride home. Why didn't you bring up this up then?" Will asked, his voice raised.

* * *

"It wasn't never the right time," Wyn stated.

"Who knows about this?" Will demanded. "How come my uncle never mentioned any of this to us? How come your mother hasn't brought it up? Maybe it's best that I talk with her about this claim."

"Look, fella," Wyn said, pointing a finger in Will's direction. "Don't go bring my momma into this."

Will laughed. "What do you mean? I'd say she's pretty much in the middle of it, if your claims are true." He shook his head in disgust, waiting for Wyn to respond, but Wyn appeared to have nothing else to say. Will's patience for the intruder into his new life had run thin. "Listen, if you need to talk with an attorney, I recommend you do that, but I'm through talking about it with you." He turned away. "I've got work to do around here."

"I don't need no damned lawyer," Wyn retorted. "I'll handle this my own way, if I have to."

It was evident that the conversation was not going as Wyn had planned. Now Wyn was mad. His anger was evident to Will. "What do you want me to do?" Will asked. "I just wrote the biggest check of my life to buy this farm. What is it you want from me?"

"I want my share, and I intend to get it," Wyn stated simply.

"This is a legal issue, Wyn. You need a lawyer," Will said, attempting to appeal to Wyn's practical side.

"I can't stand lawyers. I hate 'em. Don't tell me how I gotta' handle this. I got this," Wyn declared, as he turned and walked away.

Will burned inside with anger as he watched Wyn walk toward the cornfield behind the barn and disappeared. He was evidently walking through the cornfield toward his mother's home, about a half mile away. That didn't end well, Will thought, shaking his head in disbelief. His heart pounded. He had so much to process. At this moment, his anger was focused on Wyn and his juvenile approach to the conflict. The conversation played over and over in his mind, and then Will began to process the reality of Wyn's claims.

Who else knew about this? Is this a family secret? He wondered if his mother knew about this secret. Is this a scandal that is well known in the community? He doubted it. John would have done everything in his power to cover up a scandal like this. Was Wyn's claim even true? If it is true, why wouldn't Wyn and Eileen just hire an attorney and address the inheritance issue sooner? He imagined Eileen would rather not raise the issue at all. He was sure she'd be embarrassed and would rather just bury the past. If the allegation is true, he wondered if John supported Eileen and Wyn financially. He guessed this explained why they showed up at the house for the burial this past summer.

Will started calculating when this indiscretion might have taken place. Could Uncle John have been too old to father a child based on Will's estimate of Wyn's age? Uncle John would have been in his early sixties when he fathered Wyn if his numbers are right. Eileen was probably pretty old when she had Wyn. Why was his name Wyn? Maybe that proves he was named after the Winfield's.

Will decided he needed to call someone for answers. Calling Cat was not an option, but today's news would certainly disprove her theory that Uncle John was gay. It was Will's opinion that Cat was convinced that the South was full of uneducated hayseeds. Wyn's claim would only confirm her suspicions and give her more reasons to let Will know that the farm purchase had been a mistake.

Will walked to the front of the house and dropped into one of the rocking chairs on the front porch. He needed some time to clear his head. What did all this mean for the future of Winfield Farm? He pulled his phone from his shirt pocket and dialed his brother in Raleigh. "You're not going to believe this one, Clay," Will began, and then went on to explain in detail his confrontation with Wyn.

"Do you think it's true?" Clay asked.

"I can't tell if he's lying, but I guess I could see how it might have happened."

"I imagine Uncle John had to be gettin' it from some-where, but I didn't think he'd be tappin' the well on the prop-erty," Clay joked.

"Yes, and you met Eileen," Will replied with a faint laugh. "She's not exactly Erin Andrews either."

"It makes me wonder why John would have allowed Mom and the other siblings to put the farm solely in his name," Clay asked.

"I've thought through all sorts of theories, but the reason the estate was put in John's name alone was to allow the eight cousins to inherit the farm equally. A ninth cousin would have complicated things considerably. Why would John have drafted the will the way he did if he knew Wyn might make a claim on the farm?"

"Maybe structuring the will this way was a defensive move on John's part to try and block Wyn from claiming any owner-ship of his estate," Clay offered.

"Or maybe John wanted Wyn to inherit the entire farm," Will theorized.

"I can't imagine John would do that. My guess is that he was paying Eileen to keep quiet about things all these years.

I'm sure Eileen didn't want this scandal out in the community either."

"There are too many theories and conspiracies to process. Who do we know in Wilmington that practices estate law?" Will asked. "I think I'm going to need some help fighting this battle."

"Check with Mark Middlebrook," Clay suggested. "I think he deals in family and estate law. He can probably handle it, or someone in his firm has probably dealt with paternity issues like this before."

"That's a good thought. I'll set something up with Mark this week. I've been looking for an excuse to drive over to Wilmington anyway."

"I hate to hear this guy's shown up after all these years," Clay said. "Yeah, me too," Will said somberly. "From my perspective, his timing of dropping this bomb is pretty bad. It would have been nice to know this news before I closed on the property. But, like I used to tell my clients, it'll work out. It's just a matter of money. Worst case, it may mean having to pay this guy some 'go away' money as we used to call it when someone in Boston that would show up with a bogus claim."

"Hang in there, bro, and keep me posted," Clay sighed.

"I will. Thanks Clay."

Will buried his face in his open hands and pulled at his hair. Embittered, he leaned back in the rocking chair, staring into the cow pasture that spread across the front side of the house. *What the hell have I gotten myself into?*" he muttered.

The Homecoming

Chapter 34

A light rain hit the windshield of the metallic gray Range Rover as Will traveled the once familiar route on Highway 210, headed east from the farm towards Wilmington. Today, he was on his way to meet with Mark Middlebrook, the estate lawyer Clay had recommended. It had been two days since Wyn had abruptly disclosed his supposed birthright, so Will decided it was time to take the offensive.

Will had experienced the full range of emotions over the last forty-eight hours. He was angry with his uncle for not disclosing the issue of an illegitimate cousin in the family. He was livid at Wyn for the hostile manner in which he approached him with the news. He was irritated with Eileen for not addressing the family with the truth. Mostly, Will was disappointed in himself for falling into this debacle. Things were going so well here, he thought, as he made the sixty mile drive to Wilmington. Until this asshole showed up with claims of being his cousin. He'd get through this. He'd crush this guy. Wyn had no financial claim to the farm. If it comes down to it, he guessed he could give him a few odd jobs around the farm, but this guy was not partner material, much less employable. The thought of going into business with Wyn was absolutely not an option. In fact, he wondered what it would take to legally get him off the property. Should he pay a visit to Eileen tomorrow and demand to know the truth? Or should he keep waiting for her to come see him? One thing's for sure, he didn't want to come face to face with that SOB again anytime soon. He'd stay clear of him, until he served him papers to stay off the property.

Aside from the actual purpose of the trip, Will was excited to revisit Wilmington, the place he was born and called home for the first half of his life. Except for a few old friends and copious memories, Will no longer had many remaining ties to Wilmington. His last visit home was to bury his mother who died almost four years ago, twenty-eight months after his father's death. Since his mother's funeral, there had been no reason to come home - until now.

The drive to Wilmington from the farm, even in a light rain, was just over an hour, the route all two-lane roads. Today's sojourn between the farm and Wilmington conjured favorable memories from the many trips he and his family had made to visit the farm and see his grandparents, Uncle John, and his cousins.

Will had scheduled lunch with Wilmington native Jeff Baker, a friend from grade school who had been on Will's baseball teams. The two had been in each other's weddings. After college, the two had gone their separate ways: Jeff returned to Wilmington to work for Duke Power while Will headed to New England. Jeff and Will had made plans to meet downtown for lunch before Will's appointment with Mark at his office. Though embarrassed by the paternity conflict with his uncle's estate, Will felt Jeff would find the story intriguing. Meeting with Jeff would also enable Will to do some reconnaissance work on the whereabouts of Kaitlyn Gerrard, the girl from Wilmington that Will never found time to date in his younger years.

"So how is life as a farmer, Will?" Jeff asked as the two long-time friends sat down for lunch over a burrito in downtown Wilmington.

"I can't tell you how much I've enjoyed farming. It came at perfect time in my career. It's like running your own business, but you're not cooped up in an office all day. I don't have thirty employees with issues to deal with every day. I'm learning a new trade, and it's really been a lot of fun. Now, I'm probably still in the honeymoon phase, but so far, so good. Tomorrow marks the end of week three. The only downside is it gets lonely out there sometimes. That's why it was good for me to get away today and see a few familiar faces."

"That's awesome!" Jeff said. "There is something liberating about starting something new, particularly at our age. I've been in the same industry with the power company since graduating from Carolina. It's been a good living, but the monotony of getting up every day and doing it again, over and over can wear on you."

"There are trade-offs with this new venture," Will explained. "I hated leaving my family, but I've enjoyed connecting with my old roots down here. I didn't realize how much I missed the South until I came back. I mean, this is like an eye candy convention for me," Will said, watching some of the scenery pass by the outside seating at the Taco Tavern in downtown Wilmington. "I've seen more beautiful women in the ten minutes we've been sitting here than I saw in Boston in twenty-two years."

"They say you can't go home, but I think you've proven that theory wrong, from what I can tell. I can sense it in your voice that the move has served you well," Jeff said.

"Well, things have been going really well until this week.

So, let me tell you what brings me to Wilmington, besides having lunch with you. I told you I had a meeting downtown. I'm actually meeting with Mark Middlebrook after lunch. I've run into a buzz-saw with my uncle's estate. You're not going to believe this one, but my uncle, who was never married, may have fathered a child some twenty-five or thirty years ago. I had this guy show up at the farm on Tuesday and drop that bomb on me. I don't know if it's true. I've met his mother, but I'm not in a position to go ask her. I've done some research and a paternity test *can* be administered on a deceased person, but I'm not sure I want to go there. I've got reason to believe that this kid could be telling the truth, but he's a rough character, not the type that you and I would claim as kin, if you know what I mean. He's white trash, as they say down here in the South."

"Damn, what an ordeal!" Jeff exclaimed. "You have a real legal dilemma on your hands. What does the will say about the transfer?"

"That's what I'm here to see Mark about. The way the farm was transferred to our generation was through my uncle. He was the last of my mother's siblings to die, and the will says the surviving heirs of my uncle will receive equal shares of the farm. Well, theoretically, this illegitimate thug could claim a share of the farm or could try to make a claim for the entire portion of my uncle's estate, saying he's the sole surviving heir. The challenge is that the assets of the estate, which basically consist of the farm, have now been sold to me. I don't mind telling you that I put a large part of my liquidity into buying out my cousins and still have a substantial six-figure note to pay off each month. Given my investment in the farm, I need to know what sort of claim this asshole is making."

"Has he filed a suit or made any type of legal claim?" Jeff asked.

"Oh no," Will said, sipping sweet tea from his glass. "This guy is clearly uneducated, to put it mildly. He's apparently been in some trouble with the law in his past, because he's conjured up quite a hatred for lawyers. If he was smart, he would find someone to represent him, and we'd find a way to settle this, but I don't see him handling the claim through the court system. Then again, this whole thing could be a scam. His real father could be some migrant farm worker that was picking tobacco on our farm two decades ago. I really don't know."

"Wow, this is an interesting side-bar to your move. I hope Middlebrook can put this issue to rest pretty quickly."

"Yes, let's hope so. See, the worst of it is, the mother, and I assume the son, live on our property in an old tenant shack. The family is dirt poor, and my mom's side of the family has helped them out for years, actually for three generations. As far as I know, we've never charged them rent. I want to talk to Mark about getting them off the property. The mom appears to be a sweet lady, but based on the conversation I had with the son on Tuesday, I don't know what this character's capable of."

"Yeah, you better watch this guy," Jeff recommended. "Seems like he'd find some small town lawyer in Bladen County to help him and see if he has some claim to the farm, but I can't imagine he could claim that large of a portion, given the number of cousins in your family."

"You wouldn't think, but think about it ... he could claim to be the *only* direct heir of my uncle. In theory, he's the only child, and the rest of us were just nephews and a niece. It's really how the courts or a judge might rule, depending on how the will is interpreted," Will sighed.

"It'll work out," Jeff assured him. " I'm sure Mark's seen a few of these cases in his day as an estate lawyer."

"I didn't mean to get sidetracked on that issue for so long, but I wanted you to know why I was here in town today," Will said. He changed the subject. "So, tell me about your kids. What grades are they in this year?"

Will and Jeff caught up on each other's families, and Will made a point to ask about some of their mutual friends from Wilmington. Then he asked Jeff about Kaitlyn Gerrard. "Kate doesn't live here, as far as I know," Jeff said. "I think she's still in New York. Why do you ask about her?"

"I never told anyone this, but I had a thing for her back in high school and never pursued it. I thought she was still in New York, but I was just curious if she might be around," Will confessed.

"I don't see her in town, but the way Wilmington's grown, it's hard to know who lives here anymore. I thought she was living in New York pursuing a career on Broadway," Jeff mentioned.

"That's what I remember too, but that was years ago. She went to school up there and probably never left. Take it from me, it can happen. I got lucky and found a way to get back down here - at least part-time."

"Do you think you'll ever move to the farm permanently?" Jeff asked.

"I'd love to, but I don't think I could convince Cat to move down here. You were at the wedding. You saw how deep her ties are to New England. We have a good community in Marblehead with her parents and sister living so close. She's still friends with girls she went to elementary school with in Marblehead that she keeps up with. And I'm friends with the husbands, so it's a pretty good life up there, except the fact that I'm the odd man out as the token Southerner."

Jeff nodded in understanding as he took a final bite of his second taco.

"Like I tell people," Will continued. "I have the best of both worlds. I have my life down here during the week and get home for the weekends. Now, if you asked Cat, she'll tell you it's not what she signed up for. She hates anything to do with the farm. I'm sure I've built a wall between the two of us when I decided to buy the farm. She has agreed to bring the girls down for Thanksgiving though, so that's a start." He smiled. "Well, I felt like I did all the talking, but I better get going so I can run up some legal fees," Will joked as he stood to shake Jeff's hand.

"Yes, good luck with all that. I'm sure it'll work out. Mark's a good lawyer when it comes to estate work, from what I'm told."

"We'll get together again soon, but next time I'll have you and the family over to the farm. You need to get back over there. It'll be like stepping back in time from the days we'd go to the farm during the White Lake Little League tournaments."

"Those were some good times," Jeff remembered with a smile.

"Where did the time go? That was more than thirty-five years ago," Will calculated. "Can you believe it?"

The Counselor

Chapter 35

Will and Mark Middlebrook met in the offices of Dunlap, Murray & Landon on the second floor of the Front Street office building in downtown Wilmington. After a quick conversation with the law firm's receptionist, Will was greeted with a firm handshake from Mark as they met in the spacious lobby of the prominent law firm. Mark wore a heavily starched white shirt and silk neck-tie. For a fleeting second, Will thought he was back in the central business district of Boston. "Sorry, I didn't exactly dress up for our meeting," he apologized. "I tried to leave all my ties back in Boston." He himself wore khaki pants, a long-sleeve plaid shirt with the sleeves rolled up on his forearms, and a pair of Justin work-boots.

"No worries," Mark said, grasping a tie in one hand and a file in the other. "We see it all in here. I still wear the noose every day out of habit."

"Were you and Clay in the same class in school?" Will asked, as he glanced over Mark's shoulder in the direction of the young receptionist typing at a computer, once again allured by his attraction of another youthful Southern belle.

"Your brother was a year ahead of me at New Hanover and UNC. I wasn't ready to leave Chapel Hill, so I stayed three more years and got a law degree. I remember you from your baseball days at New Hanover. I was in eighth grade when you were the star shortstop hitting .400 as a senior," Mark said.

"I seem to recall that my batting average was more like .275 that year, but if you remember .400, then I'll take it," Will smiled. "I remember reading about your football career at New Hanover High when I came home from UNC. I'm sure you have a shrine of all those newspaper clippings plastered all over your office," he laughed.

"Not hardly. I'm just a working stiff now, trying to make a living doing family and estate law," Mark shrugged. He gestured toward the door just off the lobby. "Let's step in the conference room. Can I offer you a coke or bottled water?"

"No thanks, I just met Jeff Baker at the Mexican place down the street for lunch, but thanks anyway."

"Jeff's a good man. We see him at school functions and sporting events pretty regularly," Mark shared.

The two sat down in the large leather chairs at the conference room table and began to recap the details that Will had described in a lengthy e-mail yesterday afternoon.

"Your e-mail yesterday was helpful by framing the case, saving us sometime today," Mark explained. "I've also read your uncle's will. It was drafted by a local attorney in Elizabethtown, who was more of a generalist when it came to his law practice ... probably a friend of your uncle's. So, the will is pretty vague when it refers to the fact that your uncle's estate should be left to the surviving heirs," Mark continued. "Maybe your uncle intentionally had it worded this way, left open for interpretation. My guess is that if your uncle fathered a child who was kept a secret all these years, then your uncle probably didn't even tell the attorney who drafted the will.

On the other hand, maybe your uncle shared the truth with the attorney, and the document was drafted in a way to keep things purposely vague. It's hard to know, unless we want to try to meet with your uncle's attorney, but I don't know if that really solves anything. We can't change what the will says."

Will nodded in agreement. "My uncle was a private person. I could see where he would keep this whole ordeal a secret, not telling anyone in town ... even his lawyer. So if Wyn's claim is true, what does this mean for the farm and my ownership rights?"

"The courts could rule that Wyn is the primary surviving heir, so he should be entitled to a larger portion of the estate ... possibly all of it. On the other hand, you've made a substantial financial investment in purchasing the assets of the estate, so that can't be overlooked. It's situations like these that keep lawyers like me in business. If Wyn's able to prove the fact that he's your uncle's son, then he probably has a case, and in my opinion, could make a claim of some sort to at least a *portion* of the estate."

"I've got myself in jam with this character and want to play offense, rather than waiting to see if he takes some sort of legal action," Will said.

"Well first, if he's making these claims, we need proof, or evidence, as we call it in my world."

"Is a paternity test even worth pursuing at this point?" Will asked. "I really don't want to go there, unless we have to."

"We may want to go that route if you want to delay the process, especially if you think he has an unfounded claim, but that would mean exhuming the body, and I'm not sure you and your cousins want to go through that ordeal."

"I'd really like him off the property, but I don't want to create more of a hostile situation than already exists. Plus, his mom seems like a nice lady," Will commented.

"I could see where you might want them off the property, and from a legal right, you have the ability to request that they leave, but practically speaking, I wouldn't recommend it. If this conflict were to ever go to trial, and I'm not saying it ever would, then a jury would look very unfavorably on the fact that you evicted them, although in theory, Wyn and his family pay no rent," Mark explained.

"I'm not even a hundred percent sure he lives on property. He's a drifter from what I can tell. He may live with his girlfriend in another part of the county for all I know," Will disclosed. "Part of me wonders if Wyn is driving this decision or if his mom is counseling him. My guess is the mom is content to leave the past alone. She knows the Winfield family has been good to her through the years, and she would like to continue paying no rent. She's probably in her sixties now and might just want to let this issue die and keep the secret buried in the past."

"Unless this guy makes some sort of formal legal claim, all he's doing is making noise at this point," Mark rationalized.

"So, do we take the offensive? Should we send him a letter from your firm disputing his claims, and hope that scares him away or at least flushes him out?" Will inquired. "I don't want to provoke this guy, because I think he's got some hostile tendencies. I just want to put this to rest. If he's legally due part of the estate, then I'll figure out a way to compensate him, but let me assure you, this is not a guy I want as a partner in the farm for the next thirty years."

"Okay, I'll draft a letter that states his claims are unsubstantiated and to basically back off. We'll send it to him certified mail so we ensure he gets it. Hopefully, he'll see the light and go away."

"Sounds good," Will said, pushing away from the mahogany table.

"I'll send you an e-mail draft tonight, but let's plan to have the letter ready to go out as early as tomorrow."

"Perfect," Will said as he shook Mark's hand. Following a good-bye wave to the receptionist, Will was on his way out of the four-story building and back in his vehicle.

He had one more appointment today while on the coast. He had yet to tell Henry about the confrontation with Wyn over his supposed birthright. Yesterday, Will had called Henry and let him know he would be in Wilmington for a meeting, and wanted to come by to see how he was feeling. Will thought it would be best to tell Henry directly, in person, the full story of Wyn's visit to the farm on Tuesday. Henry, of all the eight cousins, would find Wyn's claim most preposterous and shocking.

Will drove east out of downtown Wilmington on Highway 76 toward the New Hanover County beaches. Before making the trek to see Henry in Carolina Beach, Will decided to make a slight detour to Wrightsville Beach to relive some memories of his teenage years. As he drove over the Wrightsville Beach Drawbridge on to the island, the thought hit him. Maybe Cat would agree to move to Wrightsville Beach during the winters after Lauren graduates. That would shorten his commute by at least a few hundred miles. Surely, a place like Wrightsville Beach would be a place she'd like to live to avoid the cold winters in Boston. He'd run the idea by her and drive the family over here at Thanksgiving.

Will parked his Range Rover in the Blockade Runner lot, curious to see if the resort had maintained its reputation as the center-point of Wrightsville Beach. It was late September, so the crowds Will was accustomed to during the summers would be non-existent, but he smiled inside as he stepped foot on the hallowed grounds that helped mold his teenage years.

Based on memories of days gone by at the Blockade Runner, Will speculated that the hotel would be a commendable family vacation choice next summer. He was trying his best to find ways to make the farm a place Cat and the girls would want to visit. Wrightsville Beach was only an hour from the farm and a great beach. It may not be Cape Cod, but it was a neat place. He walked through the hotel lobby toward the outdoor pool as reflections of his past flooded his mind. The one memory that stood out above the rest was the last time he saw Kaitlyn. He rehashed the encounter over in his head as he circled the pool, walking toward the boardwalk overlooking the Atlantic Ocean.

For whatever reason, he was determined to find Kaitlyn again. He wanted to know where she lived and what she was doing with her life. The missed opportunity to pursue her had evaded him over twenty years ago, right here in this very place. Not much had changed here at the Blockade Runner in two decades, he thought as he stood alone on the boardwalk, reliving the memory of a chance that had literally passed him by twenty-one years ago. Maybe his destiny with Kaitlyn was never meant to be. Was Cat really the girl he was supposed to marry? It had been a rough ride, and he was not sure they'd make it through this move, especially after the girls were gone. The thought of the two of them enjoying each other's company as empty nesters was something he couldn't envision. Still, he'd never even given Kaityn a chance, so who knows? If he had only stopped her that day, at least he would know if there had been a future for them.

Will left the Blockade Runner and drove down Waynick Boulevard to North Lumina Avenue, noting the houses and condominiums for sale as he drove to the north end of the island, home of Hanover County's most profound night-time parties in the eighties. He left Wrightsville Beach that afternoon and the high school memories behind him, but the recollection of his last encounter with Kaitlyn remained ingrained in his mind as he drove twenty miles south to Henry's beach house.

Carolina Beach was known to move at a much slower pace than Wrightsville Beach, particularly during the off-season this time of the year. Growing up, Will had spent very little time at Carolina Beach. Carolina Beach was further from his home in Wilmington, and Wrightsville Beach was where the action could be found. He had never visited Cousin Henry's house at Carolina Beach. Henry had moved here seven years ago and lived with Laura, his wife of twenty-six years, and two cats. Henry and Laura were never able to conceive, so the cats were considered their children. Will had two objectives in mind for his visit with his older cousin. First, Will wanted to check on Henry's health. Second, he was eager to tell Henry first-hand of his encounter with Wyn. The late afternoon fall breeze from the surf and a cold beer made for a comfortable visit with Henry on his back deck overlooking the Atlantic Ocean.

"So, how are you feeling?" Will asked, making note of Henry's hair loss from the radiation.

"The treatments are going well, according to the doctor. I go back for another round in two weeks. So far, the reports are positive, but the treatments are hell," Henry replied.

"Glad to hear the treatments are working," Will said, lifting his beer in Henry's direction.

"So, how are things going at the farm?" Henry asked.

"Well, I'm glad you're sitting down because I've got some news that you're not going to believe," Will said, seated on the edge of the teak chair with his hands on his knees. Henry perked up as Will began to convey the details of the Tuesday morning visit from Wyn.

Blown away by the incredulous news, Henry kept asking questions that Will could not answer, and then began offering hypothesis that only their uncle could address. The news from Winfield Farm seemed to make Henry momentarily forget that he was sick.

"Henry, this guy's a freak," Will told him. "I'm not sure what he's capable of. I want to keep my distance from him. I'm hopeful that the meeting with the attorney today will help resolve the issue."

"Let me know if there's anything I can do," Henry offered. "I'm sure your lawyer friend in Wilmington will help solve this debacle."

"Let's hope so," Will replied. "Let me know when you feel up for a trip to the farm. I'd love to give you a tour and tell you about this year's harvest."

"Let's plan on it," Henry said standing on the deck and walking Will to his car.

"Definitely," Will said. He shook the hand of his cousin tightly.

"You keep me posted on your situation at the farm," Henry said. "And keep this guy at bay. Don't let him distract you from what you're doing."

Will left Henry and Laura's house and drove back through Wilmington. It was still daylight, so he decided to visit his alma mater, New Hanover High School. The football team was practicing in full pads in preparation for tomorrow night's football game. He cruised through campus like he was a high school senior again, and the drive brought back many affirmative memories. Still, thoughts of Kaitlyn remained foremost in his mind.

After a spin down his old street on the north side of Wilmington, Will drove past Kaitlyn's home near the Pine Valley Country Club and decided to knock on the door of her childhood house. Though he had never visited Kaitlyn here, he knew where she lived from his days of working at the golf course. He decided to pose as an old friend trying to locate Kaitlyn. It was a long shot, but he timidly knocked on the door in search of her whereabouts. No answer. Just as Will turned to leave, the front door cracked open ever so slightly.

"Who's there?" the elderly female voice whispered through the meager opening of the door.

"Hello, sorry to bother you ma'am, but my name is Will Jordan. I grew up here and just moved back to town. I was looking for Kaitlyn Gerrard. She used to live here many years ago. We were in school together, and I was hoping to say hello. I don't mean to bother you, but I was hoping to find her." To Will's surprise, the door opened a little wider. The face of a silver-haired woman with perched lips, appearing to be in her late seventies, peered through the doorway.

"Kate doesn't live here anymore. She moved from here a long time ago. She lives in New York now, but she visits here every now and then. I'm her aunt. I'd be glad to tell her you came by, but you'll have to tell me your name again."

A rush of excitement came over him. Will was shocked to think that he might have found a link to Kaitlyn after all these years. "I remembered she lived in New York, but I thought I would check here anyway. As I mentioned, I just moved back in town from Boston, but if you could tell her I came by today, I would really appreciate it. Do you speak to her regularly?"

"Yes, I'm the only family she has since my sister and Kate's father died many years ago. We are close. I wish she lived here in Wilmington."

"She's a wonderful girl," Will smiled. "I'm sure you miss her living here."

"Oh, yes. Very much," the elderly lady replied.

Will reached for his wallet and pulled out a business

card. "Please tell her I came by, just to say hello," he said as he handed her his card. Her feeble hands were lily white with a spattering of liver spots that covered the blue veins that ran from her wrist to her knuckles. Her fingers were cold to the touch. "This is my old business card from Boston, but she'll recognize the name. I just moved back to North Carolina a month ago and am trying to visit a few friends."

"She'll be in town for Christmas. You should come back by to visit," she said, as she studied Will's business card like it was counterfeit money.

"I might just do that. It was nice to meet you. What is your name?"

"Esther Freeman," she replied, slowly closing the door.

Will stepped off the concrete porch, although he wanted to step back inside and hug Aunt Esther. However, he was ecstatic that his travels to Wilmington might have already led him to Kaitlyn. Amazing, he thought as he walked slowly to his car parked on the street in front of Kaitlyn's old home. He supposed it would not have been right to ask any more personal questions about her. She was probably married with seven children. It would be fitting that an only child would have seven children. Who knows, maybe he'd get an e-mail from her. He'd look her up on Facebook or Google her name when he got back to the farm.

Will's work on the Carolina coast was done for the day. It was time to head back to the farm. It had been a productive day, and after meeting with Mark this afternoon, Will felt much better about how to deal with Wyn's claim on the farm. He decided to take a different route back to the farm via State Route 87, which would take him through Elizabethtown. It had been three weeks since he moved to Bladen County, and Will was on a mission to find out the best place in the county to shoot pool. It had been a constructive day in Wilmington, so he decided to celebrate with a few beers and a game of pool. Tonight was his night to see if he still had the stick to shoot pool with the Bladen County locals. It was time to become part of his new community and seek intelligence about his newly discovered wayward cousin.

The Pool Hall

Chapter 36

The evening sun projected an ominous prism of color among the rain clouds that dominated the sky throughout the day, creating a violet illumination on the horizon as Will drove westward after his afternoon trip to the coast. A veil of darkness settled over North Carolina, signaling it was time for Will to call the family in Boston.

With every nightly call, Will was not sure whom he might catch on the home phone. Typically, by seven o'clock, he was sure to catch both Sarah and Lauren most weeknights, and if the girls were home, then Cat would most likely be there as well. The uncertainty was which Cat Will would find at home when he called. Would it be the Old Cat he married almost twenty years ago or the New Cat, the venomous wife who still carried a grudge toward her husband for the decision to buy the farm? Tonight, it was his fourteen-year-old daughter Lauren who answered the home phone. "Lar, how are you?" Will asked as he drove the last few miles westward past the open fields on Highway 87 toward Bladen County.

"I'm good, Dad. I just got home from soccer practice a little while ago."

"Okay, how was your history test today?" Will asked.

"I think it went okay. I studied for it, but it was a really unfair test."

"Was it hard?"

"Yeah, that teacher is just tough. I don't like her."

"Is Mom there?" Will asked.

"Yes, but you might want to talk to Sarah. Mom's not real happy right now."

"What's going on?" Will asked calmly, though his mind raced with uncertainty. "Is everything okay?"

"Oh yeah, things are okay. She's just having a bad day, I guess. She said I didn't study enough for my test last night, and this is not a good way to start high school. I need to be more serious about my grades now that I'm in ninth grade."

"Well, I thought you said you did pretty well on the test," Will said.

"I think I did all right. We'll see next week. Do you want to talk to Sarah?"

"Can you let me speak to Mom?" Will asked.

"She's downstairs," Lauren explained. "Really, Dad, you may not want to talk to her right now. She's kinda upset."

"Okay, I'll take your advice and wait and call her later, but I do want to speak with Sarah if she's close by," he said.

"Sure Dad, here she is," Lauren responded. "Bye, love you."

"Bye, Lauren," he said. "Love you, too."

"Hi Dad, how's everything on the farm today?" Sarah asked in a pleasant voice.

"It's pretty good, although I was in Wilmington most of today to take care of some business and see my cousin, the one who's sick. It was a good trip, so I'm headed back now," Will explained as he drove into the Elizabethtown city limits. "So, how are you? Did you have cheerleading practice today?"

"I'm good. We had a short practice today, thankfully."

"You excited about visiting BC on Saturday?"

"Yeah, I think so, but you know I'm still leaning toward NYU," Sarah said.

"Well, keep an open mind and we'll see how things work out. So, what's up with Mom? Sounds like she's not happy."

"Oh, I think she's in one of her moods," Sarah explained.

"I'll call her on her phone, and I'll see you guys Saturday morning. Love you," Will said. He hung up the phone and debated whether to call Cat. What the hell, he'd call her and check the box for the night. He dialed and waited for the answer. "Hey, how are you?" Will asked cautiously when Cat picked up.

"Don't ask," she snapped coldly.

"I just talked to the girls," Will said, trying to fend off any immediate fireworks. "Lauren said her history test was hard."

"She didn't study enough. She was on her phone most of the night. I can't do this alone, Will. It's too much trying to discipline the girls and keep them focused on school. This is not a one-parent job. This arrangement is not working out. I'm glad you're having fun playing farmer, but we might as well be divorced. This is worse, though, because you're a thousand miles away and cruise in here on the weekends when there's no pressure, no tests, and no discipline required. This just isn't working," Cat vented.

Will frowned. "I'm sorry it's been a bad day," he said, trying to show sympathy.

"It's not just a bad day, Will," she snapped. "Don't you get it? I told you this system wasn't going to work. It's one thing if it was summer and the parenting responsibilities were minimal, but now that school has started, there's so much more to be on top of with the girls. I'm glad to know things are going great down there for you, but you've left me with all the work and stress of raising these girls."

"I wish I could be there to help out, but I've got my hands full down here now," Will said, referring to the conflict with Wyn. "I'll talk to Lauren about her studies this weekend. It's probably time to take the cell phone away at night until she can learn to study. That phone is a major distraction."

"Well, you just do that and try to enforce that policy from down there, Mr. Big Talk," Cat muttered.

Will sensed Cat's frustration and knew it was time to hang up. He could only hope for a better conversation tomorrow. "I better let you guys get going. I'm sorry I'm not there to help. I didn't think it would be that hard," he said apologetically.

"Well, it *is* that hard. It's difficult for you to know since you're not here, so trust me when I tell you that this commuting system of yours is not going so well. All the work falls on the weekdays when you're not here. Your brilliant scheme has worked out splendidly for you, while leaving me with the challenges of raising the girls. I feel like it's 1998 again, home alone, raising the girls while you work your ass off and never make it home," she lamented, referring to the era when she stayed at home with two toddlers while Will worked long hours to build his investment banking practice.

Will had a difficult time showing Cat too much sympathy when she complained. In his mind, he figured Cat had enjoyed a pretty good life in Marblehead. He had been a good provider. He gave her almost anything she asked for from a material standpoint. Now that the girls were older, she had the luxury during the day to play tennis, shop, attend yoga and spin classes, and have lunch at Tedesco with her friends. "It's not like I'm down here sitting on my ass watching Sports Center," he shot back. "I've got my own set of challenges on my hands." Cat didn't respond. He didn't expect even an acknowledgement from her regarding how things were going at Winfield Farm. She appeared not to care and had never asked any specific questions about the challenges he might be facing with his new job. He had made his decision to buy the farm without her support, so he knew he must go it alone when it came to dealing with issues like Wyn's claim of ownership.

Still, he resented the fact that Cat never asked him anything about the farm. Telling her about this week's dilemma with Wyn was not an option, though a part of him wanted to share the story with her. In years past, he had shared many of his difficulties at work with her, particularly before the girls were born. Now, he faced a major issue in his new business, but he knew the standard answer he would get from Cat if he told her about Wyn would be, "I told you buying that farm was a bad idea."

Will chose to pass on sharing the story of Wyn's visit with Cat — particularly tonight. It was time to hang up. "I'll call you tomorrow, and we'll firm up plans for the visit to BC," Will said, referring to the planned college visit to Boston College for Sarah on Saturday.

"Don't bother," Cat retorted. "I can handle it by myself, just like I do every other day of the week."

"Bye, love you," Will said quickly. In instances of conflict, he made it a habit of ending a combative phone call with, "I love you."

The phone clicked. Looking at the screen, he realized she had hung up without responding or saying good-bye. Enraged, he pushed the red END button on his phone. He had grown accustomed to Cat's acrimonious outbursts, on the phone or inside their home. This wasn't the first time in twenty years of marriage that she had hung up on him. When she had a bad day, there was no cat in the house to kick, so typically the blame and rage were directed toward him. His initial response to his wife's indignations was to retreat. Typically, his retreat meant working longer hours and staying late at the office. In the investment-banking world, he could always find more work to be do, identify another prospect to call, and convince himself to work a little bit harder and longer. Now, he had found a permanent retreat: a place of refuge called Winfield Farm.

Many factors had contributed to his decision to buy the farm and move back to North Carolina. It was time for a change in his work career. He was burned out in the fast pace and pressures of the mergers and acquisitions business. Buying the farm was a favorable investment, given the timing and price of his acquisition. Family pride, and the opportunity to run a business of his own, ranked high as well. The chance to move back to North Carolina after spending the last twenty-plus years in New England was also a driver. Nevertheless, an unspoken, underlying factor of his decision to buy the farm might be summed up in the word *retreat* - a retreat from Cat. A retreat from the constant berating he had come to know as standard operating procedure. Admittedly, he had not been a model husband, and while he had been faithful to Cat, he had failed to place a priority on his relationship with her. He lacked when it came to providing her with the attention she needed.

The words of Stuart Peterson, Liberty's managing partner, echoed in his ears. "I just want to make sure you're not running away from something. If you're not running away, then I completely understand your decision to return to North Carolina." If Will was honest with himself, maybe a part of his decision to buy the farm was to flee his bad marriage. When times were good in the investment business, he could handle the conflicts at home with a little more impunity, but when the M & A business had grown more toilsome in recent years, he'd found the strife at home to be oppressive.

"Maybe I *was* running from something," Will mumbled. Had he exacerbated the hostile conflict in his marriage even more by moving to North Carolina? Apparently so. Time would tell, but so far, the decision to buy the farm and move south seemed to have provoked the anger inside of Cat and further strained their relationship.

"It's definitely time for a beer," Will sighed, turning into the parking lot of the Tar Heel Saloon, a local bar on the west side of Bladen County in the tiny town of Tar Heel. The Tar Heel Saloon was not a place a man went to meet a lady. It was a place a man went to get a drink, not a bar where one went to sip a glass of wine on the patio. However, according to the locals in Bladen County, it was the best place around to find a competitive game of pool.

The concrete block building looked just as the manager of the feed and seed store in Elizabethtown had described to Will. The parking area was scattered with a handful of older model cars, mostly pick-up trucks. Several of the trucks sported monster tires and a few displayed oversized Rebel flag stickers in the rear windows. If he wanted to get into a fight, this would be the place he'd come, Will thought as he swung open the screen door that led into the dimly lit bar. A layer of smoke settled over the crowd inside like a stratus cloud lining the sky. He surveyed the crowd. He didn't know a soul, and in the back of his mind, he wondered if he might see Wyn. The Tar Heel Saloon looked like a place that Wyn might frequent on a Thursday night.

It was still early in the evening, not even 8:00, yet the bar was crowded, its patrons mostly Southern gentlemen, but he counted a total of two girls, standing near the jukebox that played the Zac Brown Band version of *The Devil Went Down to Georgia*. He looked to his left and noticed a separate room where the pool table was located. He was in the right place.

He ordered a beer and made his way through the crowd toward the room with the pool table. Though he enjoyed the game of pool, he knew it would be difficult to break into the inter-sanctum of locals who were regulars at the Tar Heel Saloon. He didn't exactly fit the profile of a local, at least not yet. For one, he was older, in his mid-forties, and most of the guys in the bar were probably in their twenties and thirties. Second, the Tar Heel Saloon crowd represented the blue-collar working class in Bladen County. He guessed that few, if any, had gone to college. Many worked on farms, while others were employed in area manufacturing plants like Gilbarco Veeder-Root, a fuel dispensing systems plant now known as Danaher Controls, one of Bladen County's largest employers. The world's largest pork processing plant was also located in Tar Heel, just north of the pool hall.

Will stood in the corner of the room, beer in hand, and watched the game of eight-ball, assessing the level of play. The guys on the table were skilled and probably played pool five nights a week, based on his evaluation. He had not played a game a pool since a group from the office took him to play at the pool hall in downtown Boston just before he left the firm. Despite his inferiority, he wanted his shot on the table. Five or six others stood around the periphery of the table, and he wondered how many of those in the room were waiting to play the next game. He approached a tall, lean guy with a goatee beard and a tattered John Deere hat who appeared to be watching the competition on the table. He stood around 6'4, but weighed only 180 pounds. "You know who's got next game?" Will asked.

"I do," he said, sizing up Will's attire. "You here to play?"

"Was hoping to," Will nodded. "Do you know who has the next game after you?"

"Looks like you," the gangly man said, without emotion.

Will stood in the corner and sipped his Budweiser while watching as the current game ended. The lanky player approached the table to challenge the reigning Tar Heel champion, while the champion acknowledged his lanky opponent.

"You ready, Stretch?"

Stretch struggled to keep pace with the champion and fell in humble defeat after a short battle. Will pretended not to notice the thrashing that Stretch took from the Champ, but Will studied every shot, concluding his own skill level fell somewhere between the Champ and Stretch, the challenger. Stretch stepped aside and made way for Will's inaugural eight ball challenge at the Tar Heel Saloon. He went to work racking the pool balls, glancing periodically at the champ, who casually decorated the tip of his cue stick with additional chalk while engaged in conversation with a few of the locals at the opposite end of the pool table.

"Go easy on me tonight. I'm a little rusty," Will requested, carefully lifting the wooden rack from the triangular assembly of pool balls.

"You workin' in town today?" the champ asked as he leaned over the table, cue in hand, ready to rupture Will's craftsmanship of pool balls.

"Actually, I just moved here three weeks ago. I bought my uncle's farm on the north end of the county, so I'm new to town, I guess," Will explained. He watched the champ carefully position the cue ball in the optimal spot to instigate the break.

"You mean John Winfield's place?" the champ asked, looking up, as he prepared to blast the cue ball.

"So, you knew my uncle?" Will asked slightly surprised, yet feeling his first ray of connectivity to the Tar Heel Saloon and its clientele.

"Oh yeah, I've cut timber on your place, several years ago. I figure it's probably time to cut again," the champ said over the loud collision of the cue ball striking the rack.

Will watched in awe as the array of pool balls spread to the four corners of the green felt table. "Yeah, I may need you to come look at doing some thinning before too long. I'm still trying to get my arms around the operation, but the guy who cruised the timber before I bought the place said that we'd be due to thin pretty soon."

The conversation ceased as the battle began. The champ went to work, intently focused on each shot he took. It was by no means an epic battle. Will made his share of good shots, but like Stretch before him, he also fell victim to the champ's prowess. The eight ball banged in the corner pocket with a profound thud to end the game, leaving three of Will's solid pool balls scattered on the table's flat surface.

"Good game," Will said, exasperated at the hands of defeat by the champion. He walked toward the champ and extended his hand in congratulations. "I'm Will Jordan."

"Randall Shaefer. Nice to meet you," the champ responded.

"Do you ever give up the table?" Will asked with a laugh.

"Every now and again," Randall smiled.

"You schooled me," Will said shamefully. "I need to play more often. Like I said, I'm rusty."

"Your uncle was a fine man, very well respected 'round here," Randall said.

"Well, thank you. I miss him. I grew up in Wilmington, so we spent a good bit of time around the farm growing up, but then I moved up north to go to school, married a girl up there, and thought I'd be up in Boston forever ... until the chance to buy the farm came up after John died."

"You move your family here?" the Champ asked.

"No, it's just me for now," Will explained. "That's why I'm

here shooting pool tonight. I have two girls in high school back in Boston, so I couldn't pull them out of school to move here. I take the train back and forth every weekend."

"That sure sucks," Randall responded, offering a head nod to his next challenger.

"It's not so bad ... so far," Will admitted. "I'm headed to the bar for another beer. I'll let you take care of your next challenger." He exited the smoky billiards room, leaving Randall to annihilate another opponent. He ordered two Budweisers and headed back to the billiards room to watch the champion take down another inept rival.

As the game ended, Will approached Randall and offered him the second beer he had purchased at the bar, wondering if the champ ever took a rest from the table. Surely, Randall took a bathroom or beer break at some point through the night. "Good game," Will said as he handed the longneck Budweiser bottle to Randall. "Let me ask you a quick question before your next game. I wanted to see if you know anything about a family that lives on our property."

"Thanks for the beer, man," Randall said as he raised the bottle in Will's direction.

"There's a young guy named Wyn Saxon whose mom and family have lived on our property for years. He's approached me about doing some work on the farm, but I'm real skeptical about hiring him. Do you know him, or anything about him? I'm not real serious about hiring him, but I at least wanted to check him out."

"You talkin' about Wyn? The guy that doesn't have much to say? Around twenty-five or thirty? Bigger, thick fella?" Randall asked, using his pool stick as a vertical prop while gripping the beer in his other fist.

"Yep, that's him," Will replied.

"I got two words for you, sir. Hell no! That kid's bad news, far as I know. That sum bitch lives on *your* farm?" Randall asked in a surprised tone. Randall motioned with his beer toward two guys standing on the opposite side of the room against the cement block wall. The two men made their way toward Will and Randall.

"Yeah, he and his mother and sister live a little less than a mile down the road in a small frame house right on the highway. His family's lived there for years."

Randall's friends walked over and joined in the conversation. The champ introduced his two sidekicks above the noise, and Will didn't catch their names. Instead, he greeted them with a firm handshake.

"This fella' is old man John Winfield's nephew," Randall said. "He's runnin' the Winfield place now. He wanted to ask you guys about this Saxon kid. I think you guys might know him. The kid lives on the Winfield farm and is lookin' for work."

"Steer clear, my man," the shorter, stockier of the two men advised.

The second one piped in and offered his opinion of Wyn as well. He was about Will's height, but with broad shoulders and a full beard that could use a good grooming. He resembled a lumberjack, and may have been one, for all Will knew.

"He's been in here a few times a while back, and I think the last time Wyn was here, he got into a fight with some feller," the lumberjack shared. "The cops had to come and haul him off. I believe the feller's been in jail a few times. I haven't seen him 'round here in quite a while though. He may have just got out of jail again, far as I know. You need to check his criminal record before you think about hirin' him. That's my opinion, for what it's worth."

"I thought the guy seemed a little shady when I first met him at my uncle's funeral," Will said. "I'm not about to hire him, especially now. Do you guys know anything about his family? The mother seems like a decent lady. I'm not sure about his dad though. I've never seen or met him."

Randall and his comrades shook their heads and shrugged, indicating they knew nothing about Wyn's family. "Can't help you there," the lumberjack said. "Sorry."

"I appreciate your help, guys. I'll steer clear of him. Sounds like I may need him off the property, based on what you guys have told me."

"I'd watch out for him," Randall warned. "Trouble seems to find him."

"Well, I'll be back around to play some more pool, but I need to work on my game before I face Randall again," Will said. He pulled a Liberty Trust business card from his wallet. "Randall, come by sometime in the next few weeks or call me, and we'll look at the timber that needs thinning. Use my cell phone number that's on the card."

"Will do, I'll stop by next time I'm up that way," Randall said with a casual wave that resembled more of a salute.

Will turned and walked toward the exit, satisfied. His work at the Tar Heel Saloon was a success tonight. The Tar Heel Saloon was a place he would frequent again.

The Shopkeeper

Chapter 37

Will had completed his third week of work on the farm. Friday nights with Becca in Fayetteville had become a rite of passage before the overnight train ride back to Boston. The weekly routine required that Will leave the farm by six o'clock on Friday evening, arrive in Fayetteville in time for dinner with Becca, and leave his car at Java Joe's before the north-bound train left the station at 8:22 p.m.

This Friday's ritual carried a different ambience for Will. Today, he carried with him the burden of settling the newborn conflict with Wyn. The unknown of how the estate settlement would end weighed heavy on his mind. Mark's letter to Wyn would hopefully put Wyn on the defensive and back him off from any legal claims to the farm.

Will looked forward to his Friday night dinners with Becca, and their conversation mostly centered on farming and running her coffee shop. Weekend plans were also the topic of conversation, but Becca's plans seemed to always focus on the shop. Though he was not hesitant to share personal informa-tion with Becca, Will chose not to divulge the news of Wyn's visit earlier in the week with her, thinking she would find the entire incident bizarre. Wyn's claim on the farm was more of a private family matter, and something Will was actually too embarrassed to convey with too many people.

"Okay, when I get back next week, we're going to lock down the plans for you to come see the farm," he told her that night. "I'm thinking next Thursday, so get your niece or one of your other girls to cover the shop for the afternoon and evening, because I'm planning to give you the full tour and then cook you dinner." Will laid out his plans as he and Becca walked the two-block distance from Java Joe's to the Italian restaurant.

"Next Thursday works for me, but you gotta' tell me how to find this farm of yours," Becca joked.

"I already got that part figured out on my drive over here tonight," he explained. "There's a little town just over the county line in Bladen County called Tar Heel. Personally, I just like the name, but it will be a good meeting place. Tar Heel is just south of here down Highway 87, maybe twenty minutes away. There's a bar just as you come in town called the Tar Heel Saloon, on the southeast corner of the main intersection. We can meet there at noon on Thursday."

"Should I be writing this down?" Becca asked.

"No, I'll give you directions on Monday when I pick up the car," he replied. "But it'll be easy to find. We'll pick up something to eat at Melvin's in downtown Elizabethtown on the way to the farm," he continued. "The farm is only twenty minutes from the big city of E-town. I'll show you around, maybe we'll try to catch some fish, and shoot the shotguns. We'll grill out, and I'll have you back in Tar Heel by nine-thirty or ten o'clock that night. Sound like a plan?"

"I'm game. Sounds like fun, and I'll finally get to see this farm that you've been tellin' me about since we first met."

"So, have you ever shot skeet before?" he asked.

"I know how to shoot a little. It's been a while, so I'll need some instruction, especially when it comes to hitting a target. That'll be a sight," Becca laughed.

"So how have sales been this week?" he asked, changing the subject.

"Oh, not too bad. We've had a little more traffic as the weather 's gotten cooler. The morning crowd is still pretty steady."

"I hope things are going okay at Java Joe's. You work so hard, I want to see you succeed."

"You're always so nice to ask about my business. I really appreciate that."

"I'm just nosey. That's all," he grinned.

Once they sat down for dinner at Pierre's Italian Restaurant on Hay Street, the conversation turned from business to matters of a more personal nature. Will peppered Becca with questions about her family in South Carolina and her divorce. Becca described in detail how things had not ended well in her marriage.

"There you go again, asking all the questions," she griped. "It's my turn now. You're good at digging into my past while you sit there and rarely share a thing."

"That's not true. I shared way too much with you that night we had beers in your storeroom, but go ahead, ask away. I'm an open book," he offered, leaning back against the black cushion in the secluded booth in the back of the restaurant.

"Okay, so tell me about your wife. What's she like?"

"I should have seen that coming," he said, rolling his eyes. He sighed. "Let's see," he hesitated as he thought through his response. "She's a devoted mother to my daughters. She has some great attributes, but this is my assessment of her, knowing her now for over twenty years. I think she's always had her way in life. She grew up in a home of privilege. Her mother came from money and was used to being pampered, so my wife and her sister were always used to getting what they wanted. I guess you would say she was a blue blood."

Becca leaned forward against the table, took a sip from her wine glass, listening intently as Will continued with the assessment of Cat. "She hasn't had any real difficulties to deal with in life, particularly when it came to money. Money has always been there, so she's gotten most everything she ever wanted, and I don't mean this in an arrogant way at all, but I probably didn't help the situation. I gave her things, more so in an effort to keep the peace, like jewelry, trips, a nice house close to where she grew up, the car she wanted, and no limits on what she had to spend on herself and my girls."

"Maybe I could be her in my next life," Becca joked.

"I guess I thought all girls were that way. I'm no different from her parents. I'm guilty of spoiling her myself. I grew up with one brother, and we just rolled with whatever came our way. We grew up middle class in Wilmington in a modest neighborhood. We didn't take lavish trips or spend money frivolously. Shoot, our idea of a fun vacation was coming to the farm for a week." He paused. "Wealth has a way of tainting people. I just hope it hasn't affected my two girls in an adverse way. It's hard not to spoil your children, especially girls."

Becca stared intently at him as he finished his description. "Have y'all ever been to any kind of counseling?" she asked.

"No, I guess we've just endured each other through the years. The romance faded a long time ago. Maybe raising children has a way of doing that, and I'll admit that I worked long hours during those critical years when the girls were young. I regret that I let her raise the girls alone ,while I thought it was my role to make money. We're still hanging on, but this farm purchase has done more to damage our marriage than any fight we've had over the last twenty years."

"What do you mean?" Becca queried.

"She really hates the fact that I made the decision to buy the farm and leave the family in Boston. I admit, taking a job eight hundred miles away from home, is pretty radical. I get that, but she resents the fact that I didn't consult with her first before buying the farm. I admit that was probably a mistake, but she would have laughed at the idea, so I followed my heart and my gut and negotiated a price to buy the farm before getting her buy-in."

Becca listened as Will shared the story of the purchase of Winfield Farm.

"I told her about the decision after the fact. But the big thing with her, and I know this sounds terrible, is that she liked the idea of her husband working for one of the prestigious investment-banking firms in downtown Boston, so she could tell her friends what I did for a living. And now, I own a farm in this remote part of North Carolina. She's had a hard time accepting that fact. I know I've made her out to be an evil person. She's not evil. She's just been able to script out this life for herself. My decision to leave Boston and buy this farm wasn't in her script. She claims I've left her to raise my daughters during the week, and she resents the fact that I'm only there during the weekends, when things at home are easy."

"I'm sorry," Becca said with sincerity.

"Don't be sorry. I made this decision, and I couldn't be happier to be out of the corporate world and running my own business. I love being back in North Carolina. I drove to Wilmington yesterday, had lunch with a high school friend of mine, saw my cousin, and drove through my old neighborhood. I like being back home. Don't get me wrong, I miss my family, and I'll be glad to see them when I get home in the morning, but I've really enjoyed being back here."

"Will your family come down and visit?" Becca asked.

"They're supposed to come for Thanksgiving, but my wife's still fighting me on the idea. I think my girls will like the farm. It's my wife who doesn't want to come. You'll see what I mean next week when you visit the farm. It's an awesome place ... at least I think so. It's so different from a big city, and I think that's what I like about it. It can sometimes get lonely out there, but that's the only real downside I've encountered so far."

"I'm excited to see it," Becca said with a wide grin.

"You'll like it. I know you will," he said, smiling back at her.

Will felt guilty about sharing so much about Cat, but he had refrained from belittling his wife. Instead, he had psychoanalyzed Cat and explained who she was based on her upbringing. Becca had shared great detail about her divorce tonight, so he'd felt compelled to tell his story about Cat. After all, Becca had blatantly asked Will to describe her. What was he supposed to say? Lie to her and say: oh, she's awesome and is a very supportive wife? He glanced down at his watch.

"I guess I better head that way. It's about that time." He smiled at Becca. "We've covered a lot of ground tonight — maybe too much. I probably shouldn't have gone into all that detail about my wife. She's really not a bad person. We're just going through a difficult time." He took the check from the table and walked Becca to the cash register to pay for dinner. He paid for the meal in cash. Always cautious, he had decided to keep the Friday night dinners off the credit card in case Cat decided to question a Friday night dinner expense.

The two walked in silence outside into the cool air of the October night. "Well, safe driving this weekend," he said as he handed Rebecca the keys to the Range Rover.

"Don't worry, I'll look after it. In fact, I took the car to the base last weekend and drove it on the jeep course. I was really surprised. Your car held up pretty well in those fast driving conditions," she joked.

He enjoyed her sense of humor. Although he and Becca came from different worlds and backgrounds, Will respected her work ethic and liked her wit. She was easy to talk to, as evidenced by their dinner conversation. He trusted her not only to take care of his car, but now with secrets about his fledging marriage.

"Maybe you should polish up on your shooting skills at the base this weekend. We'll have a skeet shooting competition at the farm next Thursday, so be prepared," he said.

"Actually, I don't have access to the base anymore, so I'll just have to get a few pointers next Thursday and see if I can hold my own."

"That sounds good," Will said. "I wouldn't want you to show me up on the range anyway." She smiled warmly at him and he could tell she felt comfortable around him. Was he letting her get too close, though? He was mildly attracted to her, but besides his brother, she had become his closest confidant in North Carolina. So, where was this friendship headed? Next week, she would be his first visitor to the farm since the purchase. He admitted to himself that he looked forward to seeing her each time he passed through Fayetteville, but was inviting Becca to the farm taking things too far?

"Thank you for dinner," Becca said softly as they walked casually back toward the coffee shop.

"Thanks for listening. I probably said too much about my situation at home tonight. I got read the riot act just last night by my wife on the phone, so I'm probably a little more jilted than usual right now. "

"Hey, I asked the question, so don't worry about it. I've been there myself. I told you more details about my ex than I've told some of my girlfriends. I was the one that started the conversation by spillin' my guts about my divorce. Just give me one glass of wine, and you can't shut me up."

Will grew quiet as he stared into the star-lit night. It was not his style to tell anyone about his marital struggles, not even to his closest friends or his brother. In some respects, it was therapeutic to vent his conflict with Cat, but being this open went against his nature. However, Becca was such a merciful listener. She always seemed genuinely concerned.

"You okay?" Becca asked.

"Yeah, I'm fine," he said, as he stared into the star-lit autumn night. "I'm just not used to sharing my marital struggles with anyone. I've always just kept things to myself, but now that things have gotten worse, I guess it helps to talk about it. Still, I feel guilty for saying anything."

"Don't feel guilty. It helps to talk through these issues in times like this. I wish I had a solution for you, Will, but I'm certainly no expert when it comes to relationships. All I can do is listen," Becca offered.

"I appreciate it, but there's nothing you or anyone can really offer. I don't know what the solution is. I brought this on myself. Truthfully, I thought the distance apart might help things, but it's made things worse," he shared, dropping his head.

"Don't beat yourself up about it. You're tryin' to do the right thing by going home every weekend. I don't see her making an effort to come down here and visit *you*," Becca said.

They stood across the street from the red brick free-standing Amtrak station. "I better get over there and get my ticket," he said, pointing toward the train depot. "You're a great listener, and I really appreciate that." He hugged Becca until the embrace became uncomfortable, and then let go. "Thank you, I *really* appreciate it," he said, as he broke the hug, picked up his briefcase and overnight bag, and trotted across the street toward the dimly lit train station.

"See you on Monday!" she called out Inside, Will positioned himself on one of the cold orange plastic chairs that faced the window overlooking the platform. The train was scheduled to arrive in less than fifteen minutes. "Helluva week," he sighed as he stretched his head backward and yawned. His mind recounted the week's events. Tomorrow morning, he would be back in Marblehead, prepared to visit several colleges around Boston. He wished Sarah would stay in Boston, or anywhere but New York. He knew it would be a tough sell, but he'd do what he could to talk her out of NYU tomorrow. The thought of one of his kids flying the coop was depressing.

The familiar sound of the train's arrival took his mind off the events of this past week. He stood, secured his travel bags, and walked outside to the platform. The train slowed to a complete stop, and the doors opened. He boarded the train and prepared himself for the overnight trip back to Boston, wondering what kind of reception he'd get from Cat tomorrow morning.

The Visits

Chapter 38

Will sent a text to Cat around 8:20 Saturday morning, letting her know that the train would arrive right on schedule in Lynn. From the minute Cat picked Will up from the train station, the chill he felt in the air was definitely not from the October temperatures in New England, but from the cool distance Cat kept from him. Her answers to his questions were curt and calculated, and his efforts at casual conversation were met with an awkward resistance.

The weekend was dedicated to visiting various college campuses around Boston, highlighted by the Boston College-Virginia football game on Saturday night. Holy Cross was the first stop on the list, with a scheduled tour and a meeting with the admissions director. More casual tours were set up at the University of Massachusetts in Amherst, Boston University, Tufts, and Wellesley.

Sarah and Lauren both heavily favored NYU, while Will tried to sway Sarah to any school in Massachusetts. Cat appeared indifferent about the college choices, but given a choice, she seemed to favor her alma mater, Holy Cross. The campus visits were fun, and the pros and cons of attending school in New York City versus Boston were debated by everyone in the family throughout the weekend. Lauren's opinion was also taken into account as each family member weighed in on Sarah's pending decision. However, the silent treatment and snide comments from Cat all weekend had taken their toll on Will. By Sunday evening, the farm was calling his name.

Will asked Sarah and Lauren to drive him to the train station in Lynn on Sunday night. Cat elected to stay at home, claiming exhaustion from the extensive campus visits that continued into Sunday afternoon.

"We had fun this weekend, Dad," Sarah said. "Thank you taking me to see all the schools. I'm going to make out my Top Five list, but you know NYU is going to still be at the top of the list."

"Just keep an open mind," he asked.

"Okay, Dad," Sarah smiled.

The three of them stepped out of the car in front of the Amtrak station in Lynn.

"Love you, Dad," Lauren said.

Will hugged his daughters and prepared to enter the small building to wait for the southbound train to arrive. "Love you, too," he responded. "Take care of your mom. You guys behave. That will make her happy."

"We will," Lauren said, speaking for the two of them.

"I'll miss you. See on Saturday," he called out as he waved good-bye.

In a short time, Will boarded his train, his mind already focused on the week ahead. There was work to be done on the farm as the fall harvest approached, and his first visitor was due on Thursday. Becca's visit gave him something to look forward to as he planned Thursday's activities in his head. He was excited to have someone from outside of the family visit the farm.

He pulled out his tablet and began his Sunday night routine during the train trip. He checked his e-mail, surveyed the week's commodity prices, read some farming literature, and settled into the book he was reading. As the train passed through downtown Boston, he wondered if his next guest, Meghan, was still serious about visiting the farm. He pulled up his e-mail on the tablet and sent her a quick message, disguising the invitation under the heading of one of his project names.

"M, are you still interested in visiting the farm next month? It will be a good time to come, right around harvest time. Hope all is well with you. Let me know, Will."

As the train passed through New York state, his eyelids grew heavy, so he made his way to the sleeper car. By 11:15 p.m., the rocking of the train on the tracks had lulled him to sleep. After four weekends of train travel, he had become accustomed to the frequent stops the train made through the night and trained himself to sleep soundly in the sleeper car until daylight.

By sunrise, he felt well rested and ready to take on the day at the farm. At 8:06 a.m., the train stopped in Fayetteville, North Carolina. Will exited the train, splashed some water on his face in the train station bathroom, brushed his teeth, and began his Monday morning walk to Java Joe's.

He stepped through the front door of the coffee shop. "Good morning," he smiled, as Becca reciprocated with a smile of her own.

"Good morning," she replied.

He perched himself on the first stool closest to the door, which had become his personal seat on Monday mornings. He surveyed the crowd in the shop and counted five customers. "How was your weekend?" he asked.

"Not too exciting," she responded.

"I wrote down the directions for Thursday. I don't have a phone at the farm. I had it disconnected, so call my cell number if you have any trouble. We're all set to meet in Tar Heel at noon on Thursday," he said softly as Becca served him the first of two cups of coffee before his drive to Winfield Farm.

"I've got the afternoon and evening shifts covered for Thursday," she grinned. "I'm excited."

Will appreciated her excitement and wanted to make the visit eventful. "Listen, I'm not trying to be paranoid, but I hope you haven't told anyone about your little visit to the farm," he said, again keeping his voice down.

"I put an ad in the local paper and posted it on my Facebook page, but otherwise I haven't said a word to anyone," she joked.

"I don't think anyone in Boston is going to find out about you visiting, but I also want to make sure none of the locals see me bringing in some looker to spend an afternoon at the farm."

"Your secret's good with me, cowboy. I know how you married men are. You're always watching your back."

"Thanks," Will said, relieved that she was sensitive to his covert activities. "I've always been one to cover my tracks and watch my back."

"So, how did it go this weekend?" Becca asked.

"The school tours went pretty well. We visited a few colleges with my oldest daughter. She's a senior, and I'm trying to convince her to stay in Massachusetts for school, but she's hell-bent on going to NYU," he said, rolling his eyes.

"Would she come down here and go to UNC like her daddy?" Becca asked.

"I wish," he responded as he took another sip of his coffee.

"And how did it go with the wife?" she asked. "Better?"

"Not really," he shrugged, staring down at his coffee cup.

"Forgive me for being nosey," she said. He smiled. "I have a lot to do at the farm, so I'm going to take my second cup to go, Beck," he said.

"What did you call me?" she asked, in her flirtatious way.

"Sorry, I called you Beck. Is that okay?"

"Yeah, I sorta' like it," she responded.

"You got my keys, Beck?"

"Oh, I forgot to tell you about the car," she said. "You better go take a look at it before you try and drive it."

"Shut up, and give me keys," he playfully demanded, shaking his head at her failed attempt to scare him into thinking she had wrecked his car. "Here are your directions for Thursday. I'll see you at high noon in the parking lot of the Tar Heel Saloon. I'll be driving an old orange Chevy pick-up. The Range Rover will be in the shop after the weekend caretaker drove it to hell and back." He laughed and handed her the paper with the directions to Tar Heel.

She gave him her sassy look after his comment, then retrieved the keys from the front pocket of her green Java Joe's apron, and turned toward the counter to pour him a large to-go cup of coffee. "It's parked in the usual spot out back," she said.

"Okay, thanks Becca. I'll see you on Thursday at noon."

The Tour

Chapter 39

The tiny town of Tar Heel, a dot on the state map with a population of less than one hundred residents, was located on the far west side of Bladen County, less than twenty miles south of Fayetteville, where Highways 87 and 131 converge. Will drove the pick-up truck into Elizabethtown that morning to the feed store to load up on supplies, and then timed his arrival in Tar Heel precisely at noon. Today marked the first visitor to Winfield Farm since Will had purchased the farm a month ago.

He had parked in the Tar Heel Saloon parking lot for all of three minutes when an older model, black two-door Oldsmobile Monte Carlo pulled slowly into the lot. It was Becca, arriving a few minutes after twelve o'clock. He rolled down the manual window on the old Chevy truck and waved her over to a dirt parking area away from the front entry of the freestanding block structure. "You should be fine parked over here, out of the way," he instructed as he exited the truck, directing her to a suitable parking place.

As she stepped out of her car, he greeted her with a gentle hug. "You look good, like you're ready to do some work on the farm this afternoon," he joked, sizing up her attire. She wore a tan barn jacket over her ruffled shirt and snug fitting jeans tucked neatly in her knee-high equestrian riding boots. Her shoulder length auburn colored hair was pinned back with bobby pins.

"I'm ready to go to work," Becca replied.

"Let's go, then," he replied. "Did you bring anything? I thought you were bringing your gun."

"No, but I did make some brownies."

"Good, I love brownies. Good call. Let's go," he said. He opened the passenger door as Becca slid onto the bench seat of the 1978 Silverado pick-up. "You hungry?" he asked as he drove out of the Tar Heel Saloon's parking lot and headed south on Highway 87 toward the negligible town of Dublin, North Carolina.

"Little bit," Becca said. "I love this old truck. Why don't you let me take care of the truck over the weekends? I might enjoy driving this truck more than your fancy-ass Range Rover."

"I trust you with my car, but I don't trust anyone with Bo," he joked.

"Why Bo?" she asked. "Big Orange-Bo," he explained. "That's what I call her. This was my uncle's truck. Have you ever seen an uglier shade of orange on a vehicle?"

"I like it," Becca stated, looking around the cab's interior. "I really think you should let me drive the truck this weekend."

"I would, but I don't trust the truck to make the trek back and forth between the farm and Fayetteville," he admitted as he slapped the cracked leather above the dashboard, as though patting the back side of a horse. "We're headed to Elizabeth-town, the county seat of Bladen County. The farm's on the north side of the county, but I'm in town a good bit buying stuff for the farm. You get to experience the world's greatest hamburger at Melvin's in Elizabethtown. My uncle introduced us to Melvin's when I was a probably four years old. He loved the place. In fact, we put a Melvin's hat on his casket when we buried him this summer." He glanced at her with a smile. "Forgive me, but I'm going to sound like a tour guide all day, so let me know when I need to shut up."

"I like all the commentary. I can tell you have great memories of your uncle and your childhood," she said. "I like hearing about it."

"There's something about coming back to a place that you left thirty years ago, especially when your memories are so good. It takes me back to a simpler time in life when there were no worries. Remember when you were ten, and there was nothing to worry about except being home for supper?"

"Oh, yeah," she said quietly.

He cut his eyes in Becca's direction. He sensed he had said something wrong. "You okay?" he asked.

Rebecca sat in silence for a moment. "I just don't have the same positive childhood memories that you did. My parents divorced when I was eight. I just remember all the yelling and fighting between my mom and dad. After they split, we were bounced from one house to the next to stay with my dad for a while, and then back home with Mom. It wasn't good."

"I'm sorry," he said. "I have to remember that I had it pretty good growing up. Not everyone had the same childhood experience we did."

"It's okay," she said, head down. "But that's one reason I'm glad I didn't have kids. It's not fair to put them through the fights and the conflict, especially when they're young."

"I agree," Will said. He thought about the verbal battles his girls had witnessed through the years between Cat and himself. He pulled through the Melvin's drive-through and ordered lunch for the two of them. "I thought we'd eat in the truck on the way to the farm. I've got a full afternoon planned, so eat up."

On his way to the farm, Will took a slight detour on the way out of Elizabethtown to show her White Lake, another point of interest in Bladen County. "This lake is where I learned to swim and water ski. Although I grew up on the water in Wilmington, the fresh water in White Lake tasted a whole lot better than the ocean when you're learning to swim."

The early afternoon sun shined brightly over the corn crop that fronted along NC State Highway 210, as the truck approached the front gate of the farm. "It's the perfect fall day to tour the farm and see the crops in their full majesty just prior to harvest," he said as the electronic gate opened slowly to welcome Becca to Winfield Farm.

The dirt driveway leading off the highway to the house produced a sandy cloud of dust behind the old truck as Will and Becca bounced on the dusty seat with each undulation in the sandy soil. The cows welcomed the guests with a turn of their heads in acknowledgement of the truck's arrival. As the two-story structure came into full view, Will spoke. "This old house was built in the late 1700s, and it shows. The bones are in good shape, but there's definitely some deferred mainte- nance inside. My uncle, the life-long bachelor, spent a lot more taking care of the farm rather than updating the house, so not much has changed on the inside since I was a kid, including the fixtures in the kitchen."

"I can't wait to see it. It's got so much charm from the outside," Becca stated.

"The charm sorta' goes away when you see the bathroom and the dated kitchen, but those are projects I'll get around to eventually. I'm still learning how this place runs, so I've been more focused on the harvest season myself and less on the house," he explained. He pulled behind the house and parked the truck near the tractor barn. "I need to unload some of this stuff I bought in E-town this morning. Maybe you can help me? Remember, I told you I was bringing you here to work. That's the real reason you're here."

"I'm game," she said, stepping out of the passenger side of the truck with her plate of brownies in tow. "Just tell me what to do, and I'll do it."

Once the truck bed was unloaded, Will gave Rebecca the full tour of the house, explaining in detail about each room. He covered the history of the Winfield family in Bladen County, went into detail about his mother and her siblings, and even told some of the same stories his mother, grandmother, and uncle had shared with the cousins a generation ago.

"One bathroom for a family of nine?" Becca commented. "That's amazing."

"And you see that bathroom," Will responded. "It's tiny. I know my two girls couldn't get ready at the same time in that bathroom for any amount of money in the world." He gestured. "Let's go outside. I'll bore you with more details about the history of this place and the Winfield family later, if you can stand it."

"Are you kidding? This is fascinating," she responded. "I love hearing the old stories. It gives me a glimpse of what it was like to have lived here in the past. It sorta' brings the old house to life."

"You're starting to sound like Henry David Thorough," he laughed. "But it's good to find someone who appreciates what's here and the history."

The two loaded back in the truck for a driving tour of the property. Will drove Becca past the corn fields, through the planted pine, and over to the sprawling acreage planted in soybean. They stopped briefly to visit the graves at Winfield Cemetery, and then drove to the South River that bordered the northern end of the property. "We'll come back down here later this afternoon and see if we can catch some fish. The fish haven't been biting the last few times I've come down here, but we'll try our luck a little later." On the drive back from the river, Will pulled up to the doors of one of the dilapidated barns and parked the truck. "You'll like this part," he explained, motioning for her to exit the truck. "This is an old tobacco barn. My cousins and me had some fun times playing in this old barn when we were little."

He went on to explain how Winfield Farm was first established as a tobacco farm. He described how the soil in Bladen County was ideally suited to grow tobacco. "Back in the eighties, the government started paying farmers to quit growing tobacco. My uncle had the foresight to diversify into other crops, although tobacco had been the mainstay on our farm for two generations. He put more corn into production fifteen years ago, and it's paid off with the demand for ethanol in fuel products today."

"Is there any more tobacco grown on the farm?" Becca asked.

"Tobacco is such a tough crop to grow and harvest, and it's very labor intensive. Now that the demand is down, particularly in the U.S., we no longer have a single acre in tobacco today."

"That's sad for the farmer that only grew tobacco," she said.

"True, but today, this region is now known more for its hog farms than tobacco, although there's still plenty of tobacco grown around here. Like everything else in life, things change and you have to stay up with the times."

The afternoon ended at the Winfield makeshift skeet-shooting range in a pasture on the northeast side of the property, the site is where Will, Clay, and the cousins, even Virginia, all learned to shoot a shotgun. In similar fashion to his uncle, Will went through detail in explaining the mechanics of the

.12 gauge shotgun and the safety required when handling a gun. With his instruction, Becca was able to hit the flying targets on a consistent basis after a few practice rounds. "Are you sure you haven't done this before?" he asked after Becca blasted two clay targets back to back. "You're a natural."

"Just lucky, I guess," Becca responded with a sheepish grin.

As the sun started its descent over Winfield Farm, Will loaded the shotguns in the truck and the duo made their way back to the house. "It's getting late, but let's see if the fish are biting. We need something to eat for dinner, or we'll be back at Melvin's eating another hamburger," he joked, returning the guns to the rack near the bottom of the stairwell. He grabbed two fishing poles that he kept beside the gun rack, located near the back door of the house. He took four beers and a plastic container of worms from the refrigerator, placed them in a cooler, and the adventurers were off to the next activity at Winfield Farm just as the sun began to set. Will suggested that Becca drive the truck down the dirt road to the river. Quickly, she obliged. He drank his first beer from the passenger seat as he gave Becca directions on how to get back to the river. The fishing poles bounced in the bed of the old Chevy as Becca guided the truck past the cornfields and through the planted pine on the one-mile trek to the river.

Fishing was the last scheduled activity of the day before dinner. The tranquility of the South River's still water felt pleasant, the only noise detected now the occasional splash of a worm breaking the water's surface after a gentle cast. "I come down here at dusk and remind myself what I would be doing if I was back in Boston. I don't have to think about how bad the traffic will be on I-95 on the drive home or how many e-mails I didn't return today."

"It's so peaceful out here, especially at this time of the day," she commented. "Do you ever have any regrets about the move?"

"It hasn't been easy, but I don't miss the pressure of the corporate world. I had become a little cynical, mainly due to clients that would tell you one thing and do another, or go completely silent after you put together a full value assessment of their business. I'm still working on a few deals back in Boston, but I'm winding down my business up there." He paused to take a long sip of his beer as he thought about the encounter with Wyn nine days ago. "There are some days I wonder if I did the right thing. Time will tell after the harvest next month, if the move makes financial sense, but when I'm out here on the property, whether it's working or fishing, I know it's where I'm supposed to be."

"You seem so in your element out here, and you have such pride in the farm and the crops," Becca said. "I have such a different impression of you than the day we first met at the shop, when you came in wearing your suit."

"I do love it out here. It's different than working in the city. Sometimes I have to remind myself that I'm not just out here having fun, but this is my career, my life now. I can't take credit for what my uncle planted on the farm this year. It's intimidating to think I'll be on my own planting next year's crops. I have a lot to learn, so that's why I'm always reading articles and trying to learn the latest trends in farming. You know what it's like, running your own business. You don't know how many customers will show up tomorrow, and I don't know what next year's crop will bring."

Becca nodded in agreement as they stood on the flat banks of the river, waiting for the fish to bite. The lazy melody of crickets seized the night, as the sun slowly yielded its daytime light to darkness. The two fishermen ceased their conversation long enough to enjoy the still of the transition from day into night. The October harvest moon hung low over Winfield Farm and shed just enough light on the river to see the red and white bobs float motionlessly on the water's surface. While the full moon's gentle reflection bounced off the river, the fish remained elusively transient below the water's dark surface.

"It's getting a little late in the year to catch these catfish. We used to have more luck catching them in the heat of the summer when we were kids. My uncle seemed to have the golden touch. We'd come down here with him after supper, he'd hook a fish after one or two casts, and then he'd let us reel 'em in," he recalled.

"I can tell that you have good memories of the time you spent with your uncle," she said softly.

He hesitated before answering. Though he had put his uncle on a pedestal for all those years, Will couldn't help but think of the quandary Uncle John had created today by fathering this wayward son, Wyn. "He was a great American. There's so much I didn't know about him, but what I did know, I loved dearly. I only wish I could have been around him more in his later years. There are things I'm learning about him every day since I've been back. The things that the other farmers around here say about him confirm what my cousins and me all knew about him. He was really loved and respected in the community. I guess no one is perfect, but we all sure thought he hung the moon when we were little."

Will remembered vividly how sincere Becca had seemed when asking about his relationship with Uncle John when they first met at Java Joe's. "It's getting cold and these damn fish aren't biting," he remarked. "Maybe it's time to start a fire and get dinner started. You cold?"

"Not really, I could stay out here all night. It's so peaceful and quiet."

"I come down here and fish about this time of the night once or twice a week. It doesn't seem to matter if I catch anything or not. It's one of my favorite places on the farm." He watched the plastic bob float motionless on the still water as his memory took him back to a simpler time as a child fishing with Uncle John and his cousins on this same river bank. Thoughts of Wyn entered Will's mind again. Why did Wyn have to show up and complicate things? He just doesn't fit in the picture of Winfield Farm. Hopefully Mark's letter would back him off and settle the issue. "These fish aren't cooperating, so I guess we'll have to eat steak instead of fish tonight," Will joked, reeling in his final cast of the night. "Let's head back to the house."

The Dinner

Chapter 40

The logs blazing in the marble fireplace released a popping sound just as Will walked into the living room to serve Becca her first glass of red wine. She sat comfortably on the Federal-style camelback sofa in front of the warmth of the fire. "Here's a glass of Bladen County's best wine. I can't promise you how good it is, but the guy at the liquor store in Elizabethtown said it's his most expensive bottle," Will explained. "Are you good to sit here for a few minutes? I need to check on the steaks."

"I'm in good shape, now that I have my wine and a warm fire," Becca nodded, leaning back on the couch.

The grill just outside the back entry to house produced a flume of smoke that filled the outside air with an aroma that could arouse the senses of a vegetarian. Grain-fed beef had been standard fare at Winfield Farm since Will could remember. Uncle John craved beef and would traditionally cook steaks every Saturday night when family visited. Grass-fed cattle had been a part of Winfield Farm since the mid-1980s when Uncle John formed Winfield Cattle Company, converting about sixty acres in tobacco production to pasture land for beef cattle. Today, the number of cows was down to less than fifty head, but Will had ambitions to double the number of cattle and acquire his own bulls. According to Will's latest assessments, the pastures at the farm were currently under-utilized, given the capacity of the fenced pasture between the gated entry and the house.

Will moved swiftly back and forth between the grill, the kitchen, and the living room, where Becca remained seated with her wine in front of the fireplace. When the meal was almost ready, Will entered the living room, wine bottle in hand. He found Becca standing resolute in front of the fireplace mantle, studying framed pictures of his grandparents.

He paused and observed her, standing with her back to him, taking occasional sips from her wine glass, now almost empty. The glow of the fire radiated through her shoulder length hair. She appeared completely complacent in her brown leather riding boots and tightly fitted jeans that detailed every contour of her backside. "You recognize any of those folks?" Will joked. "Most of them are probably a little before your time, but you may have seen their pictures on a post office wall in downtown Fayetteville."

She turned and smiled, staying close to fireplace to keep herself warm.

"I see it's time for a refill," Will said, moving in her direction with the wine bottle.

"This is good wine," Becca commented, holding out her glass. "Can't you tell I like it?"

"Drink up," Will replied, carefully refilling her wine glass.

"I think I could stand here in front of this fire all night and drink wine."

"Well, I hate for you to move your position, but step outside for just a minute. Dinner is almost ready, but I want to show you something first." Will slowly grabbed her empty hand and led her out the front door on to the porch.

"You gotta' see the stars out here," he said, motioning toward the sky.

The still of the October night generated a calm peace over Winfield Farm. The harvest moon shed its dim light over the pasture, creating a silhouette of each cow in the fenced pasture. The multitude of stars sparkled with precise clarity, providing additional light over the acreage. "You don't see this in Boston," he proclaimed. "This is the most peaceful place on earth at night."

"It's incredible," Becca marveled from the front porch.

She stumbled closer to him in an effort to get a better look at the view, but it appeared to be a calculated move in his direction. The chill of the fall night sent a quick quiver through her torso, and sensing she was cold, Will put his arm around her shoulder. The moment soon became awkward as they observed the still of the illuminated night in silence. Becca took another sip of her wine, seemingly content in the moment. "Let's go eat, Becca," he suggested.

"Let me help you," she said. "You've been doing all the work while I've been over-serving myself wine."

"Okay, follow me," he nodded. "You get the asparagus and potatoes out of the oven, and I'll get the steaks off the grill."

* * *

After dinner, Will loaded three more logs onto the fire and poured Becca another glass of wine, and the two stood side by side facing the fireplace.

"It's been a great day," Becca commented. "Thank you for having me. You have such a wonderful place here. I needed this more than you know. It's been great to get away from the shop for the day." She paused and scowled. "I've been working way too hard."

Her speech seemed slower as she reached for the fireplace mantle to balance herself. "Let's sit down," he said, gently grasping her elbow so she didn't spill her wine. He gently took the glass from her hand and guided her by the waist toward the couch, placing her wine glass and his beer bottle on the top of his *Garden & Gun* magazine on the coffee table. He eased down next to her, staring at the glow of the fire as he calculated his next move. His emotions overtook him, he leaned toward her in an embrace, which ended in a long, deep kiss.

As the kiss ended, Will realized how long it had been since he and Cat had shared an intimate moment. Over the last few months, Cat had held firm to her vow of celibacy, punishing Will for his failure to engage her in the decision to buy the farm. True to her word, Cat had not relented and Will remained officially deprived from any physical advances until further notice. Will's patience for "further notice" had now worn thin. So here he was, entangled in the arms of an attractive single woman with whom he had bonded over the last few months. She was clearly intoxicated, to the point where her inhibitions appeared unguarded. The underlying passion of the kiss made it clear that she was a candidate to break Will's physical drought.

"Let's go upstairs," he whispered in her ear. He stood and pulled her from the couch by both hands. She gave him a heated look through watery, inebriated eyes, signifying that she was game for a change of venue. Will led her by the hand through the dining room and kitchen to the rear entry hall. The walk up the stairwell seemed endless. With each step, Will contemplated the circumstances, debating in his mind the undeniable temptation that awaited him. In one moment, he asked himself what he was doing. The next, he justified his depravity with the opportunity that lay before him. Changing course from the inevitable and turning around in the middle of the stairwell were not viable options. This was the perfect scenario, he convinced himself. No one would ever know about the incident. He was a million miles from home. In his indignation toward Cat's suspending their physical relationship, he felt his actions were justified. He was overdue in this department, and it was time to settle the score.

Though not a word was spoken between them, Will debated with his conscience as he contemplated the destiny that awaited him. As he led her down the upstairs hallway toward the back bedroom, he remembered that he had played out this fantasy with Becca a hundred times already, and now it was no longer just an apparition. She stumbled slightly on the runner that covered the upstairs hallway as she followed him, and her blatant inebriation signified that he would encounter no resistance to his advances. He prepared to manifest his fantasies of Becca into reality, and after considerable consternation while walking down the hallway, he determined that his punch card was ready for passage. He prepared himself to enter the den of adultery as the two walked through the open door of the guest bedroom.

In almost twenty years of marriage, occasional opportunities for infidelity had emerged, but none was serious enough for Will to cross the line. He had remained steadfast, maintaining his sanctity. Tonight was different. Cat and her acrimonious response to the farm purchase had pushed Will, he justified, into this plight of unfaithfulness. His lustful pursuits tonight were as much about retaliation toward Cat as any true affection he felt toward Becca.

He gazed at her before he laid her down on the four-poster bed. They locked lips in another passionate embrace before lying on the bed of iniquity. She was well beyond tipsy, to the point of incoherency. Awkwardly, he struggled to shepherd her onto the elevated mattress. "Sit down here," he coached as she settled herself onto the four-poster bed. "I'll take off your boots."

He tugged on the heel of her right boot first, and placed it on the floor next to the bed. Then he removed the second boot, positioning it uniformly next to the first. She sat unmoving, leaning slightly to the side. His mind took him back to the UNC campus as he remembered having his way with various girls who had become intoxicated and wantonly succumbed to his physical needs. Tonight was no different, except that over two decades had passed, and he was now a married man. His conscience took over as he stood beside the bed surveying his options. Did he really want to do this? She was in no condition to make a rational decision about what was about to happen. There would be other times to consummate this relationship, he rationalized.

Standing by the bed, he glanced quickly at the clock over the fireplace mantle while Becca laid down and rolled to the far edge of the bed to make room for him. He had lost all track of time preparing dinner and serving Becca almost a full bottle of wine. It was almost 9:30, later than he intended for her to stay tonight.

She was in no condition to drive herself home, and Will had polished off at least three beers himself. Driving her back to Tar Heel tonight and putting her in a car to send her home was not a rational option. His mind jumped back and forth between the alternatives that lay before him. The opportunity to break his long dry streak was imminent, but was he ready to deal with the guilt of infidelity with someone he was only mildly attracted to? What message was he sending to Becca? What if she started stalking him? He didn't really know her. She might be some sort of "clinger" and think they were having an affair. She might start showing up every night at the farm wanting to have sex. She may want to start hanging out at the farm every week. He was not ready for that. He was not really that attracted to her. He liked her personality and thought she was attractive, but he didn't want to give her the impression that they were dating.

"What are you waitin' on, cowboy?" Becca asked seductively. She gave the mattress a pat, inviting Will to join her.

Will slowly climbed on the bed and lay near her, letting his boots hang over the edge of the side of the bed. The mental debate continued to play out in his mind as he looked deep in her almond colored eyes, preparing himself for another kiss. As he drew closer, he suddenly found the smell of her perfume detestable. Her drunken state became repulsive. The debate in his conscience was over, his desire for passion squelched by her acute inebriation. Any attraction he had for her over the last three months was lost on her intoxication. "I'd like to do this more than you'll ever know," he said. "And believe me when I tell you that I haven't sex in months, so I'm ready to jump your bones ... but we're both a little drunk, and I don't want to dive into anything we both might regret. Let's just lay here for a few minutes and rest. You can spend the night. I want you to stay. I'll make sure I get you back to Fayetteville early tomorrow morning in time to open the shop."

"Just hold me," she whispered, reaching for his belt buckle. "I need you to hold me. I'm tired, but not too tired to have some fun. You lay right here with me for a minute and see how long it takes for me to change your mind."

The temptation was luring. Once again, Will entertained her invitation as he surveyed every curve of her body, inducing him to launch his invasion. "Okay, let's just rest for a minute," he relented, snuggling closer. He tucked his right arm over her back. Now side by side, they faced each other. She awaited his kiss, but Will knew another passionate lip-lock would push him over the edge of iniquity. Instead, he held her and gently stroked her long dark hair with his fingers, holding his breath so as to not to inhale the detestable aroma from her tawdry perfume. Surely, she'd pass out shortly, he imagined. He waited patiently as his lustful thoughts transitioned from a foray to a graceful exit strategy.

Within minutes, Becca drifted into a sound sleep and began to snore like a middle-aged man on a Lay-Z Boy. Will slowly reclaimed his arm from her back and rolled quietly off the bed, like an Army Ranger gyrating under a barbed wire fence. He glanced quickly back at her after his reticent dismount from the bed. He pulled up the duvet from the bottom of the bed, covered her inert body, and then tiptoed out of the room without closing the door, leaving her alone to sleep off the intoxication.

The Attack

Chapter 41

Will made his way quietly down the stairwell and secured another beer from the refrigerator. He opened the bottle and took a generous gulp, then walked out onto the porch and sat on the rocking chair closest to the front door, his mind still occupied with thoughts of Becca, fast asleep in the room just above. In his mind, he played the proverbial game of Ping-Pong, contemplating a return upstairs to awaken her. It wasn't like he felt an allegiance to Cat. She'd pushed him to this point of infidelity. He'd felt completely justified by his almost-actions and on top of that, she'd cut him off for the last two months. He could go back up there, have his way with Becca, and not feel one ounce of remorse. The only regret he might have tomorrow morning was *not* shagging her.

With each rock of the old wooden chair, however, he convinced himself that he had made the right decision. Though a part of him wanted to be tangled in the sheets with Becca, he felt better about his decision to be outside with the crickets under the stars, with a cold beer in his hand. It was too early to go to bed, and he needed more time to clear his head and convince himself that he had done the right thing tonight. It was a real possibility that Becca could rise from her drunken slumber in the middle of the night and pay him a visit in his bedroom on the main floor, and the deliberation of a midnight rendezvous upstairs was an option that he contemplated himself. He wondered if Cat would appreciate the sacrifice he had made tonight, but doubted it. He rose from the rocking chair and patrolled restlessly toward the front pasture. He drained his beer with one substantial final sip and glared back toward the front of the house.

He stared into the second story window, the dark room void of any movement or shadows, indicating that Becca was still in her comatose state. He envisioned her sleeping soundly, still snoring and completely oblivious to the mental torment that he now combatted. "I need another beer," he muttered, walking back on to the porch. Maybe he'd created too much of a temptation by inviting Becca here today. He'd gone all out to show her the farm, share the history, go fishing, and shoot skeet. It had been fun, but he shouldn't have kissed her. She probably thought he was ready to invite her to move in after today's activities. She was a friend. It was probably best to keep it that way.

By 10:30, Will lay in bed reading, nursing another Budweiser in an effort to help him fall asleep. Nevertheless, his lecherous mind continued to wander to his sleeping houseguest in the bedroom just above his. The temptation to leave his room and make a visit to the second floor danced in and out of his head. Staying focused on his book proved impossible.

A few minutes after 11:00, he turned off the light and tried to fall asleep. He had only one thing on his mind: Becca. Finally, he drifted off into a restless sleep.

A noise in the back of the house woke Will. Instinctively, he rolled toward the bedside table and checked the digital clock. It was 3:37 a.m. It must be Becca moving around the house. She had either slept off the wine and was ready to go home or she was in search of late night companionship. On the other extreme, maybe too many glasses of wine had caused her to be sick, and she was in search of the bathroom. He pictured Becca fumbling through the dark house in search of the porcelain bowl. He sat up in bed to listen as the steps grew louder. His heart pounded with each step, anticipating Becca's arrival in his room. He reasoned that she had pulled on her boots, and that her now firm steps on the pine flooring was an apparent sign that she was ready to go home.

Before she got any closer, Will rolled out of the twin bed and gently opened the bedroom door, thinking to greet her before she made it to his bedroom. Wearing boxer shorts and his favorite Carolina t-shirt, he stepped into the living room in search of his rambling house-guest. Still glowing orange embers in the fireplace provided the only source of light inside the house. He reached to turn on the reading lamp next to the couch in the living room, thinking he'd find her standing nearby. She wasn't, and he didn't hear her footsteps, either. Curious, he walked toward the dining room to find her. As he stepped through the opening that connected the living and dining rooms, a deep voice came from the far corner of the dining room.

"Don't move."

Will caught his breath, his heart pounding. Who was this man and did he have Rebecca with him? Through the shadows, he barely saw the figure of a man dressed in jeans and a dark long-sleeve shirt walking his way. He also held a gun, pointed in Will's direction. As the heavy figure stepped closer, the face became familiar. Wyn. "What are you doing here?" Will demanded as his eyes locked on the barrel of the pistol that Wyn held in one trembling hand.

"You know why I'm here. It's about that damn letter your stupid lawyer sent me," Wyn snapped. "I thought you said we were going to work out an arrangement, but you had to go get some lawyer involved to try and bully me off the property. I got just as much right to be here on this farm as you do, asshole."

"Wyn, we *can* work something out," Will replied, his voice shaking. "The letter was written to start civil discussions about how we could work out the legal issues of ownership. Coming in here with a gun isn't going to solve anything. Please, put the gun down. We can talk about an arrangement..."

"I can't afford no attorney," Wyn said, his voice growing louder. "You rich bastards think you can get rid of me by hiring a lawyer from Wilmington, but I got my own way of working things out."

It was evident by his slurred speech that Wyn was intoxicated, and the unsteady movement of his hand as he tried to hold the gun stable. However, as far as Will could tell, Wyn was sober enough to pull the trigger. Will wasn't prepared to take any chances. He watched as Wyn slowly ambled toward the middle of the dining room, making his way closer. Will took a few small steps backwards, now standing in his bare feet under the cased opening between the living and dining rooms. "Wyn, think about it. You may have legal rights to the farm, but if you shoot me, you'll be back in jail, and you'll never have the chance to own the farm. Put the gun down and let's talk about how we can work together," he tried to reason with Wyn.

"No! We're not dealin' with no courts or damn lawyers. I've been through that shit, and it's the people with money that win in that game every time," Wyn yelled.

Will thought of Catherine and his girls. Was this the end? Would he die right here in the living room of the Winfield farmhouse? He punished himself in anguish for the decisions he had made that led him to this moment.

Wyn took another step closer, leaning his right hip against the edge of the dining room table to keep himself stable. Will took another step backwards, knowing that if Wyn fired the gun, he was too close to miss, even in his drunken condition. A shot rang out. The deafening echo of the retort bounced off the walls of the house and Will dropped to the floor, his ears ringing. He smelled the acrid stench of gunpowder. A second shot quickly followed the first, and seemingly in slow motion, Wyn fell forward against the dining room table and landed on the hardwood floor with a profound thud.

Lying prostrate on the living room floor, Will watched as Wyn's body twitched in pain, gasping for his final breaths. Blood streamed steadily from his mouth, pink and frothy. Slowly, Will moved from his prone position and stood, and then looked toward the hallway on the far side of the dining room. Becca stood frozen, the shotgun she held now pointed toward the floor. She wore a blank stare as she stared down at the intruder. Will's mind went into overdrive. Panic set in. He considered the fact that a dead man was lying on his dining room floor and a female visitor stood behind the dead man with the weapon in her hands. "Who is that?" Becca asked frantically, her voice trembling in fear.

Will hesitated before answering, his eyes darting between Becca's terrorized face and Wyn's inanimate body. "He's my … cousin," he replied hesitantly.

"Your cousin?" Becca exclaimed. "Are you serious? What have I done? I just shot your cousin? But he was about to kill you!"

"I know, I'll explain later. It's a long story." Will shook his head in disbelief as he stood over Wyn's body, trying to verify that he was indeed dead. He made the decision not to touch

Wyn for a number of reasons - not even to check his pulse.

"Is he dead?" Becca asked. She still hadn't moved from the hallway, in sock feet and disheveled clothing "I think so," Will replied. "That was a good shot."

"I was afraid I was going to hit *you*, but it looked like he was ready to shoot you," she stammered. "I tried to aim for the biggest part of him..."

"You're right. He *was* ready to shoot me. You probably saved my life," Will said, and then took a deep breath. "Thank you."

Will stood over Wyn's body and stared at his face. Wyn had fallen so that he faced toward the entrance to the kitchen. His right arm was positioned under the dining room table, the gun was no longer in his hand, but lying on the floor six inches from his outstretched fingers. His eyes were closed. If not for the pool of blood that oozed from the hole in his chest onto the floor, he looked like he might be sleeping off a bad drunk. "We gotta' get outta' here, fast," Will said, turning toward Becca. "Let me see the gun."

Becca slowly released the gun and gave it to him, like a Marine handing a weapon over to her commanding officer. Will opened the breech of the over-and-under shotgun and removed the second shell from the chamber.

"Go get your boots while I wipe down the gun," Will instructed, looking down at Becca's sock feet.

"Where are we going?" she asked. "Aren't you going to call the police?"

"No, I'll call them when I get back, but first, we've got to get you out of here," he stated matter-of-factly. "You and I don't know each other, and you've never been to this farm. You got that?"

She gave him a look of uncertainty. "What do mean?"

"Trust me, we just need to get out of here. I'll explain

when we're driving," he said, motioning her toward the stairwell. "But we've got to move ... fast."

As Becca scurried up the stairwell, Will frantically wiped the shotgun with a yellow chamois cloth. He cleaned the gun a second time with the soft cloth. Once the gun was clean, he handled the gun as though he was preparing to shoot it. He hesitated. After you shoot someone, do you typically put the gun back on the rack or do you leave it on the dining room table next to the victim? This was a first for him.

He placed the gun in the upright position in the case between the .20 gauge and the .410 shotguns, then took two steps away from the gun-case and looked up the stairs. "Hurry up, dammit," he muttered. Within seconds, her silhouette appeared at the top of the stairs. "Come on," he called, motioning with his hands for her to hurry down the stairs. As soon as her boot hit the last step, Will grabbed her hand, shrugged into the coat he kept hanging on the gun-rack, and led her out the back door.

"What are we doing, Will?" she demanded as she followed him toward his car parked near the barn. "I hate to do it, but I'm taking you back to your car," Will explained. He started the Range Rover. "I'm the one that pulled the trigger. Remember, you were never here."

"I still don't understand. He broke into your house and was threatening to kill you! Tell me who this guy is that I just shot and why we're running away," Becca cried.

Will took a deep breath as the car rolled down he dark dirt driveway. "That guy on floor back there came to me last week and claimed to be an illegitimate son of my uncle."

"You mean your Uncle John?"

"Yes," Will said, looking toward Rebecca for her reaction. "Like I told you, Uncle John never married, but I guess he had his share of girlfriends. Well, the dead guy grew up in one of the old tenant farmer's houses on the property. His mother and grandmother lived on the property. Their family has done work on the farm for generations in exchange for rent. So, after he confronted me last Tuesday, I went to see an attorney in Wilmington, who writes this guy a letter. I thought the letter would bring some resolution to the situation. Apparently, the guy's been in and out of jail and hates lawyers. Did you hear any of what he said before you shot him?"

"I really couldn't follow the conversation, but the yelling woke me up. At first, I just laid in the bed, scared as shit, thinking it was a burglar, but with all the noise, I thought you might be having some trouble with someone who worked on the farm, so I decided to sneak downstairs. I thought about trying to run out of the house, because I didn't know what he was there to do. Instead, I just stood at the bottom of the stairs for a second. I peeked in the dining room. His back was to me, but I saw that he had a gun, so I decided you needed help. The gun rack was right there by the back door, so I followed your instructions - just like on the shooting range yesterday. I took a deep breath, held it, and shot him. I was just trying to protect you! I figured he was going to shoot you first and then find me!" Her voice shook and she buried her face in her hands and began to cry. "I'm so sorry. I'm scared, Will. I don't want to run away," she sobbed.

"Don't apologize," Will said, placing his right hand on her shoulder in an attempt to comfort her. "You did the right thing. You probably saved my life ... and possibly yours too. The bastard might have raped you if he found you here. He was clearly drunk and who knows what he was capable of. He's a barbarian."

"So, explain to me why we're leaving!" she demanded, tears streaming down her cheeks.

"I know this is going to sound terribly selfish on my part,

but I'm going to take the rap for the shooting. If my wife were to find out that you were here spending the night, irrespective of what did or didn't happen last night, she'd barbeque my ass."

"But nothing did happen, right? I think I was so drunk that I passed out before anything *did* happen. I woke up still wearing my clothes, so I assume that I just passed out on you."

"Something like that," Will responded, choosing to skip over the details of the night's events in the guest bedroom.

"I was really drunk last night, I'm sorry," she said, dropping her head.

"Don't apologize. I've been there before, and I had a few too many beers myself last night. We just need to get you back to Fayetteville."

"So, do you want me to be a part of some kind of cover-up?" she asked bluntly, looking directly at him.

"I know I'm putting you in a difficult position, but I really need your help."

"You know I'd do anything for you, Will. You've been good to me," she said. She turned to look out the window. "I just don't want to get you or *me* in any kind of trouble."

"I'm the one who'll take the heat, but let me ask you … who knew you were coming over here today?"

"No one," she responded.

"Are you sure?" he asked.

She turned to him. "I told the girls I was coming over here with you this afternoon and needed them to work yesterday, but they don't know anything else."

"Look, you have to keep quiet about what happened. You can't mention a word about the shooting, okay?"

"Okay," Becca responded quietly. "I shouldna' had all that wine last night. I haven't been out drinkin' in a long time. As you know, all I do is work. I guess I got carried away. I haven't been that drunk in years. I hope I didn't make an ass of myself. I'm sorry."

"Don't apologize," he said again. "Think about it. If you didn't have too much to drink and needed to sleep it off, then it might be me, instead of him, lying on that floor right now."

"If that's the case, then why do I, all of sudden, feel like I've done something terrible?"

"It was self-defense," Will said emphatically.

"Then why can't we just go back and tell the police that?" she requested.

Will also wondered about that. He wondered if he could trust Becca to stay strong, keep quiet, and not fold under pressure. After all, she was the one who had pulled the trigger, not him. He tried to empathize with what Becca might be enduring emotionally. Would she stay strong and stick with the story, if confronted? "Maybe we *should* call the police, but I can't take that risk," Will stated, then shook his head. "I've thought this through, and I've got too much at risk to go back."

Becca turned to stare at him. "Forgive me for saying this, but you can't let that bitch rule your life. From all you've told me, she sounds very controlling. You need a way out, Will. I can tell you don't love her. You're still with her because of the money, from what I can tell."

"You're probably not far off, but it's really more about my daughters," he said, his eyes on the highway. "Now, more than ever, since I'm this far away, I need to stay as close to my girls as possible. I don't want to lose them."

"So, who's got the money, you or her?"

Will resented her line of questions and sudden directness. "I can't believe we're talking about this after everything else that's gone on tonight. Let's just say this, and we'll move past the subject. If she found out that you spent the night at the farm last night, then she'd take me down. I'm sure I'd lose the farm and everything else I own, and more importantly, she'd try to keep me from seeing my girls. I can't have that happen. That's why I need your help, Becca. Can I count on you?"

Becca remained silent as she stared out the passenger side window. "I guess I understand. You do have a lot at risk. I'm not a parent, so I didn't think it through from that perspective." She took a shaky breath. "Don't worry, Will, I've got your back. I'm going to trust you. I still think you're afraid of her, though, and you'd do well to have her out of your life, best I can tell."

"We're not talking about this anymore." He glanced at her. "Listen, you and I can't talk or text, and I'm going to have to find another place to leave my car on the weekends for a while, starting tonight. You've got to promise me you won't mention any of this to your friends, your employees, your family, no one," he said. She nodded. "I'll come by the shop in a few weeks once things settle down, but I won't be stopping in for coffee for a while. I've made a point to limit my calls and texts to you in the past in case someone decided to check my phone records. But for now, they'll be no calls and no messages. Okay?"

"You're a sneaky son of a bitch, you know that?" Becca commented as the car stopped at a traffic light near the Bladen County Library in Elizabethtown.

"I'm just cautious," he responded. "I always have been. You have to be careful in my business to protect yourself and your fiduciary responsibilities to the client. Those shrewd New York bankers and private equity guys will go around your ass in a minute to get to your client, so there is a lot of CYA in the investment-banking world. It's like a second nature to me. Plus, I always kept my personal affairs to myself when it came to girls, even back in high school, and especially when I was in college."

"What's going to happen to us, Will? Maybe I'm wrong, but I thought we sorta' had a thing going. And now, you're going to run back to Boston and pretend this whole thing never happened."

"I'll be back around, but it may take some time. We did have something. I wouldn't have invited you to come see my farm if I didn't think there was something between us. Look, like I said, you saved my life back there, and I won't forget that. We just need some time. I won't disappear. I promise."

"I'm scared, Will," she admitted, turning to face him from the passenger seat. "I don't know that I can live with this for the rest of my life. Is someone going to show up in the middle of the night and find me, asking if I'm the one who shot that man, or will the police come knocking on my door at the shop one day and arrest me?"

"Look, that's not going to happen. You're strong, Becca. You did what you had to do back there. You protected me and yourself. Go back and focus on your business. I know it won't be easy, but you have to put this out of your mind. Plus, the guy was a thug. You did us all a favor by shooting him."

"But I'm worried about you, too. You've got a web of lies you gotta' live with - both here and at home in Boston."

"Don't worry about me. Believe me when I tell you, this is the best way. It's the only way," he said, appealing to her. He pulled his car next to Becca's at the Tar Heel Saloon, which had closed hours ago. Other than a few empty beer bottles and cans, the parking lot was desolate, with the exception of one abandoned truck in the parking lot. Before she left his car, Will grabbed her left hand and squeezed it. "Thank you, Becca. Thank you for everything. I owe you. I hate to leave you on these terms, but I have to." Through her tears, Becca offered him a wan smile. She exited the car without saying a word. The storyline was set. It was now all up to Will to execute it and Becca to keep it quiet. As soon as he heard Becca's Monte Carlo crank, Will pulled his car out of the dirt parking lot and began the race back to the farm. As his SUV built up speed on Highway 87, he began to rehearse his own chronicle of events and the fabricated story he was prepared to tell the police.

The Storyline

Chapter 42

By the time his Range Rover passed through downtown Elizabethtown, Will had recreated the events of the night into a sequel that even he began to believe, a timeline of when Wyn had entered the house, where Will had slept that night, the fact that Will thought Wyn was an intruder, all of it had to be crafted into a newfangled narrative. Re-entering the dark house at Winfield Farm after the round trip to Tar Heel was the most frightening part of the entire night. Rebecca's comment about whether Wyn was actually dead haunted Will's mind as he quietly entered the back door to access the scene of the crime. What if her shot to his back had only wounded him? A shotgun blast is only so powerful. Was there a chance he was sitting in the dining room with his chest blown open, waiting for Will to get home? Maybe Wyn had called his mother to take him to the hospital. What if his mother came to check on him and found him dead on the floor? What if the police and Eileen were already at the farm, waiting on him?

Still in his bare feet, Will tiptoed through the back entry hall and peered tentatively into the dining room. He breathed a sigh of relief when he saw Wyn's body still lying next to the dining room table, just as he and Rebecca had left it. He checked the clock on the mantle in the dining room as he dialed 911 to report the fact that he had just shot an intruder. It was now a few minutes past 5:00 a.m. The entire timeline of the shooting had been pushed back a little more than an hour from the time it took Will to drive Becca to Tar Heel and get back to the farm. Looking back, he should have instructed Becca to take the truck back to the bar in Tar Heel immediately after the incident and called 911 sooner. Since Wyn had been dead a little more than an hour, Will wondered if the forensic team could determine the exact time of death, but this was no time to second-guess his decisions. Did Bladen County even have a forensic staff, as small as it was? He had too many theories in his head to contemplate. It was time to make the phone call to the Bladen County authorities.

As the 911 operator answered, Will spoke. "I've just shot an intruder at my house," he stated calmly - maybe too calmly. "I'm sure he's dead, but you should send an ambulance." He gave the 911 operator his address and hung up his cell phone. Then began his wait on the police. He moved quickly after making the 911 call, making up the bed in his uncle's bedroom where he had slept. He took his boots, shirt, and some of his personal items upstairs to the guest bedroom. He ruffled the bed in the guest bedroom and checked the pillows for any of Becca's hair or other evidence that might reveal an accomplice had been in the house.

Once finished with his efforts to create the image that he had been sleeping in the guest room, Will quickly retreated back downstairs to the kitchen, where he frantically washed the lipstick stains off the rim of the wine glass that Becca had used. He hid the empty wine bottle in a cabinet above the sink. He secured the remnants of dinner from the night before in a plastic grocery bag, tied loosely, and placed the bag in the trashcan next to the refrigerator.

Now wearing a pair of jeans and his Carolina t-shirt, Will stepped into the living room, opened the front gate with the remote access, and rehearsed his story while sitting on the couch. He kept his back to the dining room where his deceased cousin lay. Then, in the distance, he heard the sirens, and then saw the flash of lights revolving red and blue through the front windows of the house as the ambulance and a single police car converged on the property. His heart raced as the revolving lights of the ambulance and police car lit up the pasture like a carnival. The scene seemed surreal, particularly when compared to the quiet nights he had become accustomed to since moving to the farm.

Two paramedics were the first of the responders to make their way through the front door. Will directed them through the front entry into the dining room where Wyn lay face down. Two officers from the Bladen County Sheriff's office greeted Will with a head nod as they walked through the entry door, removing their hats as they entered the living room. Will watched from the living room as the paramedics hovered over Wyn's corpse. The officers surveyed the scene of the crime in the dining room. The handgun Wyn had wielded lay by his side, underneath the dining room table. Between the paramedics and the officers, Will wondered what the responders might discover that would lead them to believe that this was not a normal breaking and entering case.

"We're going to look around, if you don't mind," the shorter, stockier of the two officers stated.

"Go right ahead," Will said. "Let me know if you need anything."

The two Bladen County sheriff's officers wandered through the rooms on the main level of the house. Will wanted to follow them, but he figured it was best to keep his distance and let the paramedics and sheriff deputies do their jobs. Instead, he waited anxiously in the living room, now unable to sit down. He watched the paramedics as they gingerly rolled Wyn's lifeless body onto its back. Occasionally, one paramedic whispered to the other, making Will nervous. The officers returned to the dining room, taking a moment to stare at the dead man lying face up on the hardwood floor before making their way back into the living room.

"We'd like to hear from you, Mr. Jordan, the older and heavier of the two officers asked. "Tell us what happened here tonight."

He was the quintessential Southern law enforcement officer, at least in Will's estimation. He was round from his face through his torso and stood no more than 5'8. His uniform shirt looked like it was ready to pop a button, based on the way his stomach bulged over his beltline. He made a point of remembering the name *Holloway* on his badge. "Yes sir," he replied. He cleared his throat while the officers moved to stand near the fireplace, while Will sat on the couch with his back to the dining room. "I heard a noise downstairs from my upstairs bedroom," Will began, pointing toward the ceiling. "I quietly came down the stairs, certain it was an intruder, so I grabbed my twelve-gauge that I keep in the rack by the back door. It was dark, but once I saw his shadow, I could see he had a gun. I didn't want to take any chances, so I fired. He fell to the ground. He took a shot on his way down, as you can see." He gestured toward the bullet hole in the ceiling.

"Do you live here alone, Mr. Jordan?"

Will fought back a moment of panic, wondering if the officers had found some evidence that showed someone else in the house last night.

"Yes sir, I do. In fact, I just moved down here about a month ago. My family lives in Boston. This was my uncle's place. I bought it after he died in June."

"Did you know the deceased, Mr. Jordan?"

"Not when I fired the shot. His back was to me, but afterwards, I looked at his face and realized who he was. He's the son of a lady that lives here on the property, just down the road."

"Were your doors locked last night?"

"I think so. I lock them most nights. I've lived up north for the last twenty-two years, so I still lock my doors at night. Truth be known, he may have gotten a key from his mother. She looked after my uncle before he died last summer, so she may still have a key."

"There appears to be no forced entry," the younger officer stated. "But I need to make sure I've checked all the doors."

"He could have had a key," Will repeated. "Like I said, I'm most certain his mother has one."

"We'll check his pockets," the younger officer suggested.

"Listen, I should probably tell you this now, because it could come up later," Will said. He gestured toward Wyn. "There may be more to the story as to why he was here."

"What do you mean, Mr. Jordan?" Deputy Holloway asked.

"He ... he approached me one day last week and told me some pretty profound news," Will admitted. "He claimed that my uncle was his father. My uncle was never married, so this has apparently been a secret for many years." He paused, and then continued. "The conversation between the two of us last week was not very amicable." He paused again and watched the paramedics roll a gurney bearing Wyn's corpse in a body bag through the living room and into the dining room on their way to the door.

"Officer Holloway, we're going to load up, unless you need us for any other reason," one of the paramedics said.

"No sir, we're good here. We'll see you back at the morgue in the next forty-five minutes or so."

Will watched as the paramedics carefully wheeled Wyn's body through the front door. He stood to close the door as the gurney bounced down the four porch steps and Wyn's body disappeared into the night.

"Go ahead, Mr. Jordan, finish with your story," Holloway requested as Will once again sat on the couch.

"See, I just bought the farm from my cousins less than two months ago. This is the first any of us had heard that our uncle might have fathered a child many years ago. So, I went to see an attorney in Wilmington last week, and the lawyer sent Wyn a letter about how we should resolve the issue. I assume Wyn broke in here to take matters into his own hands, with intentions to kill me, and claim the farm for himself. I wish this was just a case as simple as breaking and entering, but I wanted you to know about it because I assume it will come up when you talk to his mother."

"Have you spoken to the mother since the deceased approached you about being your uncle's son?" Holloway asked.

"No, I don't ever see her, even though she lives less than a mile that way, just off Highway 210," Will said, pointing over his shoulder. "I've steered clear from the family since he approached me last week. I didn't know what the guy was capable of, so I've kept my distance. I don't know if his claim is something he made up, or if it's true, but I wanted you to know the background."

"But the two of you didn't have any words tonight?"

"No sir," Will shook his head, confident in his lie.

"Okay, we're going to look around some more. First, where's your gun?"

Will stood. "Follow me, I'll show you. I put it back in the case." He led the two officers past the body, through the dining room, and took a right turn down the hall past the bathroom to the gun rack by the back door, near the bottom of the stairs.

He lifted the shotgun out of the rack before they could stop him, thinking to put more of his fingerprints on the weapon. He reached in his pocket and pulled out the second shell that Becca had not used. "Here's the shell that I didn't fire," he said, holding up the maroon colored cylinder shell. "I left the empty shell here," he concluded, pointing to the fatal shotgun shell, standing upright on the base of the open gun rack.

"You keep these guns here all the time?" Holloway asked.

"Yes sir, this is where my uncle always kept them. I shoot pretty often. In fact, I shot some skeet yesterday afternoon. We've got a trap thrower in one of the pastures behind the house."

"Do you own a handgun yourself, Mr. Jordan?" the deputy asked.

"No sir, I don't personally own a gun. These are all my uncle's guns."

"We'll need to take this gun and the shells down to the station with us, Mr. Jordan," Deputy Holloway stated, peering down the open breech of the shotgun.

"Do I need to come to the station as well?" Will inquired.

"That won't be necessary," Holloway responded.

Will watched as Holloway continued to examine the gun, fearful of what the weapon might reveal to the officers. "I think I also need to let you know, if you have more questions later on, that I'll be leaving town tomorrow to go back to Boston to see my family," he volunteered. "I leave every Friday and come back on Monday mornings, but I can give you my cell phone number if you need me."

"I doubt we'll need to contact you, Mr. Jordan," Holloway commented. "It might do you well to get away for the weekend. You've had a pretty eventful night."

Will nodded. "When will you contact his mother?" he asked. "I'm going to need to go see her myself at some point and explain what happened."

"I'm not sure, sir," Holloway replied. "But we'll need her to come in and identify the body. Is that his only family as far as you know?"

"Yes sir, his mother and a sister, as far as I know," Will nodded. "Can you let me know after you make contact with his mother? I want to make sure I go see her before I get out of town later today."

"Yes sir, let me get your mobile number now so we'll have it."

Will recited the number to the deputies and asked them if they needed anything else, then escorted them to front door. From the front window, he followed the taillights of the patrol car until the illumination disappeared into the night. Now alone in the house, he felt sick, empty, alone, guilty – but also relieved. His anecdotal narrative to the police appeared to have been well received. He walked into the dining room to inspect the scene of the crime. He looked at the ceiling where the bullet from Wyn's handgun had shattered the sheetrock. That errant shot had most certainly been intended for Will.

He knelt down next to the table to look closer at the blood. The once bright red color was now maroon and had puddled on the pine floors in a congealed, paste-like substance on the hardwood floor. He stared at the blood and contemplated everything that had taken place at the farm over the last ten days. He wondered if the bloodstain would ever go away. Could he really cover it up?

The symbolism of the bloodstain and Will's subterfuge effort at a cover-up were strikingly similar. Would he be able to remove the bloodstain? Would his story to the sheriff's officer's scrutiny? Did he have blood on his hands? Though he and Becca had acted for the most part in self-defense, was he the one responsible for Wyn's death? Had the letter the attorney sent pushed Wyn over the edge? Had Wyn entered the house in the middle of the night just to scare Will with the gun, with no intention of using it? Or had Wyn's intent been to actually kill Will? Had Becca's presence here tonight saved his life or had she fired too soon? No one except Wyn himself, though intoxicated as he was, knew what his motives had been in confronting Will tonight.

He contemplated these questions and more in his mind. Wyn had been a drain on society. He was a parasite - a taker, not a giver. Was he really a Winfield? He certainly didn't live his life in a way to uphold the Winfield name. Was his blood the same blood he shared with Wyn as a blood relative? He tentatively placed his index finger on the pasty substance that permeated the pine floors. He was about to find out the answer to his question when he faced Eileen later this morning. He dreaded the encounter with Wyn's mother, but he had to explain to her what had happened last night and exonerate himself from the shooting. He had never been very good at comforting people in mourning, but he needed to know the truth about Wyn and his birthright. Comforting Eileen during this time wouldn't be easy, but at least he'd find out the truth about Wyn.

The Lies

Chapter 43

As the morning sunlight penetrated the windows on the front of the house, Will scrubbed the bloodstains off the hardwood floor, but soon realized he needed something more than water and a towel to remove the blood. A trip into Elizabethtown to get a stronger cleaning compound was warranted. Maybe it would do him good to leave the farm for a while before he visited Eileen.

The drive into town would also give him time to make some phone calls to Cat in Boston, his brother in Raleigh, Henry in Carolina Beach, and his attorney, Mark, in Wilmington. He realized that his devised story to Eileen, Cat, his cousins, and even his brother would need to carry the same fabricated storyline he told the police. In many ways, lying to his family might be more difficult than concocting the story he had told to the police two hours ago. The more times he told the story, the better he'd get at telling it, he rationalized. He debated whom to call first. It would not be Cat. She would take the news worse than any of them. After some deliberation, he elected to tell her the events of the break-in tomorrow morning when he was back home in Boston.

Will decided to call Mark, his attorney in Wilmington, first. He figured Mark would most likely be in the office early, and after two rings, Mark picked up his office phone. "Mark, this is Will," he said as soon as Mark answered. "Well, the letter you mailed to Wyn sent him into action, just like we had hoped."

"What do mean, Will?" Mark asked.

"The letter must have set him off, because he broke into my house last night. I shot him before he could take a shot at me."

"Are you kidding me?" Mark exclaimed.

"I wish I was," Will replied. "I heard someone in the house last night, so I grabbed my shotgun, thinking someone was burglarizing the house. I snuck up behind him and fired."

"Did you kill him?"

"Yes, unfortunately," Will replied soberly. "I shot before he did, and he died there in my dining room. In fact, I'm headed to the hardware store now to find some cleaner to get the bloodstains off the floor."

"Are you okay, Will?" Mark asked, after a slight pause.

"Not really, but you're the first person I called. I told the police why I suspected he was there and the controversy with the estate. I even told them that Wyn claimed to be my uncle's son. I wanted to make sure there was full disclosure in case Wyn's mom brought up the conflict."

"Well, that's good you told the cops the truth," Mark commented.

Mark's words caused Will to wince. In reality, most of his story to the police was made up of lies. Except for the fact that Wyn had broken into the house, Will had told the police anything but the truth.

"So, the cops were cool when you told them the story about the letter and the fact that he might have been your cousin?" Mark asked. "I hope they didn't think that you had reason to want him dead."

"No, certainly not," Will said, his stomach heaving with uneasiness. "It was clearly a case of me protecting myself from an intruder, and I think the deputies saw it that way."

"Well, let me know if you need my help. I hate it for you, but on a positive front, at least your legal issues with him are now solved. He won't be coming back asking for ownership of your farm."

"That's one way to look at it, I guess," Will agreed. "I need to call some of my family and let them know the news, so I'll keep you posted after I talk to his mom later this morning."

"Sounds good, and I'm sorry. I had no idea my letter would create such a ruckus."

"It's not your fault. He clearly had some anger issues, and I assume he was pretty drunk when he broke in last night. It's a bad situation. I hate it for his mother, and I'm not looking forward to the conversation with her today."

"Hang in there, Will. It'll be fine. This guy was bad news, even if he may have potentially been your blood relative. I'm sorry it ended this way."

"Thanks, Mark. I've gotta go, someone is beeping in," Will said. He disconnected from Mark and looked at the number on his caller ID. He didn't recognize the number, but it came from the local area code. "Hello, this is Will."

"Mr. Jordan, this is Deputy Holloway from the Bladen County Sheriff's office. I wanted to let you know that Mrs. Saxon has been contacted and notified about her son's death. We went by to see her after we left your place. She's already been in to the morgue to ID the body."

"How's she doing?" Will asked, driving past the road sign to White Lake on his route into Elizabethtown.

"About as well as to be expected for a mother who just

lost her son," Holloway responded. "She's holding up okay, I reckon."

"Thank you for letting me know," Will said. "I'll head over that way to visit with her in the next hour or two."

"By the way, Mr. Jordan, the gun that the victim carried with him was registered to your uncle, John Winfield. Do you know if he took the gun from your house last night?"

"He had the gun with him the entire time as far as I know. But my uncle could have given Wyn the gun a long time ago, or more likely, Wyn stole the gun from the house previously to last night."

"Okay, " Holloway replied. "I just wanted to let you know about the gun."

"Thanks," Will said. He disconnected the call, wondering what else the sheriff's office might discover.

The Truth

Chapter 44

The screen door creaked as Will gently pulled it toward him. What was left of the screen in the door frame was tattered and loose, long overdue for repair. He knocked lightly on the front door of the shoddy wooden house that sat tucked behind a shield of hardwood trees separating the shack from the two-lane road. He looked down at the porch, silently hoping no one would answer the door. The untreated wood on the porch was a decadent faded gray, peppered with numerous holes from years of neglect. Will stared down through one of the holes in the porch, uncertain of the reception he was about to receive this afternoon.

After four weeks of traveling back and forth between Boston and the farm, today marked the first Friday that he actually longed to get home to Massachusetts. Today also represented the first day that he had experienced serious doubts regarding his decision to purchase Winfield Farm. Sitting in downtown traffic or behind a desk in Boston making cold-calls sounded pretty glamorous right now. He stood, holding the screen door propped open with his right arm, still hoping that Eileen was not at home. Was she grieving too much to come to the door? Had she gone to the funeral home to make arrangements to bury her son? Would she come charging out the door carrying a gun, demanding that he leave?

Finally, he heard the click of the lock as the front door opened slightly. Eileen's gray features and red-rimmed eyes appeared through the small crack between the jamb and the open door. She stepped onto the porch and quietly closed the door behind her.

"Brooke's inside. She's not doing so good," Eileen whispered, unable to lift her head to look at Will. "She's probably not ready for company right now."

"Eileen, I'm terribly sorry," Will said, truthfully.

"It's okay, I know it ain't your fault," Eileen replied. She uttered a shaky sigh as she brushed wiry gray hair from her brow.

Those words from Eileen were everything Will hoped to hear on his visit today. There appeared to be no hostility or blame from Eileen - a huge relief. "How are you holding up?" he asked gently, trying not to stare at the vintage dress she had apparently worn to visit the police compound earlier in the day.

"I'm all right, I reckon," she said.

"I'm leaving for Boston tonight, but let me know if there is anything I can do," Will said. Eileen finally looked up at him.

"That boy has given me a lifetime of heartache," Eileen shared, slowly shaking her head. "He's been in and out of trouble most his life. I always thought that one day I might get a call like I did this morning, letting me know that Wyn was dead, or that he had killed someone else. He was always so angry and thought that the world was out to get him." She paused. "He's given us fits for years, especially after he turned seventeen, dropped out of school, and was never able to hold a job. Your uncle tried to help him get a job in town a few times, but that never worked out. Every now and again, John would give him work to do on the farm, but Wyn never wanted to work, and John finally gave up on him."

"This may be the wrong time to ask, but ..." Will hesitated before finishing his question. "Is it true what Wyn told me ... that John was his father?" Eileen looked down at her feet, clearly embarrassed. She really didn't need to answer the question. Her undeniable shame and body language revealed the truth. "Forgive me for asking," he rushed to say, sensing she was uncomfortable.

"No, you need to know," she said. "Do you have some time?" She gestured beyond the porch with her chin. "Let's take a walk. I don't want to disturb Brooke."

Will and Eileen stepped off the front porch and walked around the back of the house in silence. He observed the dilapidated condition of the structure she called home, and his heart filled with compassion toward Eileen and the hand life had dealt her. Poor was all she had ever known. On top of that, she had raised an illegitimate rebellious son. This morning, she had learned that her only son had died in a shooting after a break-in last night. Will broke the silence. "How old was Wyn?"

"He would have been twenty-nine on December ninth," Eileen replied.

Will wondered why people had to suffer such heartache in life. Wordlessly, he followed Eileen toward a path behind the house.

"I guess you know where this path leads, right?" Eileen asked, looking toward Will.

Unsure what Eileen might be asking, Will responded. "I assume it leads to the house, right?"

"Yes," Eileen answered. "Do you know my mother used to walk this path to bring your grandmother eggs from our chickens most every morning?"

"I actually remember that," Will said, recalling the visits from an elderly lady who delivered eggs in a basket to the back door of the Winfield house.

"I delivered eggs to your house with my momma many a morning. Later on, I took eggs and vegetables to your Uncle John after your grandmamma passed away. After me and my ex split, Brooke and me moved back into the house that your grandmother and John let our family live in for all these years. The Winfield family has been good to us for many, many years. I told the police that this morning, when I went to the station to see my Wyn."

Will wondered what else she told them, experiencing a moment of panic as the two walked slowly along the sandy path.

Eileen paused as she tried to regain her composure. "I kept deliverin' food to your uncle after your grandmother passed away. I would walk down this same path and take him vegetables and eggs, maybe once a week. Since it was just John, there was no need to bring as much food like when your mama and all her brothers and sisters lived there." Eileen paused and took a deep breath. "We was always taught to keep our distance from the Winfields, to respect your privacy. My momma wouldn't let me walk up here and play with the Winfield kids when I was little. I was much younger than even your mama, but I was always curious to walk up here and see what the Winfield children was doing. When I moved back here after my divorce, I always remembered what Momma said about respectin' the Winfield's privacy. So I would sneak over early in the morning with the baskets of fruit, vegetables, and eggs and leave 'em on the kitchen counter. John never locked his doors, even when he went out of town, so I would drop off the baskets and leave."

Will thought about Wyn's entry last night and how he was able to access the house. He was pretty certain that he had locked all the doors before he went to bed last night. He deduced that Wyn must have used his mother's key to access the house.

"One morning, as I was fixin' to leave the house, after droppin' off the baskets, John walked into the kitchen. He had just woke up. I thought he was still asleep or already out workin' on the tractor, so he startled me when he walked in. I tried to leave outta there in a hurry, but he insisted I stay and visit for a while. I told him I should probably go, but he asked me to have a cup of coffee with him. It was kinda' funny, cause he was sittin' there with me at that little table in the kitchen in just his underwear, and he was as cordial as he could be. John asked me lots of questions about how I was doing after my divorce, and how things were going with my finances. I could tell he was concerned. I know you've heard it a thousand times, but John was always so charming, so kind, and of course, very handsome, even in his fifties." She paused momentarily to catch her breath. "After we had talked for a while that morning, he reached his hand cross the table, touched my hand, and asked me if I needed anything. My heart fluttered. I looked at those green eyes of his and without saying a word, I could tell he was interested in doing more than just talking that morning. He stood up and helped me out of my chair. He rubbed his hand through my hair and hugged me. I still remember it like it was just last week. We never had a real romantic relationship, but he was always kind and gentle with me, and I knew he cared about me."

Will listened intently as Eileen reflected back in time. It was far more information than he wanted to hear, so he looked off in the distance over the cornfields as she continued with her historical account of Wyn's conception.

"So, without getting into a whole lot a detail, John led me back to his little bedroom off the living room, and that started a weekly visit that went on for seven or eight months - 'til the morning I told him I was pregnant. He didn't take too kindly to that news. In fact, he was mad and told me that whatever I did, not to tell no one. He said he would drive me over to Fayetteville one afternoon the next week, and we'd take care of it, but I wanted another baby. I was thirty-eight and knew I probably wasn't going to have no more babies. Brooke was four at the time, and I really didn't want her to be an only child. I told him I wanted to have the child, but he said if I had the baby, he would help me out with finances, but that was it. John wanted no part of being a father. I didn't want no abortion, and I really wanted to have this baby, so I didn't tell no one who the father was. And, if anyone asked, I told them that Wyn was a result of my previous marriage before the divorce was final. No one ever had reason to question it. I had kept my relations with John a secret from everyone. Mama was still livin' with us at the time. She was old, and she didn't have no idea I was seeing John. I always told folks, if they was nosey enough to ask, that my ex and I tried to get back together a few times, and we was seeing each other on occasion. So, Wyn kept the Saxon name since that was my ex's name, and mine. I even lied on the birth certificate."

"But Wyn told me when he first came over that he had proof on the birth certificate that John was his father," Will interjected.

"That was a lie," Eileen said, shaking her head. "That boy would lie. Damn, he could lie. He would just assume lie than tell the truth."

"And what about his first name?" Will asked. "Is the name Wyn for Winfield?"

"Yes, I named him Wyn for Winfield, but no one thought anything of it. John hated the fact that I named him Wyn and said it was too suspicious, but I stuck to my story that

I was still seeing my ex from time to time. Plus, I just liked the name Wyn and it wasn't spelled exactly the same, either. I think most folks believed it, until Wyn got older and started looking nothin' like my ex. My sister used to say that it was the best kept secret in Bladen County. Hell, I didn't even tell her who the real father was until Wyn was in high school. She was always tellin' me that Wyn didn't look nuthin' like my ex, so I finally told her the truth. That was more than ten years ago. My sister's always been good at keeping a secret."

She paused, and Will nodded, encouraging her to continue.

"But John didn't want nothin' to do with Wyn when he was a baby. He wouldn't even let me bring Wyn to the house. He would speak to me when I'd see him, but he was cold and distant from me as well. He didn't want to admit that Wyn was his child, and I'm sure he was still angry that I didn't have an abortion." She turned to look at Will. "You remember how good John was with you and all your cousins when you were young 'uns? Well, it took several years, but John finally got where he liked little Wyn. By the time Wyn was three or four, John let me bring him over to the house. John eventually taught Wyn how to hunt and fish when he was ten or eleven, but when he got to be a teenager, things changed. John was getting older and wasn't able to relate to him. That's when John began to distance himself from Wyn again."

"So, when did you tell Wyn who his dad really was?" Will asked.

"About five years ago, and that was probably a mistake. The news sent Wyn into a further state of anger and rebellion. He eventually confronted John and told him he hated him. Told him he was a coward and a liar, and that he was a weak man for not marrying me. John was close to eighty by that time and was scared of him. He told Wyn to stay away from the house and off the property. John was not happy with me after that, but once John got sick a year or two later, I would sometimes drive him to the doctor and bring him meals every now and again. Things was fine between John and me by the time he died, but he and Wyn never really resolved their differences. I kept tellin' Wyn he needed to go visit John, but Wyn was out doing whatever he did and didn't want to see John — even when John was sick."

The two walked in silence for a short distance down the path. "Thanks for sharing all that," Will said. "I know it's not easy, especially today. It sounds like you were the only one around to take care of John in his older years and when he got sick. I often wondered who was here to take care of him during those times. We certainly weren't around to help, so I want to thank you for all you did for my uncle all that time."

"I was thinking about it this morning after I come back from the police station," Eileen said as her voice cracked. "I've lost two men in my life in the last four months." She began to weep.

Will gently placed his arm on Eileen's right shoulder. It felt uncomfortable for Will to try and console her in this way, particularly since he really didn't know her. However, he was among a select few who were aware of Eileen's relationship with Uncle John. After all, they shared a kindred spirit as family now — in a twisted sort of way. She had shared a part of her life that she had kept a secret for over twenty-five years. Strangely, Will and Eileen were now connected by this worn and twisted path they walked today. He envisioned Eileen walking home those mornings after her rendezvous with Uncle John. He pictured her as a more alluring female in her thirties, someone his uncle would have found attractive. He recalled the Walk of Shame at UNC, referring to the walk home many of the girls took on the mornings following an insidious night in the fraternity house after too much to drink. In his mind, Will referenced this half-mile long pathway as Eileen's own Path of Shame.

Will concluded that Wyn had walked this same path late last night, after another late night drunk, and decided he would confront Will about the letter from the attorney. Will envisioned a drunken Wyn stumbling down the dark, but familiar pathway, through the cornfields in an alcohol-induced rage, gun in hand, ready to take the issue of the farm's genealogy into his own hands. Who knew what Wyn's intentions had been last night when he stormed in the direction of the Winfield home? At a minimum, Wyn's intentions were to let Will know that he was infuriated by the letter. On the other extreme, Will considered that in Wyn's mind, perhaps the only way to solve the conflict of ownership would have been to kill Will and claim the farm as his own. The Path of Shame, as Will labeled this seemingly innocuous trail, now had a history as long as Winfield Farm itself. The now infamous, yet discrete pathway imprinted on its sandy soil the footprints of journeys from three generations of two very different families; families intertwined in secrecy, passion, friendships — even birth and death.

It started so innocently, almost a hundred years ago, when Eileen's mother used to deliver eggs and vegetables to Will's grandmother. Over time, the pathway was further worn by generations of children playing, engaged in lawful fun. Later, the licentious feet of Eileen would frequent the path to visit the prince of Winfield Farm — John Winfield. Three decades later, the Path of Shame led Wyn on a wrathful journey to vent his fury and stake his claim for his birthright. Except, last night's walk down the Path was a one-way sojourn for Wyn — never to return down this road again. As Will contemplated the events of last night, an idea struck him, and Will shared his thoughts with the grieving mother.

"Eileen, based on what you've shared with me, I think it would be appropriate to set up a grave for Wyn in the Winfield Cemetery. I don't know what you've thought about as far as a service for Wyn, but I think it would be fitting to have a plot for him next to John. We could have the preacher come back to the gravesite and have a small service. We wouldn't have to give an explanation for why he was buried there. It would be an appropriate place for Wyn to rest since he spent most of his life on the farm ... unless you have another place you want to bury him." Will knew his offer was not purely altruistic. The offer to bury Wyn next to Uncle John was made partially out of guilt.

"That's very nice of you, Will," Eileen said. "I haven't given much thought to a funeral. Unfortunately, Wyn didn't have many friends. He was a loner. I don't think too many people would show up for his funeral. He made his share of enemies through the years, constantly gettin' in fights. He once beat a man so bad, they thought he was gonna' die. He spent some time in prison for that fight, but that wasn't his only trip to jail. I had to ask John for bail money many times to get Wyn out of jail for fightin', public drunkenness, and a mess of other things. He was just angry all the time, mad at the world for some reason. I think a lot of people just didn't understand him, so they were scared of him." She shook her head as they came within full view of the two-story Winfield house as the Path of Shame terminated near the tractor barn behind the house.

"We should turn around," Eileen stated abruptly. "I can't go near that house. Not today."

"I understand," Will said as the two made a wide turn and began the journey along the pathway leading back to Eileen's house. Will searched for words of comfort as he and Eileen walked the Path of Shame under the mid-day October sun, but the irony of it was that the road they walked now represented Will's own Path of Shame. By creating a web of lies about the way Wyn died, Will had created a cover-up of his own doing. Wyn's death would become Will's sacred secret — similar to Eileen's, a secret not to be shared with anyone — not Cat, not his brother, not his cousins, nor the police, and certainly not Eileen.

Will was conscious that work on the farm had to be completed before he left for Boston this afternoon. With the corn and soybean harvests just a few weeks away, he was determined to stay steadfast on the duties that lay before him. Today was marked by multiple distractions, however — starting at 3:30 this morning. Now that he and Eileen had spoken, Will wondered what he would tell his cousins, since Eileen had now confirmed the truth about Wyn. He played out in his mind the conversation he would have with each of them, explaining the conflict over the last ten days, followed by the distorted truth of Wyn's death. It was now Will's duty to confirm to his brother and cousins that a ninth cousin had been born into their generation twenty-nine years ago. The cousins shared little in common with their youngest cousin, but he was a cousin they would never know, because he was gone — dead before they could claim him as one of their own.

The Friday Return

Chapter 45

Will parked his Range Rover in a pay lot next to the train station and walked the downtown streets of Fayetteville towards Java Joe's. The streetlights led the way down the sidewalk to Becca's coffee shop. This Friday night would be distinctly different from the ones before — no dinner with Becca, no key or car exchange, no beers or wine, no jokes or smiles — just a casual visit to see how she was doing. Though he thought better of taking a chance in seeing her, he wanted to make sure she remained committed to keep last night's incident. He entered, they exchanged a brief glance, and then he acted like any other customer. He ordered a Java Joe's decaffeinated coffee in a to-go cup from Becca. "How you holding up?" he whispered, leaning one elbow against the wooden counter.

"Not so good," she responded. "I'm not sure I'm going to be able to do this."

"You have to," he said, trying to keep his voice down. "I'm sorry I put you in this predicament. I feel horrible, but you've got to stay strong."

"I worked this morning and then went home and tried to sleep, but I couldn't think about anything else, so I just cried. I dread going home tonight. I know I'll have nightmares."

"Take a sleeping pill tonight," he suggested. "You need a good night's rest. Things will get better. Just remember, you did the right thing. I talked to his mother this morning, and she said he was capable of anything. He was a common criminal. I know this sounds harsh, but you did society ... and me ... a favor. You gotta' believe that, okay?" She nodded in agreement, but he could tell she was visibly upset. "Listen, just to be safe, I've parked my car in the lot next to the train station," he explained, looking over his shoulder to make sure no one might be listening. "I'll be by to check on you before I catch the train next Friday, but please don't try to contact me. Becca, I'm really sorry it has to be this way, but thank you for being strong."

"I just don't understand why you can't tell the truth," Becca whispered.

"It would be too much of a scandal, particularly now," he sighed. "Besides, it's s too late now. I already gave the police my statement. I know it's selfish, but I have too much at stake, too much to lose. I'm sorry." He paused. "I need to get going," he said, leaving a five-dollar bill on the counter. "Be strong, Becca," he urged as he left the counter and walked away. As he left the shop, he wondered if he could trust Becca to keep quiet. She seemed so fragile at this point, but he had a difficult time putting himself in her shoes because she was the one who actually pulled the trigger. You'd think she'd be glad to be off the hook.

Will sat inside the train station waiting room with time to kill, and decided it would be an opportune time to call Henry. He had called Clay earlier in the day, but calling Henry had slipped his mind with all the distractions. "He stepped outside into the dark and dialed Henry's phone, and after asking how Henry was feeling, he began. "Henry, you're not going to believe it, but Wyn broke into the house last night, apparently in a rage about the letter I had the attorney send him." He paused. "He had a gun. I shot him with Uncle John's shotgun, thinking he was an intruder there to rob the house."

Henry was floored. "Damn Wilbur, you seem to find trouble with every week you're down here. Is your life always filled with this much drama?"

"Not hardly," Will replied. "I need to get back to Boston and clear my head, though. It's been an interesting past few weeks. I didn't necessarily sign up for all this when I bought the farm."

"Well, you hang in there," Henry said as they concluded the call.

Now, it was time to prepare Cat with the news of the shooting. He decided to withhold telling her the full story until tomorrow morning. "Hey, how are you?" he asked when she answered.

"I'm okay. You on the way back?"

"Yeah, sorry I haven't called. It's been an eventful week here. I want to tell you all about it, so I was hoping the two of us could go to breakfast at Tedesco in the morning, alone."

"That's fine, but is everything alright?" Cat asked. "We didn't hear from you last night."

"Oh, yeah, things just got a little out of hand with one of the neighbors last night," he explained, trying to downplay the event. "I'll tell you all about it in the morning. How are the girls?" he asked, quickly changing the subject.

"Lauren's babysitting and Sarah's out with Ben, so I'm here at my parent's. We went out to dinner, but we're home now." She paused. "Will, is everything alright?"

"Everything's fine. I'll tell you the full story at breakfast. So, I'll see you in the morning, okay? Can you pick me up in Lynn around 8:40?"

"Sure," she responded.

"Thanks," he said, relieved that Cat seemed to be in a positive mood tonight. Still, he also reminded himself that she was most likely within earshot of her parents, so she was possibly on her best behavior. He hoped she would be in an equally good disposition tomorrow after receiving the news that her husband had shot and killed someone on the property last night. Up to this point, he had shared nothing regarding Wyn and Eileen with Cat and she would likely be horrified after hearing the entire narrative. She already hated even the mention of Winfield Farm, and was sure to loath it even more after hearing about the events of the last two weeks.

A small part of him wanted to avoid telling Cat anything at all about the shooting, but eventually she would find out about the incident. The cousins would know the story and the local Bladen County newspaper would most likely publish the story of the break-in and the shooting. Telling Cat his side of the story was the right thing to do, even if his details of the shooting were based on a twisted labyrinth of lies.

The November Harvest

Chapter 46

Wyn Cecil Saxon was buried next to his father, John Sumter Winfield, among three generations of Winfield's laid to rest in the unpretentious gated burial grounds on the east side of the Winfield family farm. The small crowd of eight mourners attending the graveside service all knew the reason why Wyn was buried next to Uncle John, except for Pastor Mike Watson. The burial took place on Tuesday afternoon, five days after the previous week's break-in. The ceremony was short and simple, yet still melancholy. The somber mood was less about the loss of a loved one and more about a short life lived without purpose. Will was not surprised that none of Wyn's so-called friends were in attendance, so the service was only attended by Will, Eileen, Wyn's half-sister Brooke, Eileen's sister Theresa, and a handful of other family members. As far as Will could tell, those at the service had come to support and comfort Eileen and nothing else.

Not a word was mentioned during the abbreviated service about the break-in last week, Wyn's legal claim on the farm, or why this discontented 28-year-old was being laid to rest in Winfield Cemetery. It just seemed fitting that Wyn Saxon, a man who had lived most of his troubled life on the Winfield property, and had died on the estate, should be buried here. Will maintained a comfortable distance from the attendees, though he thought it was his place to be here today. Offering Eileen a plot in the Winfield Cemetery seemed an appropriate way of expressing his sorrow to Eileen. Call it guilt, but Will's conscious felt better knowing Wyn was laid to rest next to his father. Time stood still the day Wyn was buried, but the work on the farm couldn't wait. The primary corn harvest was just a few weeks away, and the soybean crop would follow in late November.

Three weeks after the funeral, life at Winfield Farm was for the most part back to normal. A new sea-grass tinted rug covered the faint bloodstains on the hardwood floors under the dining room table where Will had scrubbed so vigorously the morning after the shooting. He'd kept a lower than normal profile around Elizabethtown over the past three weeks to avoid any questions about the break-in and the shooting.

However, he had a little different version of the story to share with his friends at the Feed & Seed store in town about the incident. The deep hidden secret of Wyn's heritage was not a fact Will, nor Eileen, wanted exposed to the community. Rumors would naturally circulate after the shooting, but Will and Eileen had agreed to maintain the veil of secrecy surrounding Wyn's real father. As far as Will and Eileen knew, the truth about Wyn's true father was known only by their two immediate families — and the police.

"It was an effort to fend off a break-in at my house," Will explained to his friends at the Feed & Seed store in Elizabethtown. "He'd been out drinking and was pretty wasted, according to the police. His mother kept a key to the house, so my house was an easy target to burglarize. I suppose he was carrying a previously stolen gun of my uncle's, and I guess he was hoping to find money or silver to pawn off. He probably didn't even known I was home, since I travel back and forth between here and Boston every week. Regardless, I heard something in the house, tiptoed downstairs, and grabbed the shotgun in the rear hallway. I saw his shadow and then I saw the gun, so I fired first. Maybe I shouldn't have shot so quickly, but when someone's in your house in the middle of the night, you don't want to take chances. He tried to take a shot back at me, but he was going down when he fired."

"Yeah, we'd heard that ole' boy was a troublemaker," Holt Register, the manager at the feed store, shared based on what he had heard in the community. "He'd spent some time in Sampson Correctional for beatin' the stew outa' some fella in a bar fight, so I wouldn't apologize for takin' him out when you had the chance."

"I heard he lived on your property," Sims Hunter, the store clerk, added, summarizing what he had read in *The Bladen Journal.* "You always hear that criminals will go back to a place they know. You'd think he had more sense than to rob his landlord, but there are some stupid sum bitches out there,"

"I'm sure the rumors around here have been flying since the shooting. I'm just glad to have it all behind me. You hearing anything more about it?" Will asked, knowing that gossip traveled fast around Bladen County. If anyone knew anything, these guys at the feed store would.

"Nothin' outa the ordinary. The talk has mainly been around the kid you shot. People seem to think he got what he deserved, knowin' his background and all," Holt shrugged, standing behind the counter next to Sims.

"I was just curious," Will commented. "Now that this is all behind me, I need to get my corn and soybean harvest sold before Thanksgiving."

"It sounds like you got a nice crop this year," Holt commented.

"Yeah, that's what I hope. The corn buyers will be in town next week to inspect the crop, and we'll start talking price the week after. If these commodity prices hold up, I should be all right," he nodded.

"We been telling you that your uncle was a damn good farmer, one of the best in the county," Sims said. "Even for a man his age, he still was able to plant an impressive crop every year."

"He was smart, rotating more acreage in corn these last few years," Will agreed. "I'm expecting a good harvest, but we'll see what these buyers have to say next week."

"Keep us posted on how things go with that," Holt commented.

Will left the feed store headed back to the farm, relieved that the shooting incident appeared to be where it belonged — in the past. Between the corn that he had already harvested in the farm's silos and the corn still in the fields, he expected a nice windfall from this year's crop. The futures trading market for corn was working in his favor, given the lofty price per bushel for corn this year. To expand his pool of commodity purchasers, he had forged new relationships with direct buyers and severed ties with some of the middlemen that his uncle had used over the last decade. Wisely, he had closely tracked corn and soybean commodity prices since negotiating terms to purchase Winfield Farm, and his timing and diligence had paid off. Now it was time to reap the benefits.

Demand for corn had sustained throughout the fall harvest season due to strong exports and the rising use of ethanol as an alternative energy source. He had timed the sale of the corn harvest fortuitously and was prepared to demand top dollar for the fall harvest. He enjoyed the negotiation process, and although he was new to farming and the commodity markets, he was skilled in bringing the top price for a seller's business or maximizing his own price per bushel for the Winfield corn crop. The soybean harvest would follow a few weeks later, once the corn was fully harvested and sold.

* * *

As the week before Thanksgiving arrived, Will had set up meetings with eight direct buyers at Winfield Farm to tour the corn crop. The first group was scheduled to visit the farm on Monday afternoon, followed by morning and afternoon tours on Tuesday, Wednesday, and Thursday. The final group was set for Friday afternoon. His anticipation of the interaction with the buyers reminded him of why he had purchased the farm. With the shooting now behind him, he was back in his element, ready to negotiate terms on a harvest projected to bring top dollar in today's market. He likened the process of selling the annual harvest to representing a business owner in a strong economic climate. In robust times, business owners who had built a solid fiscal enterprise could command top pricing in the venture capital market.

By Thursday, Will was in discussions with his seventh prospective buyer of the week. This afternoon, he would host three Cargill representatives from Greensboro, North Carolina. Earlier in the day, he had met with a smaller regional co-op, so after multiple tours with potential buyers, his pitch was suave and well-rehearsed. He savored the opportunity to tell the Winfield Farm story, its history, and show off the crops in the field as well as the corn stored in the silos. By the time the Cargill buyers arrived at the farm on Thursday afternoon, he had become quite adept at sharing the story.

The inspection of the Winfield corn harvest was well received by the Cargill buyers. Will finished the tour with the representatives late in the afternoon and drove them from the corn silos back to the house where their company truck was parked. As the Range Rover approached the farmhouse, Will noticed a car parked under the massive oak tree near the spot where the auction had been held. He didn't recognize the car because it was partially blocked by the expansive tree and the Cargill buyers' truck. He wondered if it was another representative from Cargill, stretching his neck to see who the visitor might be. As he drew closer, he recognized the Bladen County Sheriff's vehicle.

"Looks like you've got company," the buyer in the front seat commented.

Will remembered that he had left the front gate open all day due to the visits he had scheduled. However, the sheriff was not a visitor he was expecting this afternoon, and he felt a momentary burst of panic. He tried to cover up his anxiety with an antidote of humor. "Maybe the cops are here to arrest all the illegals I've hired during harvest. Can't you see them all scattering off the property?" he joked, trying to make light of the sheriff's visit.

The three Cargill reps responded with faint, polite laughter.

"I had a break-in here several weeks ago," Will explained. "I'm sure the police are here to follow up. I hate to cut you guys loose so quickly, but I guess I better see what these guys want."

"I believe we're pretty much through here today anyway, Mr. Jordan," the senior member of the Cargill delegation said. "We've seen what we came to see. You have an impressive crop of soybeans and corn this year. We appreciate the opportunity to bid on your harvest, and we should be back in touch with you early next week before the holiday with our numbers."

"Sounds great," he responded. "I appreciate you guys coming out today."

Will parked his SUV next to the Cargill truck, shook hands with the three representatives, and watched them drive down the dirt drive toward the front gate. Slowly, he turned and walked toward the officers, who now stood on the front porch, patiently waiting for him. "Good afternoon gentlemen, sorry to keep you waiting," he said, trying to disguise the nervousness in his voice. "Good afternoon, Mr. Jordan." Deputy Holloway responded.

Will surveyed his guests, dressed in full dark khaki uniform, complete with Smokey Bear hats and polished black shoes. He recognized Deputy Holloway immediately.

"You remember Deputy Butler, don't you Mr. Jordan?" Holloway said, nodding in his deputy's direction.

"Yes sir," Will said, acknowledging the young deputy with a nod. It was obvious that the deputies were not here for a social visit.

"Mr. Jordan, we'd like you to come down to the station and answer a few questions," Holloway requested. He puffed out his chest while simultaneously pushing down on his belt.

Will noted that Officer Holloway's demeanor was less friendly than it had been on his previous visit a month ago. His heart rate accelerated as he looked at their faces, searching for clues as to the purpose of the visit. The idea of riding in the police car to the station didn't sound inviting. "Can't we chat inside?"

"I think it'd be best if you came down to the station," Holloway said.

"Is everything okay?" Will asked, feeling far less certain that his cover-up of Wyn's death remained bulletproof.

"We just want to ask you some more questions about the night of the shooting, that's all," Holloway explained.

"Okay, am I following you down there, or do I need to ride with you guys?" Will asked. His mouth grew dry.

"You better ride with us, Mr. Jordan," Holloway said, motioning toward the patrol car.

"Okay," he said, his heart racing. As he sat uncomfortably in the back seat of the patrol car, he debated what to tell the officers once he arrived at the station. His mind overloaded with questions. What do they know? Did Becca break down, run to the police, and confess the truth? Would she be there to welcome him when the officers brought him into the station? What could they have found over the last three weeks to lead them to believe that his story wasn't true? Should he stick with his cover-up that he had shot Wyn, or was it time to tell the truth? He felt humiliated, riding in the back seat of the sheriff's car. He felt like a common criminal. This couldn't be good.

The Interrogation

Chapter 47

The cramped room was almost half the size of his office overlooking Boston Harbor. The scene looked just like he had seen a hundred times on television shows and in the movies: a small, well-lit room with no windows, except the one-way view window. A square table was positioned in the middle of the rectangle room, with two chairs on one side and one chair on the other side of the table. As he stood alone in the room, Will stared through the opaque glass on the wall in front of him. As he suspected, he could not see anyone or anything through the window, only his reflection in the one-way glass. He was certain that officers sat behind the glass, waiting to pounce on any deviation from the story that Will had given Officer Holloway almost a month ago. The scene was surreal, and Will could not believe he was here, inside this enclosed room in the basement of the Bladen County courthouse, waiting to be inundated with questions. What did they know? What had they found?

The door behind him suddenly opened, startling him. Officer Holloway led the procession, followed by two other personnel from the Bladen County Sheriff's office, all dressed in full uniform with the exception of the wide-brim hats. Will felt intimidated by their stoic and formal entry into the room.

"Have a seat, Mr. Jordan," Officer Holloway instructed. "This is Sheriff Alton Tucker," he said, nodding in his boss' direction.

Instinctively, Will extended his right hand toward the sheriff after the introduction, but then thought better of it. This wasn't a business meeting, you fool, he reminded himself.

Deputy Holloway and the sheriff took their seats at the table across from Will, while Holloway's assistant, one of the officers at the farm the night of the shooting, stood in the corner of the room with his arms folded over his chest. The sheriff appeared to be a no-nonsense kind of guy, maybe in his mid-fifties. His haircut, demeanor, and muscular build made Will surmise that the sheriff had been a drill sergeant as a younger man. "Do I need to have an attorney with me?" he asked apprehensively, daunted by the shear fact that three officers were in the room with him.

"It depends," Sheriff Tucker replied. "On how you answer the questions, but you are always welcome to have representation present in any dealings with my office."

"I don't have an attorney here in town, so let's go ahead," Will said. He folded his hands together as he rested his arms on the laminate tabletop, trying to stop them from shaking.

"Would you care to tell us again what happened on the night of October twenty-second when Wyn Saxon was shot in your house?" the sheriff asked, jumping immediately into his line of questions.

"I told the officers that night what happened." Will explained.

"Please," the sheriff requested.

Will again explained how he had been awakened while sleeping upstairs by what appeared to be a burglar in the house. He loaded two shells in the shotgun staged in the gun-rack near the bottom of the stairwell. "I saw a figure in the dining room with a gun. His back was to me, but I didn't want to take any chances, so I fired at him, assuming he was there to kill me." The officers stared silently at Will as he finished his diatribe of lies. His mouth was dry. His story didn't sound so good to him anymore. His eyes darted from the piercing eyes of the officers down to his hands clinched tightly together on the top of the table as he waited for their response.

"Does the name Rebecca Callahan mean anything to you?" the sheriff inquired. At the sound of Becca's name, Will knew his story was no longer valid. His lies would need to abruptly end, now. He was busted - literally. He shifted restlessly on the chair, trying to regain his composure. He felt his heart beating at a rapid pace. "Yes, she's a friend who lives in Fayetteville," he admitted. "How did you find her?"

"Let us ask the questions, Mr. Jordan," the sheriff ordered.

Will felt belittled by the sheriff's reprimand, but he was curious to know if she had come forward and confessed or if the sheriff's office had been that proficient to find her.

"Was she with you at the farm the night of October twenty-second?"

"Yes sir, she was there," Will answered, dropping his head in shame. He knew now it was time to sing like a canary and cooperate with the sheriff and his officers.

"Did she have anything to do with the shooting of Wyn Saxon?" Sherriff Tucker asked.

"Yes, she was the one who actually shot Wyn that night," Will said, his voice dejected.

"Did you, in fact, bring her to your farm and have her kill Wyn Saxon in an effort to get rid of him because he had made a claim of part-ownership on the farm you had just purchased?"

Will's disposition changed instantaneously from dejection

to defensive. He sat straight up in his chair. "Are you serious? Hell no! What sort of interrogation *is* this? I'm not answering any more questions without an attorney. I'm trying to be cooperative here, but the man broke in my house with the intent to kill me. Fortunately for me, she was there that night and shot him, which probably saved my life."

"Why did you lie to cover up the shooting then, if the shooting was self-defense, as you claim? You told the officers yourself that night at the scene that there was a dispute over the ownership of the farm. Was it your intent to make it look like a break-in? There was no sign of forced entry," Sheriff Tucker inquired.

"He had his mother's key to the house, didn't he?"

"He had a key, but how do we know *you* didn't put your own key in his pocket to make it look like he let himself in?"

"Where are you guys going with this?" Will said, shaking his head in disbelief. "This is insane."

"Isn't it true that killing Wyn Saxon was the easiest way to get rid of him without him claiming his portion of your farm?" the sheriff asked, leaning in Will's direction.

"Okay, we're done here," Will said, placing the palms of his hands on the table, indicating he was prepared to leave the room. "Ms. Callahan and I are friends. She was sleeping in a different room upstairs. She heard a ruckus downstairs and came down, saw that Wyn was about to kill me, so she shot him. I covered up the fact she was there that night because I've got a wife at home that would not understand what a woman was doing in my house spending the night, irrespective of the fact that she was too drunk to drive home and had passed out in the upstairs bedroom. There's no conspiracy here about me trying to kill Wyn to get rid of him!" Will took a deep breath and looked at each officer in the room. "Can I leave now?"

"Not so fast, Mr. Jordan," the sheriff stated. "We have some business to finish here. You told a whole mess a lies to my officers that night in order to cover up the fact that a man was shot and killed inside your house. We're not sure at this point just who pulled the trigger, or what the motive behind the shooting really was."

"The man was in my house in the middle of the night - with a gun!" Will said, growing agitated. "He fired a shot at me after he was shot. That proves he had intentions of trying to kill me that night. You guys ought to be thanking me for taking this thug off the streets. I know his background. I know the trouble he's been in before he broke in my house that night," Will seethed with anger over the accusations the officers had thrown his way.

"You best leave the law and order business in this county to us, Mr. Jordan. In fact, I've been authorized to place you under arrest for conspiring to murder Wyn Cecil Saxon," the sheriff said. He stood and began reading Will his Miranda Rights. "You'll appear before the judge at the courthouse in the morning at ten o'clock."

The deputies handcuffed Will and led him down a long, wood-paneled hall to a small room that looked like it was once used as a broom closet. On the wall was mounted a black payphone. The payphone looked out of place, even inside this archaic building that housed the sheriff's office. Will was instructed that he would have five minutes to make a phone call. His cell phone was still in his pocket, so he would have no reason to use the payphone. He considered whom he should call. He needed a criminal attorney, but in Will's world, attorneys were used for negotiating contracts and closing sales transactions. He didn't have an attorney he called his own, particularly not a criminal lawyer. Mark was the closest lawyer to the situation, but Will had also lied to Mark about the events of the shooting that night. Mark was an estate lawyer, not a criminal attorney. He was certain he could find an attorney in Elizabethtown to represent him, but maybe it was best to get Mark and another lawyer from his law firm to handle his predicament. After all, Mark was familiar with the conflict, though Will had only told him a portion of the full story. Calling Cat was not an option at this point. Clay was the logical one to contact. Besides Henry, Clay was the family member who lived closest to Elizabethtown, but he was a two-hour drive away. Will decided that Clay could get in touch with Mark and let him know what had happened.

The deputies took the handcuffs off Will's wrists and left him alone in the closet to make his phone call. He dialed Clay's cell phone. "Clay, I've got myself in a real mess," he said when his brother answered. "I'm in jail and need your help. The sheriff's office here is trying to say I intentionally killed Wyn - that I wanted to get rid of him because he wanted his portion of the farm. There's more to the story though, but I need to give you all the details later. Can you call Mark and see if his firm handles criminal defense work? This situation is pretty twisted. I'm supposed to be formally charged tomorrow morning in court."

"I can't believe this," Clay replied, clearly shocked. "I'll get in touch with Mark right away and have him call you. I'll get down there tonight if I can, but it may be tomorrow."

"You don't need to come, just see if you can get in touch with Mark tonight. I haven't called Cat yet, so don't call her until I've had a chance to talk to her."

"You gotta' tell me what's going on, Will," Clay implored. "It sounds like there's something major you're not telling me."

Will hesitated briefly, and then spoke. "I'll give you more details when I have more time to talk, but I'll tell you this now. I didn't pull the trigger that night. Someone else did. It was a lady I met in Fayetteville. She owns the coffee shop you took me to the day of the auction. Don't jump to any conclusions though, it sounds worse than it is. She was there that night, sleeping upstairs in Elizabeth's room. I was downstairs in Uncle John's room. She heard the arguing between Wyn and me, so she came downstairs, grabbed the twelve-gauge off the gun rack, and shot him in the back. We had been out shooting skeet that afternoon, so she knew right where I kept the guns. I think the girl got scared and started singing once the police found her. I thought I had this thing pretty well covered up, but I just told the police the whole story here at the station."

"So, now I see why you don't want me to call Cat. You're a sneaky son of a bitch," Clay swore. "You always were the best when it came to hooking up with girls on the sly. You could cover your tracks and keep it quiet better than any of us back in the day."

"Let me assure you, it's not what you think. She was drunk, and believe it or not, I took the high road. She passed out, until she woke up at three-thirty in the morning with Wyn yelling at me and waving a gun in my face. Thankfully, she was there to take him out."

"I can't believe this, Wilbur," Clay exclaimed.

"I've gotten myself into an absolute mess, but I'm certainly not guilty of conspiring to murder this guy," Will maintained.

"I'll do my best to get down there in the morning," Clay said. "And I'll get in touch with Mark right away. I'm sure he'll have someone in his firm that can represent you. I hate it for you, Will, but we'll get things straightened out. Do you need any help posting bail?"

"Don't worry about that," Will said, trying to hide his growing sense of urgency. "Just see if you can get Mark over here as early as possible tomorrow morning."

The Verdict

Chapter 48

The hollow clash of the steel door reverberating against the bars of the jail cell symbolized the reality that Will's cover-up had landed him in deep trouble. Spending the night in jail was a first for him. He had several college friends who had spent the night in the Chapel Hill drunk tank for public drunkenness and DUIs, but Will had typically been the responsible one to pick up the jailbirds the next morning after bail was posted. He had always been curious to know what it was like to spend the night in jail for a minor offense, so he'd peppered his friends with questions after a night in the "Tar Heel Hilton", as the boys called the jail in downtown Chapel Hill. Now, Will faced the experience of a night behind bars himself.

As he sat humiliated in his private cell, he had ample time to think through his dilemma. Why hadn't he just told the truth that night, he mumbled to himself. What was he going to tell Cat? He dreaded the thought of telling her the truth, but he knew he had to. Breaking the news to Cat might be worse than any jail time he might face in the future.

He decided to call her after the hearing tomorrow morning and rehearsed his confession to her from his holding cell in the Bladen County Jail. He preferred to convey the news of his arrest by way of phone, rather than have the conversation with her face to face. At least that way, he would be out of harm's way if Cat decided to throw anything or take a swing at him.

Mark Middlebrook arrived from Wilmington at the Bladen County Jail in Elizabethtown Friday morning shortly after 9:00 a.m., accompanied by a criminal defense attorney from his law firm to represent Will. Corey Lawson was a young associate with Dunlap, Murray & Landon who was maybe eight years out of law school at UNC. With two lawyers on the case, Will calculated the legal fees it would take to keep him out of jail.

"We just read the filing and the police report from the night of the shooting and your grill session with them yesterday," Corey explained. "The DA is trying to pin a murder charge on you, saying you had reason to kill Wyn Saxon because of his claim of ownership on the farm."

"That's ridiculous," Will exclaimed, shaking his head in anger at the accusations.

"You know that and we know that, but this is a strategy on the prosecutor's part to start with more severe charges in order for you to potentially confess to lesser charges," Corey clarified.

"This hearing will be preliminary and short," Mark explained. "And we'll hear from the judge about posting bond."

"So, should I assume I'll be able to go back to Boston for Thanksgiving, if my family will even let me back in the house?" Will asked, dropping his head in shame.

"The bond might be on the high side because they know you have a home so far away and might decide to stay up there. The judge may also know you have a higher net worth, so he may figure a ten-thousand-dollar bond is not large enough, if you decided to just check out and not come back," Corey continued. "Can't I just confess to my crime and take my medicine and skip all the proceedings?" Will asked, frustrated with all the procedures.

"We need to go through the process," Mark said. "Remember, right now, the prosecutor has a murder conspiracy placed around your neck, so we'll need to convey to the judge the truth and make sure it matches up with what Rebecca told them. So, a full confession would definitely be the best plan at this point. We'll let the judge know that you're willing to confess to the lesser crimes, don't want a trial, and then the judge will rule on the sentencing in a separate hearing."

"What should I expect? Probation? Jail time?" Will asked, looking at both attorneys.

"It's hard to say," Mark answered. "But it's our job to prove to the judge that you're a model citizen, have never been in trouble with the law in the past, and the cover-up of the homicide was a bad decision - one you regret. All you need to do today is plead Not Guilty in the proceeding, and then the judge will set the bond."

The bond hearing was as short as Will's attorneys had described. The courtroom for the mid-morning hearing was mostly empty, except for a few a newspaper reporters, a photographer who took Will's picture as he exited the courtroom, and a handful of spectators, including Clay, who had driven in from Raleigh that morning, as well as cousin Henry, who had made the trip from Carolina Beach.

Will was released on a fifty-thousand-dollar bail posting after a quick plea of Not Guilty to the judge. He would be able to make it back to the farm and meet the final group of prospective commodities buyers by mid-afternoon. He was also free to catch the evening train to Boston tonight, though the welcome mat would not be exactly rolled out for his arrival. He decided it might be best to stay at the farm this weekend and join the family in Boston next week for Thanksgiving.

His brother and cousin had come to Elizabethtown to support him at the bond hearing, and Will was grateful for their support. He also owed them an explanation and a full accounting of what happened the night of the shooting.

"Why don't you guys come by the farm?" Will asked Clay and Henry as they walked away from the courthouse. "I guess I need to tell you guys the whole story of what went on that night. I also want you guys to see the corn crop. I think you'll be impressed. Henry, do you feel up for it?"

"Absolutely," Henry responded while the three of them stood just outside of the shadow of the courthouse building under the overcast morning sky.

"Plus, I'm stranded," Will admitted. "I need one of you to give me a ride back to the farm."

"We got you covered," Henry offered. "You can ride with me if you like."

"I have a meeting with a group of buyers at two o'clock, but you guys are welcome to stay as long as you'd like," Will explained. "I really appreciate you guys being here. I've gotten myself in an absolute mess here. Who knows what'll happen after the sentencing? I'll really need your help at the farm, if I'm given any jail time."

"You let us know what you need," Henry said. "We're here for you."

"Can you guys give me a few minutes? I need to call Cat and give her the news. I haven't even told her about the arrest. This is not going to be fun, and it might take a few minutes."

"Sure, take your time," Clay said.

"Good luck," Henry said, only half-joking.

"We'll be down there by the cars," Clay said, pointing in the direction of the parking lot at the side of the courthouse.

Will waited at the bottom of the steps while Henry and Clay walked toward their cars and then dialed Cat's cell phone. She picked up on the second ring. Before she could say much more than hello, he launched into his speech. "Cat, I have some bad news. I was arrested yesterday and spent last night in jail. It looks like I won't be home this weekend."

"What are you saying, Will?" she asked after a moment of stunned silence. "Tell me what happened."

"I lied to the police about the intruder in the house that night." He paused. "Someone else was with me in the house that night - in a different room. It was a visitor, a female." He heard Cat gasp on the other end. "Please don't jump to any conclusions!" Will grimaced. He was tempted to tell Cat another lie to cover up, but he decided he had told enough lies, and the lies were what had landed him in jail last night and in court this morning. Instead, Will elected to tell her the truth. "She had too much to drink the night before, so she stayed in the guest room. She woke up while the intruder and I were arguing, came downstairs, and she shot him. I covered up the shooting because I didn't want you to find out that there was someone in the house with me that night." Silence. "Cat, I can promise you that nothing happened between us, and I have no feelings for her whatsoever. She's just someone that owns a coffee shop near the train station in Fayetteville." Will braced himself for the fury to unleash.

After several more moments of silence, Cat spoke. "I had a suspicion you were seeing someone down there! You were always so distant when you'd come home. I hope you stay in jail for the rest of your life, Will. I told you from the start that buying that damn farm was a huge mistake, and this confirms it." She started to cry. "I'm out. I'm completely done with you.

I can't believe I allowed you to buy that stupid farm, leave us up here to fend for ourselves, and then to be naïve enough to think you were down there all alone on that farm by yourself." She attempted to pull herself together, anger taking the place of her tears. "There were days I actually felt sorry for you, thinking you were down there all alone. How stupid of me! As far as I'm concerned, you can stay down there with your new girlfriend and let her come visit you in jail. You won't see us down there — ever!"

"It's not what it seems, Cat," Will broke in. "I'm not having an affair! I've been faithful to you, I promise."

"I don't believe you," she spat. "You're a liar. You just said yourself that you're a liar. The police know that. I know that. How do you expect me to believe anything you tell me anymore?"

"Believe what you want," he sighed. "She was in a completely different part of the house that night. I had no intentions of her even staying the night, but she was too drunk to drive home." He tried one more time. "I know what it looks like, Cat, but it's not what it seems," Will pleaded, pacing the grounds around the courthouse.

"Please, Will, spare me the details about your affair," she muttered. "I think I'm going to be sick, thinking what you've done to our family. You're an embarrassment. What am I supposed to tell the girls, my parents, our friends?" She paused. "I need to go. I can't talk to you anymore. Please don't call me—"

"Cat—"

"You and I are through!" she snapped, her voice filled with venom. "I hope you stay in jail forever! That would solve a lot of problems."

She abruptly hung up the phone without saying anything else. Will glared at his phone. "That went well," he muttered.

He attempted to regain his composure as he walked to the side of the courthouse to meet Clay and Henry, waiting beside Henry's car.

"You okay?" Henry asked.

"Not really," Will responded. "I didn't expect the call to go very well, and it didn't."

* * *

Will, Clay, and Henry met at the farm, where Will shared every detail of the shooting with his brother and cousin. "I know I should've gone to the police with Becca that night, but I knew the story would end up in the newspapers," he admitted. "Cat's a million miles away and may have never found out, but I panicked and didn't want a police report or a newspaper article showing that a girl was in the house with me the night of the shooting. It was too risky, and plus, the whole community would have thought that I had a live-in girlfriend. I didn't want that stigma around Bladen County either. Now, I guess the whole cover-up has blown up in my face. The locals will know the truth, Cat now knows Becca was there that night, and I'll be charged with covering up a homicide. It's now a matter of how much time I'll spend in jail, I guess. I still wonder how the sheriff's office was able to break the case. I guess I underestimated their ability to find out the truth. I really thought I had all the tracks covered. I can't figure what led them to Becca."

The Thanksgiving Visit

Chapter 49

After spending the weekend following the bond hearing in Raleigh with Clay and his family, Will took the Wednesday night train to Boston for Thanksgiving. Facing Cat and the girls was difficult. Sarah and Lauren welcomed him with open arms and forgiveness, but Cat was cold and distant. The Thanksgiving meal with Cat's side of the family was expectedly quiet and somber. He questioned why he had bothered to attend. Conversations with Cat's parents and her sister's family were awkward and strained.

Will had made plans with Sarah and Lauren to take them to dinner on Friday after Thanksgiving, to give his daughters details of the entire story regarding his uncle, Eileen, Wyn, Rebecca, the shooting, his bad decisions, the lies, and the reason he had tried to cover up the truth after the shooting. "I'm not proud of what I did, and I'll pay for the consequences for a long time," he admitted. "I've lost Mom's trust, and I won't get to see you girls as much. It was a big mistake to try to cover up something wrong with a lie."

"Will you go to jail, Dad?" Sarah asked.

"It's possible, maybe for a short while," Will replied

soberly. "A judge will pass sentence next month. Needless to say, I hope he goes easy on me and gives me probation and no jail time." He paused. "I know I have embarrassed you, and I'm sorry. You girls mean the world to me, and I never meant to hurt you. The most important thing for you to know is that I've been faithful to Mom the entire time we've been married. I'm not having an affair, and I did not have an affair. You have to believe me that I've stayed true to your mother as long as I have known her." Sarah and Lauren nodded as though they agreed with Will, despite what Cat might have conveyed to her daughters about the incident. "I don't want to break up our family, but maybe I already did when I moved to North Carolina. The decision to buy the farm and move down there part-time caused a lot of problems for me, for Mom, and for our family. I'm really sorry."

"But you and Mom fought all the time when you were here," Lauren shared, looking at her sister for confirmation. "We thought that's part of the reason why you left and moved to your farm."

"Maybe that *is* part of the reason I left," he admitted. "There are a number of reasons why I left, but it wasn't to get away from you guys or Mom. You're right, Mom and I weren't getting along too well before I bought the farm, but I wasn't running away from her. As you get older, you guys will feel the way about Boston and Marblehead that I do about North Carolina. It's your home. North Carolina was my home, until I met Mom. Massachusetts has always been my adopted home. I guess I always dreamed of moving back to the coast of North Carolina one day, but I never thought I would have that opportunity. Owning the farm gave me that chance." He paused again, and smiled at his daughters. "Once things settle down and get back to some kind of normal, I want you to spend some time at the farm, maybe come for a few days at spring break. Based on Mom's response to this whole mess, it looks like I won't be in Boston every weekend going forward, so I hope you'll come down to see me. If not during spring break, then maybe next summer."

"We will, Dad," Sarah said. "But are you and Mom getting a divorce?"

"That's up to her," Will responded. "I don't want a divorce for your guys' sake, but I think she's done with me after some of the mistakes I've made. It will take a long time to heal the wounds, but maybe she'll want to try and make it work. I hope so."

After dinner, Will hugged his girls and apologized again for what he had put them through, and then headed to his motel room near the train station in Lynn. Tonight, he was a man without a country in a land that he had once claimed as his own. Now, he was an alien in his former hometown. Staying alone at the Lynn Inn near the train station was lonelier than any night Will had spent at the farm.

Saturday morning was worse. He didn't have a car, so he took the train into downtown Boston and walked the streets of Back Bay with the post-Thanksgiving shoppers, pretending that things were normal. He shot a game of pool at his favorite pool hall, but realized that he was just burning time. As he walked through Boston Commons, Will called Meghan and left a voice-mail on her Liberty Capital office phone, letting her know that plans had changed based on a tragedy at the farm, and things probably wouldn't work out for her to visit the farm in the near future.

Will had no reason to stay in Massachusetts any longer, so he decided to take the Saturday night train back to Fayetteville. On the train ride down, Will contemplated a visit to Java Joe's before he drove back to the farm. He had not spoken to Becca since his arrest, and his curiosity wanted answers to how the authorities had eventually discovered the truth about the shooting that night. The Bladen County sheriff's office had somehow found her, and she must have immediately sung like a bird.

Will didn't blame her for telling the police the truth. Had he told the truth that night, he wouldn't be in as much trouble today. He had to know how the authorities had found Becca. His mind raced with a myriad of ideas. He had difficulty sleeping on the train ride to Fayetteville, but it wasn't the frequent stops through the night that kept him up on this trip. Instead, the uncertainty of his future that played in his head.

In Fayetteville, Will got off the train and walked to the parking lot where he kept his car. Now that Becca was no longer car sitting on the weekends, Will had found a pay-lot just a city block away from the train station. He was not completely comfortable leaving the Range Rover in the lot over the weekend, but a stolen or vandalized car didn't seem to matter as much to him these days. He had bigger concerns. Slowly, he made his way to Java Joe's, uncertain what he might say to Becca. She wasn't expecting him as he entered the shop, and in lieu of her normal friendly greeting, her face flushed with surprise as he walked through the front door.

"I didn't expect to see you in here again," she said, sheepishly.

His mind searched for a clever response, but he decided to hold off with any witty remarks for now. "Do you have time to take a walk?" he asked after ordering his usual cup of coffee to go.

"Sure," she responded, nodding at the attendant behind the counter. "I'll be back in thirty or forty minutes," she told her associate, pouring Will's coffee into a large to-go cup. She donned a coat over her apron and followed Will out the front door of the shop.

The streets of downtown Fayetteville were quiet, as expected for an early Sunday morning. The church crowd had not yet arrived, so traffic on the streets was minimal. The cool morning temperatures and the decorations on downtown lampposts signaled that Christmas was less than a month away.

The two walked quietly side-by-side for a half a block until Will broke the silence. "First, Becca, let me say I'm sorry. It goes without saying, but I wish I would have made some different decisions that night. I was trying to protect myself and thought I could keep you out of this mess as well. It was terribly selfish on my part. I'm sorry I put you in the position I did."

"It's okay," she said. "I'm sorry too. I tried to stick with the original plan, but when the police showed up at the shop two weeks ago, I knew they had figured out that I was involved in some way. I started trying to cover up the fact that I was there that night, but the police were pretty intimidating, and I got scared."

"I understand completely. I put you in a terrible position. I hope you're not in any trouble with the police." He looked at her. "Are you?"

"No, I'm not," she said. "But I'm ashamed to tell you this. The police said no charges would be pressed against me if I told them the truth and ratted you out. It was evident that they wanted to nail you. I feel terrible. They asked me a lot of questions about the man that was shot and your relationship with him. They wanted to know if I had met him, or if I had anything to do with him being in the house that night."

"What do you mean?" Will asked, puzzled by the questions the officers had asked her.

"I think, at first, the police were trying to suggest that you and I were working together to get Wyn into the house that night, so that you could kill him. I think they had me pegged as the 'other woman' who conspired with you to kill him. They were very intimidating and hell-bent on getting to the truth. They asked a lot of personal questions about our relationship, like how many times I had spent the night at your farm. They even asked if I planned to move in with you," she shared.

"I can't believe the cops got into all that with you. I'm sure it *was* intimidating," Will remarked. "It was obvious that they wanted me and intended to use your testimony to take me down. After I lied to them, they wanted to barbeque me. After they figured you were innocent and only pulled the trigger, then they backed off on you and focused on throwing the book at me. Did they say how they got to you?"

"They did. They said the plate of brownies in the kitchen tipped them off that someone else might have been there that night. In fact, one of the first questions they asked was if I had made brownies for you that night. When I said I didn't know you, the officers said the coroner estimated that the time of death did not match the timeline of what you told them. Then they asked me if I knew how much jail time I could get for tampering with evidence and leaving the scene of a homicide. Maybe all that was just to intimate me into telling the truth, but it worked, and I'm sorry. I feel terrible," Becca confessed.

"Don't apologize. I've asked myself a thousand times why Wyn decided to break in that night, of all nights, when you happened to be there. I have to hold on to the theory that you being there that night saved my life, and I'm grateful for that. Who knows what he planned to do that night, but it was evident that he was not there for a social visit. Sometimes, I wonder if he had been spying on us all afternoon. He was a creepy sort a guy. There's no telling what he knew or what he was thinking before he broke in that night. If he knew you were there, he might have thought he would kill me, rape you, and then kill you too. My mind is full of theories. I'm ready to put this all behind me and let you get on with your life."

"So, what has your wife said about all this?" she asked.

"I had to tell her the truth last week. As you might imagine, she erupted when I told her. She's convinced you and I were having an affair. I was in Boston over Thanksgiving, but I didn't sleep at home. I stayed in a low-end motel in a town near where we live. I barely saw my wife, and I'm pretty sure she didn't want to see me, so I just avoided her. I had dinner with my girls and told them the whole story. It was rough because I don't know when I'll see them again. It wasn't a good trip."

"Let me know if there's anything I can do for you. I'm glad you're not mad at me for telling the police the truth."

"You don't need to be sorry," he said, meaning it. "I got us in this mess."

"Well, I hope you'll give me another chance. I'll control myself next time and won't drink so much. It's just that I hadn't been out much before that night. I had been working so much and was stressed out about my business…"

"Believe me, I understand," Will said. "I've been there." He put his arm around her shoulder. "I think the world of you, and I owe you a debt of gratitude that will never go away. But, for a change, I need to be honest. I'm just not sure I'm ready to jump into a relationship with all that's happened over the last month. I'm still married, at least for now. I've got a lot to sort out, and I don't know what the future holds for me. I'll find out in three weeks if I'm going to jail. Who knows if I'll even be able to keep the farm, but the farm is all I really have right now. There's too much negative in my life right now, but I don't want to lose contact with you."

Dejected, Becca nodded. "I understand, but know that I'm here for you, okay?"

"I appreciate that, very much," he replied, trying to be polite, but sensing that she offered more than friendly support.

"I'm planning on coming to the sentencing, if that's okay," she stated.

"That's fine," Will said, actually preferring that she not attend.

"I hope the judge is lenient," she said, looking up at him.

"Yeah, me too," he said quietly.

"It's on the ninth, right?" she asked.

"Yes, December 9th," he confirmed, losing his fervor for the conversation. "I'm sorry," he said, looking down at her. "I'm pretty down after my trip to Boston and seeing my girls. I'm kind of rattled right now, and I've been gone for three days and need to get back to the farm. I apologize if I'm a little out of it. I didn't sleep so well on the train trip down. In fact, I haven't slept too well for the last week, as you might imagine. I'm sure you've gone through a few sleepless nights yourself over the last month."

"I have, but it's much better now since the truth has come out," she admitted.

"I understand. Look, Becca, I wanted to come by and let you know how sorry I am. I'll check in with you periodically, but I won't be making my weekend trips to Boston and back for a while. I guess a lot depends on what happens at the sentencing. I need to concentrate on finalizing a price for my soybeans, so I'll be busy between now and then." He gave her a good-bye hug. She held him tightly, signaling an uncommon bond that the two of them shared over the destructive events of the last four weeks. She didn't want to let go, but he held on as a courtesy to show his appreciation for her act of valor in the face of danger. Finally, he broke the embrace and walked briskly toward the parking lot to claim his vehicle. Emptiness overwhelmed him. A year ago, Will was with Cat and his daughters at his in-laws' house in Marblehead for Thanksgiving. He held a job with one of Boston's most prestigious boutique investment banking firms. Today, he was eight hundred miles away from his family, all alone, on the brink of a divorce, and facing possible jail time for concealing a homicide.

"Helluva year this has been!" he muttered as he climbed back in his car to make the forty-five minute drive from the train station through the back roads of eastern North Carolina on his way back to the farm.

Entering the solitary gates of Winfield Farm, his spirits lifted. The sun seemed to break through the morning's overcast skies, while the cows slowly arched their heads in the direction of his vehicle as it made his way down the driveway. Once inside and unpacked, Will dialed his brother and invited Clay and his family down to visit. "I came back early," he explained. "As I expected, the reception in Boston was bitter cold, so I came on back. Can you guys come down and visit? I could use the company. It would be a great time for the kids to spend some time on the farm, since my original Thanksgiving plans with Cat and the girls didn't exactly work out like I'd hoped."

"Sure, we'd love to," Clay replied. "We'll try to get everybody moving and be there by noon."

"That's great, but don't bring any left-over turkey. We'll ride into E town and go to Melvin's. Your crowd would probably like that."

"Sounds like a good plan. We've been inside too much this weekend. I'm glad you came back early. It should be a fun day. So, you holding up okay, Wilbur?"

"I've been a little down since I left Boston. It hit me when I got back this morning that I was actually starting to enjoy my long commute between the farm and Marblehead. It was the best of both worlds while it lasted. The faster pace in Boston was a good diversion from the slow pace down here. I got two days of Cat, which was just about enough, and five days on the farm."

Clay laughed.

"I think it hit me on the trip back that I don't have the luxury of having a place to stay when I go back to see the girls. I stayed in a fleabag motel near the train station outside of Marblehead, and that was pretty depressing. So, I talked to a few of my Boston buddies while I was up there and told them my situation. I think I'll be able to stay with them on the Saturday nights I go up to see the girls."

"You don't sound too optimistic that Cat's going to come around and forgive you," Clay guessed.

"No, I'm not betting on it. I guess I can't blame her. There's a lot to be upset about, but she's been pissed since the day I told her about my decision to buy the farm. It's not like she can't wait to see me when the train pulls in the station on Saturday mornings," he admitted. "By the time the weekend's over, I'm sure she's glad to see me go, and truthfully, I'm excited to get back down here." He paused. "I know it's just a matter of time before the divorce papers show up here in my mailbox. She'll go to her grave convinced I slept with the coffee shop girl, and I can't really blame her. Given all the circumstances, I'm sure ninety percent of America would believe that I was having an affair. Since Cat had not relented to my physical advances since August, that's evidence enough for her to think that I was getting it somewhere else."

"Are you kidding me? August?" Clay gasped.

"No kidding," Will confessed. "It's the truth. It's my longest dry streak since my first year at Dartmouth."

"*You* ought to be the one filing for divorce, not her," Clay joked. "Damn, you really must have made her mad. How do you know *she's* not tapping the yoga instructor or the mailman?

"She might be, but I doubt it," Will replied despondently. "I'm afraid she's going to clean my clock, Clay. She's got all this supposed ammunition about me abandoning the family, leaving her to take care of our girls, absentee father, a confessed felon, and even the suspicion of infidelity. She could spin this divorce thing in a really ugly way, making me out to be the villain. I've had a few long train rides to think about how she might manipulate the story. I don't think she's going to ask for full custody of the girls, but she'll hit me hard where it hurts … in the wallet."

"You certainly don't need a divorce to deal with, on top of everything else you're going through right now," Clay said.

"Her old man knows some pretty powerful divorce attorneys in Boston, and I'm sure they'll have their way with me. See, she'll want nothing to do with the farm, and that's now my largest asset and the only significant debt I have, other than around three hundred thousand on the house in Marblehead. She'll take all the stock, mutual funds, the house, retirement accounts, and leave me with the farm and the debt. Then I'll have to pay some huge child support and alimony amount based on my income over the last two years, which is a hell of a lot more than what it'll be next year as a farmer. It's a racket, but I made my bed, so I guess I gotta' lie in it."

"Maybe the judge in the divorce trial will give *her* the farm and you can go back to work for Liberty in Boston," Clay suggested with a laugh. "Wouldn't that be an interesting twist?"

Will responded with a faint laugh. "Look, I didn't mean to go so negative on you today," Will shared with his brother. "It's Thanksgiving. I should be thankful. I'm back in the Tar Heel state, living two hours away from you, the corn and soybean harvests are fantastic this year, so I'm optimistic, even if I might have to spend the next two years as some inmate's girlfriend."

The brothers laughed together at Will's humor surrounding the uncertainty of his future. "I'll see you guys when you get here in a few hours," he said. "I appreciate you making the effort to come. We'll have some fun with the kids. I'll be like Uncle John today, the single man at the farm, just like back in the day when we'd drive over to see John on Sundays."

"It'll be just like old times," Clay declared before the two brothers said their good-byes.

The Sentencing

Chapter 50

Will sprinted up the concrete stairs leading to the front entry of the Bladen County Courthouse in an effort to outrun the brisk wind that chased him from the parking spaces below. Dressed in his favorite Brooks Brothers charcoal-colored wool suit, one that he had not worn since March, Will brushed his windblown hair from his face with his fingers and followed the white marble floors toward the double doors leading into the courtroom. It was the ninth of December, and Will's sentencing was scheduled for nine-thirty.

Being late was not an option for a man with a hefty bail, so he checked his watch. Ten minutes early. He hesitated and took a deep breath before walking through the dark oak-stained double doors. He noted that the courtroom was mostly barren as he made his way down the center aisle toward his designated chair at the front of the courtroom. He nodded at his brother and Cousin Henry, seated next to each other maybe ten rows behind the defense team's table. The few unfamiliar faces in the room most likely represented the local press. Then he noticed Becca, seated just behind the defendant's table, and he acknowledged her with a forced smile before taking his seat between his two attorneys.

"We sent all the character witness letters to the judge yesterday," Mark conveyed to Will. "I hope we have a good chance to get you twelve months of probation and community service, but I can't make any promises."

"Let's hope for the best," Will whispered, glancing over his shoulder at the gallery of attendees. Eileen had just entered the rear of the courtroom, considering where to sit. He had not spoken with Eileen since his arrest almost a month ago. He still wondered what she told the sheriff about him to the authorities made them think he wanted to have him killed. He was glad they were past that assumption, as the theatric he faced today was enough. Still, he felt sure she hoped the judge would throw the book at him today.

At precisely 9:30 and on cue, the crowd rose as the bailiff introduced Judge Ray Land. The judge was a tall slender clean-cut man in his mid-fifties, most likely a former lawyer who had practiced law in Bladen County for decades before his appointment as a superior court judge. Dressed in his black robe, Judge Land looked like he could have stepped out of the choir loft as easily as the judge's chamber. He surveyed the gallery before speaking, and then glanced in Will's direction prior to commencing with his comments.

"I have read the evidence, considered the guilty plea presented by the defendant and his counsel, and I believe I understand the reasoning behind the defendant's actions. His civic record in his hometown and his letters of recommendation, along with his family's support here today, reveal that Mr. Jordan, a first time offender, is considered, for the most part, to be a respected, law abiding citizen. However, irrespective of his background, numerous indiscretions took place on the morning of October twenty-second which cannot be overlooked," Judge Land stated.

Will didn't like the sound of the judge's statement. Was he getting ready to make an example of him?

"Would the defendant please stand?" the judge requested Will did so, along with his attorneys. Then, the judge continued his ruling, his voice lilting with an eastern North Carolina accent.

"Lying to sheriff's deputies, leaving the scene of a homicide, and tampering with evidence at a crime scene all add up to serious charges. Covering up evidence to shroud personal indiscretions are not to be taken lightly. The defendant also put his accomplice, Ms. Callahan, in an uncompromising situation. She has testified to the truth and has cooperated with the local authorities, so she has been exonerated of any charges by this court, although her actions in following the defendant's efforts to cover up evidence in a crime to protect him are in no way viewed by the court as acceptable or condoned. Recognizing that the defendant has since confessed to the crimes associated with this homicide, I have chosen to evoke a lesser sentence to the defendant. However, the defendant's actions represent more than a simple lapse in judgment. The defendant made several calculated choices to cover up a homicide, fabricate his story to Bladen County authorities, leave a crime scene, and tamper with evidence at the scene. It is imperative that this court uphold and respect the laws of this State and manifest that there are consequences to any defendant's actions when in violation of the law. Therefore, I sentence the defendant, William Howard Jordan, to make restitution to the family of Wyn Cecil Saxon with a personal and written apology, and with a cash payment of twenty-five thousand dollars, to be paid within fifteen days of this sentencing." Judge Land cocked his head in Will's direction and took a breath, then continued with his vernacular.

"You will also submit a personal and written apology to Rebecca Sheila Callahan for your efforts to influence her into leaving a crime scene and covering up a homicide. And lastly, you will report to the Sampson Correctional Institute in Clinton, North Carolina, on January the tenth to fulfill a sentence handed down by this court of twelve months of incarceration. The fifty thousand dollar bond posted with this court will be increased by another fifty thousand dollars until the defendant reports to the Sampson County Institutional facility on the tenth of January." He banged his gavel on the bench, signifying the sentencing was complete.

Will stood in silence facing the judge as the verdict sunk into his mind. The courtroom was silent as the judge signed the bailiff's paperwork. The judge had ruled harshly, despite the fact that Will had confessed to his offenses. He wondered, if he had hired a Bladen County attorney and was a permanent resident that maybe the sentence might have been less harsh. The judge presides to rule fairly, but he said himself that he wanted to make an example out of Will for what he did. Will dropped his head in disbelief and shame. Then, he faced his attorneys.

"I'm sorry, Will," Mark said.

"You did what you could," Will told Corey and Mark. "The judge was prepared to make an example of me. I get that. I just hoped that pleading guilty would have gotten me probation and no jail time."

"We thought the same thing," Corey commented, stacking papers inside his briefcase, clearly disappointed in the judge's decision.

Becca was the first to approach Will after he shook hands with his attorneys. She gave him a look of condolence. "It's okay," Will said to her. "Really, it's okay." She reached across the waist-high railing and hugged him, and he thanked for her for being there. "I'll come by the shop to see you before I have to report," he said. "I'm sure I'll go back to Boston for Christmas, so I'll stop by for one last cup of coffee to say good-bye. According to the judge, I guess I owe you an official apology as well." He noticed that Becca had been crying. He appreciated her concern, but he also wanted to keep his distance. He stepped away and faced Henry and Clay, next to greet him. He shook his head in disbelief. "Not only am I guilty, but I guess I'm a flight risk too," he attempted to joke with his brother and cousin. Not exactly what I had hoped for," he admitted as the three walked side-by-side down the center aisle toward the courtroom exit. The crowd inside the courtroom amounted to less than ten attendees, much to Will's relief. He wanted as little fanfare to the debacle as possible. Although his sentencing was stiff, a Not Guilty plea and a trial by jury would have been mayhem, with more press overage. Pleading guilty was still the right decision, he thought.

Before the three reached the door, a young female reporter with *The Bladen Journal* stopped Will, turned on a hand-held recorder, and asked him a question. "Do you have anything to say, Mr. Jordan?"

Will hesitated, prepared to say, "No comment," but the words gushed out of his mouth instead. "There are most likely many rumors circulating around this community about what happened that night, but let me make this statement to clear the good name of my family. People like to talk, especially if there's speculation that an affair was behind a crime. Ms. Callahan is in this courtroom today, and she can testify that she is a friend, nothing more, and there was absolutely no affair, nor have there been any relations of a sexual nature that took place between the two of us. Let me be clear on that point." He paused. "Otherwise, I have confessed my bad error in judgment that I made to cover up the details of what went on after the break-in at my house. I'm sorry to Ms. Callahan for what I put her through, and I'm equally sorry to Eileen Saxon and her family for what happened. I have apologized to both of them privately already, but let me make a public apology today. I'm very sorry to both of them, and that's all I have to say."

The young reporter started to ask another question, but Will waved her away with his right hand. As he, Clay, and Henry were about to exit the courtroom, he glanced to his left and recognized a familiar face. He stopped abruptly and turned to get a better view of the woman standing in the last row of benches. "Kaitlyn?" he asked.

"Hi," she said with a gentle smile.

"I'm glad you came, but how did you know about the sentencing?"

"I've been following the story online since my aunt said you came by last month. I wasn't sure how to find you because you left your card with just your Boston address, so I did an internet search for you. My aunt said you had just moved back to Wilmington. I guess she was wrong. This isn't exactly Wilmington. When I Googled you, the articles came up online. I guess I was curious to see what happened and hear your side of the story, so I decided to drive over from Wilmington. I hope you don't mind that I came," Kaitlyn said.

"Ironically, I was in Wilmington to meet with my attorneys the day this whole ordeal started," Will said. "I figured I would stop by your old house and ask about you. I had no idea I'd find your aunt, but I'm glad I did. I thought that my guilty plea would keep the story out of the press, but I guess there's too good of a story line here. After all these years, I'm embarrassed that this is the way you had to find me, but I appreciate you being here." He paused and gestured to his brother. "Do you remember my brother, Clay?" he asked, pointing over his shoulder toward his brother. "And this is my cousin, Henry Winfield."

Will stepped aside as Kaitlyn acknowledged Clay and Henry with a warm smile and a light handshake. Astonished by the fact that she was here to witness the events of today, he stared at her face while she greeted Clay and Henry. "I thought you were in New York," he said as Kaitlyn stepped toward the door leading out of the courtroom.

"I'm out of school now and came to spend the holidays with my aunt. I try to spend Christmas with her every year."

"Go ahead guys," Will motioned to Clay and Henry. "I'll see you back at the farm."

They nodded and left him to his catching up. "Where do you teach?"

"I teach drama at NYU," Kaitlyn replied.

"I guess the semester is over already," Will inquired as their steps echoed through the marble hallways of the courthouse.

"Yes, I try to come visit my aunt in Wilmington in the summer and around Christmas. My son and I flew down on Sunday."

"How old is your son?" Will asked.

"He's eight."

"What's his name?"

"Chandler," Kaitlyn said with a wide grin. "He's in Wilmington with my aunt."

Will stopped and faced Kaitlyn as they stood on the top step of the courthouse overlooking downtown Elizabethtown. "I took a chance last month when I was in Wilmington that I might find you, or at least find someone who knew where you were. My life's just gone from bad to worse today, so I might as well tell you why I came by your house that day. I've got nothing to lose. I don't know what your aunt said when I came by two months ago, but I told her I was an old friend from

513

high school. The truth is that I wanted to find you that day so I could apologize to you."

Kaitlyn glanced back at him with a perplexed look. Will studied her face, remembering her familiar features from almost twenty-five years ago. Her olive colored complexion still required very little make-up and her shy smile expressed her humility - just the way he remembered. Her piercing green eyes stared back at him, curious.

"Apologize for what?" Kaitlyn asked.

"Look, I admired you for a long time, from when we first met at that camp in high school. Since we were at different schools, I never saw you, and we ran in completely different crowds, but I never forgot about you. I wanted to ask you out, but I guess I was too shy. I should have called, but I never did. That's why I wanted to apologize."

"You, shy?" she smiled. "I don't see it."

"You'd be surprised. Back in the day, I was pretty shy. I saw you perform in a few plays at Opera House Theater in Wilmington, and then I ran into you that last time on the boardwalk at Blockade Runner. I wanted to talk to you then, but I didn't. I was with three friends of mine from Dartmouth, and you walked by us. You seemed to be in a hurry, so I decided not to stop you. Do you remember that day?"

She nodded gently. "Oh, yes, I remember," she said. "Quite well."

"See, I left Wilmington that next week after I saw you and always wondered what might have been, because I moved to Boston that next weekend and never came back — until three months ago. If only I had talked to you in high school, college, grad school, or just asked you out one time, who knows what might have been? " He shrugged. "But I never did, and I regret that. It seemed like we were always at different schools, in other cities, and never around each other long enough to really get to know each other. We may have never made it past the first date, but I never even gave us that chance. And for that, I owe you an apology."

"Our stories are not really that different, you know," Kaitlyn said. "I left home to go to Yale, followed my dream to act, fell in love with New York after college, and never left the Northeast, except to visit my aunt twice a year after my parents died."

"So, are you still married?" Will asked, glancing down at her left hand, void of a wedding ring.

"Not really. We're separated," Kaitlyn responded. "For almost ten months."

"I'm sorry," he said.

"Things between us have not been going well for a while, and I have some decisions to make. I'm not sure the city is where I want to raise Chandler. He needs a back yard, a neighborhood, and a rec department where he can play on a real lacrosse or basketball team. He's constantly around adults and needs to be around more kids."

"I can understand that," Will agreed, studying every aspect of her face while she spoke.

"Wilmington was a great place to grow up, as you know, so we're looking around while we're here. I have a contract with NYU through May, but I don't want to keep putting off the decision. Chandler's at a critical age. I just want him to be a boy, and do things that boys do. Plus, New York has lost a little of its luster for me."

"I can relate," Will smiled. "Boston is a great city, and I was ready for a change myself, but you see where that got me."

"I love New York, and we live downtown in Chelsea. It's neat, but it's not the place I envisioned raising a family," Kaitlyn shared.

They walked slowly along the marble floors of the second

floor of the courthouse. "Well, not that you would be interested, but it looks like I'll have a farmhouse for rent about fifteen minutes up the road from here," Will said half-joking, referring to the fact that his house would be vacant in January.

Kaitlyn offered him a faint smile.

"I'm serious, now that I think about it," Will continued. "I'm sure you have no interest in moving from New York to Nowhere, North Carolina, but I'm going to need someone to live on my farm for a year while I'm in prison. Free rent. Think about it." She smiled back at him.

"I couldn't do that," she said.

"No pressure, but think about it," Will proposed, his voice now gearing into sales mode. "In fact, there's a private school in Clinton, just twenty minutes from my farm. Chandler would love it there, and I'm sure they could use a good drama teacher. You should check it out. Harrells School in Clinton. It's where my cousins went to school."

Kaitlyn considered the offer momentarily. "I need to be near my aunt," Kaitlyn replied. "She's eighty-four and all alone. She's all the family I have here since my parents passed away."

"I understand," Will acknowledged. "I wish I would have spent more time with my uncle down here. He was living on the farm all alone, and after I moved to Boston, I never made a single trip down here to visit him, until I came back for his funeral. We lost him this summer. You're doing the right thing, making plans to be close to your aunt."

"I've held you up long enough," she said, gesturing outside. "Your brother and cousin are waiting. You should go catch up with them."

"I'm meeting them back at the farm, so it's all right. I should probably go, but I'd like to see you again, before you leave Wilmington ... if you'd even consider being seen with a jail-bird like me."

"Oh, we haven't even talked about your sentencing," Kaitlyn gasped. "I'm sorry for the way things turned out today."

"It wasn't what I was expecting, but I guess I shouldn't be surprised."

"I heard your statement to the press. You seemed emphatic about what you said," she noted.

"You mean what I said about the affair?" he inquired.

"Yes," Kate answered.

"Maybe I came on too strong, but I wanted to be clear that it was a plutonic friendship. I wanted to make that clear to the press. I know there will be plenty of people in town that don't believe it, but I wanted to state my position, nonetheless."

Kaitlyn nodded in agreement.

"Would you give me your number?" he asked. "Maybe we could go out for dinner while you're still in Wilmington. Are you staying here through Christmas?"

"Yes, I have a flight back to New York on January second."

She gave him her phone number. "Good, then I'll call you in the next few weeks before you leave town," Will said, programing her number in his phone.

He hugged Kaitlyn good-bye and thanked her for coming. He was still reeling with surprise, but elated that she had come from Wilmington to Elizabethtown to see the sentencing. He walked down the courthouse steps, a free man for the next thirty days. He had three weeks to get together with Kate, and seeing her again was something to look forward to.

As he opened the door of his uncle's old truck, he knew what awaited him. He had to let Catherine know the judge's sentencing. "Calling her today with the news might be worse than walking through the gates of Samson Institutional in a month," Will muttered.

The Goodbyes

Chapter 51

Will made the familiar drive from the courthouse in down-town Elizabethtown toward White Lake on Highway 701. Clay and Henry were already at the farm, waiting on him. The fifteen-minute drive back to the farm would be ample time to call Cat and break the news about the prison time. Part of him hoped she would not pick up the phone, but she answered on the third ring.

"Hello."

"Is now a good time?" Will asked.

"I guess. What's up?"

Cat spoke bluntly, oblivious that today had been the day of Will's sentencing. He had purposely spared her and the girls the details of the legal proceedings, until now. "Cat, before you read about it or hear about it, I wanted to let you know I just left the courthouse. The judge ruled harshly and sentenced me to a year in jail," he said in a matter-of-fact tone. He waited for her response.

"That's terrible," she said after a moment of silence. "I don't really know what to say. Part of me wants to say you got what you deserved, but I hate that you're going to jail. Will, I know you get tired of me saying it, but this decision to buy that farm has been a complete disaster. It's by far the stupidest decision you've ever made. It marks the end of us. I can't go on. I've hired a lawyer, and my decision has already been made. This news just sealed that fact that I'm doing the right thing."

Will wanted to say that the stupidest decision he ever made was in marrying her, but a degrading rebuttal like that was not his style. Instead, he took the high road. "I understand. You need to do what you need to do." Oddly, he felt almost relieved by the news that Cat had hired an attorney. He had expected it, and in some ways hoped for it. Divorce represented closure, an end to an era of turmoil and angst. The value of his estate did not matter anymore. His life as he knew it was over. He was about to spend the next twelve months of his life in state prison, and his net worth meant very little at this point. He would spend his forty-sixth birthday imprisoned, but in many respects, he had already been incarcerated for the last nineteen years. "I want to come to Boston and spend a few days around Christmas. I'll drive up and move all my stuff out. I want to spend some time with the girls before I have to report to prison. I'll stay out of your way. I just want to tell the girls good-bye."

"Are you bringing that girl with you?"

"What girl?" he asked.

"Don't be foolish, Will. You know who I'm talking about. Your accomplice, the girl you were sleeping with the night of the shooting."

"Look, believe what you want, Cat," Will sighed, tired of trying to convince her of his fidelity. "I've never cheated on you in the twenty-one years we've been together. I stand on that truth, whether you want to believe it or not. There is plenty you can accuse me of over the years, but being unfaithful to you is not something I'm guilty of."

"Whatever," she snapped. "I just know I'll be glad when this nightmare ends."

Not half as glad as he would be, Will thought. "I just wanted to give you the news and see if it was okay to visit the girls in a week or so."

"That's fine, but whatever stuff you leave here at home is going to get thrown out, just be aware of that."

Will shook his head. He'd just told her he was going to jail for a year and all she can think about was his leaving a few shirts in the closet. Good riddance. "That's fine. I'm sorry, Cat. I know I've made some bad decisions lately. I've caused you a lot of pain and heartache. I know I've embarrassed you and the girls, and I'm sorry. I don't expect you to forgive me." There, he said it.

"Embarrassed doesn't even scratch the surface," Cat seethed, her voice now full of emotion and anger. "You have no idea. It was hard enough trying to explain to people why you moved ten thousand miles away to buy a farm, but now what am I supposed to tell my friends, people in the neighborhood, my parents? Oh, Will's a great guy, but he's in prison for the next year because he and his North Carolina girlfriend killed a man inside their house. However, it's really not that big a deal. He's still the same great guy everyone thinks he is." She paused. "It's not a story I look forward to having to explain."

"I know, I hate it for you," Will said, astounded by the fact that she had no compassion for him after learning about the verdict the judge just handed down to him. She only worried about her reputation.

"Will, I don't even know who you are anymore," Cat said coldly. "I don't know what you're capable of doing next."

"I'm the same guy you always knew, just capable of making a few stupid mistakes - some bigger than others," he stated.

"Well, I'll call the girls later today when they get home from school."

"Yes, you better call them tonight and break the news. I've got my own news to tell them," Cat shared, apparently referring to her intentions to file for divorce.

Will dismissed Cat's disparaging comments from his mind and began to think about the fate of the farm. Who could he trust to take care of property and keep the farm operational while he was away for the next year? The two most likely candidates to assist were waiting for him back at Winfield Farm. Could Henry and Clay take care of things while he was away? Henry was sick, and it wasn't fair to Clay to ask him to leave his family to clean up after his mess. Maybe he should sell the farm. Still, it was all he had to come back to when he got out of prison next January. Maybe he should hire one of the other farmers in the county to run things for the next year. He knew that Lucius Cody and his sons were very capable farmers, and folks he could trust to keep the farm operational for the next year. He could partner with them and let Lucius share in the profits or pay the two of them a retainer to oversee the operations. He would probably need their help next spring anyway to help him during planting season.

Will pulled the truck through the front gate of Winfield Farm. Clay and Henry were there, waiting on him. It was good to have the support of his brother and cousin during the adversities over the last month, but he would need to lean on them for the next twelve months as well.

"Guys, thanks for being here for me today," Will said as they walked into the house. "I've got some decisions to make as it relates to the farm. I have thought about selling, but this farm is all I'll have when I get out of jail. I'm going to need some help to keep the bills paid and make sure I don't lose this place, but I don't want to tax you guys any more than I already have." He paused as he looked around the room. "I think I'll need someone here locally to run the day to day operations of the farm, so I was thinking about hiring Lucius Cody and his sons to do that. However, I'll need the two of you to oversee what he's doing, if you guys are up to the challenge."

"I like that idea," Henry nodded.

"Sure," Clay concurred. "We're here to help you out in any way we can."

"Thanks guys," Will replied, humbled by their loyalty.

"Well, I just told Cat my news," Will shared.

"How did that go?" Clay inquired.

"Not well at all," he admitted. "And she let me know that I'd be receiving some correspondence from her attorney in the next few weeks."

"That's not good," Henry offered.

"It's been coming for a long time," Will shrugged. "I'm sure I made it worse when I bought the farm and moved down here, and then after the arrest, she was done. She's also convinced I'm having an affair with Becca."

"Well, speaking of girls in your life, you have got to explain how Kaitlyn Gerrard showed up at the sentencing today," Clay inquired, ribbing his brother.

"That was a shocker, seeing her there," Will responded. "I hadn't seen her or talked to her in twenty-something years. I guess she was bored and drove over from Wilmington after reading about the story online. I purposely haven't looked at the internet, but I guess this scandal is written up in more than just the Bladen Journal."

"But she lives in New York, or so I thought?" Clay asked.

"Yes, she does, but she's in Wilmington visiting her aunt. Her aunt lives in the same house in Forest Hills where Kaitlyn grew up. I stopped by to the old house to see if I could find her when I drove over to see the attorneys a month ago. That was the day I stopped by to see you, Henry. After I left Carolina Beach, I drove over to Wrightsville Beach, by the high school, and through our old neighborhood, just to see what's changed in twenty years. That's when I stopped by her old house."

"So, what's going on between you and Kate?" Clay inquired. "I never knew the two of you had gone out."

"Nothing's going on," Will said. "I had always had a thing for her back in high school, but I never went out with her. She had been on my mind since I moved down here, so I told her aunt I'd just moved back to town and wanted to see her, just to say hello."

"You work fast, Wilbur," Clay offered, shaking his head in amazement. "I'll just say that. I didn't know her that well, but I remember she was a good girl, back in the day. She didn't exactly run in our crowd in Wilmington - which was probably a good thing."

"Yeah, that's probably what I liked about her, but don't get any ideas. I don't think I'm in any position to get involved with anyone at this stage of my life. I'm not exactly that marketable right now. I'm a confessed felon, destined for state prison in thirty days. I'm not exactly at the top of my game."

Henry laughed at Will's comments and at the bantering between the brothers.

"It's like we're all back here on the farm, teasing each other about girls, like it was thirty years ago," Henry laughed.

"We had some great memories here, didn't we?" Will reflected.

"We did," Henry acknowledged.

The Dinner

Chapter 52

The Christmas visit to Boston was over. His final trip home for the year had gone as well as Will might have expected. He spent more time with friends than he spent with the family, although Cat had agreed to allow Will to spend Christmas Eve in the guest room at the house in Marblehead. The traditional Christmas Day lunch with Cat's family, however, was off limits. Will used the time to pack up his belongings, while Cat and the girls spent the afternoon at the Key's house.

Will tried to fight back the tears as he hugged Sarah and Lauren good-bye, uncertain when he might see them again. Part of him wanted the girls to visit him in North Carolina at the prison next summer, but he really didn't want them to see him locked up behind bars. "I'm sorry," he told them both. He hated himself for what he had done to separate himself from his daughters.

The ten-hour drive back to the farm was a time of reflection for Will, recounting the last twenty-two years he had spent in New England, starting with his two years in business school at Dartmouth and ending on the drive home today. He now faced the certainty of a contentious divorce and twelve months of time in a rural North Carolina state prison. Decisions, he pondered. "They have everything to do with molding our lives. What if he had not made the decision to go to business school at Dartmouth and stayed at Duke or UNC? Where would he be right now? What if he had stopped Kaitlyn on the beach that day at the Blockade Runner? What if they had gone out, just once, to see if there really was a spark all those years ago? Maybe it was his destiny to marry Cat, although it certainly didn't end well. She was going to clean his clock financially, but he was prepared for that. The decision to accept the job at Liberty seemed to be a good one at the time. It provided a good living for a number of years and enabled him to accrue the capital to buy the farm, but what if he had taken a job as an investment banker in Charlotte instead right out of grad school? Would Cat have moved to Charlotte way back then? Boston seemed like the right place at the time.

Was buying the farm another bad decision? Maybe so, or was it really just a bad decision to lie about what happened that night? Being truthful would have gotten him right where he was today. Cat would still be filing for divorce, but he'd be a free man and facing no jail time. But, maybe there's a reason he was going to jail. He couldn't imagine why, but who knows? He had two wonderful daughters who loved him despite the fact that he'd embarrassed them. It's hard to imagine that Sarah and Lauren were the by-product of a bad decision. He didn't know if he could handle being away from them for a full year. He would miss Sarah's graduation and half of her first year of college. What kind of father was he? Imagine a man who couldn't be there for his daughter's high school graduation because he's locked up in prison. What a deadbeat dad! Maybe they'll let him out for good behavior to attend her graduation next spring.

Once back at the farm, the battle of good decisions and bad decisions continued to play out in Will's head. After a few days of being back in North Carolina, he made peace with the fact that the farm was where he belonged. North Carolina was starting to feel like home again. He made the decision that he would serve his prison time and return to the farm permanently next January.

As a belated Christmas gift to Eileen, Will delivered his court-mandated check and a handwritten letter of apology to the Saxon's diminutive home. A newly framed picture of Wyn hung on the wall in the living room. Wyn's face haunted Will during the visit with the Saxons, so he shortened his apology in an effort to evacuate the house as quickly as possible. Eileen seemed to understand Will's logic behind the cover-up of the shooting. After all, Eileen had been involved in a cover-up of her own for three decades. Brooke felt differently regarding her brother's death. She did little to hide her anger toward Will. On the way out that night, Will asked if Eileen would watch out for the house while he was away. She was happy to help, and Will offered to pay her for keeping watch over the house.

"I won't accept no more money from you, Will. You done paid us plenty with what the judge required. I'm glad to look out for things. I don't think you'll have no trouble, although these crooks know when someone's not home for a long period of time, and they might try to break in or vandalize the house. But I'll keep an eye out on things."

Will couldn't help but think about Wyn as Eileen referred to vandals breaking into the house, but Wyn was no more of a criminal than Will. Wyn had paid for his trespass with his life. Will would pay for his crime with twelve months behind bars. Both were capable of corruption.

With the apology to the Saxons behind him, Will was determined to make good choices when it came to the farm.

The fall harvest had proven to be profitable, and he felt excited about the future of the farm and his career as a farmer. Over the course of a two-hour meeting at Winfield Farm, Will worked out an agreement with Lucius, Cy, and Luther Cody to operate the farm for the upcoming year.

The Cody's were honest, hard-working people who would take good care of the farm and keep Will updated on their plans and progress. As part of the arrangement, Mr. Cody or one of the boys would make the twenty-two-mile drive to the prison in Clinton once a month to update Will on the status of the crops and cattle.

"We'll take pictures and coordinate with you and Henry on what crops to plant next spring. We'll run any expenses by your brother and let him handle all the books and expenses. I'll have my son, Cyrus, take care of the cattle. He's had experience raising cows working at the Richardson farm. We'll treat your farm like it's our own," Mr. Cody promised.

"I know you will," Will replied.

The day following the meeting with the Cody's, a large envelope from Boston arrived at the farm by overnight delivery. Inside were divorce papers from Cat's attorney. Will had expected the package before he was due to report to Sampson Institute, but the reality of the documents hit him like a blast of cold air from Massachusetts in wintertime. He read the first paragraph of the cover letter and tossed the documents on the dining room table for review at a later time.

The arrival of the divorce papers prompted Will to make the deferred phone call to Kaitlyn. It was December twenty-eighth and Kaitlyn was leaving for New York in five days. If Will was serious about seeing her again, he knew had better quit procrastinating and make plans. Maybe a casual dinner in Wilmington on New Year's Eve would be a good end to an otherwise bad year, Will thought as he debated whether to call Kaitlyn. Was this really a good idea? She's separated. He wasn't even divorced yet. He was less than two weeks from reporting to prison. She lives in New York, and he wasn't sure where he lived anymore. What the hell? What does it hurt? He could use the company, and maybe she needs someone to talk to as well. Plus, he couldn't imagine her doing a whole lot while she's in Wilmington, other than seeing a few of her friends from home."

After convincing himself that she was expecting him to call, Will finally dialed her cell phone and asked her to join him for a date that had taken twenty-eight years to arrange. He booked an early dinner on New Year's Eve at Dockside, one of Wilmington's classic waterfront restaurants. He picked her up at her aunt's house at six o'clock, had the chance to meet young Chandler, and thanked Aunt Esther for babysitting during their night out in Wilmington.

In a period of two hours, Will was able to recapture what he had lost in Kaitlyn's life over the last two decades. She shared her experiences at New York University, her decision to move to New York City after college, the loss of her parents over a three year period while living in New York, and the challenges of a conservative Southern girl trying to start a career on Broadway. As a starving actress, her experience in acting led her to teach drama in schools and community theaters in the city. She had given up on acting in her late twenties, wrote and directed a few plays in community theaters, and began teaching drama full-time at age thirty-two. She met her husband a few years later through friends in the movie production industry. He was much older than Kate and had been married once before, the father of two grown children. He had not been prepared for parenthood again at age of forty-eight when Kaitlyn announced she was pregnant. After Chandler was born, Kate and her husband of four years drifted apart, so teaching drama and raising Chandler became her world.

"We've lived separate lives for eight years," Kaitlyn shared. "He had his career and was not prepared to be a father again. I loved being a mother and really wanted a sibling for Chandler, but that wasn't going to happen. I didn't want Chandler to be an only child like me, but that wasn't a choice I got to make. He's not a bad man, but we should have never gotten married. We had all these same interests ... except when it came to family. We talked about having a family together before we got married, but when Chandler was born, he had forgotten how hard it was to raise a child, particularly a toddler. He was too old to change diapers and left all the parenting to me. I don't know that I ever resented the fact that he was past his parenting years, but it certainly did push us further apart."

"I'm sorry," Will said. "What does he do in the film industry?"

"He owns a film production company. The company has done well, so he spends most of his time focused on his business. He still loves Chandler, but even now, he leaves the parenting part to me. We finally separated earlier this year. It's not that we don't get along. Like I said, we just lead separate lives. I just haven't felt the need to file for divorce yet, but I have no hope that we'll ever get back together."

"I can tell you and Chandler are close, just in the short amount of time I was around the two of you. How does he do staying with your aunt?" Will asked.

"Pretty good. They get along real well. He's used to being around adults - maybe too much of the time."

"What about his school?" Will inquired. "Where does he go?"

"It's a small private school right in the city. It's a place where a number of artists, musicians, and people in the theater world send their kids. The school goes only first through fifth grade, so the options will be really limited in a couple of years."

"Sounds like a unique school, probably pretty conservative with a strong emphasis on athletics," Will commented, laughing at his take on things.

Kaitlyn rolled her eyes at Will's comment.

"I'm sorry, that wasn't a nice thing to say about your school. I'm sure it's very strong academically ... and athletically," Will smiled.

"I told you a few weeks ago that I thought Chandler needed some diversity in his activities. He's learning to play the piano and gets overexposed to the arts, but I want him to learn how to play sports and be on a team with other kids."

"I really wish you would consider moving into my house at the farm for the summer and see how you guys like it. Chandler needs to get out of the big city with all that smog and traffic and breathe some of this North Carolina fresh air. I'm not asking you to move here for me, but do it for him. He needs some of that Southern culture like his mother grew up with. He would love spending time on the farm. He needs more wide open spaces in his life. You could get him on a baseball team this summer and in a lacrosse league this fall. Has he ever played a sport or been on a team?"

"Unfortunately not, I'm embarrassed to say," Kaitlyn responded.

"You have to do it, before it's too late," he told her. "Let me tell you a story about a kid in my class that moved to Wilmington in sixth grade. His name was Leland Hall. He moved from New Jersey, and his parents had never let him play sports because they were afraid he'd get hurt. A few of the guys in our class convinced him to play baseball with us that spring. He showed up for practice and hardly knew which hand to put his glove on. He embarrassed himself, struck out every at-bat, quit after the third game, and never came back. I know it crushed his self-esteem. He just started too late. It wasn't that he was uncoordinated or wasn't athletic. He just didn't start playing sports early enough and was too far behind to compete, especially when he got to be eleven or twelve years old."

"Poor guy. Did you guys heckle him?"

"Oh yeah. There were times we tried to encourage him and help him, but we were kids. Of course, we gave him hell. Looking back, we shouldn't have, but we did."

After dinner, Will and Kaitlyn strolled along Riverwalk near Chandler's Wharf under the Cape Fear Memorial Bridge. It was just after eight o'clock on a chilly New Year's Eve, the calm before the storm that always erupted in downtown Wilmington for the New Year's celebration.

"Have you ever brought Chandler downtown to see his namesake, Chandler's Wharf?" Will asked.

"No, but he would like this place," Kaitlyn said, looking across the Cape Fear River from the brick walkway.

"He might enjoy walking through the battleship North Carolina," Will said pointing to the massive World War II fighting vessel across the wharf. "I remember when my dad brought my brother and me here to see the battleship when I was ten and Clay was probably Chandler's age. If he's into it, you should take him to see the ship while you're in town." He stared off across the water toward Wrightsville Beach. "This was an incredible place to grow up," Will stated. "I don't know why I ever left. Boston's a great city and has a lot to offer with the water and the beaches, but Wilmington is heaven and North Carolina is God's country. Don't you miss it?"

"I do, I really do," Kaitlyn whispered as she bundled her coat to protect herself from the cool night's winter breeze off the Cape Fear River. "I never thought I would say this, but I'm really not looking forward to going back to New York."

"I think the road is calling you home. It sounds like it's time for you to start making plans to move back to Wilmington."

Kaitlyn smiled at Will's statement as they walked along the wharf in silence. Will calculated that Kate was considering the same issues he went through when deciding to move home to North Carolina. He could offer her advice, but this was her decision to make. "I have a plan, if you and Chandler are up for it," he said with a flair of excitement in his voice. "Let's go get Chandler and take him to the farm. He can stay up until midnight, then we'll let him see the farm and all the fun he can have there."

"We can't do that. It sounds like something he would enjoy, but I don't know if I'm ready."

"Ready for what? To have some fun?"

"No, to spend too much time with you. It's no secret that I felt the same way about you back in high school, but so much has changed and there's so much going on in both our lives. I just want to be cautious."

"Look, I'm still working through the details of my divorce, and I'll be in jail in a matter of days, so I'm not exactly dating material right now. I just get excited about people visiting the farm, and I was just trying to give you and Chandler something fun to do tomorrow."

"I appreciate that," Kaitlyn said quietly. "Plus, I'm not sure how Aunt Esther would react to us grabbing Chandler and leaving her there by herself."

"She's obviously welcome to come with us," Will suggested.

Kaitlyn laughed. "She could probably use the adventure, but I can just see the look on her face when we'd come charging in and tell her to pack her bags because we're going on an overnight trip."

"I understand," Will smiled, yet disappointed that his late

night ride to the farm was met with resistance. "Let's get out of this cold. How about a warm cup of coffee, and then I'll get you home to see Chandler," Will suggested.

"Sounds good," she concurred.

The night ended with Chandler, Kaitlyn, and Will playing a card game of Go Fish back at Kaitlyn aunt's home. As he prepared to leave, Will spoke. "Let's stay in touch. I want to hear how things are going in New York," he said.

"This was fun," Kate agreed. "I'm really glad you called. I felt a little awkward when I showed up at your sentencing. I guess I was more curious than anything, after reading the article on the internet. I didn't picture you being in that kind of trouble. I was surprised when Aunt Esther said you came by that day. I didn't know what to think, but I'm glad we got to spend some time together … after all these years."

"Well, I don't know if I'll ever see you again, but I'm glad you agreed to see me. It took me a while to arrange it, but I'm glad we went out tonight." After a quick kiss on the cheek and a long hug at the front door of Esther's house, Will made it home just in time to bring in the New Year — alone at Winfield Farm.

The New Year

Chapter 53

New Year's Day marked the ten-day countdown to the end of Will's freedom before reporting for his twelve month incarceration at the Sampson Correctional Institution. The timeline signaled that limited time remained to take care of his financial affairs, settle the divorce with Cat, and insure that any special projects around the farm were complete. Will was determined to keep the farm fully operational and profitable in the upcoming year. After all, returning to the farm was the one thing he had to look forward to after his prison term ended next January.

New Year's Day back in Boston would typically be spent watching football games with friends at home or at Tedesco Country Club, but with only ten days left before he had to report to Sampson Correctional, Will decided to use the time to complete some work on the farm. The Tar Heels were not playing in a New Year's Day Bowl, and Will wasn't really that interested in the outcome of any of the other games, so he elected to work today. Plus, unless it was Carolina basketball, watching sporting events on television by himself was not as exciting to Will as it used to be.

With colder weather approaching, Will opted to spend the rest of the morning on the tractor, moving hay bales from the barn behind the house to the cattle fields. The temperature was in the low fifties, considered warm for New Year's Day in North Carolina. The sun was shining, inviting him to be outside - even if it meant working. He attached the long metal forks to the front of the tractor and transferred the first five-foot rolled bale from the barn to the gate of the pasture directly in front of the house. As Will opened the gate on the north end of the field, the putter of the diesel engine prompted the cows into a slow trot to a more remote part of the pasture.

Quickly, Will dismounted the tractor and closed the gate. He had already learned the hard way how difficult it was to get just one cow back into the pasture after one went AWOL. "Get out of the way, ladies. We got some of North Carolina's best hay coming your way," he yelled in their direction as he put the tractor in gear and headed toward the fence-line. Carefully, he dropped the hay bale a few feet from the fence with a slight tilt of the forks, then put the old Ford tractor in reverse and quickly backed away, leaving the fresh bale of hay for his Herford cows.

He found first gear, turned the wheel sharply to the left, and headed back to the barn to load another bale. As he shifted the tractor into second gear, he noticed a car parked at the front gate, either turning around in the driveway or seeking entry into Winfield Farm. He was not expecting company, and his first thought, based on the look of the sedan, was that it was another county official here to ask more questions.

Surely there's not more they intend to nail me with, Will pondered, and not on New Year's Day. Maybe the judge changed his mind and decided he was too harsh in his sentencing. Could be that he realized that what he really deserved was community service? He didn't allow his hopes to rise as he drove the tractor through the pasture toward the entry gate, curious. Maybe it was Clay or one of the Codys, but he didn't recognize the car as one that belonged to either one of them.

Still unsure, he put the tractor in neutral and dismounted. As he walked toward the car, the driver's side window rolled down and a female's voice yelled out. "What does it take to get in this farm?"

It was Kaitlyn. Will trotted across the pasture, leaving the tractor idling in the field.

"We've been waiting out here, hoping you would notice us," Kaitlyn explained loudly over the drone of the tractor's diesel engine. We tried to call your phone, but I guess you couldn't hear us."

"Sorry about that," Will yelled. "Is Chandler with you?"

"Yes, and Aunt Esther too."

Will leaned down and greeted Aunt Esther through the open window as she sat stoically in the passenger seat next to Kaitlyn. Chandler rolled down the window in the back seat and waved at Will. "Chandler, hop out," Will commanded. "I'm going to let you drive the tractor back to the house with me."

"Please be careful," Kaitlyn pleaded.

"I will. Don't worry," Will assured her. "Come on, Chandler. We're going to race them back to the house."

After procuring final approval from his mother, Chandler sprung from the back seat of the car and climbed to the top of the top of the wooden fence that separated Will from Aunt Esther's car. He instructed Chandler to free-fall off the fence, insuring the eight-year-old that he was strong enough to catch him when he jumped. After Chandler's successful landing, Will yelled the four-digit entry code over the fence to Kaitlyn and requested that she give the tractor a head-start in preparation for the race to the house.

"Please be careful," Kaitlyn requested again, uncertainty in her eyes.

"Don't worry," Will responded. "You've seen how slow this old tractor moves, even at top speed. You've got nothing to worry about."

Chandler took the race to the house seriously and held tightly to the thin black steering wheel as the tractor navigated the grassy racetrack through the pasture, weaving its way past the cattle. As the tractor trudged toward the house, Will wasn't sure who was smiling more, him or Chandler. Somehow, the need to move the next two bales of hay into the pasture didn't seem to be a priority anymore.

He welcomed the visitors into the house and offered the New Year's Day travelers a beverage. "I'm curious, how did you find the farm?" Will asked, still amazed that Kaitlyn, Aunt Esther, and Chandler had driven over from Wilmington.

"It wasn't that hard," Kaitlyn joked. "Once we drove past White Lake, we didn't have any trouble. All we had to do was stop and ask where your farm was located. For some reason, people around here seemed to know where your place is."

"There was a time, not too long ago, when no one even knew I lived here," Will chuckled at his own expense. "I'm glad you found me," he continued. "I know you guys have been in the car for a while, so let's walk around for a few minutes. I want to show you the old house, and then we'll walk out back to see the fields."

Will gave Aunt Esther, Kaitlyn, and Chandler the full tour of the house and conveyed the short version of the farm's history, as well as some minor detail on the background of the Winfield family. Then, the four of them took Will's standard driving tour around the farm in his Range Rover. The dirt road took them past the corn and soybean fields, now barren from the recent harvest. They drove through the planted pines down to the South River and made a stop at the old tobacco barn on the way back to the house.

The stench from the curing tobacco had faded over the decades, but Will imagined himself in Chandler's shoes as an eight-year-old, standing inside the tattered wood barn with his baseball teammates, listening to his uncle tell the boys about how tobacco cured in the barn.

"Do you still grow tobacco on your farm, Mr. Jordan?" Chandler asked as he looked high into the rafters of the empty barn.

"No, unfortunately not. Tobacco is not as popular as it once was. People, cars and animals consume more corn than tobacco these days," Will shared, looking at Esther and Kate while he spoke. Today Will felt like he had assumed the role of Uncle John. Like his uncle, he was able to share with visitors the history of tobacco grown at Winfield Farm. Why not plant tobacco on Winfield Farm again, he thought. Nostalgia might play a role in bringing the crop back to Winfield Farm one day, but certainly not in the next twelve months.

"I have a surprise for you, Chandler," he announced once the tour of the farm was complete and the entourage back at the house. "Hang on for two minutes, and I'll be right back." As promised, Will returned shortly with two baseball gloves and a hat from the back of the house. "I found my old Little League glove when I was cleaning out some things in Boston last week," he said. He handed Chandler the smaller glove, helped him fit it on his left hand, and jammed a baseball securely in the pocket of the worn mitt. "The Durham Bulls are a minor league baseball team that plays right here in North Carolina. You wouldn't know about the Bulls, but I bet you've heard of the Mets or the Yankees. What team do you like best, Mets or the Yankees?"

"I don't really know," Chandler answered shyly.

His uncertainty proved Will's assumption that Chandler probably had not had much exposure to baseball — or sports in general. "Well, I think you should be a Bulls' fan since you're in North Carolina for a few more days," Will recommended. "And you should wear this old Bulls hat of mine, too." He dropped to one knee and secured the Bulls cap over Chandler's shaggy jet-black hair. "The hat looks good on you," he proclaimed. "And now you're ready to play baseball with your mom and me. Let's go outside and throw."

Will looked up from his kneeling position on the living room floor, seeking Kaitlyn's approval. Her face seemed to confirm that she was in agreement with the plan to play some baseball. "Aunt Esther, you need to try out one of my uncle's old rocking chairs on the front porch. You can watch Chandler practice his curve ball. I think you'll like the view from the porch, and fortunately, the temperature is tolerable today."

Once outside in the grass between the front porch and the fenced pasture, the instruction began. Will crouched next to Chandler and showed him the basics of throwing and catching a baseball. "Point at the target with the glove in your left hand, then throw hard toward my glove," Will coached. "Step forward with your left foot before you throw, and that will give you more power and accuracy." Chandler tried it.

"Hold the ball close to your ear, and then fire it at my glove." Will backed about ten paces away, and Chandler modeled Will's pitching instructions. "Now, let's work on catching. Hold the glove open like this and use your right hand to secure the ball in the glove," Will instructed, using his own glove to teach the art of catching a baseball.

Will rolled Chandler a few ground balls before advancing to the drill of actually catching a slow pitch and a fly ball. Once Chandler got comfortable stopping the ball with his glove, Will tossed a few underhand throws toward the boy. After a few tries, Chandler was catching the ball in his glove. Will was pleased with his progress. "Let's go practice throwing against the barn," Will said, motioning to Chandler and Kaitlyn. "Follow me." He turned toward the porch before heading behind the house for more practice. "Esther, we'll be back shortly," Will called out to her. "We're going around back to practice some grounders. You're welcome to come with us!"

"No, I'm enjoying my seat right here. I'm fine," Esther said, waving her hand.

Kaitlyn, Will, and Chandler walked around the side of the house through the grass toward the tractor barn. "Now, throw this ball against that barn over here," Will said, pointing to a spot on the barn door about four feet off the ground. "See if you can hit the door right here and pretend this is the other player's mitt. Throw the ball at the barn ten times and catch the ball when it rolls back to you, like this," Will modeled, bouncing the baseball off the barn door. "Stay low, like me, when you field the ball," Will instructed as the ball rolled across the sandy drive in front of the barn. "You'll have to throw it hard against that door, so the ball will roll back to your glove," Will coached. "Keep throwing at the barn and squat down low with your legs wide apart to stop the ball when it rolls back to you. This is how I used to practice when I was your age. Practice is important in any sport, but especially baseball. Doing something over and over will make you a good player. Now it's your turn. Start throwing the ball hard against that barn door. I'm going to talk to your mom for a minute."

Will stepped away from the barn and stood next to Kaitlyn while he and Kaitlyn watched Chandler throw the ball against the barn and attempt to field each throw. "Throw it hard," Will said. "You can't hurt that barn."

Kaitlyn and Will watched in silence while Chandler threw

the ball against the barn. "He's got potential," he said, grinning. "He just needs to keep practicing."

"He never gets this at home," Kaitlyn said. "He needs this, more than you know."

Will and Kaitlyn stood side-by-side at a comfortable distance away from Chandler and the action, watching the baseball thump against the barn's wooden door with each throw.

"I thought all night about what you said last night," she said. "I couldn't sleep. I kept thinking about the little boy who quit your baseball team in sixth grade. I don't want Chandler to be that kid. He needs to be around some boys that are interested in sports. I want to get him on a team - baseball, soccer, football, anything," Kaitlyn explained. She watched intently as Chandler followed the instructions to master his throwing technique, impressed with the progress he made with each throw. "I checked on that private school you mentioned close to here in Clinton. While I was up in the middle of the night, I searched the internet for schools down here. I kept coming back to Harrells, the school your cousins attended. Then I couldn't get the school out of my mind. We just drove by the campus on the way over here. I want to do some more research, but I think it's a place he could be happy. We'll come back at spring break and tour the school. I made up my mind last night that it's time to leave New York and move south before Chandler gets too old."

Will was shocked, but pleased. "I think that's awesome," he said.

"We'll finish spring semester and move down in May. I need some time to prepare myself, and others in the city, that we're leaving," Kate explained. "I broke the news to Aunt Esther this morning that we were considering a move closer to her. I'm the only family she has left. She's eighty-two, and

I need to be close by if she needs me. We might even let her move in with us."

"So does that mean you're moving to Wilmington?" Will asked.

"Well, Wilmington is still a possibility, but this friend of mine from high school has this house on a farm that needs a caretaker," Kaitlyn said. "He's an old friend that I'm just getting to know again, but if his offer's still good, I want to explore that option and see if I can reestablish my roots in North Carolina."

She glanced his way, anticipating his response. Will responded only with a smile.

Kate continued, "This place may be too rural for us, but I need a drastic change from New York. It's time to come back home. I've been gone too long. I decided last night that I want to raise Chandler as a Tar Heel, not a Yankee."

Still stunned by Kaitlyn's words, Will searched for the right response. "I think that's a good idea, a *real* good idea."

"Me too," Kaitlyn said as she glanced in Chandler's direction.

"Welcome home," Will said. He faced Kate and entrapped her in a prolonged hug.

THE END

About the Author

Charlie Fiveash is a native Georgian, raised on the Georgia coast in Brunswick. He currently lives in Atlanta with his wife and three children. A graduate of the University of Georgia, he has been in the commercial real estate business in Atlanta since 1987. Return to Tobacco Road is his first published book. He has also authored Moonlight in the Pine, a novel based in Georgia.

26178613R00318

Made in the USA
Lexington, KY
20 September 2013